SEVEN SHOES

by Mark Davis

Stark House Press • Eureka California

SEVEN SHOES

Published by Stark House Press
1315 H Street
Eureka, CA 95501, USA
griffinskye3@sbcglobal.net
www.starkhousepress.com

ISBN-13: 978-1-944520-97-7

Book and cover design by Mark Shepard, shepgraphics.com
Proofreading by Bill Kelly

First Stark House Press Edition: March 2020

SEVEN SHOES

by Mark Davis

She strides out of her office into the shadow canyons of downtown wearing a new cashmere sweater—perfect for a spring day—and a pair of woven, low-top walking shoes to break in on her way to meet an old friend for lunch. With the ice finally vanished from the sidewalks, Elizabeth looks forward to stretching her legs and feeling the warmth of the sun on her face and hands.

A screech of car brakes.

An SUV lurches to a stop on Vermont Avenue, then more screeches and mechanical shrieks as the cars behind it chain-react. A fraction of a second later a high-pitched squeal of tires lances her eardrums and Elizabeth's whole body clenches as if she expects to be struck.

The car that stopped the noontime traffic is a big, blue box of an SUV in the middle of the street. Horns blare in an angry chorus.

The driver emerges from the other side, shirtless. He walks around the front of his car and she sees that he is naked. The driver is a young man, around thirty, his white skin mottled with pink blotches in the cool spring air.

He walks toward her at an even, unhurried pace.

Elizabeth laughs to herself, incredulous, fingernails at her lips.

The naked man's arms swing and his hips twist slightly as he walks. He is rangy, with long, hairy legs, a sunken chest, and a white stomach cut inward from years of wearing a belt. His penis, shrunken into the bird's nest of his pubis, bounces slightly as he strides forward. He has a light beard and a round face framed by stringy, unwashed hair.

Elizabeth focuses on his face—the faint smile, the bland look of an intelligent man whose mind has gone vacant—and recognition hits her like a flush of ice water through her heart. She doesn't know the man, but she knows that expression from a thousand faces.

I'm on deck.

Passersby on the sidewalk keep their distance, watching the

naked man silently, warily. A petite Asian woman listening to music on her earphones is slow to notice. When the woman finally does see the naked man, she makes a little pip and jumps backwards into a protective crouch.

All the bystanders stay back, afraid that the naked man might come over and touch them.

"Excuse me," the man says, stepping around Elizabeth to pass through the glass door and into the foyer.

Last line of defense.

Elizabeth spins around and follows him.

When the naked man passes the security desk, the guard looks up from her reading. She is a middle-aged black woman with dreadlocks that contrast with her starched, white shirt with a corporate logo.

"Sir. Sir? Sir!" The guard pulls her walkie-talkie and barks commands into it.

The naked man keeps his even stride into the massive glass and teakwood lobby that rises 10 stories to a rounded, white cupola—a modernist comment on the dome of the U.S. Capitol just two miles away.

The naked man heads toward the elevator.

"You can always do this, at any hour of any day," Elizabeth says, keeping pace behind him, trying her best to sound conversational. "But first, let's talk options."

"I know there are other options," he says. "But none of them appeal to me."

He gently pushes the 'up' button.

"Look at me."

She pulls on his bare shoulder and he turns to look at her.

His eyes stare into hers, but without intensity. He is not interested in discussion or negotiation.

"Come up to three," Elizabeth says. "We can go to my office and talk."

He laughs, a natural and calm laugh that sets Elizabeth back on her heels.

"You a shrink?" he asks.

"Yeah, sort of."

He laughs again.

"That would be quite a sight. Me naked, talking about my

dreams on your couch."

Elizabeth gets the picture, a *New Yorker* cartoon brought to life, and laughs as well. And that is a good thing, making a connection like this. She tries to hold his eye contact, but his gaze keeps shifting downward, then to the sides.

Personalize it. Keep 'em talking.

"What's your name?"

The man gives a wan smile, a naturally shy person now walking naked in public.

"Jeremy."

Ding.

The brass door slides open to a woman holding a stack of folders. She does not see Jeremy until she is halfway out. The woman screams and steps back inside the elevator. Jeremy follows her into the elevator, and Elizabeth jumps in right behind him. The woman eases around the naked man in an exaggerated bend to keep from grazing his shoulder. As soon as she comes out of the elevator she trips, goes down to her knees, and spills her folders across the marble floor.

Elizabeth hits three.

Jeremy hits nine.

"There's no coming back from something like this Jeremy," she says. "We can fix whatever is wrong."

Jeremy stares at the two illuminated buttons.

"I am what is wrong. And I don't want to come back."

He is the calm one. It is Elizabeth who feels light-headed and flustered. She had talked down patients hundreds of times before. She had the playbook of questions and discussion points, all the best practices. And yet this time, for some reason, she can't think of a thing to say.

So Elizabeth slaps both hands on Jeremy's right wrist.

The young man gives her a look of indolent contempt.

The elevator chimes and the door opens at three.

She pulls on his wrists, leaning back, straining her slender body into a fulcrum. Jeremy, surprised at her strength and sudden ferocity, leans backward. Elizabeth wrests him toward the open elevator door, and manages to pull him off balance and a few inches forward.

"I'm not letting you do this, I'm not, so you might as well . . ."

She puffs out the words until she is breathless.

A man pushing a handcart shouts something when he sees a naked man wrestling with a woman at the door of the elevator. His shout is just enough distraction for Elizabeth to weaken her grip for a fatal instant. The elevator door slides to a close and they fall away from one another, riding upwards again. Elizabeth is exhausted by exertion and fear, like a boxer after several tough rounds, the muscles of her legs trembling. Jeremy leans against the elevator wall.

He looks relieved.

They ride in silence for a few seconds as the floors chime by.

"Really, I am fine," he says. "I'm cool with this."

"Is it a job or a woman?" Elizabeth asks.

"You know how they say you should never shit where you eat? They were right."

"There is so much more for you, Jeremy, so much better to come. Believe me, I know."

Jeremy looks her in the eyes again.

"Do you really believe that?" he says and glances up at the changing digits of the floor indicator. "Or are you just trying to keep yourself from holding my hand on the way down?"

Elizabeth feels heat rise into her eyes. A blush always blooms against her pale skin like strawberries on cream. This was going so wrong. You never let them get inside your head. Elizabeth stares back at him, trying to make his eyes connect with hers again, trying to control him by force of will.

Jeremy looks away from her.

"Stay with me Jeremy. Stay with me, please."

After a beat, Jeremy returns her gaze.

"Look, lady, this is hard, but I am actually in a place where I can kind of enjoy it, the release you know. Don't ruin it for me."

The door opens at nine. Jeremy saunters toward a wall of plate glass with a keypad by a door. Behind the glass is a large desk of white quartz that looks like the bridge of a television starship. The young woman is wearing an ear bud and in mid-conversation when she sees Jeremy and screams.

Jeremy punches four digits into the entry keypad. Elizabeth grabs the edge of the glass door and follows him inside.

"Is Belinda here?" Jeremy asks.

The woman, wide-eyed, shakes her head 'no.'

He is at a slow trot now. As he passes each cubicle, Jeremy creates a wave of reaction from former office mates who shout or scream. The staffers peek out from their cubicles at their former colleague, now naked in public like an anxiety dream made flesh. Some point, some laugh, some just stare in mute incomprehension.

Jeremy turns a corner toward the darkened conference room and runs through it. He grabs a black, ergonomic chair from the head of the long faux-mahogany desk and pulls it along the carpet and out onto the balcony.

Elizabeth follows him outside. They are out in the cool spring air again. Nearby office buildings cast a permanent shadow on the balcony and muffle the sounds of downtown traffic.

"You might kill someone on the way down, did you ever think of that?"

"I did," Jeremy says. "On this side it's all alley."

He is breathing rapidly. An artery pulses in his neck.

Jeremy balances himself awkwardly on one foot on the chair and heaves himself up to the ledge, where he stands precariously, arms flapping in the air for balance, like a comedian pantomiming flight.

His face has a beatific cast—the expression of saints. But this young man is not about to be beatified.

"My brother!"

Elizabeth screams so loudly it feels as if someone raked a key across her larynx.

Jeremy turns to look at her, astonished and displeased at the interruption of his last act.

"He killed himself when we were in college."

Jeremy wavers and flaps on the ledge some more, and then turns his gaze straight ahead, saying nothing.

"When Mike and I were kids, our father had done it as well. Do you know what that did to us? What it did to Mike, and what he did to me? Do you know what it will do to your—"

But Jeremy had already closed his eyes and gone over the edge with a hop. She hears him slap the pavement an instant later.

"Not only is suicide a sin, it is the sin. It is the ultimate and absolute evil, the refusal to take an interest in existence; the refusal to take the oath of loyalty to life. The man who kills a man, kills a man. The man who kills himself, kills all men; as far as he is concerned he wipes out the world."
G.K. Chesterton

"Make no mistake about people who leap from burning windows. Their terror of falling from a great height is still just as great as it would be for you or me standing speculatively at the same window just checking out the view; i.e. the fear of falling remains a constant. The variable here is the other terror, the fire's flames: when the flames get close enough, falling to death becomes the slightly less terrible of two terrors."
David Foster Wallace

ONE

The American ambassador to the United Kingdom was a cheerful man, bald and rosy cheeked.

"Our planner had you pegged as a salad and salmon girl," he said from Elizabeth's right while she surveyed the room from the head table of the ornate ballroom of the London Savoy. Elizabeth smiled at the ambassador and cut into her Beef Wellington. She generally didn't eat a heavy meal before a speech, but this cut of meat with its soft, red center looked too delicious to resist. She generally did not drink before a speech, either, but the claret went well with the beef.

"I'll keep your introduction mercifully brief," the ambassador said. "How has your day been?"

"I met with some psych students from King's College this morning," Elizabeth said, holding a napkin in front of her mouth. "The rest of my days are spent reading and doing research."

"You're an academic," the ambassador said. "Such a summer must be your idea of heaven."

Elizabeth's summer was off to a glorious start, a three-month grant to plum meta-studies and share her findings with colleagues at the University of London. Practically speaking, this meant that she had nothing to do but to read things that interested her, delve into deep conversations and take long walks in Regent's Park. Who knows what else could happen in the days to come?

A buzz in her purse.

Elizabeth pulled her smartphone and glanced down at it in her lap.

>**Lizzie!**<

Only Max, her 19-year-old son and a rising sophomore at Rutgers, called her that. Then—

>**Hi mom how r u?**<

She knew, of course, that Max really wanted to tell her how he was. Elizabeth looked down into her lap as discreetly as possible while she texted.

>About to give a speech how are you?<

She set the phone down and ate another forkful of the Beef Wellington and took a sip of wine. Another buzz.

>Still lonely here a little weird to tell the truth<

>Will you be okay tonight?<
>Yes, Mom, definitely<
>Be sure and take your meds<
>OK, never forget, you know<
>Got to go, talk tomorrow<

"A significant other?" the ambassador said.

"Very significant," Elizabeth said. "My son. He's staying at Rutgers over the summer to redo the math class he bombed out of last semester. The dorms are largely empty now, so he gets lonely."

"And then he remembers how much he needs mom," the ambassador said, smiling and resting his hand on her arm in a solicitous gesture—or was he flirting? She glanced at his hand and the thick, gold band on one finger.

"I've got one like that myself," he said. "A little needy."

"They all are. Some show it more than others."

The ambassador withdrew his hand.

Five minutes later, the ambassador introduced Dr. Elizabeth B. Browne of Georgetown University and Georgetown School of Medicine to the Royal Council for the Prevention of Suicide, a ballroom full of psychologists, psychiatrists and activists, many of them the parents, siblings, widows and widowers of suicides. Elizabeth did a mental inventory of her speaking points while the ambassador rattled off her resume . . . Smith College and Harvard Medical School, board certified at Brigham and Women's Hospital, a fellow at the National Institutes of Health.

Elizabeth always felt a flutter of stage fright when she glanced around a room and saw so many well-dressed people looking at her expectantly. While the ambassador droned on, she quietly drew in a breath for four seconds, held it for seven, and exhaled over eight. Elizabeth was able to do this three times by the time the ambassador finished introducing her.

The 4-7-8 breath always calmed her down before a talk.

Elizabeth walked confidently to the podium and made a few American-in-London quips. She spoke of her background before medical school, how she and her brother Mike were in a fragile state after the death of their mother and then torn to pieces by the subsequent suicide of their father. She spoke about Mike's suicide while they were both in college, and how hard it was for her to survive the loss of the last member of her family.

She told of her successes and her failures, including the story of Jeremy, three months before. As she spoke, Elizabeth marveled at how easy it had become to speak about such things in public, the first time she had talked about Jeremy outside of therapy. Being so open was not possible in the first such speech she had made, or the tenth. But she had talked about her life for so many years in therapy, first as a patient, then as a resident, that she was finding it was becoming second nature.

Elizabeth told her stories because they were useful. It gave her credibility, connecting with audiences in a way no academic talk ever could. Above all, it gave Elizabeth Browne the ability to communicate with potential suicides as a peer. *I know,* she said, *I've walked in the valley of the shadow of despair just as you have. I've turned a pill bottle in my hands and thought about it.* In this moment, there was a hush in the room, a quiet intimacy with people who were no strangers to her struggle.

At these moments, when she spoke about Mike, she seemed to stand outside of herself, listening to herself speak as if she were sitting in the audience. That felt good, felt right, her story more important than all her credentials or presence as a speaker.

Yet there were times, thankfully it did not happen tonight, when the retelling of her family story seemed like a recitation, even, she sometimes felt, a vulgar display of the special qualification of victimhood that was such a hallmark of these times. When that feeling came over her, she felt inauthentic, false, even a betrayer of her lost loved ones.

Such thoughts posed the danger of becoming intrusive, even disabling. They threatened to make her choke in front of an audience. But Elizabeth had learned to dismiss that little voice of self-condemnation and carry on.

Elizabeth came to the close of her speech. It had become a part of her, and she felt like an old stage actor coming to the most important part of a famous soliloquy.

"If it had not been for the intervention of a mentor—a remarkable man who had guided me through my own analysis—I very well may have been the final victim of suicide in the Browne family."

The only sound in the room was the clinking of plates from the kitchen.

"That is when I came to know what I had to do with my life, to pull others from the pitiless gaze of the abyss," she said. "Yes, I've lost some patients. But I've saved many more—as I know every practitioner here tonight has done. We've saved enough people to fill this room many times over. Like you, I have yet to find a better purpose for a career, for my very life."

The applause was explosive. It always was.

As Elizabeth smiled appreciatively at her audience, the thought came to her that for all their admiration, no one in the room would be terribly surprised to read one day that she had finally killed herself.

———

The castle stood high and lonely, perched on a plug of land surrounded by a long stretch of purple sand fast by a purple sea. In her dream, Elizabeth labored under the weight of a basket of laundry she had to take to the king. It was supposed to be clean, of course, but wind-borne sand kept dirtying it up.

A murmur, slight and tinny, caught her attention. The sound was coming from the basket, pathetic little mouse voices crying out for help, but there was nothing funny about them. She set the basket down on the sand. She fished through sheets and found that the cries emanated from a cord of multi-colored knots. When Elizabeth examined the knots of the cord more closely, she could see they were made of people, human figures with limbs tied tightly together, binding them into a single chain of agony.

She began to untie them with frantic haste. She wanted to save them, but the more she pulled on their tangled arms and legs, the more she hurt them.

Elizabeth couldn't stop and she couldn't save them. So she kept hurting them. Even killing them.

A dull, insistent tone called out to her.

She looked up at the castle. The king was waiting, impatient, upset . . .

The sound again, two dull tones in rapid succession.

The king was angry.

She stirred, unwilling to rise from the depths of sleep.

That obnoxious British ring tone.

The red lights of the digital clock said 3:33 a.m. She answered with her name. Elizabeth didn't mind that she sounded scratchy and half-asleep. She wanted the caller to know how rude he was. But she was also grateful to be pulled away from such a disturbing dream.

"Sorry to call so late, but this is an emergency."

The voice was American, not familiar.

Something must have happened to Max.

Elizabeth bolted upright in bed, gripping the phone like a weapon.

"Is my son okay?"

"Oh no," the voice said. "Nothing like that. Put yourself at ease. This is a business call."

"A business call or an emergency? Do you know what time it is in London? We're ahead of you, not behind you."

"Yes, I am in London too. Townsend Gray, chargé d'affaires at the American embassy. Again, I'm sorry to have awakened you. You are here for the whole summer, are you not?"

Townsend as a first name? Did the State Department have a secret breeding facility for fops?

"Academic exchange, King's College . . . What can I do for you, Mister Gray?"

"There has been a mass suicide, four are Americans."

Elizabeth cleared her throat. Four. A pact of some sort, obviously.

"And you need me—?"

"The ambassador was impressed by your speech. He asks that you come to the scene, advise Scotland Yard and the Norwegian

Police Security Service."

"Norway?"

"Yes, we would like you to gather your things for a short trip to Stavanger first thing in the morning. Scotland Yard will make a jet available. And please don't forget your passport. You'll be paid of course, one hundred dollars an hour out of embassy funds, surely below your standard rate, but . . ."

"Norwegians?"

"No, three Brits, seven people in all. Several of the Brits and the Americans were, well, prominent. A senior oil company executive from Houston, a pharmaceutical CEO from Delaware, a famous British writer, although I never heard of her . . . And then there is how they, how they . . ."

"Don't tell me."

"How anyone could do that to themselves. I would be . . ."

"Don't tell me," she said.

A long silence.

"Why not?"

"I like to go into a scene naïve, without preconception. It helps me see it fresh, through their eyes. Please let everyone know that."

It took Mr. Gray a few more beats to assimilate what she meant.

"Very well. Will you help us?"

"My schedule is light, mainly summer research before I have to be back in Washington. My Georgetown classes don't start until, uh, August twenty-eighth. And this is the kind of case that I do, so yes."

And besides, she thought, Mr. Gray described a case that certainly qualifies as research, perhaps the sort that could be the basis of the kind of study that would attract a big grant.

"Thank you, Ms. Browne. Please be at Victoria Station, the Krispy Kreme bar, five a.m. And don't forget that passport."

———

The coffee at the doughnut shop was surprisingly good. Elizabeth hadn't been able to catch much sleep after the call, so she needed every drop.

Instead of being met by the American chargé, Elizabeth was met by a Scotland Yard detective. The inspector was dark and pretty, with a heart-shaped face that came to a fine-point chin, almond eyes accentuated by mascara, and black hair that was too long and lustrous for a policewoman.

"Detective Inspector Nasrin Jones, Metropolitan Police." Her voice was steady, handshake firm.

"Pleased to meet you, Inspector Jones," Elizabeth said. "I hope I can be of help."

"We hope so too."

There was no time for further introduction. They rolled their bags down the escalator and boarded the 5:10 to Heathrow.

Elizabeth took the seat directly opposite Inspector Jones facing the back of the train. She was soon staring at a backwards roll of dreary landscape in the dishwater light of a summer morning, public housing complexes of gray concrete and satellite dishes, cottages with rippling roofs, junk piles of car parts and appliances, and sidings bright with phosphorescent graffiti.

"I did some online research on you last night," Inspector Jones said. "Browsed several of your papers . . . *Ideation and the Adolescent Mind . . . In-Group Ideology and Mass Suicide* and, of course, *Suicide as Epidemic.*"

Elizabeth smiled.

"Then you must have had a good night's sleep," she replied.

I sure didn't.

The Battersea Power Station rolled backwards into view, a relic of Elizabeth's childhood come to life. Not two weeks after the death of Elizabeth's mother from cancer, Dad had tacked up old record album covers on the walls of the dining room and set up his amps and electric guitar, converting it into his music room. A beloved, vintage album cover was tacked on the wall depicting a giant pig floating in the air over the power station's four smokestacks.

"So is suicide your area of investigation?" Elizabeth asked.

"No, homicide," Nasrin said. "Doctor Browne—"

"Elizabeth, please."

"Do you truly insist on going to the scene . . . *naïve?*"

"I should have found a better word to use on the call with Mister Gray. Not at my best at three in the morning."

Elizabeth glanced out the window again as the power station slipped from view. Pink Floyd, *Animals,* that was the album. How Dad had listened to that record over and over wearing his clunky, giant headphones. How Mother would have hated what he had done to her dining room.

The inspector leaned forward, noticing Elizabeth's distraction.

"But yes," Elizabeth continued, "going in fresh helps me see things, the scene and all its clues to what the victims were thinking. It helps me to experience the site as the victims approached it, to feel a little of what they felt. Homicide, you say?"

"Even suicides are homicides."

"Of course."

Elizabeth knew that. Too little sleep had left her brain as dim as the early morning landscape. And, of course, prominent, international suicides would attract high-level police attention.

A car and driver waited for them at Heathrow Station. They were whisked through a gate and out onto a tarmac with a fleet of small government jets with royal seals.

Elizabeth followed Inspector Jones up the tiny metal ramp into a small Brazilian-made jet, a Legacy 500. The beige interior had little headroom, but the seats were plush. Elizabeth again found herself in a chair that faced backwards, this time across a small walnut table from Inspector Jones.

"Will we be met by the Norwegian police?"

"Of course, it's their country, even though it presently appears that none of their subjects were among the victims. An Inspector Stenstrom will be leading the investigation."

"What do we know about the victims?"

"One was an oil company executive from Houston. Kenneth H. Woods, vice president for safety, health, security and the environment at XRO Energy."

The largest publicly held corporation in the world. To be an XRO vice president was better than being the CEO of many Fortune 500s.

The engines roared, the craft vibrated and rolled into takeoff. Once airborne, the small jet tilted one way, then the other, before nosing almost straight up into a Wedgewood-blue sky. Once they leveled off, sunlight broke over a pleasant English farmscape of green and yellow squares. The land soon ended at a broken coastline of rock followed by pewter-gray sea dotted with an array of wind turbines like enormous white daffodils poking out of the sea.

"And the pharma CEO from Delaware?"

"Sandra Armstrong. She had led Therapso for almost eight years."

The name was familiar. Elizabeth had a vague memory of meeting Armstrong at a medical convention. Tall, striking-looking woman, confident and charming. A suicide?

Sun glinted off the mirror of the North Sea.

"And the writer?"

"Anne Shrewsbury. Wrote a mystery series, I read a few. Main character was a widow who was a famous painter in a small village in the Cotswolds. There always seemed to be a murder in the painter-widow's local parish, which of course, she always solved."

"Others?"

"Lionel Jacobson."

"The playwright?"

"Yes," Inspector Jones said.

Elizabeth remembered a *New York Times* profile piece on Jacobson, with headline something like, 'Weaving Success Out of Tragedy.' She recalled a photo of an earnest-looking man with short-shorn, salt-and-pepper hair on a round head. Proudly gay, intense work ethic, a history of feuds with other writers and endless lawsuits against his producers and others he felt had wronged him.

"The rest?"

"Still working on them. We should have their files by this afternoon."

"Clearly, they all had to be members of some sort of group," Elizabeth said.

"I thought you wanted to go into this naïve?"

"Enough of that."

"Very well," Inspector Jones had a pleasant smile. "Please call me Nasrin. The truth is, we don't know exactly what happened. But yes, when you see the scene, there will be no doubt. They were all in some sort of group, we just don't know what kind."

TWO

They were greeted on the airport tarmac by a small delegation of police.

An athletic-looking man in a dark blue uniform stepped forward. The gold-leaf clusters that framed his cap made him look more like a NATO general than a cop. Next to him was a trim, blonde woman with a severe expression. She wore a white shirt with epaulettes of brass-colored cords and a dark-blue skirt. Parked behind them were a dark-blue armored Volvo and a white VW station wagon with police stripes.

"I am Chief Inspector Stenstrom and this is my assistant, Inspector Dahl." Inspector Stenstrom's handshake was as firm as Nasrin's had been.

Several others stepped forward. There were introductions all the way around.

"Inspector Jones, you are to ride with me," Stenstrom said. "Ms. Browne, you are to ride in the white car with Inspector Dahl. We will be stopping in about thirty minutes, and then we shall ride on to the entrance to the park, which should take a further hour."

On that brisk note, they were off. Elizabeth sat in the back seat while Lieutenant Dahl drove. Elizabeth had never been to Norway before and was eager to drink in as much scenery as she could. All she saw at first were strip malls, high-end car dealerships and gas stations. The suburbs thinned out and they came to a stop at a large store, an outfitter of fishing gear, camping equipment and hiking apparel.

"Do you have any medical conditions that would prevent you from undertaking a strenuous hike?" Inspector Dahl asked.

"No."

"What is your foot size?"

"Seven-and-a-half, but an eight will do."

Dahl had a blonde ponytail and a face that would have been pretty if her expression were not so hard.

"Come inside."

The store was a steel cavern with hanging canoes and kayaks, not unlike any big box outfitter around the Washington Beltway.

"Ready for a hike?" Nasrin Jones, the Scotland Yard inspector, had crept up behind her. She had just been speaking with Inspector Dahl.

"Always," Elizabeth said.

"Get something warm," Nasrin said. "There will be altitude changes, and the winds can get pretty brisk up there."

"Up there?"

Her response to Nasrin made Dahl smile for once.

"They told me about you and your French word," Dahl said. "I am told not to say it."

Elizabeth picked out a pair of nylon hiking pants, a green, long-sleeved hiking shirt and a windbreaker. Inspector Dahl presented her with a pair of women's hiking boots with a pair of water-resistant socks.

"These should be sufficient," she said. "Seven-and-a-half. Want to try them on?"

"I am sure they'll fit."

"Try them on, if you would."

Inspector Dahl motioned Elizabeth to go to a changing booth. The hiking clothes fit well and the boots were snug. Elizabeth folded her business suit and put it into the bag. She walked toward the counter to pay for the clothes she was wearing, but Inspector Dahl held a hand out for the tags.

"The Crown will pay for all this," she said.

"Great, can I keep my new outfit?"

"No. It will be cleaned and go to charity."

Stenstrom and Nasrin Jones were off in a corner talking heatedly while keeping their voices low. Nasrin too had already changed into hiking gear. Stenstrom remained in his uniform. Elizabeth noticed that his uniform included black leather boots, sufficient for a hike, as did Dahl's.

Inspector Dahl shot her a look of displeasure, as if she had just caught Elizabeth eavesdropping.

"Please wait in the car," she said.

Back on the road, the last vestiges of suburbs gave way to the bucolic Norway that matched Elizabeth's expectations. The overcast day couldn't bleach out the vivid colors of the countryside, iridescent grass, Van Gogh bales of hay, red barns with green thatch sprouting on their roofs. The farmland rolled to a horizon that looked as if giants had once played marbles with boulders. The road rose into highlands and soon split a forested mountain chain. They crested a hill and a fjord opened before them.

A ferry sat by a dock, the gate up and the attendants waiting to lead the two police cars into an empty lane with reserved spaces at the bow end of the ferry. The craft was off in a minute. Elizabeth rolled down the window of her police car. Wind cut through the strait and raised small white caps and flecks of foam off the gray waters. After a night of interrupted sleep, the cool air made Elizabeth feel fresh and alert.

Ten minutes later, the ferry slowed to moor into its berth at the other side of the strait. Their caravan went straight out as soon as the metal arm was up. They took a winding ribbon of a road that followed the mountainous terrain up and down. A half-hour later, the driver parked next to the dark blue sedan on a hillside.

Reporters were waiting for them, a clot of television cameras and upheld smartphones tracking the inspectors as they walked by. No one barked a question. Elizabeth had been at a few public crime scenes in her career, but she had never encountered a press mob that was so respectful.

One question finally came from the leader of the pack.

"Inspector, sir, can you please tell us the identities of—"

Stenstrom waved him off.

A park ranger bounded forward to lead the inspectors to huddle over a map. A thin, balding man, with the world-weary expression of a detective, joined them. Stenstrom said something and they lined up behind the park ranger. Nasrin motioned for Elizabeth to get in line behind her. Several policemen guarded the entrance to a hiking trail. A sign in Norwegian and English said that the trail to the Preikestolen was closed for the day.

They began the ascent, leaving the journalists and a small crowd behind.

"How long?" Elizabeth asked.

"Two hours at brisk pace," Nasrin Jones said.

"I do it in an hour and a half," Inspector Dahl said.

"I have no doubt that you do," Nasrin said.

"Elevation?" Elizabeth asked.

"Six hundred and four meters," Dahl said.

Almost two thousand feet.

"And the name of this place, preka?"

Nasrin shot a village-idiot glance at Elizabeth.

"You've really never heard of this?"

"Humor me."

"Preikestolen—means the Pulpit Rock, or preacher's rock," Nasrin said. "World famous. You'll recognize it when you see it."

The trail, all loose rubble and gravel, became suddenly steeper. Elizabeth felt the burn in her chest and her breathing edge into a pant. Nasrin gave her an 'are-you-all-right' look. Elizabeth often ran along the C&O Canal and did a fair amount of hiking in the Blue Ridge two hours west of her U Street condo. Exertion always began like that for her until she adjusted, her breathing regularized, her pulse—still quickened—leveled off.

The trail became less steep as it wound through piney woods, a large blue lake glinting through the trees. The trail grew tough again as they stepped up stairs hewed out of natural stone.

Catching her breath, Elizabeth glanced backwards and saw the radio towers and church steeples of a nearby town. The trail flattened and became a wooden walkway across a green, mossy bog. Back on the trail, they climbed through birch woodland surrounded by giant boulders. The air was cool and sweet and the sun stung her cheeks and the backs of her hands.

They reached the top of the mountain in a little more than two hours. Sweat clung to her skin, making Elizabeth feel clammy inside her hiking clothes. They came to a crest and clambered over a ridge of stone.

"This is the Lysefjord," Dahl said.

The blue of this water was as dark as that of the deepest, coldest ocean. But it was no ocean. It was a thick channel that ran between gray cliffs topped by green pastureland and massive trees under mountain tops riven by bright-white glaciers. Most of the ridges and peaks of granite were well below them.

The Pulpit Rock was an enormous spade-shaped outcropping that tapered to an irregular point over the vast space overlooking the fjord. A diagonal crack ran across its flat base. It was big enough to hold a hundred people.

"It is 25 meters by 25 meters at its widest and longest," Dahl said, as if reading Elizabeth's mind.

The rock had only two people on it, a Norwegian policeman and a policewoman standing guard at a line of yellow police tape where the precipice joined the mountain. Several dozen hikers, like spectators at an amphitheater, had spread out on cliffs that rose behind and above the Pulpit Rock. Many had raised their smartphones to capture the investigators arriving at the scene.

Inspector Stenstrom led the way and came to a stop in front of the police officers. Elizabeth stepped around him, over the tape and out onto the rock.

The policewoman shouted something in Norwegian at her, but Stenstrom barked a countermand.

The wind rippled Elizabeth's windbreaker and ran her hair sideways. She stiffened for a moment, as if the wind might lift her up and send her soaring over the fjord.

Elizabeth looked around. Above the vista of mountains and vast waters was a realm of pure nothingness. Space defined the scene, carving the mountains and the bowing horizon, an emptiness filled only with the molecules of thinning, light-blue atmosphere.

"No further," the policewoman said in English.

Elizabeth nodded.

She looked straight up to the dark purple zenith, dome of the cosmos. She looked down and studied the seven shoes set in a neat line two-thirds of the way to the tip of the rock.

An elegant pump, metallic blue, sharp heel jutting into a surface fracture in the rock.

A white running shoe with creases, breaks and grass stains from many runs.

A man's executive shoe, highly polished and black, strings neatly tied.

An old tattered house slipper.

A lady's boot, high and sexy, the dark leather slick and shiny in the sun, top-half folded over.

An open-toed Birkenstock flat.

A light-brown man's penny loafer.

The toe of each shoe pointed at the cliff's edge like a compass needle aiming at magnetic North.

THREE

After catching up her on sleep at a small hotel for tourists and hikers, Elizabeth met Inspector Dahl, who drove her to the Lysefjord nature center.

Outside, the museum was a modernist take on an old stave church. Inside, a bored girl in a park service uniform behind the reception desk chuckled at something as she scrolled on her smartphone. Behind her were set pieces on the birch forest, stuffed mountain goats, replicas of giant cod and the history of the area that lit up when one approached.

Inspector Dahl motioned Elizabeth to a side door and led her into a birch-paneled conference room with a long table of unstained birch. On a sidewall a long mural of the Norwegian forest unfolded, a bas-relief of light, blonde wood representing trees against a dark-brown background. The front of the room was a panel of windows that afforded a spectacular view of the sun creeping down the opposite cliff of the Lysefjord. A bell pitcher of stainless steel sweated beads of moisture on a mat in the middle of the table.

Nasrin Jones and Lars Stenstrom both nodded at Elizabeth as she entered. Next to Nasrin was the same thin, bald man who had joined them yesterday. There were three more men she had not seen before. Inspector Dahl took a seat and motioned to Elizabeth to do the same. She took an empty chair next to Nasrin.

Stenstrom made introductions all around the table.

The bald man from yesterday was introduced as Harold Kober of the *Politiets sikkerhetstjeneste.*

"PST is their Scotland Yard," Nasrin whispered in Elizabeth's ear, leaning in close enough for Elizabeth to feel the warmth of the inspector's breath.

One of the strangers was a counselor official from the British Embassy, but she did not catch his name.

Another, a burly, red-headed man with a round, ruddy face and a chinstrap beard was Charles Bowie, from the U.S. embassy. Next to him was a thin, man with strands of hair across a bald pate and a hang-dog expression, Jim Norris, an FBI agent.

"And I am Lars Stenstrom, Chief Inspector of the *Direktoratet for naturforvaltning.*"

Nasrin looked up, startled.

"I appreciate you conducting this meeting in English for our benefit," Nasrin said. "But you say you are chief inspector of what?"

"The *Miljødirektoratet,* to be precise," Stenstrom said with a bland smile. "The Directorate of the Environment, parks division."

"You're a bloody park ranger?" Nasrin said. "And you're leading a homicide investigation?"

"Yes, that is the protocol," he said. "Bloody or not."

"And this is fine with you?" Nasrin said to Kober.

"Why yes, of course, Inspector Stenstrom has jurisdiction within the park," the little man said with a friendly smile. "I am more than happy for him to take the lead."

Elizabeth smiled inwardly. In the many investigations she had assisted in the United States, federal agents had been ready to draw guns over who got to unwrap the yellow crime scene tape. Kober acted with all the deference of a pastor passing the salt at a church picnic.

"After all," Kober said, "Lars Stenstrom is chief inspector over all of the park service." He turned to Stenstrom and dipped his head. "I am honored to work under your direction, sir."

Nasrin snorted.

"So what's this all about?" asked Bowie, the redhead from the U.S. Embassy.

"Seven victims, three from the UK, the rest American," Stenstrom said. "Among them, two senior corporate executives from the U.S., one a recently retired pharmaceutical CEO, a semi-famous British novelist, a very prominent playwright from London. All seem to have left a single shoe with an ID in that nice little row and jumped together to their deaths."

"Time?"

It was Norris, the FBI agent, who barked the question, chin down while taking notes.

"We can narrow the jump to between 7:40 and 7:50 a.m.," Stenstrom said.

"Witnesses?" Nasrin asked.

"We are canvassing the locals, putting out the word on social media for hikers who might have been in the area," Stenstrom said. "Cruise lines frequent the fjord, but not that early, otherwise we would have abundant video."

"They would have had to have started hiking up the mountain at what time?" Norris asked.

"Around 5 a.m., if they took time to compose themselves before jumping," Stenstrom said. "We believe they each carried a torch to manage the trail in the dawn light, and took them with them over the edge."

"A torch?" Elizabeth asked.

"That's the Queen's English for flashlight," Nasrin said. "Where are we now on bodies?"

"District water police picked up one more last night, giving us only three," Stenstrom said. "No notes found on any of them. Just the drivers' licenses left in the shoes. None of the seven have returned to the hotel."

"So how could four bodies still be missing from a straight fall down to the rocks?" Norris asked.

"They must have hit outcroppings and shot out over the Lysefjord, or rolled down the rocks and got pulled into the water," Stenstrom said. "These channels cut as deep as the mountains around them, with roiling currents that move up and down with the water column. The current runs straight to a large channel that empties to the North Sea. So we're currently checking every skerry between the point of impact and the outlet to the main channel."

"Skerry?" Norris asked.

"Small islands of rock and coral at the mouth of the fjord," Nasrin said.

"Who do we have?" Norris asked.

"Let me take you to the morgue in Stavanger later today," Stenstrom said, "and we can all countercheck identities there."

"Mobiles?" Nasrin asked.

"None were recovered with mobile devices," Stenstrom said. "But they had all left plenty in the hotel—smartphones, pads, laptops. So we still have to regard the ones whose bodies were not recovered as potentially alive, if they jumped at all. We've collected—"

"They all stayed at the same hotel?" Elizabeth asked. "In Stavanger?"

"Yes, at the Victoria," Stenstrom said. "And credit card receipts show that they had dinner together at the World Tree Pub the night before. A preliminary look into their email accounts shows no direct contact between them prior to that dinner."

"How could that be?" Norris asked.

"It is a suicide pact," Elizabeth said.

All heads turned to her.

"Most likely," she continued, "they were joined together by the same website."

"So they were all depressed, just got together in a chat room and decided to take a swan dive into a fjord?" It was Bowie, the embassy counselor.

"No, this isn't that simple."

"Then what?" Bowie leaned back. He wore a silver tie that cascaded down the ridges of his gut like a waterfall.

"There is a belief system at work here," Elizabeth said. "Intelligent, imaginative people who were highly successful in very different domains. Something brought them together. Something shiny that lured them in and took control of them."

"How could this be?" Kober asked.

Lars Stenstrom sat back, eyes narrowing as he appraised her.

"Yes," he said, "something like that."

Elizabeth loved a hearty lunch, but on this day she had a cup of yogurt. She had enough experience with morgues to know that it was never a good idea to have too much in one's stomach.

A caravan of police cars delivered the party of investigators to the examining room of the Stavanger coroner, a modernistic steel and concrete structure attached to the side of a hospital. A policewoman signed them in. She led them down a hall and through glass doors into an autopsy room of white tile and a dozen steel dissection tables with faucets, runnels and steel basins.

The room was chilly and thick with a familiar scent of hospital bleach and floral spray. Elizabeth always found that scent accentuated rather than masked the underlying stench of decomposition.

Three naked bodies were splayed out on steel tables under pivoting medical lights. One of them was a pear-shaped woman in her late fifties, with an apricot patch of pubic hair and dark-red hair slicked to her skull. The woman's body bore the characteristic Y-shaped incision of an autopsy. Around the back of her hairline, Elizabeth could see the subtler suture marks from the removal of her brain.

"Anne Shrewsbury?" Nasrin asked. "The mystery writer?"

Stenstrom nodded.

"Front is too fine, almost undamaged," Kober said. "She must have landed on her back."

Shrewsbury's face had a composed expression, as if she had just closed her eyes to prepare for a writing session.

"And so she escaped the heartache and the thousand natural shocks that flesh is heir to," Bowie said. "Sucks for her."

Stenstrom locked eyes on Bowie for a moment.

"There will be respect in this room," he said.

The next table held a young man's body, the head exploded like a pulpy fruit that had burst in a microwave. His one remaining eye stood out on a stalk, like the eyeball of a crab.

"Hit a rock on the way down," Norris said.

"His name is Mike Drummond, thirty-one," Stenstrom said. "He was rising up through the ranks of PubX, the global PR firm, vice president, North America. Resigned last year to pursue outdoor activities in . . . uh, Bend, Oregon . . . Lots of Facebook postings on rock climbing, hikes, kayaking."

"I guess the outdoor life didn't fill the void," Bowie said. "Could've done this at home."

Stenstrom cast Bowie another hard stare.

"Actually, Bowie is right," Nasrin said. "Why come all the way from the Rocky Mountains—"

"Cascades. I grew up outside of Eugene. And it's Charlie."

"—Cascades, Charlie, just to jump off a cliff halfway around the world?"

"For a belief," Elizabeth said. "And to join with his companions in that belief."

"Even though they may not have known each other?" Stenstrom

asked.

Elizabeth could only shrug. There was still so much to learn.

The third body was a slender woman, blondish hair with a sole strand interwoven purple and green. Her face was swollen on one side and mashed like a boxer's on the other, arms and legs broken and twisted into unnatural angles. She had a small tattoo under her left collarbone that spelled out a message in Gothic letters: "Think It and It Will Happen."

"Sophia Goddard," Stenstrom said. "An administrative assistant to the CEO of a small Internet firm in Milton Keynes."

His voice went down an octave.

"Only twenty-four years old."

"And whom are we missing?" Nasrin asked.

"Sandra Armstrong, CEO of Therapso . . . Kenneth Woods, executive vice president of XRO Energy . . . Lionel Jacobson, playwright ... and one Daryl Parnell, fifty-eight, a widower and restaurateur from Atlanta."

"How many were married?"

"None," Stenstrom said. "Armstrong, Woods and Shrewsbury were divorced. Parnell widowed, as I said. The others had never married."

"I can see the headline now," Charlie Bowie said. "Suicide of the Singletons."

Stenstrom turned to Bowie to say something, shook his head instead, and then turned to Norris and Nasrin.

"I will leave it to you to bring me whatever information Scotland Yard and the FBI can collect from next-of-kin and other sources," he said. "We will meet at 9 a.m. By that time, our digital forensic expert will be ready to report."

As the others gathered into the caravan of police cars, Elizabeth told the group she felt like walking the city. As Elizabeth turned, Lars Stenstrom smiled for once and waved goodbye.

Elizabeth turned a corner and went down an alley between tall brick walls. It was becoming an effort to walk, as if her feet had been packed with sand. She slowed down and rested a shoulder against the bricks.

"You all right?"

Nasrin had followed her.

"Just need to catch my breath, Inspector," Elizabeth said. "From the smell of that place."

"I know what you mean. And again, please use my first name. We're going to be working together for a while."

Nasrin lit a cigarette and handed it to her.

"Hell of a way to catch one's breath," Elizabeth said. "And I don't smoke."

"So one won't hurt you."

Elizabeth took the cigarette, tasting the residue of Nasrin's lipstick, tart like apples. The aroma of the freshly lit cigarette was as pleasant as brewing coffee in the morning. Elizabeth drew it deep into her lungs, the narcotic effect almost immediate. She let the smoke out through her nostrils like an accomplished smoker.

"Better?"

"Yes," Elizabeth said.

"You look like you could get used to this."

Elizabeth took another drag.

"I smoked for a year, just after my father died when I was in college."

"Did it help?"

"It gave me a cough. And a bad taste in my mouth in the mornings."

"Fair enough," Nasrin said, taking the cig back and inhaling. "I don't do this often myself. Just one a day. Takes discipline. Going for a walk?"

"Going shopping. I can't come to Stavanger without getting my son a sweater."

"Could you use some company? I know I can," Nasrin said. "Bloody weird day. Bloody weird case."

Elizabeth nodded.

They took a cab to Old Stavanger, a neighborhood of winding, cobblestone streets and shops in small white homes that looked like doll houses.

One shop sold only sweaters. After much deliberation and trying on, Elizabeth selected a Nordic wool sweater, a dark blue one with a large, white snowflake. It would look good on Max … if he would wear it.

Elizabeth held the sweater up for Nasrin's approval.

Nasrin stared at Elizabeth for a long moment.

"It also would look very good on you," Nasrin said.

They walked around. Stavanger had a charming fish market along a wooden pier, with stalls selling every size and color of fish on ice along with the occasional chunk of whale meat. Elizabeth used her phone to snap pictures of the old Hanseatic-style mansions and simpler, wooden homes, which she texted to Max. They browsed the tchotchkes and curios in a string of intriguing little shops along the harbor and then stopped at an outdoor café for a glass of wine.

Elizabeth felt safe around Nasrin. And it was good to have a new friend. Over a glass of wine, the conversation turned from the case to their pasts.

Nasrin's mother hailed from a prominent family that included the personal physician to the Shah. Her mother had studied at the London School of Economics, where she had fallen in love with a skinny Englishman named Jones. Nasrin's maternal grandparents had never approved of the marriage, even though Mr. Jones had gone on to become a prominent barrister and Nasrin's mother had flourished as an academic, both happily married and devoted to their one child.

"Did you grow up speaking Farsi?" Elizabeth asked.

"Yes, my mother made sure of it," Nasrin said. "I am really quite good at it. Comes in handy these days in my line of work."

"Men?"

"One or two," Nasrin looked down at her nails. "I was actually married to a man for six whole months."

The way she said it made Elizabeth laugh.

Nasrin leaned forward.

"Tell me about yourself."

And so Elizabeth did, from her mother's death, to her father's suicide, then Mike's … Elizabeth's mentoring at the university, finding salvation in her work. A difficult marriage to a difficult man. Hard divorce. Raising Max as a single mother while building a career … tenure, licensing, practice, publishing and not perishing.

Nasrin's eyes scanned Elizabeth's with interest and compassion as she told her story. To Elizabeth's surprise, by the time she finished, Nasrin's eyes were glistening with held back tears.

"You might think yourself vulnerable," Nasrin said. "But from what you say, you have survived things that would slay the strongest."

"I am a survivor," Elizabeth said. "That much I know."

After they finished their wine and went back out on the street, Elizabeth caught a glimpse of copies of a London tabloid in a kiosk. It had a front-page picture of the Pulpit Rock under a headline in a huge font.

"Terror on the Cliffs," screamed *The Daily Mail*. "Playwright, Author, CEO and XRO Exec Take the Plunge," read the subhead. "They held hands all the way down," read a quote from a supposed witness in a box.

"Barmy press," Nasrin said and then checked the time on her smartphone. "I've got to go. Got to pick up a package at the UK consulate."

Nasrin gave Elizabeth a warm smile.

"It's been lovely, dear. It's nice to know I have a friend on this assignment. Perhaps I'll check in later in case you want to share a late-night cocktail?"

Elizabeth nodded. She kept walking around the old city. By 7 o'clock in what in most parts of the world was the evening, the summer sun was as strong and bright as mid-afternoon. The sunlight made everything crisp and clean—the blue-gray harbor, the blinding-white hulls of cruise ships and fishing boats, the pubs with murals of Norwegian history and pop art on their walls— all of it underneath bright red flags with blue crosses that snapped in the wind.

Elizabeth realized she had eaten nothing since her morning yogurt.

She easily found her way back to the Hotel Victoria, where the members of the little investigative group had checked in after their Lysefjord excursion, a definite improvement over the hikers' inn where they had spent their first night. The Victoria was a block-long rectangle of red and brown brick with subdued Edwardian accents. It was a practical choice that—however unintended—kept the team in communion with the dead they studied.

Elizabeth went into the hotel's Holmen Pub and saw Lars

Stenstrom sitting at the dark wooden bar, nursing a beer alone.

"Good evening Inspector," Elizabeth said.

Stenstrom turned slowly, even a little lazily, no sign of the brisk manner he displayed on-duty.

"Doctor Browne, I hope you have had a nice day since the unpleasantness at the morgue." Stenstrom's blue eyes seemed electric when he smiled.

"We all deserve a little vacation after the horror show of this morning. May I buy you a drink?"

"You certainly may," he said.

Elizabeth took an adjoining stool.

"And please, call me Lars."

"Likewise," Elizabeth said.

"So you want me to call you Lars?"

A warm smile broke across his face when he made her laugh. As Lars Stenstrom lifted his glass, Elizabeth couldn't help but notice how the low sunlight inflamed the blonde hairs that bristled along his thick forearms and the backs of his large hands. A worker's hands. She also couldn't help but notice that his left hand, flat on the bar, was without a ring.

The bartender took her order, a local microbrew, which he pumped from a beer tap. The beer arrived, a clean lager with a slightly sweet head.

"I would never have thought you to be a beer drinker," Lars said.

"I am a bit of a fanatic about it, actually," Elizabeth said. "If I won the lottery, there would be nothing to stop me from doing a microbrew tour of the world. Mind if I eat?"

She ordered a cheeseburger with Swiss cheese and a reindeer patty.

"Another surprise," he said.

"You had me pegged as a chardonnay-sipping, salad eater, right?"

"You must work out," he said.

"I like to walk. A lot. And yoga. Occasional hikes."

"I thought Washington was a flat swamp."

"There are mountains nearby. Nothing like yours."

The hamburger was good and juicy, the meat not at all gamey. Elizabeth ate half of it, and washed it down with the ice-cold beer.

"So any new thoughts?" he asked.

"With a complete absence of suicide notes, we won't know until you tell us what you find when you crack their computers and phones. You must already know some new things?"

Lars Stenstrom nodded.

"Want to share anything?"

"Don't you want to hear it all tomorrow *naïve*?"

"Oh not you, give that a rest. I mean for good."

"Before I tell you anything, I truly would like to know what you think beforehand."

Elizabeth sipped her beer.

"Well, as I said, they were definitely indoctrinated and turned into an affinity group. Probably online."

Lars ran a big hand across the blonde stubble of his jaw. The sunlight was getting low now, casting a golden glow on the brass fixtures in the bar.

"And," Elizabeth added, "there is a belief system at work here."

"Reasonable," he said.

"I will go farther," she said. "This is something fervent, some shared sense of the sacred they concocted. A small-group religion."

"Nothing we have seen to date would suggest that," Lars said. "They just had one meal together, at the World Tree."

"Any details?"

"The pub's just down the street," Lars said. "They were there for a good two hours." He squinted as he searched his memory. "A Caesar salad, small pizza, two orders of local salmon, one order of swordfish, two hamburgers, one of them a reindeer burger like yours. Fourteen beers and … uh, two bottles of an expensive California pinot noir, followed by, I believe, some cheesecake, vanilla ice cream and coffee. Three thousand and thirty-nine Kroner, or about five hundred and fifty dollars, U.S."

"Who paid?"

"Does it matter?" Lars said. "I believe it was Woods, the oil company executive, who put it all on his credit card."

"What does the wait staff remember?"

"They remember them as all relaxed, jovial, a bit loud. Nothing out of the ordinary."

The people Elizabeth had seen on the metal trays in the morgue had, a mere two nights ago, been out in the fun part of this small city, sharing a hearty meal, drinks and laughs. They went back to their rooms, set their alarms, woke up in the pre-dawn hours to dress warmly in appropriate hiking clothes, and then marched to their doom through the dark forest like the seven dwarves.

Elizabeth looked out the window at the last rays of the sun glinting off the metal bands and handles on the sailboats in the harbor. She tried to register some insight in reaction to the disparity between these chosen deaths and the cheerful city outside, but she couldn't.

The knock on her door was soft.

It was Nasrin Jones, her jacket off but still wearing a starched white shirt neatly tucked into a gray skirt.

Nasrin smiled.

"My chores are done. It's been an absolutely shambolic day. I thought it might be nice to end it with a friendly face."

"Please come in."

The detective padded into Elizabeth's room like a cat, the scent of her jasmine perfume trailing her.

Elizabeth closed the door. By then, Nasrin had walked to the center of the room, and performed a quick pirouette to face Elizabeth.

"I caught a glimpse of you and Lars talking in the bar on my way through the lobby," Nasrin said. "He is just a highly promoted park ranger, you know that, don't you?"

"He seems like a trained investigator to me. We talked about the victims' last meal at the World Tree," Elizabeth said. "Lars also told me something I didn't want to know. This is the room that Sandra Armstrong had stayed in."

Nasrin stepped toward Elizabeth, a pert smile on her nicely formed lips.

"Don't tell me that you believe in ghosts?"

"That would be an occupational hazard in my profession," Elizabeth said.

"Me, too. I enjoyed our afternoon together."

"So did I."

"Tell me, Elizabeth, are you okay? You seemed troubled when I caught up with you in the alley."

"Well … despite the late sun and beautiful scenery, I can't shake the feeling that this place is gloomy."

"I know what you mean," Nasrin replied. "A little lonely, too, perhaps? I know I am, especially given the prospect of having to stay here and follow such a dismal inquiry. Do you ever feel lonely here?"

"A little, yes."

Nasrin stepped in a bit closer.

"I don't want to be presumptuous, but over our two days together, I think I may have caught a sense …"

Elizabeth thought, *Did I do something wrong at the suicide scene?*

". . . of a kindred soul, of shared sensibilities."

"Yes," Elizabeth said. "I feel that."

"You have a pretty way of cocking your head when you're perplexed, did you know that?"

Nasrin took one more step into her personal space, gently lifted Elizabeth's chin with a long, slender finger and kissed her.

Elizabeth had never been kissed by a woman before, not like that. Nasrin's lips were soft and pleasing. Nasrin's breasts, tight against her shirt, pressed against her own.

Elizabeth felt a brief quiver of pleasure bolt through her chest.

Nasrin pulled back, a little breathless.

"Do you desire me?"

Elizabeth said nothing, her heart hammering from the surprise.

"Do you want to lie down with me?" Nasrin said, nodding in the direction of the bed.

"If you like," Elizabeth said. "Never really thought about it."

That put her off a beat. Elizabeth decided it would be best to let Nasrin down gently by making herself the odd duck.

"But you do want to, with me?"

"Not especially, but I will."

The truth is, it was not entirely out of the realm of possibility. The kiss had been sweet and there was something about Nasrin that intrigued Elizabeth.

Nasrin stepped back, incredulous.

"Haven't you ever been with a woman before?"

"No."

"Not even in college?"

"No," she said. It was true, and a little astonishing, considering that Elizabeth Barrett Browne had earned her B.S. in biochemistry at Smith, where Sapphic experimentation was practically a requirement.

"And yet you would just be compliant?"

"Sure, why not?"

Nasrin shook her head, whether in astonishment or disgust it was hard to tell. Her pretty face fluttered with powerful and conflicting emotions.

"I misread the signals, sorry," Nasrin said. "Please, do me a favor Elizabeth and let us just wind this back."

Elizabeth tried to imagine what signals she might have given off.

"Wound back it is," she said.

Nasrin smiled and nodded a bit too energetically, embarrassed. She left without another word.

Her jasmine scent lingered in the room.

Elizabeth stood frozen for a moment, too astonished for a moment to know what to do next. She washed her face, brushed her teeth, rubbed her face with night cream, put on a nightie and went straight to bed.

She thought of reading, but took a sleeping pill instead, followed by a half pill. She turned off the light. The room was dark and cool and Elizabeth wanted to keep a tight rein on her imagination.

FOUR

They met in a conference room inside a structure of stacked steel and concrete boxes, each box with an acrylic window to provide a view of the city below. It could have been the headquarters of a top-flight creative ad agency, but it was instead the Oslo headquarters of the Directorate of the Environment.

Elizabeth took a seat in a webbed chair to join the others around a glass conference table. Charlie Bowie, the American counselor official from Oslo, stroked his beard compulsively. He was even ruddier than usual this morning, his eyes unfocused and bloodshot. Agent Norris leaned forward over the glass, as if he were begging some unseen master for a treat.

Lars Stenstrom walked briskly into the room and announced there was plentiful coffee and scones in a galley down the hall, promoting Bowie to bolt up and leave the room. Lars nodded at Elizabeth with a slight smile. Nasrin made eye contact with her immediately afterward. A brief smile started and faded on her lips and she looked away.

"We'll start in a moment," Lars said. "I have asked our lead digital investigator to give this morning's presentation."

A young woman with a thin ring sprouting from one nostril and a line of rings embedded across one ear entered the room. Her black hair was shaved into an undercut, the longer half in rooster tails, the shorter half revealing runic tattoos made fuzzy by the black bristles of her scalp. She turned on a projector and connected a laptop to it. The desktop of the computer had a screensaver with anime renderings of the cast from a popular cable-TV show about fantasy kingdoms and dragons.

Elizabeth looked out the wall window. To the west, container ships in the harbor vanished into a rolling curtain of white fog.

"Thank you Ingrid," Lars said.

The young woman with the facial rings and the runic head symbols left, almost bumping into Bowie as he returned with an oversized cup of coffee.

Bowie turned in her direction and looked back, astonished.

"How are we going to manage to conduct this investigation without Goth girl?" Bowie said. "Bit of a cliché, isn't she?"

"Ingrid is a university student and our intern," Lars said. "Believe it or not, the regular park service actually has a grooming code."

A fat, blonde man in his mid-thirties bounded into the room, breathing heavily.

Lars spoke again, "Colleagues, allow me to introduce Thor Magnusson, lead digital investigator the PST has been kind enough to detail to the park service."

Thor set down a folder, fished around for something and came up with a remote. He turned, saw the anime screensaver and cringed with embarrassment.

"Ingrid," he said under his breath.

A few clicks brought up a virtual folder with a title, *"digital rettsmedisinsk etterforskning."*

Digital forensic investigation.

"Good morning," Thor said. "I regret that happier circumstances have not brought us together."

"Yeah, like fairies and dragons," Bowie said.

"Or smartasses with thin covers," Nasrin said, looking straight at Bowie.

Bowie stiffened in his chair and shot Nasrin a cool look as he raised his coffee mug to his mouth. Nasrin smiled at Bowie, then turned to Elizabeth, displaying the satisfied look of a person with a delicious secret barely held.

"We have recovered fifteen devices in all," Thor said. "Seven people who left behind eight smartphones, two laptops and five smart pads in their rooms. Not a single one of them left behind a suicide letter in their devices, even in draft form. Nor did there appear to be anything unusual in their many email accounts, at least in regard to a planned suicide or unorthodox ideologies."

"So we have nothing," Norris said.

"I did not say that," Thor said. "They all communicated, but used a common ruse favored by terrorists and adulterous generals. They shared a Gmail account into which they deposited messages in draft folders. The drafts were never sent, but I am sure the accounts were shared and the drafts read."

"But they had to have started with a direct communication, to be led to this point?" Norris asked.

"Yes," Thor said. "All of their devices and accounts were purchased and signed on to at most six months ago. We should ask their relatives or executors to look for older devices."

Thor turned to Bowie again.

"Or perhaps we could just ask our American friends to simply ask the NSA to look up the records."

"I'm a diplo, so signals is not my area of expertise," Bowie said. "But I do know that recent law makes private phone companies responsible for keeping international records, but they don't keep them that long."

"What I don't get is why they didn't leave a note for loved ones, for the world?" Norris asked.

"What they left is a collective message," Elizabeth said. "In the form of performance art, spelled out by seven shoes. What was the name of the account that they shared?"

Thor grimaced. He hit a toggle.

Black letters on a screen read: "Fólkvangr_or _bust@gmail.com."

"What is bloody Fólkvangr?" Nasrin asked.

"It is the afterlife for heroes," Lars replied.

"I thought that was Valhalla," Nasrin said.

"Half of deserving warriors go to Valhalla, the other half to Fólkvangr," Lars said. "Fólkvangr is not the realm of Odin, but of Freyja . . . goddess of erotic love, receiver of the slain."

"Sounds like the better deal," Nasrin said.

———————

In the morning, Elizabeth took a morning flight back to Stavanger. At the airport, she found the dark-blue armored Volvo and slipped into the front passenger seat. Lars Stenstrom sat behind the wheel, grinning like a man about to go on vacation.

"You really enjoy this," she said.

"I love to get out into the field," Lars said.

"And why didn't you ask Nasrin to join us?"

"You didn't mention anything to her?"

"No," Elizabeth said with an edge of irritation, rejecting any implication that politics between inspectors was somehow her responsibility. "I followed all of your instructions to the letter."

Lars pulled away from the curb and entered the slipstream of traffic.

"So why didn't you ask her to come along?" Elizabeth asked.

Lars pondered the question as he navigated a roundabout.

"The better question is why I asked you to come along."

"I'll bite. So why?"

"We finally found a witness. I need you to evaluate him as I evaluate what he tells us."

"So who is he?"

"Mountain folk."

"A Norwegian hillbilly?"

Lars chuckled and then lapsed into a thoughtful silence as he concentrated on the tight curves that led to the backcountry. They retraced the route toward the Pulpit Rock and crossed by ferry, this time no one holding a special spot for them. Lars took a quick turn at speed onto gravel road that cut through thick forest. The forest opened to the Lysefjord, where a forest ranger waited for them in a police boat with a thick rubber siding and two powerful Yamaha engines rumbling at idle.

"After you."

Lars followed Elizabeth down a short pier and onto the cruiser.

As soon as Lars jumped aboard, the ranger pushed the throttle forward and sent Elizabeth wheeling backward. Lars caught her in his arms and held her closely in the grip of his large hands.

"Are you okay?"

Elizabeth looked up at him and nodded. He grasped her waist and gently eased her to back onto her feet. Lars went to the ranger behind the wheel of the boat and shouted something into the man's ear. The ranger accepted the reprimand with a brisk nod.

The craft cut across the gray-blue surface of the water. Seen from this vantage point, the cliffs that seemed so sheer and straight from above were now irregular columns and blocks of light granite. The stone walls had the hue of beach sand. White mist that wafted from the forest above, infiltrated the rocks and trees and went to the water line.

Lars smiled at Elizabeth and pointed at something. A waterfall spouted over a cliff high above them and cascaded down the rocks to roil the waters. In the high cliffs, trees jutted out of the rock face like sprigs of parsley.

As they approached the opposite bank, Elizabeth saw Inspector Dahl standing next to a dark blue Range Rover with "Politi" in big block letters, lest anyone imagine that such a gas-devouring beast was used for fun. The ranger cut the engines—taking care to make a slow transition this time—to push the bow of the rubber-bottomed boat onto a gravel beach. Elizabeth rolled up her pants leg and took off her shoes.

"I hope you don't mind a little wet," Lars said, offering her hand as she stepped down a metal ladder. She waved him off.

The water was ankle deep and glacially cold.

There was a towel inside the Range Rover, which Elizabeth used to dry her feet and ankles. They buckled into their seats. Inspector Dahl took the wheel and ground up a pitted road of rock and dirt. The gradient was soon so steep it seemed as if they would lose traction and roll back a hundred feet into the water.

The Range Rover leveled off on a narrow roadbed between a wall of granite on one side and a sheer drop no more than two inches from the edge of their tires on the other.

"Next time, can we phone this in?" Elizabeth said.

"Fear of heights?" Lars asked.

"Not so far," she replied, "but I think Norway might help me cultivate one."

They rose again. Elizabeth felt her breath catch as the Range Rover slipped again on gravel. Inspector Dahl expertly maneuvered the SUV, letting off the gas and slowly reapplying it to regain traction.

They came to a flat place, a green glade where a house stood just off a granite wall. A carpet of grass covered the roof. In the yard, the boney hoop of a pilot whale's lower jaw stood upright like a giant croquet wicket. Soccer flags flapped from its serrated teeth. The house was a rectangle with weathered siding of dark wood. It took a moment for Elizabeth to realize that the antique siding covered a manufactured home.

A face flashed by the window.

"He is here all right," Inspector Dahl said.

Elizabeth looked to Lars.

"Magnus Norland," Lars said. "A loner, trapper, with rights to this land that go back farther than anyone can remember."

"An eccentric?" she asked.

"Eccentric would be kind," Lars said. "He is, how to say this for our consultant, folkish?"

"Ásatrú," Dahl added.

"Which is?" Elizabeth asked.

"The old religion, true to the Ása gods" Lars said. "In these back-country places, the Christian cross has never taken root in this stony soil. When you step out of this car, you find yourself on Odin's land."

"Magnus's wife was Sami, white people who live in tee-pees, much like your Indians," Dahl added. All Elizabeth could recall about them was a TV documentary about people who lived near the Arctic Circle and raised reindeer.

The door opened and an elfin face, white and weathered, peered out from the shadows. Lars shouted a loud greeting. A liver-spotted hand thrust out into the sunlight to make a welcoming gesture.

As they approached the house, Elizabeth flinched at the odor of decaying flesh. Off to the side, several animal traps hung from a rack. A small skin, like a black blotch, dried on a smaller rack.

The inside of the house was dark and cool. The old man waved but did not shake their hands. He motioned for everyone to sit. He took a chair and lit a cigarette. Elizabeth followed the two inspectors inside. Lars and Dahl sat side by side on a ratty couch. Elizabeth took a seat in a thick chair upholstered in corduroy.

Lars spoke in rapid Norwegian, smiling. Elizabeth could read the sentiments— *thank you for allowing us to visit, we are so lucky to have a witness, I appreciate your willingness to talk to us.*

The old man lifted a glass from a small table and took a sip of something clear, giving Lars a suspicious look.

Magnus was a small man, with long whitish-gray hair pulled back into a ponytail. He had clear blue eyes and a pointed nose broken by a tracery of red and blue veins. His hands rested gently, palm side up on dirt-stained blue jeans. But his eyes remained alert, as if the outward gentility of this meeting might unexpectedly burst into violence.

Elizabeth guessed he had a gun tucked in the seams of his chair.

Lars lapsed into silence. Water from the kitchen tapped a beat in metronomic time, as if to measure the pauses. Elizabeth looked around the dwelling, first at the steel and plastic and Formica of what had originally been a mobile home, then the rest, which told a less modern story. Caps and coats in the colorful, indigenous patterns of the Sami people were tacked to the walls alongside the skulls of foxes and the antlers of reindeer and a bull moose.

The floor was covered with skins—bears, seals, foxes.

Lars finally broke the silence with questions, got the old man's answers, and then related them to Elizabeth. Magnus eyed her suspiciously as she listened to Lars' translations.

How long has it been since Ádá passed?

I'm going on three years. I get lonely and I never see the children. But Ádá visits from time to time to let me know she still waits for me.

How has the hunting been this year?

If it wasn't for the traps, I'd starve. The occasional grouse. I haven't felled a moose in a year.

Do you need anything from social services? I can have some people visit?

No, I don't want any visitors. I am happy to talk to you because you are a ranger and you take care of the land. You keep people away from the sacred places. And you need to know what I saw.

What did you see?

I saw people jump from Hyvlatonnå.

Lars explained to Elizabeth that he used the old Norse name for the Pulpit Rock.

"Were they holding hands?" Elizabeth asked.

The old man's eyes narrowed with suspicion at the strange English-speaking woman.

Lars said something that seemed to put Magnus at ease.

No, they just jumped in a neat line, all at once.

No one appeared to have been pushed? Lars asked.

Not that I could see.

And you watched them fall?

Yes. They went off together, as I said. Then they began to fall in their own ways. Some tumbled. One man put his hands above his head, put his feet together, to drop through the air fast like a rocket. A fat woman rolled over and over.

Did you hear anything?

Some screams, both men's and women's screams. Most hit rocks that veered off the wall on the way down. Those that hit outcroppings went into the channel. The rest bounced off the bottom while the others hit the water like cannon balls, almost at once.

Did you see other witnesses, boats?

No.

Did you see anyone on the Pulpit Rock looking down?

No.

Did you count them?

Six plus one.

Please explain.

The old man took a draw from his glass and gave his visitors that suspicious look again. He took his time, as if trying to decide whether to divulge something.

I saw Freyja.

"Does he mean a real person?" Elizabeth asked.

Lars shook his head at her in a dismissive gesture, cautioning her not to interrupt again.

What was Freyja was doing?

She flew straight above the jumpers, looking down on them with pity as they fell into the water.

You saw the goddess?

I did. I think these poor fools imagined they would go to the meadow-place with her. Freyja only flew above them, never gathering them to her bosom. I am sure she knows that those who choose to die so foolishly surely belong to the kingdom of Hel.

FIVE

The gray trunk of a large ash tree rose out of a stone pit installed in the wooden floors of the old warehouse, now converted to a dining room. The broad branches of the tree and its green fronds towered over the tables and pressed against the opaque glass ceiling twenty feet above. Dark fissures streaked the bark of its massive trunk, making it look as if it were truly as old as the world.

"So what's with the tree?" Norris asked as a hostess led the group to a table under the limbs of the tree.

"It's supposed to be Yggdrasil," Bowie said.

"Yeeg-what?" Norris asked.

"Yggdrasil, the tree that holds up the nine worlds of Nordic legend," Bowie said. "At its base are the Norns."

"The whats?"

"Beings the Greeks and Romans called the Fates," Lars said as they all took a seat. "They are the spinners who weave the destinies of our lives."

"And the victims sat down here for dinner, where the Norns should be?" Elizabeth asked.

"Because their fates were almost fully spun," Nasrin said.

She did not look at Lars or Elizabeth when she spoke, but straight ahead as if addressing some unseen diner. Elizabeth could only imagine her reaction when Lars Stenstrom had divulged to Nasrin that they had interviewed a witness without her. Ever since, Nasrin had avoided eye contact with Lars, and only glancing contact with Elizabeth, never smiling. Lars had explained that he didn't want to overwhelm Magnus Norland with visitors, and absolutely needed Dr. Browne to assess the hermit's mental condition. It was clear that Lars was also letting Nasrin know her place as a guest in his country.

So Nasrin kept her eyes away from Lars and Elizabeth.

"Tell me something," Lars turned to Elizabeth. "Just as we were leaving Magnus, you turned at the door and had me ask the old man if he detected any kind of odor when Freyja flew by.

Why?"

"The hallucinations of schizophrenics are sometimes attended by olfactory sensations," Elizabeth said. "He said he didn't experience any unusual smells."

"Just an old man's flight of fancy?" Nasrin asked, looking at Elizabeth's direction but slightly above her eyes. "Not that I would have any first-hand impressions of my own."

"No," Elizabeth said, "I think he's just interpreting something he saw."

"Like what?" Bowie asked. "Lady Gaga?"

"Maybe a bird?" Agent Norris said.

"Or one of the jumpers falling at an odd angle," Bowie said.

Thor Magnusson arrived late, breathing hard, blonde hair darkened by sweat.

"I am sorry," Thor said. "I just had to review a few things to be sure."

"Sure of what?" Nasrin asked.

"The digital forensics," he said. "We have got them. Almost, I think."

A young woman with pink hair took their drink orders. Bowie ordered nachos for all to share.

"As you know, they communicated by posting emails into a drafts folder of that Gmail account," Thor said. "It took me all night, but I was able to trace Fólkvangrorbust to an IP address here in Norway."

"Do you have a physical destination?" Lars asked.

The waitress arrived and set drinks around the table. They paused their conversation until she was gone.

"Yes, I do," Thor said, taking a swig from a local microbrew. "It is just outside of Hommelvik."

"Which is where?" Nasrin asked.

"Just outside of Trondheim. Traces to an open field on public land a few kilometers from a small clubhouse."

"Clubhouse?" Bowie asked.

"Called Sessrúmnir, the mead hall where Freyja receives the dead," Thor said. "In the real world, it is the headquarters for the Trondheim division of the Hammers, a biker gang."

"You have these characters in Norway?" Elizabeth asked.

"A few years back, they went after each other hammer and

tong," Inspector Dahl said. "The Hammers scare even the Bandidos and Hells Angels."

"Yes," Lars added, "if by hammers you mean RPGs stolen from Norwegian Army bases, and if by tongs you mean Glock 17s smuggled from Estonia by way of a Russian freighter. Let Inspector Dahl and myself pull together more information about these gangs and we shall convene another meeting within a day."

The train to Trondheim was a clean, modern marvel with wood accents. Green farmland and hay rolls slid by at an even clip.

Nasrin unfolded a leaf from the wooden table between her and Elizabeth and set down a dark folder with a royal seal and a logo stamped with the insignia of the Metropolitan Police Force. She slowly undid the string on a fastener to reveal a pile of papers and photographs.

"The Hommelvik Hammers," Nasrin said. "Founded by Norwegian bikers who had lived in New Orleans and been associated with the Banditos there. Their leader—"

She slid forward an image of a man with receding black hair, a square jaw with dark stubble. His brown eyes suggested unexpected sensitivity.

"That's Karl Pedersen, president of the Mother Charter. He did a few years in Norway for rape, though he is suspected of multiple rapes. He is into just about anything you can imagine, and probably more."

Nasrin slid a single sheet of paper at Elizabeth.

"Pedersen has links to organized crime in the UK, so I asked a friend at MI5 to return a favor. He gave me this."

Elizabeth read the short report.

"GHCQ reports suspicious dark web activity from roaming mobile users connected to Hammers motorcycle gang in 12-mile radius around Hommelvik, Norway. It is believed users rotate cheap mobiles and disposable laptops for the purpose of selling unlicensed pharmaceuticals and introducing criminal elements for the purpose of establishing a digital bazaar for services ranging from murder-for-hire to trafficking in Eastern European girls and women for prostitution."

This Pedersen had been talking with someone when the clandestine photo was taken. His expression had an open and friendly look, which could be a display of genuine warmth or the mask of a sociopath.

"When I think of cybercrime, I don't exactly think of bikers," Elizabeth said.

"Cyber is the only game in town—easy to learn, hard to catch and harder to prosecute," Nasrin said. "One-percenter bikers are pure organized crime. They would be fools not to get into this. Imagine all the heavy artillery that they can now buy by phishing for industrial secrets and hawking phony impotence pills over the Internet."

Elizabeth nodded and sipped her dark coffee.

"Do they actually believe?" Nasrin asked.

"What?"

"I mean all these locals," Nasrin said, gesturing at the train window with her coffee cup, "out there. Do they actually cling to the old religion?"

"By old religion you might as well mean the Evangelical Lutheran Church of Norway," Elizabeth said. "Most, I am sure, believe in soccer, high definition television and white quartz kitchen counters. And serial marriages."

"But the country folk, like the mountain fellow you and Lars interviewed, people at the margins?"

"I am sure they are all baptized Christians," Elizabeth said. "But from what I am reading, their parents would have told them the old stories at bedtime. They carry these tales in their hearts."

"But gods and goddesses? I mean, really. I have trouble enough believing in the possibility of an abstract God, much less the Allah of my mother's people. But Valhalla and Freefuck!"

"Freyja," Elizabeth said. "Mythology is just the surface of any religion. Like a Jew recounting the story of Jonah, or a Hindu retelling of the exploits of Krishna, the sophisticated believer sees the story as a portal to a deeper truth."

"But a Jew, Muslim, Hindu or Christian asks for wisdom, or divine guidance, or salvation," Nasrin said. "In this religion, the—

what are they called?"

"Lars calls them the folkish ones," Elizabeth said. "Ásatrú"

"The folkish people are seeking material help from nature gods. They want money, or children, or good health. And when they die, all they can look forward to is slamming down their beer goblets and singing in Valhalla or Fuckvanger or wherever. And then I understand from what I've read that they and the gods eventually expect to be killed—again—in their heaven. Even their gods will one day die in battle, including top god Odin."

"It is a stoic religion, well suited to the harsh environment from which it sprang," Elizabeth said. "It is also a propitiatory religion, one that connects to the deepest wellsprings of human fear and desire."

"All to go to a mead hall, to drink and feast and tell of one's exploits," Nasrin said. "Some religion."

"Tell me, Nasrin, when a jihadist pulls the line on his suicide vest, do you think he truly imagines he is going to be serviced by seventy-seven virgins?"

"Seventy-two," Nasrin said, straightening up a little. "Very well, I see your point—the gazelle-eyed *houri* of the Garden are seen by scholars as an earthly metaphor for the spiritual delights of a paradise that defies description."

"In a similar way, Fólkvangr is a meadow paradise that modern believers see as a metaphor for something numinous, heavenly beyond description," Elizabeth said. "Are we doing this to spite Lars?"

"Someone has to get out front in this investigation," Nasrin said. "And I need to wrap this up. I've got a full plate waiting for me back in London."

More farms slid by, this impossibly green country with its ridiculously blue sky.

At the end of yesterday's meeting, Lars had told Nasrin to sit tight while Thor Magnusson continued to complete his forensic digital work. As the meeting broke, Lars confided in Elizabeth that he was taking a day off to escort his daughter to a chess tournament. Like practically every other adult Norwegian, Lars seemed to be amicably divorced and raising children with a happy village of old lovers, extended family and community of friends.

A short time later, Nasrin had called Elizabeth's room. She could have knocked, but Elizabeth suspected that she would have been embarrassed to do that again.

"I'm up for a little trip," she said. "How about you? I could use a psychologist, especially if we are to find ourselves in the company of bikers."

"Lars won't like it."

"We could just do a little reconnaissance, that's all," Nasrin said, "I will make sure that you get to keep backups of any data we come across, digital or forensic. You could use that, couldn't you, for your next paper?"

"I suppose," Elizabeth said. "Why not tell Lars?"

"Three British subjects are dead," Nasrin said. "All I suggest is that we do a little looking around."

Trondheim was a college town with massive wooden homes and storehouses on pilings along the broad and gray-blue Nidelva, which merged into the immense expanse of the Trondheimsfjord.

"Every bit of scenery here seems to top the last," Elizabeth said.

"That fjord is very deep," Nasrin replied. "The Nazis built an enormous sub base here."

They soon found themselves drifting through knots of people thickening into a crowd of families with strollers, men with plastic cups full of beer, children with painted whiskers and cheetah spots, packs of kids on skateboards, throngs of college students, milling around, eating pizza, dragging balloons, joking boisterously.

"I had no idea Trondheim would be so festive," Nasrin said.

"Today is the last day of the St. Olaf's Festival," Elizabeth read from her phone, while Nasrin consulted a map on her own phone.

They pushed through the crowd toward a center square in front of the large, gray mass of a Gothic cathedral. On the steps of the cathedral, a blonde woman in a Lutheran pastor's vestment and an Africa-themed stole cheerfully tapped a tambourine against her palm while a rock band played a bland hymn.

Nasrin walked up to a hot dog kiosk and bought two mustard-slathered dogs for thirty kroner. Elizabeth bought two cold

Ringnes lagers to wash them down.

"What's all this about?" Nasrin asked. "Did you Wikipedia St. Olaf?"

"Yes," Elizabeth said. "He was an incompetent ninth-century king, but did manage to convert his kingdom to Christianity, for which his reward was to get torn apart in battle."

"And he apparently didn't do a thorough job of that—of conversion, I mean, Lutheran lady ministers notwithstanding," Nasrin said.

They wended though the crowd trying not to trip on the cobblestone streets, past a large expanse of green by a lake with an abstract, metal sculpture. At periodic intervals, there were more bands—rock bands playing old standards, Norwegian folk ensembles and Trondheim teenagers doing their best American hip-hop.

"The car rentals should be over there," Nasrin said, pointing to a small shopping center.

Off to the side of the center was a storefront for a large American car rental chain. They went inside to rent an SUV for the drive to Hommelvik, only to be immediately stopped short by the bulk of a Norwegian policeman, a substantial man with a trim blonde mustache who placed himself between them and the counter.

"Detective Inspector Jones? And you, uh, doctor? …"

"Elizabeth Browne."

"You are both to come with me," he said.

"Are we under arrest?"

"You will be if you do not come with me."

The policeman led them outside where a marked cruiser idled in a parking spot. It had not been there a moment before. Another policeman stood by the side of the car, holding out a cellphone with the speaker activated.

"Did you get a good look at Nidarosdomen?" The voice on the speaker asked.

"Come again?" Nasrin said to the phone. "Is that you Lars?"

"The Nidaros, Trondheim's cathedral, one of the largest in Europe," Lars said. "You see, we take pride in our ability to do anything as well as or better than our larger neighbors."

"What would you like me to say?" Nasrin replied.

"That you are getting on the next flight back to London. I can do that, you know. Expel you from this investigation and from this country, if I choose."

A long silence.

"I am certain that you can. I only wanted—"

"You, or you and Elizabeth. Are you there Elizabeth?"

"Hello, Lars," she said.

"Enjoying St. Olaf's Day?" he asked.

"The hot dogs are worthy of any ballpark in America."

"I have two hot dogs on my hands right now, and I don't know what to do with them," Lars replied. "Nasrin, tell me your plan of action."

"Well," Nasrin began, "we plan to drive to the social club that the Hammers use as their public front, just to assess the scene, the people. We didn't anticipate it, but St. Olaf's Day makes the perfect excuse for strangers to wander by their beer hall. We could make contact with Pedersen, tell him who we are, and make a deal."

"Before or after he rapes you both."

"He won't do that," Nasrin said. "He has not stayed in business for this long by being stupid."

"And under what authority do you plan to do this?" Lars asked.

"Acting on behalf of Scotland Yard, through Interpol, under the color of the Council of Europe's Convention on Cybercrime."

"Why don't you spend a few kroner and get yourself a child's sheriff's badge while you're at it? There is only one authority under which you can act in my country, and that is my authority. Are we clear on this point?"

"Crystal," Nasrin said.

The sounds of children laughing and splashing water came through the speaker.

"I will allow you to proceed on this adventure, provided that you activate your phone to this number when you arrive in Hommelvik and slip it into your purse or pocket," Lars said. "I will detail several police units to be no more than five minutes away from the Hammers social club. If anything truly dangerous begins to occur, just say, 'I guess I should have never left Oslo,' and say it twice, and we shall save your boney ass."

"Very well," Nasrin said. "Will do, boney ass and all."

They wanted an SUV but settled for a Fiat 500, a small, boxy car that killed any bad vibe they could have hoped to muster. The drive to Hommelvik took less than twenty minutes, a winding road through coastal forest broken by the occasional estate and ramshackle hunting cottage. Nasrin drove while Elizabeth kept an eye on their progress on Nasrin's phone.

"Take the next left," she said.

Hommelvik turned out to be a bit less scenic than Trondheim, a hardscrabble fishing and lumber town by a port on the Trondsheimfjord.

"We go through town, take the E-12 for three miles, then a left at the intersection," Elizabeth said. Five minutes later, she handed the phone back to Nasrin. They parked and stepped out onto a gravel parking lot, packed with cars. A long row of Gold Wing and Harley choppers with 24-inch ape-hanger handlebars stood in a neat row in front of the hall. They were parked with military precision, each handlebar an exact foot apart.

Sessrúmnir was a single-story structure of rock and timber with a shingle roof.

Nasrin wore leather boots, blue jeans and a blue camisole under a white shirt. Elizabeth wore her one pair of leather cowgirl boots, brown, with black jeans and a black T-shirt. Perhaps that would be bad enough.

As the heels of Elizabeth's boots crunched the gravel, she hitched a thumb in a belt loop and attempted a bored expression. The front door burst open and several young mothers with children spilled out. Music blared as the doors opened and muted as it shut.

"Poison," Nasrin said, stepping up onto the wooden porch. "Late-century glam metal."

"You a Poison fan? That's a surprise."

"Come clubbing in London with me and you can learn all kinds of things."

Nasrin opened the door and they went inside.

Elizabeth had imagined that their entrance would stop the music, prompt all heads to turn to them in a deadly silence, just as it does when the movie tenderfoot steps into a saloon full of desperados. But no one took any notice of them.

"The phone!" Elizabeth said.

"Oh bugger!"

Nasrin looked into her purse, hit a button to autodial the number Lars had left for them, and slipped it back in. Elizabeth worried this might look suspicious, but still no one took any notice of them. And why would they? People check their phones all the time and the room was packed with celebrants in rowdy conversation. Almost all the men wore denim jackets with the club's emblem on back, a large yellow hammer tumbling through the air and a logo in a cartoon explosion that ran above it—819-MC— and "Kongeriket Norge" in a semicircle underneath.

Some of the men looked like refugees from the Golden Horde of Genghis Khan, with tattoos rounding their shaven scalps and scrollworks that rolled around the bony protrusions on the backs of their heads. Others had faces obscured by blonde or grayish-black beards. Some had their thick hair pulled into ponytails. Others allowed their long hair to unfurl in pyramids that framed big, round faces with porcine eyes.

Some were giants, with massive jaws, like Viking warriors ready to man a shield wall. Some were wiry men, lithe and agile, the sort who could run the back line of the shield wall to supply fresh water and replace broken spears. Some wore no shirt under their jackets, showing off elaborate prison tattoos over torsos that varied from buff to potbellied. Rings sprouted from lips, nostrils, eyebrows and occasionally from an ear.

Some of the women looked like housewives on a weekend picnic, blue jeans with tasteful blouses and makeup. Others wore leather pants that gleamed like black glass. The leather-wearers also wore black T-shirts and leather jackets with the arms cut off to sport tattoos, mostly abstract runic designs. These women had the same assortment of facial rings as the men, but they wore makeup, just like the housewives-types.

Children played and scurried between the adults like hungry rodents in a maze.

"Let's saddle up to the bar," Nasrin said.

A fat man in civilian clothes gestured to them. The music had died down, and Elizabeth could hear him saying something in

Norwegian. As soon as she addressed him in English, he switched to almost perfect, unaccented American English.

This was something she had noticed throughout the country. Once she addressed any Norwegian in American English, there was always a slight of flutter about that person's eyes, a switching of linguistic tracks. Then it was almost like speaking to someone from Kansas. Their proficiency shamed Elizabeth. She had earned an "A" in all her French courses at Smith, but all that meant was that she had a talent for memorizing conjugated verbs. For all her degrees, Elizabeth could barely understand French or Spanish.

"One hundred kroner each," the fat man said. "It's all going to the children's wing of St. Olaf's hospital."

They paid him and maneuvered through the crowd toward the bar.

The scent of beer, perfume, cigarette smoke and male sweat was almost overpowering. Nasrin found an opening at the bar large enough for her to squeeze through and order two local craft brews. The beer was cold and crisp and tasted of apples. A new round of music started up, something that sounded like a fresh take on Norwegian folk music. The bikers and their old ladies began to sway, some singing along with the lyrics. Men with women, women with women, and parents with children, all shuffled and swirled. A circle of dancers began to form.

As the people moved, Elizabeth caught glimpses of motifs painted on the wooden wall behind them. She saw vibrant and well-executed Thors and Odins and other gods standing in front of Bifrost, the rainbow bridge between worlds. They were not at all like comic book characters or their heroic derivations in the movies, but realistic people with expressions of haggard defiance drawn in lines of dark, ink-like paint and filled in with faint colors, weathered on the wood. At the opposite end, she saw a formidable-looking Freyja, tall and strong with a tilted head and penetrating expression. She held an unsheathed sword at the ready in one hand, and a falcon high on a gloved hand on the other. The falcon had fierce humanlike eyes, observant and ready to pounce. Freyja stood in the shade of Yggdrasil, which dug thick roots toward the floor and stretched its thick limbs ever outward.

"Looks like St. Olaf might have done a little more converting in this area," Nasrin said.

"You could say the same anywhere in Europe now," Elizabeth said.

In between the dancers and the men talking, Elizabeth caught a glimpse of a man looking back at them, watchful, brown eyes like the falcon's.

Karl Pedersen.

The song changed and they watched the dancing awhile longer. Nasrin spotted a clear table of rough-hewn wood and led Elizabeth over to it.

"One of the dancers might be sitting here," Elizabeth said. "This might piss someone off. Like Karl over there."

"Good," Nasrin said. "We could stand a little attention. I am positively begging for trouble."

Elizabeth imagined Lars on the other end of the phone, plonking his head.

Some dancers moved and Elizabeth saw Pedersen standing as immobile as one of the figures on the wall, eyes slitted and head arched back. After a moment of eye contact with Elizabeth, he spun around and disappeared behind the thicket of Hammers and their old ladies.

"He looks as dangerous as his Q.E.," Nasrin said. "Queen's evidence."

"Do I want to know it all?" Elizabeth asked.

"As his file says, suspected of this, linked to that," Nasrin said. "Rape, murder, murder-for-hire, arson and lately, cybercrime. Except for a two-year stint for that rape, he's been positively catlike in his ability to slink around the law."

They finished their beers. The music went back to something from ten years ago, and the dancers spun to a stop and began to gather around the bar. A woman of about thirty walked toward them.

"Hello, may I join you? I am Sonya."

The accent was Eastern European, maybe Polish.

Sonya pulled out a chair and sat down.

"Are you enjoying yourselves?" she asked.

"Not yet," Nasrin said.

Sonya had a dissipated beauty, high cheekbones and a pretty mouth, offset by a sallow complexion and an unhealthy-looking translucence about the corners of the eyes.

"We won't truly enjoy ourselves until we've talked to Karl," Nasrin said.

"Then go home unhappy," Sonya said. "We know the stink of *snut* and we don't want it in our house."

"What did she call us?" Elizabeth asked.

"Here's my warrant card," Nasrin said, and flipped open a leather case to show her ornate badge and a holographic card with her picture.

"You've got no jurisdiction here, *snut*," Sonya said. "Go back to Scotland."

Nasrin laughed at her. Sonya's eyes narrowed and she brought up a cigarette clipped in her nicotine-stained fingers, took a long drag and blew smoke at them as if she were laying down a curse.

"It's because I have no jurisdiction here that I think Karl will want to speak to us," Nasrin said. "We just want information. I think the last thing you want is for us to come back here with the PST."

Sonya turned from Nasrin to inspect me.

"And this one, she is from Scotland too?"

"No," Nasrin said. "She's with the American FBI."

Elizabeth felt a clench in her gut.

"If she is FBI, then I want to see her warrant card also."

"We don't have warrant cards, we have badges," Elizabeth said. "And by law, we are not allowed to take them outside of the U.S."

That seemed to satisfy Sonya.

"So what do you want?"

"You saw the Preikestolen suicides?"

"How could I miss it? Fools."

"We want some background on it, how the Internet might have been used to bring these people together."

"And this has what to do with the Hammers?"

Nasrin leaned in.

"Ever hear of GCHQ? No? It's a big silver building in the country in Gloucestershire they call the Doughnut, though personally I think it looks a bit more like a flying saucer that landed. Saucer or doughnut, when GCHQ turns its eyes and ears to Hommelvik it sees a digital spiderweb that laces out from near here to shady accounts in Cyprus, to Hezbollah and its sale of copycat pharma in South America and Russia, and—"

"So someone's bad," Sonya said. "Look around if you like. There are no computers here. We don't even have WiFi."

"Of course you wouldn't, not exactly here at Sessrúmnir," Nasrin said. "But we can see your assets seeded about the farms, the wharfs, the places you think we don't know about, including those most nearby."

Sonya stared at us, put her cigarette down and threw her hands open in a gesture of mock surrender to an arrest.

"And we do not care," Nasrin said. "At least, I do not. But one of those spider threads links to a site that brought the suicides together. We want you to give up one small, sketchy customer. Do that, and I will never darken your door again."

Sonya sneered and gave a short laugh that was more like a snigger.

"*Snut*, you will never leave us alone."

Sonya left.

After waiting for fifteen minutes, Elizabeth went to the bar and got two more beers. She felt someone too close behind her and she turned.

"I think you should leave when you finish those two."

It was the fat man who had sold them tickets. Elizabeth nodded.

She took the beers back to the table and informed Nasrin that they had overstayed their welcome. They quaffed their beers to the halfway mark and took their leave.

Once in the car, Nasrin pulled her phone from her purse and hit the speaker button.

"Did you get that?" Nasrin asked.

"Most of it," Lars said, the connection making his voice several octaves higher. "At least enough to ask Agent Norris to indict Elizabeth for impersonating a federal officer. Not that I would care."

"So what is *snut*?" Elizabeth asked.

"It means 'snout,' the idea being that police officers are always sniffing around like dogs," Lars said. "Which I have always taken as an accurate description, if not exactly complimentary. I want you to come back to Oslo now. And I want to see the two of you in my office at 8 a.m."

Nasrin told Lars that the long call had left her phone without power, although she had already plugged it into the car charger.

"Cheerio," Nasrin said suddenly, and terminated the call.

"So that went well," Elizabeth said.

"Didn't it?"

Nasrin started back for Trondheim. Soon they were coasting between a lonely stretch of shadowy forest on either side of the road.

"So why didn't Pedersen speak to us?" Elizabeth asked.

"My guess is that was never in the cards," Nasrin said, taking a particularly sharp turn with ease. "He would never expose himself to actual contact. He leaves that to flunkies like Sonya."

"Doesn't this now mean the PST will show up with an army in a day or two?" Elizabeth said.

"Perhaps Pedersen doesn't care," Nasrin said. "Perhaps he appreciates the fact that we have tipped him off, giving him time to clean up. Either way, it probably doesn't matter."

"Why?"

"Because I think after we meet with Lars, you and I will be on the first jet back home."

Nasrin glanced at the rearview mirror as the road straightened. "Trouble."

They gained speed.

Elizabeth craned around to see a motorcyclist a good hundred yards behind them. He was large man whose bulk made his black Harley-Davidson appear absurdly small, like a trained bear on a tricycle. The motorcyclist's long dirty blond hair whipped in the wind from underneath a black helmet that was also too small for him, almost sitting on the top of his head.

"Be a dear and reach into my purse for me."

Elizabeth did as Nasrin asked.

"Now kindly pull out my G43."

Elizabeth felt the cold polymer skin of a semiautomatic pistol. She carefully lifted it from Nasrin's purse, lightly holding the grip to keep her fingertips as far away from the trigger as possible.

"What is this?" she asked.

"My Lady Glock, courtesy of a friend at the British Embassy. Don't worry, the safety's on. Now, please gently place it on top of my lap, barrel pointing toward the door."

Elizabeth again did as Nasrin asked.

"Wouldn't you get in big trouble if Lars knows you're carrying?"

"We'll be in bigger trouble if Pedersen sent that chopperhead to kill us."

The gunning of an overpowered engine split the air and needled their eardrums. The sound became a guttural rip to make the distant mountains vibrate as the motorcycle shot forward like a black cannonball. The rider brought his front wheel right behind their back bumper.

"I feel conspicuously outmatched in this little box," Nasrin said.

She whipped the Fiat onto the side of the road and quickly slowed to a stop.

Nasrin turned to Elizabeth, eyes wide and bright.

"Be ready in an instant to dart out that door and make for the woods," she said.

Elizabeth unlatched her door and undid her seatbelt.

In one quick motion, Nasrin spun out her seat, planted her feet firmly a yard apart and aimed her gun at the motorcyclist with two hands.

The loud, rasping rumble of the bike sputtered, coughed and died. The big man lifted one leg over the chopper and stood tall. He stretched his arms, displaying his broad shoulders and massive gut. The biker removed the black helmet from the top of his head. Elizabeth could now see that it was shaped like an old German army war helmet, a deliberate Nazi resonance that seemed to be the default fashion statement for outlaws everywhere. With insolent slowness, the man hung the helmet by a strap on one handle and shook out his hair. He ambled toward Nasrin, big boots grinding the pavement.

"Close enough," Nasrin said.

Without a word, the man pulled a folded napkin from the front pocket of black leather pants and set the napkin down on the road. He placed a loose pebble on it, turned and walked back to his motorcycle. He gunned it and spun around to return to Sessrúmnir.

Nasrin stuck her Glock into her waistband and bent over to lift the napkin. She unfolded it.

"What does it say?" Elizabeth asked.

Nasrin held it up. Elizabeth expected some cryptic message, but not actual numbers.

63.36915526,10.89277578

"A code?" She asked as Nasrin slipped back behind the wheel.

"GPS coordinates," Nasrin said, and slipped her gun back into her purse like a pack of mints.

"Wonder where?"

Nasrin keyed the numbers on her smartphone and read the screen.

"Well, it appears we've just been invited to go to somewhere in the vicinity of Hell."

SIX

The Radisson was a modernist take on a Hanseatic storehouse, with immense glass walls in its lobby that overlooked Trondheim's oceanic fjord. Nasrin asked Elizabeth to meet her at nine for dinner in the hotel restaurant so they could go over the events of the day, plan their next steps and concoct a pitch to mollify Lars when they failed to show up in the morning.

Elizabeth smiled and said good evening to Nasrin. She hoped it wasn't a weak, sickly smile. Although Elizabeth did not want to repeat what had happened the last time they were in a hotel room together, she didn't feel like being left alone, either.

Elizabeth's room, with its Scandinavian retro décor, was a large box, cool and empty. It felt strange to walk into a hotel room with no bags. She could stand to wear the same clothes another day in this cool climate. The greater problem was with what was roiling inside her. The room felt closed, like a tomb.

Elizabeth pulled a bottle of water out of the minibar and fished a plastic container with a few pills out of her jeans pocket. She swallowed one, a half a milligram of benzodiazepine, with a sip of water.

She pulled off her boots, stretched out on the bed and let it come.

Elizabeth always appreciated what an observer watching her would see, as if she were outside herself, seeing her body tense, then ball up as she gave into a red-faced crying jag with gritted teeth, bobbing head, and spastic movements. Elizabeth struggled to let out the maximum amount of tears with the minimum amount of grunts and whines.

The observer would not know, however, that on the inside Elizabeth was feeling far less than one would imagine, as if the powerful emotions being released by her body didn't belong to her, just a fast-moving storm passing through.

In this disassociated state, Elizabeth watched herself from the other side of the room, impassively, even contemptuously for the curled weakling crying in her bed.

Her episodes always ended with feelings from which there was no disassociation and no escape. This stage was Elizabeth's hell. She balled up even tighter, silent and wet-faced, trembling at the final arrival of her old familiar—dread like a physical thing that crept across the room until it wormed its way inside her and into the marrow of her bones. Since she was a teen, Elizabeth had always called this unwanted visitor the Edge, that thing that lurks in the periphery, a watchful predator waiting for her to get into the wrong situation and falter so it can return and prove to her that all her coping and her therapy and her tactics and her learning means nothing.

The return of the Edge did not surprise Elizabeth. It always gave her warning.

It had been building up since the visit to the morgue. It showed itself after the encounter with the motorcyclist. Elizabeth's hands had trembled in her lap as Nasrin calmly drove away, as if pulling a gun on a biker was as ordinary as pumping gas. While speeding along in the car, wind rushing through the open windows, Elizabeth caught sight of her nemesis in the corners of her eyes, welling up in the dark recesses of the forest like a rising tide of ink, lurking in the shadows that were satisfied with the knowledge that the sun would eventually set so the darkness could merge and cover everything.

On the drive back to Trondheim, Elizabeth had studied Nasrin. The detective seemed to notice nothing off about her passenger. As Elizabeth had stared, she silently wished to be like Nasrin, to be able to face the world with simple, unexamined courage.

It had been almost three months since the last episode. It had come just after Elizabeth's failure to stop Jeremy from leaping from the 9th floor of a building in Washington, D.C. For the first time in years Elizabeth had to return to therapy and renew her prescription.

She thought it was done, just a minor relapse brought on by fresh trauma. But now the Edge was back.

And it was in the room with her.

It advanced toward her stealthily, slithering like an ancient sea creature, a bilious horror, its skirt of black flesh undulating in a sickening and obscene motion.

The Edge is both omen and the terrible thing the omen points to.

She performed her breathing exercises, focusing on the hot breath on her nostrils and the expansion and recession of her diaphragm. Elizabeth felt clenched muscles unlock and begin to relax. She lay still, resting, imagining the drug dissolving, spreading in her bloodstream, slowing and cooling her hot brain, bringing peace.

She opened her eyes. The room was clear.

Elizabeth picked up her smartphone and rolled the contacts until she came to Dr. George Adler Abelman.

She sent him a text.

>Had a bit of a scare today. Turned out to be a trigger. Maybe we could Skype sometime?<

The reply from gaableman@georgetown.edu came back immediately.

>**I can do better than that. I am in Oslo. Can we get together tomorrow? I am looking forward to seeing you again, my dear Elizabeth. <**

She replied.

>Thank you, a Godsend for real.<

Elizabeth didn't have the strength to ask what her old faculty advisor, therapist and savior was doing in Norway. He was just close, a good sign that comforted her like a warm blanket. She set an alarm so she could make dinner with Nasrin, an hour would be enough. The meds were now taking a firm hold. The tick of time slowed to thuds, and she fell into that state of numb grace that always guarantees peace.

Elizabeth Browne was asleep.

After breakfast at the Radisson, Elizabeth and Nasrin took the little Fiat through Hommevik and past the turnoff to Sessrúmnir, while Elizabeth's phone voiced directions to the GPS coordinates. They had decided over dinner to try to talk Lars into letting them pursue the thread a little further. He knew, as well as they did, that Karl Pedersen was too sophisticated to lure a British Scotland Yard Inspector and what he thought was an FBI agent to face a pointless death in the woods.

"I told you to be in my office this morning," Lars said sternly. But the new lead was tempting. After some arguing with Nasrin, he let them go, with the promise that Nasrin would again dial him and keep the line open. As before, he would station several armed units nearby in case of trouble.

Along the ride, Elizabeth could not shake the feelings from last night. She didn't need any more episodes, not on this trip. She thought of George, marveled at the coincidence of her mentor and therapist happening to be in Norway, and tried to balance her anxiety about the possibility of future episodes with her gratitude that he was here.

Seeing George would keep the shadows away.

"You have arrived at your destination."

Elizabeth's phone had spoken with certainty, but there was nothing around but woods on both sides of the road. The town of Hell was two miles away. Nasrin eased the Fiat onto the side of the road. She retrieved the Glock from her purse, stepped out, double-checked the safety and slid the gun into a small holster on her right side.

Getting out of the little car felt liberating. A slight wind rustled the forest, the hood of the Fiat snicked and the fan rumbled.

"So this is what Hell looks like," Nasrin said. "Just as I expected, it's boring."

Elizabeth saw the hazy outline of a path in the tall grass, almost grown over.

"There," she said.

Nasrin threw the keys to Elizabeth.

"If anything happens to me, run to the car and drive for your life," she said.

Their boots crunched on a gravel pathway. Nasrin insisted on walking in front of Elizabeth, keeping her right hand on her hip, taking it slow, making as little noise as possible. The path curved several times until a clearing came into view, and after that a green stretch of mowed lawn with lawn chairs, plastic tables, golf balls and red plastic cups all scattered about.

Beyond the lawn was a log cabin, its wood weathered and gray with a roof of curling shingles that came halfway down, obscuring the top halves of two narrow windows. A door in the middle of the cabin was painted an incongruous bright red. The door opened, and a tall, thin man in his early thirties stepped out. His round head was covered in strands of thin, brownish-red hair. He wore dark jeans and an untucked, plaid shirt of blacks, blues and reds.

"I thought you were coming yesterday afternoon," he shouted.

"Too late in the day," Nasrin shouted back.

"ID please."

As they approached, Nasrin pulled her warrant card. Elizabeth noticed several cables snaking through the grass and a large satellite dish on the roof. Off to the side, under a narrow wooden shed, sat an electric generator on a table, with shelves underneath that stored several red canisters of gasoline. In the opposite direction was a barrel to catch rainwater, with a hose connected to the side of the house.

"I'm Detective Inspector Nasrin Jones, Scotland Yard, and this is one of our consultant investigators, Elizabeth Browne."

"Everett Walleen," the man said in a slow-as-syrup American Southern accent. "Come inside."

Inside was single room, a utilitarian kitchen with a wood stove, a table littered with papers and a single laptop computer, its screen glowing with the TechCrunch landing page. A shotgun leaned against the opposite corner.

"This place is clean," Walleen said. "The only equipment you will find is this old Dell with nothing on it that would be of any use to you."

"That's just as well since this little inquiry is off the books," Nasrin said. "We're just looking for some leads."

"Lady, nothing is off the books with you folks, ever."

"We want to know why an IP address that sources to this area was used to set up a web account accessed by all the Preikestolen suicides," Nasrin said.

Walleen pulled a pack of Marlboros, tapped a few out and offered them, a token gesture to the unlikely. When the two women declined, he struck a match with his thumbnail, lit up and took a deep drag. His eyes narrowed in satisfaction as he exhaled blue smoke. Walleen was wiry as well as tall, with large, expressive brown eyes like a child's.

"I wouldn't know anything about that," he said.

Nasrin snorted. Elizabeth could sense she was about to get tough, perhaps too tough, a mistake that would shut down this interview.

"I believe you," Elizabeth said. "But hypothetically, in your expert opinion, suppose a black hat hacker was sitting out in the woods here, how would he construct that?"

"Well," Walleen drew out the vowels, "*hypo-thet-tically* speaking, I suppose a scenario could be envisioned in which the hacker received a request for a proposal on a black auction site—"

"Which site?" Nasrin asked.

She was bearing down again, the trained interrogator trying to flip the script back to obtain dominance. It was a gamble. It could shut Walleen down. But if he answered her, a little bit of the patina of this being a hypothetical scenario would be worn off, and Walleen would be answering more directly.

"Zerodaygasm.ru," he said.

"What was the RFP for?"

"It wanted a domain proxy, setting up a message board to be operated remotely, through a tier of nested domains. Which was kinda weird."

"Weird, how?" Elizabeth asked.

"Weird like he could have done this through a legitimate proxy service. He was being extra careful with redundant layers. I had no … I mean the hacker in the woods … would have started with no idea about the purpose of the site. Just the technical requirements of the RFP."

"Do think the customer can be traced?" Nasrin asked.

"No," Walleen took another drag, "I do not. Not if he was smart on his end, using cheap, throwaway devices in wireless cafes. And if he was smart enough to get to someone like me, he was smart enough to do all that."

Nasrin's pressure had worked, prompting Walleen to open up and drop the hypothetical pretense, a cool shift that Elizabeth had to admire.

"Did you construct the site for him?"

"No, but I went back and looked it up. At first it was a soft, touchy-feely kind of board where people posted about their troubles and fears and dreams, wanting to end it all and such. A special level of subscribers who logged in were given all kinds of secure codes, all meant to assure them of the anonymity of the site. Then the dialogue took a mean turn. I could see this host manipulating people, making them feel worthless instead of making them feel better. But you see a lot of that online."

"How were you paid?" Nasrin asked.

"I wasn't paid at all," he said. "But your average hypothetical hacker might accept untraceable bitcoins."

"We'll see about that."

Walleen's eyes narrowed.

Elizabeth looked around the cabin. An open box of a chocolate cereal with a cartoon vampire, an empty box of chocolate-covered raisins on the floor, a pack of sausages in plastic wrap.

"Where are you from, Everett?" Elizabeth asked.

"Slidell, St. Tammany Parish," he said. "I got in a bit of trouble with the local constabularies, and decided that my best work could be done somewhere else. I've been in Europe for six years now."

"Where?" Nasrin asked.

"Slovenia, then Czech Republic, mostly. And here."

"Business good?"

"Good enough for me not to want to be mixed up in something like this."

"You mean something too public," Nasrin said. "But you are mixed up in it."

"Not me, just the hacker in the woods," he said.

Nasrin stared at him for a half beat.

"Agreed."

Walleen shuffled over to the computer. He pulled a USB stick and slapped it into Nasrin's outstretched palm.

"That's everything. That's all that can be known from the hacker end."

"How did you come to work for Karl Pedersen?" Elizabeth asked.

Elizabeth was also trained to read people, to catch the slight register of a tic or a lip bite. At the mention of that name, Everett

Walleen looked away for a half-a-beat.

"I have no bosses, only clients."

"So you are not a Hammer?"

Walleen snorted.

"The last time I was on a hog, I wound up in a tree. And my mamma was part Creek, which in Slidell means some African way back there too, so I guess I'd flunk their little Nordic-Nazi test."

"But you do work for Pedersen?" she asked.

"Karl had nothing to do with any of this. That is why he wanted you to talk to me. This is business he don't need."

"Don't go far," Nasrin said. "The PST will be by."

"So much for hypothetical and off-the-record."

"I believe it was you who said that nothing is off the record," Nasrin replied. "But for what it is worth, I just gave you a heads up."

"Okay, so let 'em come," Walleen said. "They'll find nothing here but boudin sausages and some Ringnes beer in the icebox. And they can have the sausages."

He smiled.

"Thank you for coming by. And please don't come again."

"Come to Jesus?" Lars asked.

His wood-paneled office, more birch of course, was backed with a bookcase dedicated to collecting oblong blobs of clear plastic on stands, along with pictures of his two impossibly beautiful offspring—a girl and boy, each with cornflower blue eyes, blonde hair like spun gold.

"It's an American expression and it means a coming to terms," Nasrin said, and then smiled. "And you get to be Jesus."

"I see," Lars said. "I do in fact get to be Jesus."

Nasrin and Elizabeth stood before the landscape of the chief inspector's bare, wooden desk like two delinquents before the principal. It was all but decided that they would be expelled.

"I could cite for you all the procedures and even some laws that you have broken," Lars said. "I could play the role of bureaucrat. But I won't do that. I will simply characterize what you have done as a breach of trust. I trusted you both, and now I don't."

"I understand your position," Nasrin said. "But we did uncover digital forensic evidence that will be of use."

"Which, thanks to you, comes with a contaminated chain of custody that may not stand up in a Norwegian court of law, which I remind you, still governs jurisprudence for the Kingdom of Norway. A quaint distinction from your point of view, I am sure."

"We respect your position," Elizabeth said.

Lars turned to her, head tilted like a curious bird.

"My position is that of a man crouched under a flimsy umbrella as hot steaming piss rains through my ceiling from the Ministry of Justice and Security."

"I am sorry to hear that," Nasrin said. She sounded sorry, investigator to investigator.

"You can dwell on that on the way home," Lars said. "And you both will fly economy-class."

"Just one thing before we go," Nasrin said. "Did you look at the data on Walleen's thumb drive?"

Lars leaned forward in his chair, eyes narrowing.

"Not yet, did you?"

"Yes."

Elizabeth had watched as Nasrin had put the thumb drive straight into Thor's palm a few hours before, but that did not—she now realized—preclude her from copying it somewhere along the way. This infraction was, of course, another demerit for Lars to add to both of their columns.

"And has Thor come around to informing you of how much of the data was being routed through Iceland?"

"That is all to the best," Lars said. "We have excellent relations with the *Greiningardeild Ríkislögreglustjóra.*"

"Goodness me," Nasrin said. "And I can't even say the first few consonants without choking. You surely know—and if you don't, Thor can explain it to you—that there are old warehouses along a wharf on the south end of Reykjavik that act as server farms for drug deals, money laundering, as well as a lot of legitimate but secretive business."

"We know that."

"And they do that because the peculiarly lax laws there make it hard to get the government to trace anything. Remember, Ice-

land is the country that expelled the FBI for looking into Wik-
iLeaks."

"What's your point?"

"Just how many months, years or centuries do you think it will
take you to get Reykjavik to tell you anything revealing about
what is being routed through their server farms?"

"Fine, if Iceland is a dead end, I can always go to Agent Norris
and ask him to query the NSA."

"Ah, yes, sounds smart," Nasrin said. "And do you know what we
mean at Vauxhall Cross when we say 'Washington Time'?"

Silence, which deepened as the inspectors stared at each other
like two animals squaring off. It was Lars who finally spoke.

"Bitch," Lars whispered the word.

"When I need to be."

Elizabeth looked at them, reading their expressions, trying to
make sense of what was being said.

"So you're MI6?" he asked. "Why the Scotland Yard cover? Why
did MI6 send you over for this?"

"As I was saying, 'Washington time' is Vauxhall for 'you're holding your cock in your hands,'" Nasrin said. "I can say that if you
and Thor are relying on Washington to unscramble this for you,
you might as well gently stroke your hands up and down. It will
feel better."

Lars bolted up, slamming the back of his chair into his bookcase
and rattling his forest of plaques. In Elizabeth's experience, an
American bureaucrat in his position would have hurled expletives
and violently thrown them out of his office, but Lars kept his voice
down and eyes locked on Nasrin.

"Washington cares about this too," Lars said.

"Yes, Washington cares because several prominent Americans
were killed. And you'd best go through Charlie Bowie—you do
know that counselor title is pure bullshit, that he's CIA? Charlie would be your most direct route, the ambassador's an idiot, as
you know. But your request would have to make it to the office
of the DCI, and from there to the ODNI, to be farmed out for comment among its 17 committee members who represent the U.S.
intelligence community, and from there go to the one agency that
could actually do the job— the NSA with its big ears—where a
request from Norway about suicides would wend its way through

their priority intelligence process, competing for their processing time against active threats like ISIS, Russian hacking of elections and Chinese penetration of U.S. defense companies. Good luck with that."

Lars sighed out a deep breath, smiled, looked down at his desk and shook his head. He raised his head again, looking directly into Nasrin's eyes.

"You actually think there is a deal to be made here?"

"I do indeed," Nasrin said. "I was, by the way, on the Greater Manchester Police force for a good ten years, homicide, before being recruited by the Secret Intelligence Service. I was selected for this assignment to do double duty, as I often do in foreign cases that involve fatal action against British subjects."

"Why this case?"

"There is an interest in it at the highest levels," Nasrin said. "A prominent playwright. And it is said that the Duchess of Cambridge herself is a devoted reader of Anne Shrewsbury mysteries."

"Now you are the one doing the stroking," he said.

"There could be other equities in this case," Nasrin said. "But keep us on and I promise to keep you in the loop on anything we discover. That's a personal pledge I am authorized to convey to you direct from C. So you don't need the American NSA. If we have a deal, I can get Thor and his thumb drives into GCHQ tomorrow to participate in a full forensic."

Lars sighed again, walked to the window and looked out at the clutter of tall triangular white sails cutting against each other like shark fins across the Oslofjord.

He looked back at Nasrin.

"How do I know you will not park Thor in some sanitized visitor's room in some remote corner of the Doughnut?"

"The Doughnut has no corners. I promise Thor will be taken straight to the war room, and that he can be as hands-on in this matter as he wishes, provided he signs certain releases."

"I can make that deal," Lars said. "But if Thor is not physically within the walls of GCHQ by sunset tomorrow—or if he reports back to me that you are withholding anything, a hashtag or an umlaut—the ministry will expel you. And then I will have a friendly drink with some friends in the press. Your cover will be blown for life."

"I can accept those terms because we do not renege."

"And total discretion afterwards? No James Bond fables at my expense in the press?"

"Total discretion," Nasrin said. "We have no interest in that kind of publicity. That would be MI5."

"Me too," Elizabeth said, and instantly regretted it.

Lars and Nasrin both turned to Elizabeth in dead silence. In the heat of their negotiation, they had forgotten that there was a civilian in the room.

SEVEN

They met with a hug at a dockside café, but George was too fidgety to sit still.

"Mind if we take a walk?"

"Sure, it's late in the day and I'm already well caffeinated," Elizabeth said.

"How are you doing today?"

"Well," she said. And she was. It wasn't just the brightness of the long summer days and the cheeriness of the scene of shoppers and strollers along Oslo's main dock. Elizabeth had just finished a long Skype talk with Max. He seemed to be doing well for a change, chattier than usual, with an A-minus on a calculus midterm. And there were hints of a girl, though that worried Elizabeth a bit.

College romances are always the toughest. And this would be his first. That is the way it was with a vulnerable child, every bit of happy news—getting into a tough school, try-outs for the lacrosse team—became a potential ordeal.

"Let's stroll by City Hall," George said. They passed by the steps that led to the twin brick towers done in a Brutalist style that either evoked admiration or disgust, but never indifference.

"I heard Nelson Mandela give his Nobel Peace Prize acceptance speech in the great hall. Did you know that?"

At sixty-four, George walked briskly with the stride and natural ease of a much younger man.

"I believe you may have mentioned it once or twice or forty times before," Elizabeth said, which made George laugh. He had a habit of name-dropping and bragging about every notable event in his life, a tendency toward braggadocio that for Elizabeth only brought George's more sensitive, vulnerable side into stark contrast. Elizabeth loved him more for his little eccentricities.

A steel clock face on one of the towers struck one o'clock, prompting 49 carillon bells to chime a popular rock tune from the 20th century. They walked in silence until the bells were done.

"George, I can't tell you what it means to me to have you here."

He stopped and turned to look her in the eye.

"You had a relapse," he said.

"I'm consulting on a case that is more than a little disturbing."

"No matter how clinically detached we try to be, we can't help but get caught up in the horror of some of the things we see. I would be worried for you, Elizabeth, if it were otherwise."

"And there were some rough moments in our investigation," she said. "Also, some … unwanted feelings of attraction. Not at all appropriate to these circumstances."

"A man you're working with?"

"Yes," she said. "And a woman."

Professional to the core, George only emitted a quick chuckle.

"This is a new side of you," he said, smiling.

"Tell me about it."

George Adler Abelman had a squat, strong frame. As an undergraduate at Yale, he had been a champion wrestler, an air of athleticism he retained decades later. George's most distinctive feature had not changed, his blue eyes, clear as cut glass after cataract surgery. Those eyes appeared moist and slightly magnified by his glasses, which combined with his ever-present slight smile and salt-and-pepper mustache, gave George an aura of beneficence.

George's unkempt hair had now gone completely white, a wreath framing his pink face.

"I will always be when and where you need me," he said. "You were my best student and my worthiest successor."

He turned to walk again before he could see Elizabeth blush.

"But I came to Oslo for other reasons," he said. "Research, something that may wrap up my lifelong quest to map the suicidal impulse."

"Really, what's that about?"

"Elizabeth, my dear, you know all about it. I just arrived here to begin research on the Pulpit Rock suicides."

"What?"

"Clear examples, I believe, of cult manipulation. It will make a hell of a paper. Probably a book."

They walked in silence for a few beats as Elizabeth took in this news.

"But George, I am here to do the same thing."

"I thought you were working on this as an active consultant to the U.S. government, through the State Department, I believe."

More likely, Elizabeth realized, through the CIA budget, given what she had learned from Nasrin. That meant she was really working for Charlie Bowie.

"Yes, I am an active consultant," she said. "What better way to conduct research?"

"And you think that is ethical?"

George's question wounded like a pinprick, though he voiced it in that friendly way of his.

"I wouldn't be planning it if I thought otherwise."

George nodded.

Elizabeth knew what he was thinking—that it would be hard to balance the act of active analysis for the authorities while also organizing the data in front of her into theoretical constructs. Promises would be made, data parsed for certain confidentialities.

But it was not impossible. And certainly not unethical.

"There are many mysteries in this one," George said. "Clear signs of cult conversion and indoctrination."

"And yet most cults physically and socially isolate the subjects," she said. "These people probably never met each other until their last dinner together, which apparently was quite festive."

"Festivity is common before these events," George said. "I'd be festive too if I focused only on all the things that I would no longer have to do … no longer attend faculty meetings, no longer make my TAs clean the lab, no longer have to floss or pay taxes."

"No longer see a sunset," Elizabeth replied. "No longer trace the lines of a lover's palm."

"Or eat chocolate," George said.

"Or drink a really good indie beer on a hot day. This case leaves us with the likelihood that all the work of conversion and reality distortion occurred over the Internet."

"That is what brought me over here," George said. "Internet cults are common, but they exist to lure one into the trap. They have never before, at least in my experience, been the trap itself."

"And there is something else," Elizabeth said. "There is a distinct religious element at work."

"That does not surprise me in the least, as you would know,"

George said.

"What will surprise you is the religion that was used to foment this ideation."

He turned his palms to the sky, looking to her for the answer.

"Ásatrú," she said.

He laughed.

"You mean Odin and Thor and other cartoon characters?" he said. "Are you telling me that these erudite people became Vikings?"

"I am convinced they became followers of Freyja, the goddess who receives the honored dead and leads them to a paradise hall much like Valhalla."

George stopped again, his expression fierce.

"That's preposterous," he said in a tone with which one would admonish a dog or a graduate student. "An XRO executive. A drug company CEO. An award-winning playwright and a bestselling novelist. Worshippers of a goddess last seen painted on the side of vans at stoner concerts!"

"Their belief was subtler than it sounds. They saw Freyja as a symbol, a guide to a numinous reality."

"Sounds like the Heaven's Gate suicide so many years ago, only that was about a …"

"Comet."

"Yes, a comet," he said, looking a little embarrassed by his memory lapse. "Hale-Bopp now, wasn't it? Supposed to take them to a new realm. But Heaven's Gate was a full-on indoctrination cult in San Diego, if I recall correctly. And yet you say this was all done on the Internet?"

"So I can see you are just getting started," Elizabeth said. "When I find out, George, you can read about it in my paper."

He laughed, but his eyes didn't.

———

"What is N, uh, Dimethyltryptamine?"

A moment before hearing this question, Elizabeth had given George another hug and had agreed to discuss the issue of research further. Her little jibe had prompted George to bring up the prospect of working together, a paper that could be "our final collaboration." He seemed thrilled at the prospect. Elizabeth was not. This was her find and he was poaching.

But she didn't say that. Not yet.

After bidding goodbye to George, Elizabeth walked down Karl Johans gate, a broad avenue lined with T-shirt shops and over-priced restaurants. She heard a ringtone coming from her purse—Abba's "Mamma Mia"—programmed by Max, another sign of his puckish humor.

But it wasn't Max on the line. It was Nasrin with her question.

"It's called DMT," Elizabeth replied. "A hallucinogen—*ayahuasca*, or Vine of the Spirits—used by some Amerindians in the Amazon for spiritual journeys. Why, are you thinking about taking some the next time you go clubbing?"

"Not yet, though a few more meetings that include Charlie Bowie and I might," Nasrin said. "It's been a while since I've been a real inspector, and the drug beat was never my thing. Tell me you don't have to actually go to the Amazon to get it?"

"No," Elizabeth said. "DMT was first synthesized by a Hungarian scientist in the Fifties. As a recreational drug it is not common, but not unheard of, either. Why?"

"DMT was apparently the drug of choice for our suicides," Nasrin said. "There were no surprises in the coroner's final report except for this notation of N-Dimethyltryptamine. Traces were found in the bloodstreams of Shrewsbury, Drummond and Goddard."

"Does the report put any numbers to that?"

Elizabeth heard the rattling of paper over the line.

"Yes, uh, 'widespread lipophilic binding in all subjects let's see—87 mg, 46 and 78 ...'"

"Are you sure you read that right?" Elizabeth said. "Even if it had been in their fat for a while, at these levels they had to have taken a substantial dose a few hours before, probably on their way up the mountain. They must have been merrily tripping all the way to the top."

"Like LSD?"

"No, more like psilocybin, you know, mushrooms."

"And with it you might see God or unicorns or anything?"

"Not quite," Elizabeth said, and paused. "Now this is interesting. The odd thing about this drug is that in majority of users it induces a particular kind of hallucination, usually an encounter with a shamanistic entity. There is something about how DMT interacts with the human brain that causes these entities to often appear to users as shapeshifting elves. Aficionados call them 'fractal elves' and sometimes, 'machine elves.'"

"Or perhaps Freyja's elves?" Nasrin asked, voicing what Elizabeth was already thinking. "Ready to escort one to Fuckvanger or some such?"

Elizabeth thought of the beings the seven might have seen in the dark shadows of the early morning forest on their way up to their deaths … sprites, fairies, trolls, strange and dark divinities of the forest. Those images made her shudder.

"If they took it in the morning at the start of their journey, it would have partially worn off by the time they jumped," Elizabeth said. "Their exertion would have helped burn it off."

"Determined lot," Nasrin said.

———

"Sign this."

Charles Bowie set down a glowing tablet. Elizabeth read the contract. It contained a non-disclosure agreement just between her and the U.S. State Department—I, Elizabeth Barrett Browne, M.D., Ph.D., agree not to disclose, discuss, by omission, commission, any business of such and such and so and so, by which and forthwith, so help me God.

She signed it with her fingertip.

"I was supposed to have taken care of that right away," Bowie said. "I should have flown back to London and brought you here myself, instead of letting you catch a free ride with Nasrin. I gave her a chance to get her hooks into you."

"I've always understood that my work was for the U.S. government," Elizabeth said.

"Still, I got a demerit all the same for waiting to make it official," he said.

Bowie tucked the tablet away in a briefcase next to his seat. They sat in adjacent pools of lights, just the two of them in the cabin as the government-issued Gulfstream roared through the black, moonless sky over the North Sea toward Britain.

"I want to impress upon you, Elizabeth, you're not just working for Uncle Sam," he said. "You're working for me. You have been all along."

"You mean the CIA."

"I mean not MI6. Friends though we are with our cousins across the sea, you may not share intel with any foreign government. And do watch out for Nasrin. I hear she can be a nasty piece of work, though she's not bad looking for a dyke."

"Are we in the same century?"

"Probably not."

Bowie rested a scotch and water on his stomach. Elizabeth picked up her little plastic cup with Ringnes beer from her tray and took a sip.

"Why bring me along?"

Bowie looked down at his drink, his bearded jowls spread like cake batter.

He bit his lip, weighing a decision.

"Did you really understand that contract? What we discuss, you can never reveal."

"You can see all my fingers," Elizabeth said. "None of them are crossed. Besides, I don't want to be sued by my own government."

"We need you because what we're dealing with here involves the science of the mind," he said. "None of the agency shrinks are quite up to this, not anymore. We once had top-notch research psychologists. But the shrinks we have now are mainly for PTSD and rooting out problem people. And when it comes to theoretical research, everyone says that you're the tops."

He took a sip of scotch. He had something more to say.

"You've surely come across MKULTRA in your reading."

Elizabeth nodded, wary, not sure where this was going.

MKULTRA was the CIA's infamous mind-control experiment in the Fifties and Sixties to develop push-button mind control through psychedelics, hypnosis and abuse—mental, physical and sexual. It was a front-page scandal when it spilled out of a Senate investigation in the 1970s.

"Today's kinder, gentler CIA can't touch anything like that, but we still have all the research, miles and miles of paper," Bowie said, leaving her to wonder if he was dangling forbidden data like a treat before a dog. "The sensational stuff with drugs and sex got all the headlines. But the really intriguing results have to do with RF."

"You mean radio frequency?" Elizabeth said. "For what?"

"For brain hacking."

She set her drink down on the armrest.

"Are you telling me the CIA found a way to control someone's brain remotely? With radio waves?"

Bowie smiled.

"Why not?" he said. "It's no secret that we can use RF to resonate and control cellphone circuits. Why not RF for the brain?"

"I'll tell you why not. A cellphone is digital. It has discrete on and off circuits that electromagnetic waves can ping. The brain is wet tissue. It is analog. And it is supremely complex. We still don't know how it all works. So there's no way to ping a wet, analog brain with RF."

"We don't understand quantum mechanics, either," Bowie countered. "But modern technology is based on it."

"Are you telling me that you made RF control of people work?" Elizabeth said. "Should I make a tin foil hat?"

"Not quite," Bowie said, lifting his drink again, which had left a dark ring on his blue shirt. "But the agency was convinced back then that Remote Neural Monitoring and Control was possible with the right kind of electromagnetic signal."

"And this has what to do with the Pulpit Rock?"

"Think about it. Leading executives and cultural figures fall for an implausible cult my stupid cousin Vern would see through, to kill themselves in such a preposterous way. Something had to be working on them."

"DMT," she said.

"I've read the autopsy results, too," Bowie said. "The drug was a factor. But the eggheads at Langley wonder if the drug was the charge and RT was the trigger."

"Why do you persist in thinking that?"

Bowie stared at her, as if he were noticing something on her mouth that needed brushing off.

"Are you seeing someone?" Bowie said, leaning in a bit, smiling for once.

"I'm not seeing you," she said, looking right at him.

Shafts of golden light broke through low clouds to inflame barns, bushy oaks, meandering lanes and villages of stone and thatch. They touched down at a private airport near the village of Kemble.

A black sedan from the embassy idled a few steps beyond the stepladder of their jet. A young driver took Bowie and Elizabeth along a winding Cotswold road for the half-hour drive to GCHQ, stopping once to let a shepherd herd his flock off a narrow road.

The hulking mass of the Government Communication Headquarters rose like an alien thing out of a landscape of mossy rock. Morning sunlight glinted off glass walls framed by brushed steel under a round roof of bright aluminum. While their driver presented his credentials to a military guard with a submachine gun, Elizabeth noticed children running around a swingset in a playground behind razor wire.

"Welcome to GCHQ," the guard said.

Nasrin, Thor and a young lady in a corporate uniform waited for them on the other side of the security checkpoint. The young woman's name was Glenda, and she was pleased as punch to be escorting them around "the Doughnut" on this fair morning.

"How was your flight?" Nasrin asked Elizabeth, sotto voce.

"Fine," she whispered back. "Only one clumsy attempt at the mile-high club."

Glenda led them down an open walkway just inside the structure's three-story glass walls. The heels of many shoes echoed off the native limestone interior as they circumnavigated the Doughnut. British officers in crisp blue-gray RAF uniforms walked among nerds loping about in short-sleeves, jeans and tennis shoes.

Glenda took them into the office of Bureau and Legal Affairs, where under Charlie Bowie's guidance, Thor, Nasrin and Elizabeth signed further statements promising not to disclose anything they happened to learn or accidentally see while inside the Doughnut, so forth and such with, so help them God.

"Iceland, always bloody Iceland," Thor said.

A digital map of Europe glowed on a large HD screen. An animated redline shot straight from Reykjavik to Hommelvik, and then a blue line shot back.

Glenda had turned them over to Ian, a wiry young man in a thin gray sweater and jeans. Ian's head was thatched with an unruly tuft of straw. After some introductions, and the mutual sniffing of nerd pheromones with Thor, Ian led them through his digital tracking of what he called the "Hommelvik intercept." As he spoke, Ian rocked back and forth in his executive chair in front of a large Apple monitor. All the while, an officer in an RAF uniform stood erect against the wall behind them. She had not introduced herself and did not say a word.

"No surprises there, Thor," Ian said. "All roads do tend to lead to Reykjavik."

Ian performed a few clicks, and the globe swiveled and Iceland took on geographic features. Reykjavik swelled until the whole screen was filled with a crystalline image of five or six large structures along a dock. A man smoked a cigarette at the water's edge.

"That is about a ten times improvement over Google Earth," Thor said.

"Oh, that's nothing, you should see —"

The female RAF officer in the back of the room ahemed.

Ian glanced back at her.

"Sorry," Ian said.

He hit a few toggles and the image of the buildings fluoresced, the roofs turned a dark magenta, bright red blobs floating off the heat vents.

"The servers in there must have the power of a small city running through them," Thor said.

"Good thing the Icies have geothermal energy," Ian said. "There's a little fish restaurant just a hundred feet to the south of there by the way. Spectacular crab soup."

"So all this digital illustration is impressive to look at," Nasrin said. "But it tells us nothing we didn't already know."

"I need to assimilate the data from Thor's stick," Ian said.

Ian clicked away as long strings of code filled a smaller screen on the side of the wall.

"There," he said. "We're in the dark web now."

The code moved down the screen and resolved. The image on the large screen popped back out to a wider aperture of the Northern Hemisphere and animated a green line from Reykjavik to somewhere in the mid-Atlantic region of the United States.

"Can you netstat this to the Hommelvik IP?" Thor asked.

"Just did," Ian said. "When I run a tracer, the link to the American IP is only stronger," Ian said. "That can be traced …"

He clicked some more.

" … to a standard Gmail account."

"What does that tell us?" Bowie asked.

"It tells us that after the owner of this IP address built an online relationship with his victims, he taught them basic security techniques," Nasrin said. "Standard drop box, right?"

"Right," Ian said. "You communicate by leaving a draft message in a Gmail draft's folder, then delete once read. Leaves no metadata traces, no IP address behind, although we can easily —"

The officer in the back of the room ahemed again.

Ian worked some more and an address came up, "freyja.onion."

"Dot onion?" Nasrin asked.

"A pseudo top-level domain on Tor," Ian said.

"You might as well tell me it's a bloody rag on Mars," Nasrin said.

"Tor is an Internet address that works, but doesn't register in the global domain name system," Thor explained. "To put it simply, onion routing is hard to trace and heavily encrypted. Fortunately, all those hackers out there are oblivious to the virus that NSA—"

The lady officer gave another loud "ahem" and now it was Thor's turn to shut up.

"Show us the IP," Bowie said.

The Earth expanded again, this time the image swelling toward the East Coast, the Chesapeake Bay, then Washington D.C., rolling north to a large technical-looking complex with several water towers surrounded by the perfect rectangles of a suburb of row houses in straight lines.

"Cheeky bastard," Ian said.

"Fort Meade, home of the NSA," Thor said.

"You're telling us that the NSA is behind this?" Nasrin asked.

"Can't be," Bowie said.

A few more clicks, a long string of numbers—IP address, GPS coordinate—ran across the URL bar.

"Looks like we just caught him," Ian said.

The image reduced again to a strip mall with cars parked within diagonal lines.

Ian clicked furiously, and web images from the inside of a hipster coffee house flashed by, with candid shots from an online review site of young and middle-aged professionals with laptops, handhelds and large mugs of lattes and coffees in front of them.

"Café Mata Hari," Ian said, reading copy off a website. "Great java from Java … Lattes, cappuccinos, iced coffees."

He paused.

"And free WiFi."

EIGHT

A fingertip lightly grazed Elizabeth's cheek, stroked her jawline, caressed the side of her neck down to the hollow of her throat.

Lars smiled at her, his blue eyes studying her reactions. He had his shirt off, and she ran her fingertips over the swirl of blonde hair on his well-formed chest. His arms were powerful, heavily muscled, but his touch was gentle and solicitous.

Desire quickened her breath and her blood coursed with new power. Lars slowly undid her blouse and the latch on her bra, his fingertip running across her nipples and down her stomach, grazing and sliding and teasing. He began to sculpt her inner thigh with that finger, teasing her by rolling it under the edge of her panties, shaping her as the ancient rhythm began to roll from her center and through her hips like a tide.

Lars kissed Elizabeth, lightly at first, just a grazing of lips and tongue, then a full kiss, open and greedy. His hand went under her panties. He touched her and she began to feel the pressure build in the center of her body, a small knot squeezing itself, reducing to a quivering singularity that would continue to tighten inexorably until it exploded.

Elizabeth opened her eyes …

She said something, but the word came out as a croak and Nasrin did not stop. And Elizabeth was too far gone to stop her.

She cried out and latched onto Nasrin, her face cradled in the starched white fabric of the other woman's shirt as she came to a ragged finish. Elizabeth clung to Nasrin like a child gripping its mother. Then she pulled back, pulled up her panties, quickly snapped her bra in place, sat upright and buttoned her shirt.

"I thought—" Elizabeth caught a breath.

"I thought—" she caught another.

"You were —"

"Going to stop?" Nasrin said. "No dear, not when you're like that."

"Someone."

"I am certainly someone."

"Someone else."

"Someone else? Why would you think that? Sorry, dear, but you really did seem to be in the moment with me."

The pilot had dialed the cabin lights down for sleeping. Nasrin's face was barely visible in the twilight gloom. Elizabeth glanced at the wooden door that separated the cabin of the small jet from the cockpit. She wondered if the pilots had cameras that watched the cabin and if they could see anything. Not likely, but if they did, they had just seen quite a show.

Elizabeth grasped the aluminum armrest.

Nasrin had touched me while I had been asleep.

"I did not ask you to do that," she said. "Not any of that."

"You didn't stop me," Nasrin said.

"I was asleep. How could I ask you anything?"

"Could have fooled me from the way you were responding."

"That's why I thought you were someone else."

"One of your dreamboats, perhaps?"

Elizabeth slapped her, hard enough to make Nasrin turn completely away.

She brushed past Nasrin and bolted for the lavatory. Elizabeth locked herself inside. A stab of brightness from the automatic lights came up.

She splashed water on her face, rubbed the sleep from her eyes and studied herself in a steel mirror. Her breaths were fast and shallow, pulse still elevated.

What the fuck?

Nasrin's jasmine perfume was all over her.

Elizabeth washed it off along with makeup she had applied just two hours before, at 4 a.m. in a hotel room in Kemble, England.

Elizabeth could make a federal case out of this. She could do nothing. The truth is, the residue of pleasure still tingled throughout her body. She had not felt release like this in a long time. It had been more than nine months since she had been with someone, a lawyer she had met in Georgetown, and he could not bring her to the edge like that. But she was still angry. She had been manipulated in the most literal sense of that word.

Like a puppet on a string.

Elizabeth felt a crying jag coming on, and she gave into it. It was not a long cry, not a hard one, just good enough to vent her conflicting emotions and let her regain herself.

She dabbed mascara from the corners of her eyes, redid her lipstick and powder and went out. Elizabeth knelt to look out a window. It was still pitch black outside, another early morning run before dawn, this time back to Norway. Back in the cabin, she could see Nasrin in silhouette, still as a statue. Elizabeth stood over her, her head bent under the small bulkhead.

The pilot upped the light. Landing couldn't be more than forty-five minutes away. Elizabeth continued to stand over Nasrin.

Nasrin looked up at her. A ruddy hand-sized imprint was fading on her right check. Her eyes brimmed with tears, threatening to overrun her mascara and make a mess of her face.

"The last thing Elizabeth that I wanted was for you to feel overpowered by me. I thought I was being gentle."

"Gentle?"

"Truly, you seemed to be in the moment with me."

Elizabeth closed her eyes. Intake for four seconds, hold for seven, out in eight.

"I guess I can believe that."

"Can you forgive me?"

A large tear rolled over the lid of Nasrin's right eye, tracing a blob of ink down a cheek.

"It wasn't what you thought, Nasrin."

"It is a grief to me to think that I've made you uncomfortable."

Elizabeth stared at her. She let the silence grow for a moment.

"I know it's almost dawn, but after all that I need a drink," Elizabeth said. "You?"

Nasrin making a puffing noise, a gesture of relief, and dabbed her face.

"Scotch dear," Nasrin's voice was thick and scratchy.

Elizabeth found glasses of cut crystal in the back. There was a very British choice of a fine single malt and gin. Elizabeth made two scotches, neat.

She handed one to Nasrin, which she took gratefully.

"You can sit next to me again. I won't bite," she gave a congested laugh. "At least, not this time."

The events of the last few minutes began to seem unreal, dissipating Elizabeth's anger. But she still didn't want Nasrin to touch her, not even a handshake. She continued to stand in the aisle and took a sip of her scotch.

After an awkward moment, Nasrin spoke.

"Let me voice the obvious," she said. "Again, I am truly sorry. If we are going to work together, I know that there must be boundaries."

"If we are going to be friends, Nasrin—and I believe we are becoming friends—we have to have those boundaries."

Nasrin took another sip, tilted her head down and gazed upward directly into Elizabeth's eyes.

"I accept boundaries. But tell me dear that you are not the least bit attracted to me."

Elizabeth felt heat rising up from her body, up her neck.

"Tell me that you haven't thought about it, fantasized about us together …"

The red light on a phone installed on the wall of the cabin illuminated and began to blink.

Nasrin pulled the wireless handset and answered it.

"Detective Inspector Jones."

She relaxed and settled back into her seat.

"Hello Lars," she said, glancing at Elizabeth. "Sorry about GCHQ, but I kept up my end of the bargain. Please don't tell me you want to have another come-to-Jesus?"

Nasrin's dark eyes darted back and forth as she listened.

"When? How? Any notes? Yes, yes, we will, I will ask the pilots, but I see no reason why we cannot, we are still a good ways out. Yes. Hold on."

Nasrin rose, slid around Elizabeth and knocked on the cabin door. After a cautious moment, the co-pilot stuck his head out the door. They conversed in voices too low to be heard above the drone of the engines.

The door shut and by the time Nasrin retook her seat, the jet tilted, already veering toward a new course.

Nasrin retook the phone.

"The pilot says we will be there in an hour and fifteen. Right, we will meet you there. Thank you Lars."

Nasrin rested the phone into its cradle and turned to Elizabeth.

"We are going to land in Trondheim and go straight to Hommelvik. We need to draw once again on your suicide expertise, Elizabeth. So it is especially good that you are with us."

"Another high-profile jumper?"

"No. Everett Walleen."

Elizabeth took a seat behind Nasrin and they didn't say a word to one another for the rest of the flight.

———

A chill wind swept in from the fjord, brushing up water drops from the wet pavement of the tarmac.

Lars stood in a dark, blue raincoat in front of a cluster of police cars and SUVs, looking as grim as the gray blanket of low clouds over Trondheim. Behind him Bowie, Agent Norris and Harold Korber of the PST milled about sipping coffee and trading jibes.

After a perfunctory greeting, they rushed down the Hommelvik road to arrive at the gravel strip that led to Walleen's cabin. Police cars and an ambulance were parked at some distance, while technicians in white, hooded clean suits went about their business. Every now and then, the cabin's windows exploded with the flash of a camera.

They waited down the gravel path for a good forty-five minutes, until the white-suited technicians finished carrying their black cases and white plastic tubs to a van.

Charles Bowie ambled over to Elizabeth and leaned into her ear.

"You should have flown back with me," he said. "Not as a guest of the British government."

Elizabeth shrugged. She didn't tell him that as things turned out, she wished she had.

They stepped aside to let the caravan depart. Inspector Dahl came out of the cabin door, slipped covers off her polished shoes and removed a plastic cover from her head that hardly seemed necessary for blonde hair pulled back into such a tight ponytail.

"What do we have?" Lars asked.

"If he left a suicide note, it would have to be an email," Dahl said. "We're taking his laptop back to Thor to check it out. His fingers were not on the grip of the shotgun, but that is to be expected from recoil."

"Were any his fingers broken?" Agent Norris asked.

"This appears not to be the case," Dahl said. "But your instincts are correct. This could actually be a homicide."

"Any signs of coercion?" Lars asked.

"No, but then there wouldn't be if an intruder surprised him, keeping a gun on him at all times," Dahl said.

"Footprints or track marks?" Nasrin asked.

"Not on this gravel," Dahl said.

"But how do you get a man to stick a shotgun in his mouth and pull the trigger?" Bowie asked. "Threaten to shoot him?"

"All you need to do is to surprise the victim," Agent Norris said, "holding him at gunpoint with his own loaded shotgun, thrust it in his mouth as he starts to scream or say something, and pull the trigger. Then pose the body. Voilà, apparent suicide."

"What do you think?" Lars asked Elizabeth.

"The man I met presented no suicidal affect," she said. "He seemed resilient and wary, preparing to extricate himself from a legal situation he wanted no part of."

"So we could have a murder here," Lars said.

They walked down the path. Ambulance attendants stood around a stretcher, waiting for Lars and his crew to finish the inspection.

They stepped inside.

The air was thick with the scent of cordite and the iron tang of congealing blood.

Elizabeth closed her eyes, did her 4-7-8 breath and took a moment to orient herself before looking. With preparation, she could force herself to see but not feel, just as she had done at the Oslo morgue.

There is always a preternatural stillness about the dead that makes one imagine they are about to move.

Walleen had the posture of a man resting comfortably, sitting in a slouch with his back against the vertical logs that made up the back wall. Two thick lines of dried blood ran from his nostrils to the sides of his chin. The top of his head looked like the remnant of an exploded volcano. Far above him, a crimson spray of blood and brain covered the wall, tendrils of gray and white tissue clinging to the wood. Walleen's eyes, half open and dilated, stared at nothing.

"This is not right," Norris said. "The spray is high, where you would expect it to be if Walleen had been standing further from the wall when the trigger was pulled."

"You are correct," Dahl said. "Then there is this."

The inspector pulled out her smartphone and brought up a crime scene photo. It was a photo of Walleen's right hand, opened, holding a tab torn from the top of the box of chocolate-covered raisins.

"I cannot show you the torn paper now, it has been removed for testing," Dahl said.

"Think it means something?" Norris asked.

"Possibly a clue, or some statement," Dahl said.

"Or maybe the guy just thought raisins with chocolate were to die for," Bowie said.

Elizabeth scoured the cabin with her eyes. The boxes of snack food that had been on the kitchen table were gone.

"Was there a box of chocolate-covered raisins when you arrived?" she asked Inspector Dahl.

"Yes, the one Walleen had torn, and a box of children's cereal. But we checked, there was nothing inside them. They went to the lab just the same."

"May I look in the pantry?" Elizabeth asked.

"I didn't know you were a forensic investigator," Dahl said.

"I want to see if I can read Walleen's thinking, that's all," she said.

Dahl handed Elizabeth a pair of Latex gloves.

"Look all you want. There's nothing there."

Elizabeth opened one cabinet door after another. Tuna cans by the pack. Warm beer and cigarettes. An unopened box of chocolate cereal and an unopened box of chocolate-covered raisins.

"Did you look in these?" she asked.

"No, they have not been opened," Dahl said.

"So let's open them," Elizabeth said.

"It hardly seems necessary," Dahl replied.

"Do it," Lars said.

Dahl retrieved a small knife like a letter opener from a kit. She removed the boxes and began to probe the seams at the top of the cereal box.

"It should not be this difficult," Dahl said, then looked surprised by something. "I believe this item has been re-glued."

Inspector Dahl worked the tab, gave up, and finally tore it open with her gloved hands.

"Hand me a bowl," she said.

Elizabeth found a large plastic bowl in the lower cabinet.

Dahl poured out crisp puffs of cereal in a chocolate waterfall. An object fell in the stream, making a plopping sound, then another.

"Oh goody," Bowie said. "A decoder ring."

Dahl fished out the objects and inspected them with the intensity of a jeweler evaluating an uncut diamond.

"A good discovery, Doctor Browne, I must admit," Dahl said. "Two standard USB drives, 8 gigabytes each."

Elizabeth found a Pyrex casserole dish. Dahl once again tried the knife, gave up and resorted to tearing the top off the box of chocolate-covered raisins. She came up with two more flash drives.

"Thor will be busy," Elizabeth said.

"We will all be very busy," Lars said.

NINE

"What are you taking?"

"Lithium. Occasionally, one of the benzodiazepines," Elizabeth said.

"Sleep?"

"Satisfactory, if I walk more than two miles a day and do my yoga stretches at night," Elizabeth said. "If I don't get exercise, sleep is patchy."

"Dreams?" George asked.

She did not want to talk about that. George let the silence grow, the hook every psychiatrist uses to elicit more information. The fact that Elizabeth knew what he was doing didn't make it any easier to resist him.

"Disturbing," she said. "Like before."

"That's the second time you've used that word with me," George said. "The first time was about the case we're working on. Would you like to explore your dreams with me?"

Elizabeth took a bite of reindeer steak. She almost responded that she did not know "we" were working on anything together.

"No," she finally replied. "Their meaning is manifest. They are about my work, trying to help people. And not succeeding. Nightmares, really, although they don't wake me up."

George laughed.

"As we noted years before, those dreams of yours just show that you truly are a shrink. I've never told you, but should have, that I have had those kinds of dreams since my residency."

"Thank you for telling me," Elizabeth said. George could not have professionally spoken about his own dream life when he first led her through psychotherapy. It was good to hear it now.

He paused, weighing something on his mind.

"Elizabeth ..."

"The paper?"

"Yes."

"I now realize that I surprised you when I showed up here, horning in on what I can now see is territory you had staked out."

"Yes, you did. How, George?"

"I came here years ago on a Fulbright, and from the first minute I arrived I felt at home. I came back for two summers, six and four years ago. I'm not one for mysticism, but if there is anything to reincarnation, I was definitely a Norwegian in one of my lives."

"Maybe you were a Viking, George."

He chuckled.

"Norwegian summers are glorious. Winter is not as harsh as you might think, either, especially if you don't mind a little cross-country skiing to the local market. In fact, I am considering retiring here."

"How is it that I never knew that about you?" Elizabeth said.

"It's not a secret, exactly, but Norway has become my retreat, my special place," he said.

"Norway is lovely," Elizabeth said. "But how did you come to this case George?"

"I have friends in the Norwegian government," he said. "They know me well and thought I might be interested in this case."

"Who specifically?"

"The PST."

He looked down at his food, took a sip of beer, and said, "And Lars Stenstrom."

"You know Lars? How?"

"I wasn't taking patients, but he was a friend of a friend, so four years ago I saw him over the summer in Oslo. About twelve visits, that's all."

"Lars was your patient?"

George nodded.

"And what was his ..." Elizabeth stopped herself.

George smiled.

———————

Elizabeth sipped her coffee and stared out the giant windows of the Oslo Park Service office. Nasrin had not chosen a chair next to her, but did take one directly across the conference table from her. Looking out the window was a good strategy to avoid eye contact.

This morning, the Oslofjord was a serene waterscape of sails under a blue sky. Even a master artist would struggle to keep it from appearing trite.

"I have been up the better part of the night," Thor said, standing by an illuminated screen with a control in his hand. "And the better part of the night is not something to be missed on a Saturday in Oslo."

Agent Norris and Charles Bowie chuckled. Was it Sunday? Elizabeth had lost track of the days.

"Normally, I know you would all be holding your hymnals in church at this time," Thor said to more chuckles. "But I am sure you are really more curious about what is in Walleen's thumb drives."

Thor advanced the digital presentation.

"Until now, we had to guess what might have been passing between the victims through the dark web. Now, thanks to the late Everett Walleen's hidden data, we have this—"

The screen filled with the image of a landing page. The background imagery was of a light, misty forest in gray-green with silhouettes of light-green pines. All of this was behind the almost translucent image of a woman's face. She had high cheekbones, knowing blue eyes that seemed to follow the viewer. Her blonde hair parted into golden waves, and around her elegant neck was a bejeweled torc of gold.

Freyja's hair shimmered and waved slightly, like golden wheat in a light wind. There was no other movement.

The landing page had no text, no links to other sites or a menu of other pages. All that could be seen was the image and its slight, rippling motions of a breeze stirring the branches of trees in the forest and individual strands of Freyja's hair.

"How could they use something like this?" Lars asked.

Thor paced and pulled on his lips in a nervous gesture.

"There is a lot we have yet to figure out. Here is what we know. There is an unusual data packet attached to this site. When we decoded it, what we got were two things. First, a link to those drafts folders in an associated Gmail account on which the communications took place. I have asked my colleague Ian at GCHQ to negotiate with Google to retrieve the files. This I believe we can do, perhaps for all of the victims in their discussions with the—

" Thor glanced at Freyja—"host."

"Will you distribute what you find?" Nasrin asked.

Ingrid wheeled a cart of coffee and pastries into room. Her eyes were narrow and bloodshot, lips drawn. She looked as pleased to be in the office on a Sunday morning as she would have been at an evangelical foot washing.

"Yes," Lars said, "we will distribute the British files to you, and the American files to Agent Norris. If you wish to share them between you, or to ask Elizabeth to review them, that is your business."

"You said, 'first,' about the Gmail files," Bowie said to Thor. "What else did you find?"

"Hidden in this website is a large subset of packets that the users could access on an audio line."

"What was it?" Lars asked. "Freyja's speaking?"

"No human voices at all," Thor replied. "Just this."

He hit a toggle and nothing happened. From the back of the room, Ingrid spoke out what was obviously a Norwegian obscenity.

"What do you hear, Ingrid?" Thor asked.

"Tell me you don't hear that for real?" she asked, setting the tray of Danish in the middle of the table. Charles Bowie grabbed one and took a large bite.

"How can you miss it?" Ingrid asked, her face twisted with irritation. "Such a weird scream, almost painful."

Slowly, a thin note at an extremely high-pitch came out of the speakers. Elizabeth looked around, as one by one they heard it.

"The note is at 15,000 hertz," Thor said, "but I am pulling it down to a more audible range. If we were all in our twenties again, we would have all heard it along with Ingrid."

"I still hear nothing," Agent Norris said, prompting everyone to laugh, since he was the oldest in the room.

"That sound is embedded in the data stream," Thor said. "With a simple code, anyone on the receiving end could have heard it. With the right software, they could have pulled information out of it."

Bowie set down the remnant of his Danish, brushed crumbs from his chinstrap beard, rose and left the room.

———————

After a long, technical discussion about the website and the mysteries of how it had been covertly hosted through Tor and the dark web, they broke at noon. As Elizabeth gathered her papers, Nasrin walked around the table toward her. Elizabeth felt her pulse quicken, her body involuntarily stiffen.

"Yes, Nasrin, what do you want?"

Nasrin stared for half a beat, taking in Elizabeth's new coldness.

"Jesus just asked the two of us to lunch," she said.

Elizabeth made eye contact with Lars, who acknowledged her with a nod. He walked over to them and assumed a friendlier demeanor than he had shown the last time the three of them had a conversation.

"I know a good little place," Lars said. "Perhaps we can have a spot of lunch? If we are going to continue to work together ..."

Elizabeth smiled at him and nodded.

Lars drove them in his government-issue Volvo down a throughway into the heart of the city. They passed through a mountain tunnel. On the other side, vast, sloping sheets of white marble emerged along the harborside like a jagged piece of floating ice, the Oslo Opera House. Lars turned right on a city road that rose upward through a forest of boutiques and elegant homes to take advantage of a rare open parking space near the concrete mass of a museum. It was the Munchmusett, dedicated exclusively to the works of Edvard Munch.

"I always rather liked him," Nasrin said as they got out of the car. "Never fails to cheer me up."

"Over here," Lars led them down the street a good block to a bistro with outdoor seating in a recess in an office building. The manager smiled and nodded at Lars in recognition and sat them outside at a table in the shade of an awning along the small boulevard. Across the street, tourists lined up to buy tickets to the latest Munch exhibit, "The Frieze of Life."

Lars said something and the manager put a "reserved" sign on the other three outdoor tables, and one-by-one leaned the chairs inward.

When the waiter came, Lars favored hierarchy over chivalry by ordering first. He asked for a hamburger and water. Elizabeth asked for the same. Nasrin ordered a salmon salad with a white wine, defying the dry mood set by Lars.

When the waiter was safely gone, Lars spoke.

"It is clear to me that we are in new territory," Lars said. "Soon we will be examining the personal files of the victims."

"And perhaps that of the perpetrator," Elizabeth said.

"Perpetrator?"

"She means the host of the website," Nasrin said.

"But is that person necessarily a perpetrator?" Lars asked.

"If he or she deliberately manipulated vulnerable people, then yes," Elizabeth said.

"Assuming that the perpetrator, as you call him or her, did not go over the edge himself or herself," Lars said. "If the host wasn't Everett Walleen all along."

"He or she would still be the perp," Elizabeth said. "That's often how suicide cults work. Mother duck jumps and all the little ducklings follow."

"What interests me is the audio signal," Nasrin said. "Did you notice Bowie bolt up and leave the room to report something to somebody?"

"Yes, he knows something," Lars said. "For a spy, he could have been subtler."

"I wonder what might be encoded in those sounds." Nasrin said. "And how the victims deciphered them?"

"And why go to all that trouble?" Lars asked.

Elizabeth sat back and studied Lars. His demeanor was noticeably more cooperative. Lars had not suddenly become friendlier, she realized. He just needed allies to help him to stay ahead of Bowie.

She pondered what she could say that would not violate her agreement with the U.S. government.

"Maybe it's not a code," Elizabeth said. "Maybe it's—"

A detonation hurt her ears, strummed her jawbone. The boom made the metal table vibrate like a tuning fork and the plate glass windows of the restaurant ripple.

At the same time she felt the blast, Elizabeth watched the doors of a parked, red VW Golf across the street blow out sideways, the front windshield implode, and the hood crumple inward. The whole front of the car buckled as if pounded with a giant fist.

Then came the sounds of falling debris and tinkling glass.

Lars tossed the table to the side and knocked Elizabeth flat to the ground— Nasrin pulled a gun from her purse and screamed "RPG." Elizabeth realized that her eyes and brain had captured, like a single frame of film, the cone of a shell rotating in the air just before it had hit the car. But that car, parked and empty, had not been the intended target.

A dark-gray Audi squealed out from behind the flaming car and came to a quick stop in the middle of the road. Three men emerged—two big men and one smaller fellow—all in shiny, cheap suits with shirts half-unbuttoned, with black or dirty blonde long hair pulled back in ponytails … Vikings with guns. The three men poised in shooting stances and hammered shots down the road in rapid succession. A few shots answered back, but an outcropping of office building obscured the other shooter.

There was another torrent of shooting by the Vikings as they stood firm by their Audi, until the shooting finally stopped on both sides.

One of the Vikings ran forward, a big, black-haired man with a gold chain bobbing on his hairy chest, arm outstretched to point his gun at something in the road. He passed behind the out-cropping, out of their sight. There was only one more shot.

A coup de grâce.

The man returned toward his comrades in a skulking stride. He glanced to his right, saw Nasrin and the barrel of her Glock tracking him. His comrades made Nasrin at the same instant, pivoting their guns at her.

"No trouble here, fellows," Nasrin shouted. "We're not your enemies."

She continued to track the black-haired Viking until he returned to his pack. Then she flipped the Glock upward, both arms raised.

"See? Run along now."

The men starred at Nasrin, predators still assessing the threat.

"We're the bloody PST and MI6 rolled into one. Believe me, you don't need this trouble."

The car doors slammed and the tires of the Audi squealed as the car pivoted and roared away.

"Christ, that was close," Nasrin said. "Some timing. And you had to knock over my bloody wine."

Lars lifted himself off Elizabeth and helped her up with one hand. The restaurant manager and waiter ran out as Elizabeth brushed herself off.

Nasrin still clutched her Glock, now pointed just below the horizon line. She crept to the side of the building, raised the pistol and took a quick look. She walked gingerly out into the street, scanning both ends of the boulevard.

Lars and Elizabeth followed.

A single figure lay in the road. Beyond him, the green cylinder of the RPG launcher, with instructions in red, Cyrillic lettering. Elizabeth looked at the man. He was skinny and pale, about thirty, with thinning light blonde hair and an expensive, all-black Italian suit. Dark, arterial blood spurted in gouts from a hole in his shiny silk shirt like the intermittent spray from a geyser. The bullet hole in the side of his forehead looked like a bloody tree knot.

"He's still breathing," Lars said. He pulled out his phone, hit a speed dial and began to bark commands into it.

Nasrin knelt beside the man. Blood streamed out between the man's teeth. He made a gurgling sound.

"Though not for long," Nasrin said, slipping her gun into her waistband.

Part of Elizabeth's training included basic first aid. She could use her belt as a tourniquet for a slit wrist. There was nothing she could do here but compress the chest wound, but even that seemed useless.

Nasrin pulled the man's shirt apart, buttons popping and skittering.

"Wait for the paramedics," Lars shouted.

"I'm not looking for wounds," Nasrin said. "I'm looking for this."

She raked off a film of blood with the edge of her hand to reveal a pale tattoo of light blue and rose ink across the dying man's white chest. A tableaux of dragons, saints, angels, demons, all dancing in the air around a red castle with crenelated walls. Nasrin pushed the shirt upward to reveal neat, eight-pointed stars below each shoulder.

She pulled her phone and snapped a picture.

"Authority stars, he's a made man," Nasrin said. "He got them in prison, probably in one of the labor camps run by the prisoners."

"Stop that," Lars ordered.

Nasrin released the man's shirt, thick beads of blood forming on her fingernails.

The man burbled more blood, spasmed and groaned. The air bled out his mouth and chest wound like the final bleat of an expiring bagpipe.

"Lars, please check his pockets before your detectives arrive," Nasrin said, standing up. "I'm going to the restroom to scald my hands under hot water. You wouldn't believe the diseases these characters pick up in prison."

Nasrin calmly walked back toward the restaurant in search of soap and hot water.

"Have you seen a gun on her before?" Lars asked.

"Does it matter?" Elizabeth asked.

Lars glanced at Nasrin disappearing into the restaurant.

"No," he said. "I am rather glad she has it."

Lars' phone trilled. He answered, listened and shouted something into the receiver and snapped the phone shut.

"There are battles going on all around us," he said.

But he didn't have to tell Elizabeth that. She could hear it, small arms fire echoing off the hills around the city.

TEN

Thor's plaid shirt was indifferently tucked into his blue jeans. His blonde curls bounced when he walked and sweat rolled from his hairline down the sides of his forehead and face. Thor glanced up at the flat screen Nasrin and Elizabeth were watching in the conference room and froze.

The news showed Norwegian Home Guard soldiers piling out of military transports sporting berets, automatic weapons slung across their heavily padded chests. The news cut to a scene from earlier in the day that showed policemen hunkered down behind large concrete barriers as windows shattered and chips flecked off the sides of buildings. The next cut showed images of the Russian Night Wolves motorcycle group, big men with black vests, black knit caps and long hair, along with photos of the gang's leaders. The news cut to an old mug shot image of Karl Pedersen, president of the Mother Charter of the Hommelvik Hammers, who was on the run.

A rolling shot moved across an outdoor food court, metal tables and chairs turned over, a pool of blood under a black Harley-Davidson. The motorcycle looked like a crumbled insect as it lay on its side riddled with bullet holes, leaking fluorescent-green antifreeze into a red pool of blood. Another cut showed police officers milling around two bodies under white sheets behind yellow crime scene tapes.

"I am sorry I am late, but I had to check in with my mother," Thor said.

"Is she all right?" Elizabeth asked.

"She lives in Tromso, way up north," he said. "She was worried about me. I have really been too busy with these files to pay much attention. I need to go see her. What is the latest?"

"Well," Nasrin said, "the little war on the streets of Oslo between the Russian Night Wolves and our very own Hommelvik Hammers seems to be finally winding down. It seems they were resolving some sort of commercial dispute without resorting to a court-appointed mediator."

"Who won?"

"Both sides are losing now that they have the Norwegian Home Guard, the PST, Interpol and every European intelligence service hunting them down," Nasrin said. "Russia's president for life, of course, is protesting Norway's inhumane treatment of his respected citizen-diplomats who merely brought Norway a message of peace on their motorbikes."

"Nice," Thor said. "Shall we get down to business?"

"Let's," Nasrin said, leaning back in her chair.

"Allow me to begin, Detective Inspector Jones, by thanking you," Lars said. "GCHQ was true to your word. Ian complied with all our requests overnight, which is stunning speed. We have found that in addition to our seven victims, there are dozens of other people around the English-speaking world who were connected to freyja.onion. All but one of them are still alive. That one, an Australian, committed suicide last week at his home in Perth. Local authorities are being notified to check in with the families of anyone who spent any significant amount of time with Freyja."

"What do we have on our seven?" Elizabeth asked.

"Each one submitted a kind of video interview, a suicide letter in the form of a long, biographical testimony spoken into a camera," Thor said.

Nasrin swung forward so fast that it caused the back of her chair to snap against her back.

"Let me see them."

"There is a point to us having this particular conversation in this particular room," Thor said, meaning *without the others.* "I am sure you will see them."

Elizabeth bit her lower lip, trying to chart any unspoken subterfuges. Lars was holding up his end of their deal, all right, sharing information with MI6 first. Elizabeth was being brought in not just to offer her professional advice. The fact that she was an American who saw the videos would undermine Bowie's standing to mount a protest once he discovered that Nasrin had been given a head start over him.

But what about Elizabeth's contractual obligations to Bowie and the CIA? Elizabeth would have to work to pull them all together—Brits, Americans and Norwegians—or she might find herself in legal jeopardy. And playing with subversion did not suit her, even if the issue was somewhat less than a burning matter of national security.

"When do you want us to review these files?" Elizabeth asked.

"I have an office set up for your discreet review," Thor said. "I thought we could begin first thing in the morning. The files are long, with writings, diary entries and hours of self-disclosure."

"Does Freyja ever speak?" Elizabeth asked.

"She is never heard from," Thor said. "At least, not in what we have."

————————

Elizabeth slid her card key into the lock, waited for the little green dot to illuminate and opened the door to her hotel room. The room was a twilight cave, only a thin, blinding line of light coming from between curtains almost pulled to a close.

She didn't like being in the dark, not even during the day. She let the door swing to a heavy close and ran her fingers over the wall where she guessed the light switch would be. She felt only the rills of wallpaper. Elizabeth turned to the wall on the other side of the door and ran her fingers up and down, wondering how it could be so hard to find a light switch in the dark until she found the switch to the little chandelier that illuminated the room in a sickly yellow light.

"Tell me why I shouldn't just fuck you right here and now," Karl Pedersen said, one leg hooked over the armrest of a chair by the reading desk.

Elizabeth made a short puffing noise. She edged back toward the door, but Karl lifted a small pistol at her and made that clucking noise parents use to warn their children not to do something disobedient.

"Quiet, my love," he said softly.

Elizabeth nodded, the fingers of one hand splayed across her chest, her heart pounding against her breastbone. She stared past Karl's vulpine glare, drawing in her breath slowly, holding it in, letting it out, trying to calm her mind.

"Do you know New Orleans?" Karl asked.

"What?"

"The city in Louisiana," he said. "Fast by the Gulf of Mexico."

"Not well," Elizabeth said, taking in air. "I've been there for a conference or two. I've had beignets for breakfast."

Karl Pedersen laughed and gestured with the pistol for Elizabeth to sit on the bed. She walked to the front of the bed, continuing to stand.

"You are so pretty and athletic, you remind me of the fine-looking girls I used to watch jogging in the Garden District," he said. "You can find nice everything in New Orleans. Above the stench of poverty is the sweet smell of oil money, pipelines full of cash and ever flowing. That's where I got started, you know. My father was a welder, see, and he took us to live in Fat City when I was a boy. Would you believe I first hung out with the Banditos?"

"Aren't they your mortal enemies?"

"Not as mortal as the Russian Night Wolves, as it turns out. I said I hung out with the Banditos. Never patched with them, obviously. But we did do some sweet jobs, mostly warehouses. Why rob a bank when the Port of New Orleans is so easy? Of course, I had to get used to killing warehouse dogs. I didn't like that part at all, even when they were Dobermans."

"Is that when you met Walleen?"

"Basically," he said. "I had a job and his talents were very useful, crazy Cajun bastard. I want to lay you face down across that bed and give you the rogering of your life. Hard, like you deserve."

"I'm on my period."

"A little blood never bothered me. It obviously doesn't bother you. Tell me, my dear Elizabeth … *cara mia Elizabetta … mi Isabella* … what did you feel when you saw my friend's brain smeared across a wall? Anything like remorse?"

Elizabeth's mind raced to catch his meaning.

"Frankly, we assumed you had done it."

Karl's eyes narrowed and his lips became a flat line.

"Why would I kill Walleen, one of my best?"

"So you didn't. I believe you."

Karl laughed. It sounded forced.

"You'd believe anything I tell you if you thought it might help you."

"I'd believe anything you tell me now because you have no reason left to lie to anybody," Elizabeth said.

"You're hardly in the same position," Karl said. "Fix me a drink."

Elizabeth walked over the mini-bar, grateful for the chance to turn away from him. She turned the key and opened it. She almost asked, 'name your pleasure,' but caught herself.

"Scotch or vodka? Beer or wine?"

"Gin."

"How do you like it?"

"Neat. Right out of the little bottle."

She walked it over to him. Karl Pedersen's eyes tracked her. He stared at her hips and made the rapid sniff-sniff sounds of a dog.

"I can always tell when a woman is bleeding," he said, smiling. "A faint metallic scent, like licking a krone."

Elizabeth stared at his forehead to avoid direct eye contact and stepped two paces back. He was right. She was, in fact, not lying about being on her period.

"What happened to start a war with the Night Wolves?" she asked.

"Ever the detective," Karl said. "Unto death, you might say … One of Walleen's talents was his ability to spoof Russian hackers. Not easy to do. They are very cagey. He got us inside and had … well, he made certain transfer payments from their ill-gotten gains in their offshore accounts to other offshore accounts. After I fuck you, I will put a pillow on the back of your head and fire through it. In the next room, it'll sound like someone dropped a book."

"If you kill a federal agent, you will be extradited to the United States and will spend many miserable years in a Supermax prison awaiting your execution."

Karl took a swig from the little gin bottle. He sucked in some air to run the flavor over his tongue.

"That will never happen. Tell me something. Is your British partner a bean flicker? Has she flicked your bean?"

"Let's talk deals."

"Let's. Let's do it with your crikey-dykey friend. Give me your phone."

"Why?"

Karl straightened his arm, the borehole of his pistol seemed to expand. He was aiming at her heart.

Elizabeth retrieved her smartphone from her purse.

"You want me to make a call?"

"That gash would hear it in your voice. Hand it over."

Karl set the little bottle on the nightstand. He raised the pistol with one hand, and manipulated Elizabeth's phone with the other. She hated him for the way he so casually controlled her with his pistol, insolently holding it on her while seeming to give his complete attention to the phone. She knew that if she flinched, Karl would instantly flex the gun back at her. He found a text thread with Nasrin and laboriously typed out a message with one thumb, a letter at a time.

"May I ask what you just said on my behalf?"

"Just 'need to talk, urgent and private. Come down to my room.'"

Elizabeth's phone made the silly whoosh sound of a sent message.

He stared at her and sipped his gin for a few minutes. Elizabeth's phone emitted the xylophone tinkle of a reply.

Karl looked down at the screen and broke into a broad smile.

"She says, 'I'll be right down dear, just give me twenty.' Fancy that, you're a couple of dears."

Anger warmed Elizabeth's veins. She wanted to bash in this man's head with the hard lamp on the nightstand. But she knew she wouldn't make it two feet across the room.

"As it turns out, twenty minutes is all we need, love," Karl said. "Now take off your clothes my darling Liz."

Elizabeth's mind raced. She had to do something, anything, to confound him and slow him down.

"I'm not FBI."

Karl's mouth twisted.

"CIA?"

She shook her head.

"Then what the hell are you?"

"I'm just a shrink. I was brought in to deal with the suicides. As a consultant."

This time Karl's laugh was genuine, from the belly. He raked a tear from the corner of one eye, and took another sip.

"Now that's rich. You realize that you just threw away absolutely any leverage you may have had."

"What I don't understand is why you blame us for your war with the Night Wolves?"

Karl sucked down the last of the gin and gave Elizabeth a long look. He knew what she was doing, stretching it out like this. He seemed to waver for a moment between raping her, killing her outright or answering her question. From the expression on his face, Elizabeth guessed that it was a close call.

He finally spoke.

"We got ahold of one of them and encouraged him to be talkative. Someone had told the Wolves that an American hacker working for our Mother Charter was skimming them. We had no leaks, of that I am sure. So who else could know that except British and American spooks?"

Elizabeth thought about it a minute. NSA could track something like that. It wouldn't be out of character for Charles Bowie to disturb the hornet's nest and see what flies out. But not likely.

"It doesn't sound right," Elizabeth said, "I mean—"

Karl stood up, his face contorted and red.

"You fucking *purks* you can't help but thrust your *snuts* into our arseholes, and now I've got five of my men in the morgue and twenty-two in prison."

He slapped his hand on the back of Elizabeth's neck, pulled her toward him and rammed the muzzle into her left temple. Elizabeth stepped back and he kept in step with her, pressing the gun harder, hurting her. They did a slow minuet around the middle of the room, the only sound that of his breathing. He stank of dried sweat and gin. The chapped, broken skin of his lips parted as he spoke in a guttural tone.

"Five of my men in the morgue and twenty-two in prison."

There was a strong rap on the door.

Karl gave Elizabeth one more hard press of the gun muzzle and made an unspoken gesture that conveyed the message, 'quiet or die.' He spun Elizabeth around, his big hand on her throat, the gun now boring into the opposite temple.

"Open it," he whispered. "Wide as you can."

He walked her to the door and Elizabeth swung the door open.

Nasrin's eyes went wide, then narrowed.

"I'm sorry," Elizabeth said, barely audible. She felt shame at how weak her words sounded.

"Hands in the air, walk in, slowly," Karl ordered.

Nasrin came forward, her hands raised just above her shoulders. The self-closing hinges of the door made it close slowly, a creaking horror movie cliché.

Nasrin followed Karl Pedersen to the center of the room as he stepped backwards. Her eyes were alert, a slight smile of command formed on her lips.

"Throw your purse on the bed."

Nasrin's purse landed on the edge of the mattress.

"Over there," Karl gestured with his gun for the two women to stand by the bathroom door.

He fumbled around the purse with one hand, keeping his eyes and gun locked on Nasrin. He held the purse upside down, and shook it without looking. A mascara kit and blush fell out, a gun, tissues and gum.

Karl glanced at the bed.

"Is that a Glock?" he asked, feeling for it with his left hand. He picked it up. Now he had two guns trained on them. "It's so small."

"It's a G43," Nasrin said.

"Single stack?" Karl asked.

"Yes," she said. "Easy recoil."

"But not seventeen rounds, surely?"

"Just a standard six," Nasrin said. "Good enough for most jobs."

"It will be good enough for this job."

"If you want to die," she said.

"I do," Karl said. "I want to die and join my brothers in the mead hall. After I kill you and fuck your friend and then kill her."

"Blaze of glory, huh?"

"Got any better ideas?"

"As a matter of fact, I do," Nasrin said. "Consider Anton Breivik. He dressed up like a policeman and gunned down almost seventy people, most of them teenagers."

Karl Pedersen looked startled, like he had just been bitch-slapped. Both guns shook as his grip tightened and his arms straightened.

"Are you comparing me to that *h'stkuk*?"

"No," Nasrin said, "whatever that means, my goodness no. But even Breivik, Norway's very own homegrown bin Laden, terrorist and mass murderer of children, can only be in prison for 21 years, max. He has a comfortable cell, a legal right to cable TV and the Internet, hobbies, a gym worthy of a millionaire and full access to social media, from which he maintains a constant stream of his vile opinions."

"I know that. I did a stint. What's your point?"

"My point is that the PST and prosecutors will have a hard time making a case that you are personally responsible for everything that has happened today. Sure, they'll nick you for currency violations, gun violations, and some other things. But Norway has no racketeering law. If no street CCTV caught you killing anyone, you can expect to spend three years, five years max, in a Norwegian prison. And if IKEA designed resorts, they would look like Norwegian prisons. Much of the world would gladly commit a crime here just to live in one."

"Except that now I have kidnapped and threatened two foreign women in a hotel room with a gun," he said. "Add that to my list of charges."

"Or subtract it," Nasrin said. "Leave your gun with me. I'll dispose of it. Just toss both of them on the bed and walk out. There is a police station at the end of this street. Walk in and calmly present yourself for arrest. Then sit back and enjoy your vacation in the Norwegian prison system for the next few years."

"I cannot know it will go down like that."

"You can, because I have friends in the PST."

"Why won't you put a hole in the back of my head and return to London to receive your medal?"

"I'm a woman of my word."

"What can you give me?"

Elizabeth marveled at Nasrin's cool, her level eyes and level voice, both soothing and yet somehow commanding.

"We weren't the ones who caused your trouble with the Russian Night Wolves," she said. "We didn't even know about that particular side activity."

"So?"

"Someone messed with you. Someone discovered what you were doing and alerted the Wolves. That someone did it to cover tracks and mess with our investigation. The same someone who killed Everett."

"So?"

"We have an enemy in common. And I bet it is the same person who is behind Freyja. Help us find Freyja and we'll fuck her for you."

ELEVEN

Elizabeth watched and waited.

She had asked for a change in hotel rooms, for a room with a western view.

As the line of sunlight sank across her new room, she rested on the bed in a long T-shirt, alert for any sign of the Edge. But it wasn't there. No, that wasn't quite right. It wasn't making itself known.

Elizabeth kept the bottle of benzodiazepine on her bedside table and left the bathroom light on. But all she did was sleep that night, and rather soundly at that.

Before breakfast, she went for a run along a river trail that led into forest that was surprisingly dense and wild to be so close to the city center. The morning air had a hint of coming chill, and the white noise of water over rock was a comfort as she jogged along the river.

Elizabeth felt great. But she knew better than to assume the Edge had left her. No. It was still there, somewhere, a sly creature, biding its time, almost as if it wanted her to relax and believe it was gone for good so it could catch her cold.

———

Thor walked into his office, rocking back and forth like a wobbling top. He eased himself into his ergonomic, black carbon office chair and made a sound of relief. The desk and shelves behind him were full of nerd collectables from movies, parts of old machines, an Alan Turing bobble doll.

"My knees," he said. "The doctor tells me I am either going to have to lose weight or I am going to have to get a pair of new knees."

Thor leaned back and smiled.

"I think it will have to be the knees."

"You're entirely too young to be facing such an issue," Elizabeth said.

"I forget that you went to medical school," Thor said. "I will manage, thank you very much."

"Sorry," Elizabeth said. "I've also got a master's degree in busybody. But I am grateful you've set up some time just for me."

"Why did you not want to see it with Nasrin?"

"It helps to experience something like this alone, without distraction," she said.

Elizabeth understood why Thor would be confused. His focus on technology was total. Once Thor began to scan code, he would be oblivious to distraction, no matter how many people were holding conversations around him. Not so for Elizabeth. It helped her to have solitude to read people, whether one-on-one, or as she would today, on a computer screen.

"It's all set up in the office to our left," he said. "The first one is loaded. You'll forgive me if I don't escort you."

Elizabeth thanked him. The office next to Thor's was spare, with an identical ergonomic chair of black carbon webbing.

She closed the door, turned off the office lights, sat down and touched a key to awaken the computer. A folder entitled 'Kenneth Woods' occupied a central place. Elizabeth clicked it open and started the video file.

At 53, Ken Woods had had a lithe, athletic frame, a long and lean face, expressive eyes under eyebrows that arched into shaggy, black chevrons. He had not shaved in days, his chin speckled with tufts of salt-and-pepper. He sported a golf shirt, blue jeans and a wry expression. Behind him, wooden banana-shaped boats plied a turquoise sea beyond a strip of white sand and dwarf palms.

"Howdy, you there. Whoever you are. This is my testament, the story of who I am and how I came to be at this, impasse, and why I need to move forward to the next level. You were probably wondering why. I am here to tell you why. If I go through with it, this will be record enough. If I chicken out, no one will see this or know what it is about if they do. So here goes.

"The particulars. Good family, daddy a municipal engineer, mom a teacher. Geology degree at Texas A&M University, MBA from Harvard. Married to Jane, née Jane Hughes, for 28 years until our divorce. No children, just didn't happen for us though, Lord knows, we tried. Also married during that same period to my only employer, XRO Energy, in Houston, Texas, with some postings in the UAE, the Philippines, Brazil and Brussels. Became vice president for safety, health, security and the environment at age forty-eight. Big job. Paid 900k a year, with stock options that had made me a millionaire many times over. Officer rank. Brass. Got to lunch once a week in the small dining room with the big boys."

Ken Woods took a sip from a cocktail glass and winced.

"Great life. And now I am about to throw it all away." He smiled. "Literally, if I go through with it. And I am grateful to the good goddess for that second chance."

XRO Energy was kept safe from disgruntled ex-employees and paint-splashing activists by massive bollards that mechanically descended into concrete slots and a black wrought-iron gate that could stop an 18-wheeler going sixty. Once past the guardhouse with the magic of one's corporate pass card and a wave from a guard, the road meandered for a full country mile through the shade of semi-tropical East Texas forest. It was meant to be relaxing, but Ken never found it a bit relaxing.

At least not on the way in.

Like most executives who had risen to his level, Ken awakened at five in the morning, ran like a locomotive on the treadmill in his home gym and got to the office no later than 6:15. Getting in early was key.

It was necessary to get in early just to catch up on emails that trickled in throughout the night from around the world, from the elastomer plant in Dubai, the new refinery in Singapore, the offshore field near Darwin that had come into the company portfolio through an M&A. If he missed that precious window, Ken would pay for it throughout the day, sitting through endless meetings, tapping his feet, worrying what might be going wrong that he didn't know about. That is why slugs who came in after eight never advanced beyond a certain level.

XRO's exterior, designed by a famous architect whose name Ken couldn't remember, was made of marble and burnished steel. It looked like the progeny of a university library and a spaceship. Once through the cavernous interior and past the ever-smiling guards and the card-activated revolving door, the mood changed from cold science to pseudo-warm tints and colors meant to sooth. The lighting was low, the walls done in pleasant tans, every room linked by two hundred-thousand square feet of bronze carpet. Scattered throughout the complex were large oils, mostly pastoral landscapes from the countries in which XRO operated, though not a one of the mountain lake scenes or pristine deserts included an oil derrick or a diesel cracker.

Ken's admin, Karin, would not be in for another two hours. She preset the coffee maker every night so the odor of brewing black roast would stimulate him as soon as he came in through the door. Ken poured himself a cup and sat down to work.

A baker's dozen of new emails.

Dubai: Report on worker fatality from last March. Ken sent it to the printer so Karin could put it in his binder for tonight's reading.

Singapore: There was a draft press release for the inauguration of the new catalytic steamer. He scanned it, hit the 'read' receipt and sent back a one-word response, 'approved.'

Russia: The Arctic project was ready to announce the one-year delay. The delay was blamed on a backlog in construction, but it was really about Russian anger over Western sanctions.

Headquarters: It was from Margo O'Donnell, Corporate Vice President and General-Counsel. It had a one-word subject line, "Iran."

Ken felt a squirt of anxiety. He clicked.

Ken,

We need to discuss this matter as soon as possible.

Margo J. O'Donnell

That was it, like an invitation to discuss theology from the Inquisition or a knock on the door to have a late-night political chat with the Stasi. As soon as Ken heard Karin dropping her things he called her in. He had her set up a meeting with Margo for 11 a.m.

For the next few hours, Ken met with the social media team assigned to disseminate health goals to employees. He spoke with media relations about NGO allegations over the recent fatality. But in his mind, through all the discussion and questions, the 11 o'clock meeting had already begun.

Iran.

It had been but a brief encounter two months before, just a minute with an Iranian delegate to the World Petroleum Congress in Vienna. Ken remembered being dog-ass tired through the whole trip. The older he got, the less well he handled jet lag. That, and the required ceremonial drinking and whirl of people and presentations had made him seem disconnected from his body and the convention dreamlike.

The world's private and national oil companies, with a scattering of big contractors like Haliburton and KBR, had set up booths, and dispatched delegates to present papers and hold discussions on best practices on environmental quality and safety principles. The whole purpose of the event was to share information, so Ken tried to mask his tiredness and slid into his friendliest and most helpful mode as corporate ambassador. When it was almost over, Ken had to host a cocktail reception with 500 people before going up to his room for blessed sleep. Ken remembered that the Iranian delegate at the reception, a shy, diminutive man whose nametag said Eshan, had presented a paper on safety and flaring.

A Canadian Club on the rocks in hand, Ken walked up to Eshan. He noticed the Iranian's small fist was wrapped around the stem of a wine glass. Ken thanked Eshan for his paper.

After some small talk about their respective careers and families, Eshan asked a polite question about the Arctic.

Ken took a sip and replied, "Actually, the whole project could be on ice, forgive the pun. Probably will be."

"I understand," Eshan said. "What's the timeframe?"

"Eight months for a final decision," Ken said. "Then it's go or no go."

Eshan took a sip.

"Big stakes, I sympathize," he said. "If you had to guess?"

"No go, for sure."

Eshan said it was a pleasure and Ken turned to a young woman from the PR department of Total who had a question about managing the communications around estuary spills.

And that was it. In a few seconds, Ken Woods had not only divulged sensitive corporate information, he had also likely violated the Iran and Libya Sanctions Act of 1996. Worse, he had been overheard by Jerome Robinson, standing behind him, alone. Jerome was close to the chairman. He was an eager, true-bluer without an ounce of give who would immediately report Ken Wood's indiscretion to Compliance.

It took months for Ken to come to appreciate the potential cost of his little slip. He had subjected his company and its 70,000 employees and millions of shareholders to the risk of a decade of import restrictions and excommunication from the Import-Export Act. Of course, it would never come to that. The U.S. government couldn't afford to destroy the nation's largest energy corporation. They could just settle by agreeing to the prosecution of one Kenneth H. Woods.

A violator could get 15 years in prison. Of course, it wouldn't come to that or anything like that, either. With a guilty plea, Ken would probably get fired, lose his stock options and serve a few months tending bean fields in a minimum security facility near Beaumont, never to work in a serious job again.

Ken imagined what his mugshot would look like on social media. He imagined himself working the fields wearing an orange jumpsuit. He imagined himself after prison, living in disgrace on whatever savings the government allowed him to keep.

Ken ran up the stairs from the third floor to the fourth floor. Margo's office was just under the "God Pod," the fifth-floor structure that capped the building and housed the four humorless and largely unseen imperators who oversaw the global strategy of the company. Margo's receptionist was a polite young man with short hair who dressed like a Mormon on Sunday. Everyone dressed that way at XRO. Men never wore sports jackets, only suits. Shoes had to be polished to a sheen. Infractions were noted.

The young man smiled and said, "Mister Woods, Margo will see you now."

Margo's office would have been the right size for many company presidents. Tall windows looked out over the bushy green canopy of forest and the jogging trail that no one used after eight in the morning, except in the dead of winter. There was a plush couch, rarely used, in front of a coffee table with books on corporate history that were too boring to read and could only have been written by someone well paid to write them.

Several chairs faced the couch around the coffee table, but they would not be used. Only schmucks were greeted at the couch. In the domain of a corporate officer, the real business always took place around the chairs in front of the desk.

In one of those chairs sat Jerome Robinson, doing his best to look glum. He had started as a speechwriter to an executive vice president, who had gone on to become President and CEO of XRO. As his boss had risen, Jerome had wormed his way into become a free-floating assistant without portfolio.

The chairman's enforcer.

Jerome was overly fashionable, wearing a tailored three-piecer over his stocky wrestler's body. Jerome had a round head, pale skin and a sharp, Roman nose. That visage always brought to Ken's mind the image of a jack-in-the-box.

Margo was still sitting behind her desk, finishing a signature on a contract. Behind her were several photos of Margo with her teen-aged son and daughter on a ski vacation. Margo looked up and smiled at Ken and said something friendly, but Ken did not take in the words. He waited for Margo to come around and take a seat before he took a chair across from her. They were equals in the corporate hierarchy, but he still could be a gentleman.

"So Ken," Margo said, "let me get right down to it. We've reviewed your account of your conversation with this, uh, Eshan, and I am afraid to tell you that after much discussion and reading of the case law, it appears that you may have inadvertently violated the sanctions act."

She let that sink in.

"And Ken," Jerome spoke slowly, as if the very act of speaking was somehow a valiant defiance of shared pain, "this little incident is known and I must tell you that it is considered to be a disappointment."

Known. Meaning known by the God Pod, as if the very names

of the Chairman and his three cohorts could not be spoken aloud. For a moment, Ken thought he was being fired. But no, that wasn't it. If that were the case, there would be a senior HR person and another lawyer in the room.

"We are going to have to report this incident to the U.S. Justice Department," Margo said. "Don't be alarmed. It is just pro-forma at this point."

"What … should I do?"

Margo leaned against her hard-back chair and bit the stem of her reading glasses.

"Ken, I think this would be an appropriate time for you to consult an attorney of your own."

It took a week to locate a lawyer with the right background and credentials, a Big Law partner who had a way of eliciting admissions and evidence by giving his client a silent stare from behind rimless, polycarbonate eyeglasses. After a lot of listening and few questions, the lawyer told Ken to carry on as if nothing had happened. Behind the scenes, there would be an exchange of letters, meetings, talks with the DOJ.

"Really, the more you can relax and settle in, the better chance this has of blowing over," the attorney said.

The long summer days dragged on for six weeks with no news from either side. In his daily work, Ken tried to hear what people said, read what they wrote, learn what they knew and then give them instructions on what to do. But it all seemed at a distance, as if he was straining to listen from the inside of a steel diving helmet.

Only when Ken left the office on those summer evenings, windows down all the way, the sun still absurdly high, did he feel any direct contact with the world. This feeling lasted until Ken pulled into his driveway. His home was a two-story mini-mansion of chalky-white brick with a sloping gambrel roof that gave it a storybook appearance.

Jane always seemed to be feeding her bird whenever he came in.

This mystified him. Surely she didn't feed it all day long. Surely she didn't run to feed it when she heard him coming up the driveway. Still, Jane always seemed to be doing this when he came through the door. She doted on her parakeet, which she had named Tony, after the Dallas Cowboys quarterback.

Jane gave him a glance, smiled and continued to pour seed for the bird. She was pretty and petite, ass still firm from Pilates and yoga, bare heels lifted off the floor, lips pursed as she cooed to her pet.

It had been several weeks since Jane had last asked Ken how his day had gone. It had been a habit of years, but now she knew better. Jane clearly thought her husband was overreacting, being too negative. But she had no idea what it took to go to work and put on a face for meetings while one's guts churned in acid.

Ken went to the kitchen and fixed himself a glass full of ice and splashed it with rye. He sat on a stool at his kitchen counter made of white quartz picked out by Jane's decorator. Jane went to the stovetop and churned stir-fry. The scent of onions and spice made Ken's nostrils flare and eyes water. A recipe Jane had picked up on their stint in Thailand.

"Smells good," Ken said.

"Shrimp," she replied. "Just like you used to order."

Ken dashed some more rye into his drink. The ice cracked and melted, an oddly pleasing sensation.

"Honey …" she said, turning to look at him from the stove.

"Yes."

"I know how tough this is for you."

Jane had grown up in Highland Park, but she had a serious accent like someone from the piney woods.

Ken sniffed the vapors of his rye and took a draw.

"I just thought you might come with me on Saturday."

"With you where?" he asked.

"To my Saturday yoga class, you know. Vinyasa. Might help."

Ken smiled at her.

"Might. Just might."

Ken took another draw of rye.

On Saturday morning, he woke up early and went to the office to catch up on protocols for the new Singapore refinery.

———

Bemelmans Bar in the Carlyle was a yellow cavern, walls illustrated with old cartoons in dim, romantic light. Ken took a sip of his rye and rested his head on the back of the leather booth. He had just had a celebratory drink with Lyle "Scooter" Jackson, the head of investor relations, after a half-day with shareholders and the trade press over a pending acquisition of a big natural gas field in North Dakota. Scooter had left for a dinner, but Ken stayed, feeling the need to nurse this one a bit.

The day had gone well. The acquisition, which had made sense to the board, now made sense to the investors. Best of all, XRO had achieved dramatic reductions in reported incidents since that one last, regrettable Dubai incident, so Ken had a good story to tell about instilling XRO's safety process into the corporate culture of the acquired company. It was an old-line natural gas firm that would soon lose the name of its long-dead founder and wastrel children as it was added to XRO's global empire.

After Ken had spoken, the Chairman asked him to stand on the stage among the senior ranked executives as they took questions from investors, the usual social justice nuns and elderly cranks.

Ken had taken one question about risk management from a hedge fund stand-in and felt he had acquitted himself well. As he spoke, he could feel all eyes on him—the Chairman, Scooter and off to one side, Margo.

Now he looked down and watched the last little fleck of ice dissolve into his rye. He thought about ordering another.

"Would a little company be welcomed?"

The warm light of the bar softened Margo's appearance. She was what used to be called a handsome woman, with a strong jawline and wide shoulders, a firm look nicely offset by her eyes—green, with a hint of smoky eye shadow—a graceful neck, and a generous bosom pressing against her business suit.

Ken recalled that Margo was reputed to be a fierce competitor on the tennis court. She obviously did something to stay in shape.

"Only if you're ready to drink," Ken said, "and we can speak frankly, just confidentially."

Margo took a seat and ordered a scotch on the rocks.

"Ken, take this advice from me, and I mean it as a friend," she said. "With a company lawyer, there are no confidences. Not in my world … Still, I'd like to do you good turn."

"I would like that too. I could use one about now."

The drink came. Margo took a sip and leaned forward.

"Ken, I'm not going to kid you. You are still in jeopardy. Everyone knows that you did nothing wrong. Everyone knows the law is stupid and mindless. But the fact remains that you gave an Iranian useful information about our Arctic ventures with the Russians, which he no doubt proudly took back to their intelligence service."

"I told him nothing that you couldn't infer from *The Financial Times*," he said.

"Maybe. But now they've got it from the horse's mouth."

Ken took a sip. It was good to let the ice melt, let the grass flavors of rye pop.

"Okay, so what now?"

Margo stared at him for a few beats, her large green eyes taking him in.

"There is a way out of this," she said.

"You have my full attention."

"Well," Margo looked down at her drink, and then back up at Ken, "you could sign a 499."

Ken shot her a quizzical expression.

"It's an internal XRO legal product, a limited culpability disclosure document," she said. "It represents a kind of an 'oops' on your part. If the government is serious about prosecuting this, they could. But given a 499, they won't. They'll see that you've admitted fault and that you won't do it again. That always works."

"Always?"

Margo took another sip.

"Well, in cases like yours. Believe me, this is a misdemeanor compared to some of the felonies and blunders DOJ sees every day. It will satisfy their file."

"I'll need to run this by my lawyer."

"Of course."

"Why didn't we discuss this before?"

"Because before, we needed to gauge DOJ's intent, gauge our options."

Like hanging me out to dry, Ken thought.

They took their time finishing their drinks. In that space, small talk crept in, little disclosures and confessions. Margo, who had grown up in Tarrytown, New York, and graduated from Boston University Law, spoke of the culture shock of Houston when she first started with the company. She talked about taking her kids skiing and how much she loved her tennis, and then engaged in some light gossip about a few peers and subordinates.

As she spoke, the low light of the bar accentuated light freckles on the bridge of her nose, like a light dusting of cinnamon.

"Would you like to see it?" Margo asked.

Ken felt his pulse quicken.

"See what?"

"The form."

"The form?"

"The 499."

She reached into her purse and fished out a room keycard.

"I'm in 502. Give me 10 minutes. Just be discreet. We don't want give our colleagues unfounded reason for gossip."

"I … uh, wonder …"

"No big deal," she said. "I just thought given the importance to you, you'd like to read it all now on paper, that's all."

Ken stood in front of 502 for almost a full minute. He finally gave the door a soft knuckle wrap. Nothing happened. He turned to walk away when the door cracked opened, slightly.

"I don't mean to bother you I just …"

"Come in."

Ken entered.

The room was as dim and warm-looking as the bar, mustard walls made moody by light from one lamp on the bedside nightstand.

Several stacks of paper stood on a credenza next to a laptop and an open bottle of scotch. Margo found a plastic drink and took a sip.

"Want one? No rye, sorry."

"Sure."

Margo scooped a fresh plastic cup in an ice bucket and poured it to just under the rim with scotch.

She handed him the drink and began to rifle through her papers.

"Here," she pulled a sheet out and handed it to him.

Across the top, in bold letters, it read: "Declaration of Disclosure and Limited Liability." In the thick continents of legal text Ken noticed that his name and title and the date of the offending incident had already been inserted.

Ken took a sip of the scotch, which had a similar grassy flavor as his favorite rye. Margo drained hers until the ice chips clinked on her teeth.

"Let me ponder this," Ken said. "And thank you, I can see that you're trying to help."

"I want to help you, Ken. I do."

"I appreciate that. I know that this can't be easy for you, either."

Margo set her drink down and gave Ken a searching stare for an uncomfortably long time.

"Margo?"

She went over to the window and pulled the curtain fast and walked right up to him.

Her kiss was delicate at first, a light brush of the lips.

Ken edged back.

"Margo?"

She stepped forward again, the scent of her perfume like a secret garden.

"Margo?"

She kissed him again, and so he kissed her back, lightly at first, then openly, as he pulled her in close and felt her bosom press against his chest. There was a mad dash to untie and unbuckle and toss aside. Ken hastily found a condom in the mini-bar and plunged into her. For hours he wallowed in the pure sensation of her, her scents, the smoothness of her skin and the strength of her body.

The following Monday, Ken received an email from Margo.

Ken,

I want to thank you for what I consider a very productive meeting in New York. To come away with so much done in one session is most gratifying. I hope you feel the same way.

Margo

Elizabeth had to stop.

Ken Woods' story promised long hours of more talk. She was beginning to feel uncomfortable. Elizabeth had listened to patients tell the story of their lives. She had read many suicide notes. Never anything quite like this. To listen to a long, intimate testimonial felt uncomfortably close to a séance, a communion with the dead, Ken telling how he had arrived at this particular avenue of damnation.

Were they all to be like this? A *Decameron* of the damned.

Elizabeth went out for a lunch break and crossed through a tiled tunnel that led to the Oslo Metro to get to Karl Johans gate. Homeless teenagers watched her from the corners of the station, clutching their skateboards and scanning the scene for someone dropping money or a wallet for the next fix.

It was a burden, taking on so many secrets of others. If you weren't careful, they accumulated and the weight of them could make you drown.

But she wouldn't stop, not with Ken, not with the others.

Elizabeth had to know why.

It made her uncomfortable to ask an even deeper question of herself: Why did she so desperately need to know their reasons?

TWELVE

Ken stared at the email. The nerve of Margo, to send such a juvenile double entendre. Karin, as part of her job, read every email in Ken's inbox. Ken re-read it until he was satisfied that in the Scout's honor atmosphere of XRO, no one would see its real meaning.

As he pondered whether to reply, Ken had to struggle to control his breathing. What was this sensation? Was it desire? Was it fear? Was it suspense? It was some combination of the three. It was unpleasant and pleasant at the same time, what a skydiver must feel an instant before jumping. It was horrifying and delicious.

Ken's finger began typing before he had made a conscious decision.

Margo,

I agree, it is a rare meeting that produces as many good outcomes as the one in New York.

Some due diligence is in order. I propose we carefully retrace our process and see if we can yield even better results next time.

Ken

His index finger paused a moment above the "send" button.

He had never done anything like this before. If he stopped now, he could write this off as a vulnerable moment, something that was foisted on him, an excusable weakness. He continued to think about it until he realized that his finger had already come down.

Ken sat there for long minutes, awaiting a reply. There were a thousand urgent issues that needed his attention, but he just sat there, waiting. While he waited, memories of New York flooded over him. So did memories of the weekend, the awkward guilt he felt as Jane asked him about his trip, which led him to give in and go to one of her yoga classes in Bellaire. All weekend long, Ken had to constantly fight the impulse to check for a message on his phone, to see if Margo was thinking about him too.

His smartphone trilled the fight song of Texas A&M University.

"Do you know that string of motels you pass along Bissonnet going west?" Margo asked.

"Yes," he said.

"I think the first's one a pink one."

"Yes, I believe it is."

"I'm taking off at 5 today."

The motel was advertised by a neon flamingo that had long since lost its glow. A gated area in the middle of the parking lot contained a swimming pool the size of a small sedan. Margo waited for him by the door of a first-story room, key in hand, smiling at Ken as he parked. She led him inside. Once the door was shut and the chain slide fastened, Ken pulled Margo into his arms and kissed her deeply. Margo pulled back and looked at him for a long time, her eyes scanning his, searching for some secret or confirmation, as she had done in New York.

Was she testing him? Did she think he was too good to be true? Did she not trust him? Ken could give that look a thousand different interpretations.

As he was formulating something to say, Margo turned around and slipped out of the jacket of her business suit. She briskly unbuttoned her shirt. Ken unsnapped her bra and cupped her ample breasts in his hands as she unzipped her skirt and let her slip and panties drop to the floor.

Margo stretched out on the bed. He undressed and joined her. They kissed for a long time while Ken caressed her body with his fingertips. Their lovemaking started out slow and passionate but quickly built into a frenzy. When they were done, Margo rested her cheek on the sweat-cooled skin of his chest.

A breeze wafted through an open screen in the bathroom window, bearing the ozone scent that always preceded a big storm off the Gulf. Thunder came, distant and muffled. Rain tapped on the cars outside.

The Texas A&M fight song went off. Jane would be calling now, asking Ken to pick up a spice or some fish or some such on the way home. He ignored it and closed his eyes, resting … perhaps a short nap, the rain now a torrent, drumming on the cars outside, Margo warm and close.

Ken felt a splash of wet on his chest and for a moment he had the impression that a drop of rainwater had leaked through the ceiling.

"What's wrong?"

Margo's shook her head, not wanting to speak. Ken gently nudged her chin upwards with a finger. Running mascara had given her raccoon eyes.

"What's wrong?"

"It's Mike."

"Mike?"

"My husband."

Ken realized that he had never heard the name of Margo's husband. In fact, he recalled seeing no pictures of him in her office, just photos of Margo skiing with her teen-aged children.

"What about him?"

"It's getting impossible to be around him."

When he asked why, Margo went into a crying jag, her body suddenly tense and heavy, shuddering against him. Ken retrieved some tissues and wiped her cheeks while her story poured out of her, her voice strained and unnatural. Margo and Mike had had a great courtship and a strong marriage at first. After the kids were born, Mike began to change, spending more and more time building up his construction company. When he was home, Mike became controlling, jealous of the time that Margo spent in her career at XRO. He grew suspicious and belittling, verbally and psychologically abusive.

Margo snorted and laughed. She looked up at Ken with a smile.

"I guess he had reasons to be suspicious after all."

Ken laughed. Hearing Margo speak, he had begun to feel heavy in the chest. He had to tell his story, and so he did, the story of Ken and Jane, a loving couple who grew apart. If they had had kids, it might have been different. Their childlessness was a bad break, leaving them with less and less in common.

"I'm sorry," Margo said, sounding more like herself.

Ken wiped her face some more, the raccoon eyes gone, just a smudge at the corners of her eyes.

"And now this," she said, starting to laugh.

"And now this," he said, smiling at her.

Margo grabbed Ken's smartphone, thumbed an app. She leaned over him, her breasts draping his shoulder and smiled at the phone. A flash popped from his smartphone and it made the noise of a camera click.

She had taken a selfie of the two of them.

"Give me that!"

Margo rolled off the bed and toggled the phone some more. She went to the other side of the room. Her phone made the whooshing sound of mail being sent.

"What the hell did you just do?"

Margo smiled, set the phone down.

"Do you trust me?"

"What did you just do?"

"I just sent a little pic of you to my private email, that's all," she said, slinking toward him with exaggerated hip movements like a burlesque girl. "My very private email account."

"Why?"

Margo's fingernails raked his chest, sending a shiver of pleasure that traced every nerve in his body.

"So whenever Mike starts chewing me out, I can just shut the bathroom door, lock it and gaze on my beloved."

She eased him down on his back and lowered herself on his prone body. Margo moved slowly at first, teasingly, until he grew hard and slipped inside her.

They made love for the better part of an hour. Afterwards, they took a quick shower. Ken looked out through the screen of the tiny bathroom window. It was after eight, the sulfur lights of the refineries making a sickly glow on low, murky clouds that trailed the storm. The parking lot was pockmarked with puddles. It was time to go.

Ken kissed Margo goodbye, a chaste kiss so as not to smear her freshly applied lipstick. He went outside, got behind the wheel of his car, and began to formulate his response to Jane: *Sorry I missed your call, I went down to the company gym and got into it, what can I pick up?*

It was a believable account. It would explain why his hair was still wet from a shower.

Margo tapped on a window. He lowered it. She thrust some papers and pen at him.

"The 499?" he asked.

She nodded.

"Let's get this out of the way," she said. "Sign this and I can get all the paperwork done tomorrow."

The document had yellow sticky tabs denoting every place to sign. Ken wrote his initials at the bottom of each page and scribbled his name at the appropriate line at the end.

Jane called him on the way home, asking him to pick up some tilapia.

THIRTEEN

"Makes me think of the Beatles' song," Elizabeth said. "This lovely Norwegian wood."

"The birds behind these walls are not about to fly," Lars said.

Lars drove slowly after passing through the tall concrete walls of Halden Prison down a ribbon of road that rolled through thin, well-trimmed forest. A walkway bisected the forest, with park benches set at even distances along the way.

Lars pumped the brake of his police Volvo to make way for a prisoner jogging across the road.

"Bloody ridiculous," Nasrin said from the backseat. "A perp's paradise."

"With your talent for alliteration, Nasrin, you should find your calling as a headline writer for one of your country's more lurid tabloids," he said.

The prison rolled into view, a sprawling two-story structure, modernist and concrete. There were no bars on any of the prison's panoramic windows.

They were going to see Karl Pedersen.

As part of his deal, Karl had suffered no trial. He and his attorneys had agreed to a guilty plea with prosecutors in a matter of days, mostly gun and drug charges, in exchange for a short sentence he could begin serving immediately. The prosecutors were grateful. Lacking RICO statutes, they had precious little on Pedersen that would stick in court. The deal still had to be ratified by an appellate judge, who would not approve it unless Lars reported to him that Karl Pedersen had fully cooperated on the Preikestolen matter.

Lars parked and led Elizabeth and Nasrin straight to security, where a guard took their cellphones. Each of them had to undergo a pat down from a blonde female guard who could have moonlighted as one of Wagner's Valkyries. They had no guns to check. Lars generally did not carry a gun and he had asked Elizabeth to tell Nasrin not to bring her illicit weapon. Elizabeth found it interesting that he did not want to make the request to Nasrin directly, whether for deniability or because he did not like nego-tiating with Nasrin, she wasn't sure.

The Valkyrie led them through an outdoor basketball court sur-rounded by whitewashed walls. The walls were illustrated with enormous, modernist murals depicting men in striped prison uni-forms trying to dribble and shoot while attached to balls-and-chains.

"I read that these are gifts from some of the most famous street artists in Norway," Lars said.

"Do they bring in world-renowned chefs as well?" Nasrin asked.

The guard unlocked a metal door and led them to a room with walls painted in soothing colors of forest-green and tans with framed watercolors depicting forests and fjords. Amid the mid-century modern furniture done in primary colors, Karl Pedersen sat waiting for them in a rented tuxedo with a blue shirt with ruf-fles. His black hair was slicked back, making him look like a movie vampire.

"Elisabetta, *mia cara*, it is so good to see you again," Karl said.

"How has your stay been?" Lars asked. They had come to know each other through the interrogation and prosecution.

"The food is borderline," Karl said, giving Lars a sidewise look. "I am enjoying my daily runs and the weight room. The art class is very relaxing, although frankly, I am coming to terms with the fact that I am not particularly talented. And then there are the outside excursions. We had the first of our weekly summer swims in Oslo just yesterday. We're told we will be doing some spectac-ular nature hikes in some of the nearby fjords."

"Why the tux?" Nasrin asked.

"I am about to get married," Karl said. "To Margita, one of our top girls."

"Your regular squeeze?" Nasrin asked.

Karl shook his head.

"She was Sven's old lady, so I had to order them to split up."

"Why get married now?" Elizabeth asked.

Pedersen seemed astonished by such an obviously stupid ques-tion.

"I have to have someone to enjoy in the conjugal rooms, don't I?" he said. "You're more than welcome to attend our ceremony. It's in a half-hour."

"No thanks," Nasrin said. "I prefer to throw up in private."

Karl gave her a cat-with-a-canary smile, then turned serious.

"I'll say this for you, Nasrin, you keep your word," he said. "Not many snuts do. That goes a long way in my book."

"The deal works only if you are forthcoming about everything to do with the site, everything Walleen knew or did," Lars said. "Remember, you're in prison on a conditional sentence. We can extend your stay by years with a single email."

"Tell me, Inspector, do they let you carry a flashlight on your belt, or would that be too militaristic?"

"I carry a weapon when I need to," he said. "You should also know that the Norwegian prison system includes places less nice and closer to the Arctic Circle."

Karl Pedersen hunched in his seat and gave Lars a sullen look. In the hotel room, when he believed his life would soon be over, Karl had been expansive. Now, living in comfortable confinement, he appeared smaller, like a trapped animal ready to either roll on its back and present its stomach or burst into attack.

Elizabeth looked down at Karl's strong, fidgety hands and felt a momentary return of fear. She could feel the pressure of the bore of his pistol at her temple. Elizabeth had felt the onset of an attack last night and had taken a half a mil of benzodiazepine. She had taken another one this morning. It was clearly working, the feelings lurking at the edges of her mind, but not close to take hold of her.

"Let's get back on point," Nasrin said. "We agreed that we have a common enemy ..."

"Right," Karl said, eyes locked on Lars.

"And we can help each other take down the person who got your people killed by the Russians and facilitated the suicides of seven British and American citizens."

"Right," Karl said, turning his gaze on Nasrin.

"So do you have anything?" she asked.

Karl stood up and looked down, a reflex from years of stamping out cigarettes and grinding them with his feet. But there were no cigarettes allowed here. He motioned for them to follow him down a hallway, lined with more paintings. The Valkyrie followed.

"So why is my *donna Elizabetta* with us today?" Karl asked Nasrin, nodding in the direction of Elizabeth as if she were an inanimate object.

"She is here to evaluate you," Lars answered instead. "To tell us if she thinks you're telling the truth."

"When have I not told you the truth?" he asked.

Karl came to an open door that led to a Spartan room with blond walls, a nightstand with a small lamp next to a single bed, a bureau and a small, flat-screen TV on the wall.

"Catch any good soccer games here?" Nasrin asked.

"Movies, mostly," Karl said, rummaging around his desk to find a pen and a pad of paper. "I watch the games in the main hall with the other prisoners, livelier that way."

He picked up a slender pad full of notes.

"What is this?" Lars asked.

"It is my recollection of everything Walleen told me. Phrases, technical terms, words, all about this weird client."

"Walleen told us that he had told us everything," Nasrin said.

"He gave you enough to get you off his back."

"So who was the client?" Lars asked.

"The one behind Freyja," Karl said.

"I know that, but who?"

"Walleen never said."

"A man or woman?" Elizabeth asked. "Young or old? American or European?"

"Never said," Karl replied. "But he told me that this was the gateway."

sromonov@goaskalice.tor

"That's it?" Lars could sound intimidating when he wanted to. "I am putting you up in this studio for this?"

"The password is 'snowdenru83,'" Karl said.

"Get ready to move," Lars said. "Where we're sending you, the only conjugal visits you'll get will be with a polar bear."

Karl was nonplussed. He checked himself in the mirror and straightened out the lapel of his tuxedo.

"This will lead you to Freyja," he said. "You will be talking with her in a matter of days. And I will be enjoying Margita for the next few years. Of this I am certain."

The Valkyrie appeared at the door of Karl's room and led them all out into the hall. She punched a code and two large metal doors opened, slow and silent.

In the large social room beyond was a small, cheerless wedding party of surviving Hommelvik Hammers, looking uncomfortable in suits. In the center of the cluster of sullen men, Sven looked every bit as dour as the disapproving Lutheran pastor who stood next to him. Standing before them all was Margita in a white dress.

Elizabeth recognized her as one of the wives she and Nasrin had seen in the middle of the crowd in the Fólkvangr social club. Margita was an attractive woman, tall, statuesque, with a pinched nose. She stood in the middle of the room clutching a bouquet of white tulips in plastic wrapping with the price tag still stuck on it.

Margita smiled grimly at her new husband, ready to do her duty.

Lars' phone trilled. He voice-activated the pick-up because, as an officer of the law, it would not only be illegal for him to hold a cellphone in one hand as he drove. In Norway, it would be a scandal.

It was Harold Kober, federal police force.

"Lars … where are you? I have some news to tell you."

"I am driving. You are on speaker with Nasrin Jones and Elizabeth Browne."

"It is bad news. You might want to pull over to receive it."

"I am fine."

"You truly might—"

"Just tell me."

"Thor is dead."

"What?"

Lars momentarily lost control of the Volvo, and steered into the center lane.

"What?" he said, slowing down. "How?"

They left in a federal police plane, a Fokker turbo prop that jerked and bounced on bruised cloud tops over the North Sea. After decades of travel, Elizabeth still had not reconciled herself to severe turbulence. So she sat upright in her seat, eyes closed, concentrating on her calming breathing technique. Nasrin sat across from her, studying Elizabeth's pretty face, reading her discomfort and deriving amusement from it. Agent Norris and Chuck Bowie had stretched out in the back to sleep. Lars looked out the window for the entire flight, lost in thought for the two hours it took to get to Tromso.

The temperature fell a good thirty degrees when the flight attendant unsealed the door. Wind whipped across the tarmac as they descended the metal jetway down to the pavement and their police-escort Volvos. Dark, roiling clouds confirmed the wisdom of their packing umbrellas and rain coats. Mountains ringed the small cityscape, some rounded, some sharp and riven with ice.

"Welcome to Tromso, Paris of the North," Lars said glumly. "First time above the Arctic Circle, Elizabeth?"

"Yes," she said.

"We are going directly to the site."

Elizabeth started to ask if Thor's body would still be there. Surely not, she hoped. It was one thing to see a stranger's body in a morgue, quite something else to see someone you had just been working with, someone you liked.

Elizabeth said nothing.

They wended around the city and through a suburb of tidy wooden houses painted in vibrant reds, greens and yellows. They passed by a university of low brick with a broad, green campus, rode up a hill and parked in a gravel lot. A sign read:

Arktisk alpin Botanisk hage

"Artistic, alpine …?" Elizabeth asked.

"Arctic, alpine botanical garden," Lars replied.

A police van was parked near the entrance. A young man and woman sat in the sunlight on fold out chairs, smoking and drinking coffee. They did not wear the clean suits of the forensic team at Walleen's murder. At the sight of Lars and his uniform, they put down their cups, crushed out their cigarettes and stood at attention in their jeans and woolen shirts.

Lars conversed awhile with them. One of the technicians, a young woman with sallow hair, made a right-this-way gesture. Her name was Marte and she was from the National Criminal Investigative Service.

All around them was grassland and stone, with small ponds and gravel walkways.

Before them was a small ridge covered in boulders, some sharp and some rounded. Some were ochre, others dark red or the color of sand. Running up the middle of the ridge was short staircase of flat stones of the same variegated colors.

Marte led them up the stone steps. They all stopped for a moment at a rise. Dark clouds scudded fast toward the mountains, opening a patch of pale blue sky. Even in summer, the Arctic sunlight was as thin as weak tea. Elizabeth surveyed the low profile of the city, the mountains and fjordlands beyond.

It suddenly seemed wrong to be taking in the view. The others had the same thought, turning as a group and following the steps down a ridge. In the grassland below were flowers—violet, pink and orange—in thick tufts.

"I read the Gulf Stream keeps this place warmer than you'd expect," Agent Norris said. He smiled and pointed out Rhododendrons and Aster. "Well, will you look at those."

"Let's keep going," Lars said.

"Reminds me of my flowerbed back in Annenberg," Norris said.

"It is just up this way," Marte said.

Elizabeth wondered what the technician meant by "it" and shuddered.

Up ahead was another ridge of boulders, with a similar set of flat stone steps leading up to the crest. A short line of yellow police tape had been wrapped around two poles at the entrance. The technician ripped it away.

They climbed to the top. They were all a little out of breath.

"He was in this place," the young woman said.

There was nothing to see. Elizabeth tried to imagine she could make out an imprint of Thor's body in the gravel, but there was no pattern that she could make out in the pebbles.

"He was found face down," the technician said.

"Lividity?" Nasrin asked.

"Around his chest," the technician said. "The EMTs had turned him over to find his shirt was already half off. Bruising about the ribs and nipples from blood pooling. My guess is that he had been deceased for several hours."

"Ligature?" Agent Norris asked.

"No marks," Marte said. "No wounds of any kind."

"What's your prelim?" Nasrin asked.

"Classic myocardial infarction," Marte said. "Hands were frozen, like claws. He had been in obvious agony. Buttons along the middle of his shirt had been torn off as if he were trying to get to his chest."

Elizabeth shuddered.

"Time of day?"

"Mid-afternoon, there were many people who saw him running along the back street by the university," Marte said. "He passed behind the garden's ticket office and made his way over there ..." she pointed to a muddy trail in a patch of grass between boulders.

"Running?" Lars asked. "Up that steep slope? For what?"

"It was some University of Tromso students who had seen him," Marte said. "There were astonished to see such a ... excuse me, fat man ... running so hard. One of the students caught a picture of him on a smartphone."

Marte pulled her phone and produced a slighted blurred image of Thor taken at a cocked angle. Sweat pasted a mat of blonde hair onto Thor's forehead. His shirt was untucked, wings flying as he ran. The silver clam of a laptop was tucked between an armpit and the grip of his left hand.

"Any idea of what he was trying to catch?" Agent Norris asked.

"More likely, he was running away from something," Nasrin said.

"There is one more unusual thing," Marte said. "The laptop was not here when the medical technicians arrived."

"So a bystander stole it," Agent Norris said. "Perhaps another visitor to the garden?"

"No," Marte said. "This is Tromso. You could leave a laptop laying on a park bench in the middle of town and the only thing that would happen is that someone would take it to the police station."

Three soft raps on the door.

The bedside clock showed 12:30 am.

Elizabeth resented being awakened. She wasn't about to have a Sapphic dalliance or a sister-to-sister talk with Detective Inspector Jones. The almost endless days played with her sleep cycle, throwing her off, with fits of drowsiness in mid-afternoon. There was no escaping the near-constant days in Norway in late July. No matter how tightly one drew the curtains, random photons still managed to leak through, declaring that the middle of the night was day. And there would not be much sleep. They were to be in the lobby at 4:45 a.m. for the return to Oslo.

Then Elizabeth remembered Pedersen and how close she came to being raped and murdered in an Oslo hotel room. He couldn't be here, could he? No, he was in prison. Surely there was no danger. Not like that.

Elizabeth looked through the peephole. Lars stood in the hallway wearing a T-shirt and blue jeans. He was motionless, a rind of stubble across his jaw. Elizabeth undid the chain and opened the door.

"Yes," she said.

"Forgive me," Lars said. "But I think this is something that you will want to see. May I come into your room?"

"Give me a minute."

Elizabeth slipped into her running shorts and T-shirt and let him in.

"Let me show you," Lars said. He crossed the room and pulled back the curtains that Elizabeth had kept tight to block the midnight sun of Tromso in late July.

Night had finally arrived. The city was dark, no one bothering to turn on lights for an evening that would only last for about one hour.

"Okay," Elizabeth said. "What am I looking for?"

"Come here," Lars said, leaning onto the large windowpane. "Look."

In the dark sky Elizabeth saw a moving labyrinth, translucent, electric green drapes that crackled and shifted, snaked and danced. The shapes shimmered at the edges, swirled like fast moving clouds in the center. For all their color and beauty, the most spectacular thing about the Northern Lights was their obvious depth, tracing the immensity of space and exposing the smallness of man.

What choice did the ancients have but to believe in gods?

"I have never seen this before," Lars said.

"That cannot be true."

"I mean in summer. This is a once in a lifetime spectacle for late July."

"Thank you," Elizabeth said. "It is worth losing a little sleep over this. I have never seen this before, at any time of the year."

They stood in silence for a long time, shoulders touching, their breathing the only sound in the room. Within minutes the spectacle faded as weak light suffused the evening sky, herald of the relentless summer sun.

Elizabeth closed the curtain, tight.

"How are you Lars?" she asked.

"Not so well right now," he said.

Elizabeth sat on the bed. Enough light was already leaking through the curtains that they could see each other. She patted a spot on the bed. Lars sat next to her.

"Tell the good doctor."

Lars chuckled then turned serious.

"I spent the afternoon with Thor's mother," he said. "He was her only child. We had to admit her to hospital."

"And what else?"

"I feel responsible."

"You heard the technician. Thor had a myocardial infarction."

"Thor had a heart attack because he was being chased. For his laptop."

"It was an accident."

"It was a murder."

Elizabeth realized that Lars had put it all together while they were still in the car leaving Pedersen and the prison, just from details he had heard over the phone. That is why he brought the team with him and demanded that the site be treated as a crime scene. This park ranger was quite a good detective.

Elizabeth rolled across the bed. She bunched up some pillows for two heads and patted the mattress again. Lars scooted next to her and lay down with his back to her. She rested against his back, her arm draped over his hip, her fingertips lightly grazing his stomach. They lay in silence like that, her breath on the back of his neck.

Their breathing gradually fell into sync and within minutes they were asleep.

FOURTEEN

The conference rooms scattered throughout the leviathan complex were named after large-scale XRO projects. The name plaque for this one was "Orinoco River," although the Venezuelans had expelled XRO and nationalized its properties decades ago.

"Mind if I ride up in the driver's box?" Scooter asked.

Scooter Jackson, the wizard of IR, had no official reason to be at this meeting, but Ken was pleased that his friend had come to sit next to him in what promised to be a hard meeting.

"I don't know," Ken replied. "Did you bring a shotgun?"

They both sat in silence, facing the glass wall that looked out to a small pond with fleshy lily pads and a line of snapping turtles sunning themselves on a log. Beyond that was a green wall of steamy, East Texas forest.

Margo walked in at 10 a.m. sharp, looking fresh in a smart, beige business suit. She took a seat opposite Ken and Scooter. Jerome entered with several MBA factotums on detail to the God Pod. They scattered around the table, with Jerome taking a spot next to Margo.

Jerome cleared his throat.

"The purpose of this meeting is to discuss the continuing implications of the Dubai fatality," Jerome declared, "and the death of a contractor, Rakesh Sharma."

"Mister Sharma, as you know, has dependent children living in Charlotte," Margo said. "They have filed suit against the company in the Western District of North Carolina alleging that XRO covered up the circumstances that led to the death of their father. XRO contests their accusation, supported by amici from Dubai Petroleum and the National Association of Safety Professionals."

"Margo, correct me if I got this wrong," Scooter said, his oscillating twang undiminished by living in posts around the world. "But this is a very well understood, well documented event."

Margo said nothing, so Ken stepped in.

"Yes it was," Ken said. "It was a simple but egregious error, for which the company is liable. A pressure control at Dubai's isomerization unit had been documented to be unstable—"

"The main poppet was sprung," Scooter said.

"And should have been rectified immediately, but the plant supervisor elected to continue operations while waiting for a replacement part from Manchester, England, without objections by his deputies," Ken said. "Our response has been to terminate the supervisor, downgrade the deputies by one level and apologize to the family. Clearly, we're talking settlement."

Margo handled a small pair of black reading glasses and leaned back in her chair. She rubbed the stem of her glasses at the corners of her mouth as if she were going to chew on them, but didn't.

"Ken, I wish it was that simple."

A turtle on the other side of the glass wall, having had enough morning sun, dropped off the log into the pond.

Margo sat up slowly, made a show of slipping on her reading glasses and opened a briefing book.

"We have here a memo you put out from HS&E, less than four years ago, allowing managers to elect to wait for a replacement if the part can be secured in under two weeks."

"Hold on there, counsel," Ken said. "That's for non-critical parts. Pressure control—"

"It says nothing here about a criticality threshold," Margo said.

"It is understood," Ken said. "Every engineer would know that."

"But the law is about what we put on paper."

Margo tossed her reading glasses, letting them clatter across the walnut tabletop.

"Ken, this was an exceptionally brutal incident."

"Everyone here appreciates that," Scooter said.

The valve had popped, firing a jet spray of superheated condensate onto Sharma's face and torso, scalding him to the bone. He had lingered in the hospital for three days.

"So what exactly are you saying?" Ken asked.

Margo looked to Jerome, who glanced down at Ken with his best I-feel-your-pain expression. Ken stared back at that pallid jack-in-the-box face, the pomaded bristles of his short hair gleaming under the fluorescent light.

"Ken," Jerome said, "the view upstairs is that what we're looking at here is not just a large payout over an errant engineer, but a significant issue of internal control."

———————

There was always little traffic at the pink hotel on Bissonnet, so the one who got there first could always indicate the room by parking directly in front of it. The front of Margo's dark blue two-door Mercedes pointed at the door. She let him in without a word. Margo had already placed their bottle of scotch on the table, so Ken took an ice bucket, filled it and returned to make them two drinks.

"What the fuck Margo?" he said. "What was that about?"

"Ken, it's not me," she said. "It's Jerome."

"I get that. But do you have to be his enabler?"

"You have no idea what I do for you behind the scenes."

"No, I don't," he said. "What do you do for me?"

Margo shook her head, disgusted by his lack of appreciation. She picked up her drink and took a sip.

"What?"

"Ken, he still won't let the Iran business go. He wants to take this and take that and tie it all up in a nice little bow."

"Around my neck."

"Yes," she said softly.

"Then I'm fucked."

"Maybe not. You've still got a champion with the Chairman."

"I haven't spoken to him since the presentation."

Margo took a hard belt of scotch.

"Enough of this, for now, okay, honey? We can talk conspiracy later."

"Okay," he said.

Despite all that had happened, Margo looked fine this evening and he wanted her. She threw the plastic cup on the carpet and began to unbutton, unsnap and slide out of her clothes.

While they were making love, Margo pulled above him and looked down on him for a moment with that intense, searching look. When they were done, she remained on top for a while, wet and cooling, gazing silently into his eyes. There was a tremor around her lips, her mouth pulled down and tears welled up in her eyes, mascara ran down her cheeks and black tears spotted his stomach.

What is that look, Ken thought. *Anger? Sadness? My God, is it pity?*

He couldn't think of anything to say or ask. At that moment, he really didn't want to know. Ken slid from underneath her and went to take a quick shower. He had to be alone for a moment, gather his thoughts. Ken stood for a silent moment under the rush of warm water. What was really going on? The Iran business again? Hadn't the 499 dispensed with all that? Jerome? They never liked each other, but why was he on such an anti-Ken jihad? And Margo? What was up with that look?

Sadness over impending breakup, perhaps? No. It was more than that. It was the look one gives to the innocent guest being ushered to the ceremony, just before he realizes that the ceremony is a human sacrifice.

Ken came out the bathroom in a bath towel and roll of steam, determined to get some answers. But Margo was gone.

Jane had long begged Ken to take her on a two-week, phone-free vacation to the Caribbean. After all he had been through, Ken was ready for it. He turned his work over to his deputies, leaving them with meticulous instructions on how to respond to this and that, and left with Jane for St. Barts. By the fifth day away from the phone, Ken could feel his shoulders come down a notch. He enjoyed a solid week of sleeping late, making love to his wife in the mid-morning, swimming in the late afternoon in turquoise waters, reading novels on white sandy beaches, lolling in a hammock and dining every night on white, succulent fish filets with buttery Chardonnays. The Gordian knot in his stomach began to dissolve. He felt lighter, younger. He even went willingly to several yoga classes with Jane, though he found the task of twisting his body into pretzels unrewarding. After two weeks, Ken returned to Houston a new man, lean and tan.

Back in the office, the first call Ken had to return was to his lawyer.

"Glad you finally called me back."

"Sorry," Ken said, not sounding at all sorry. "I decided to take a real vacation."

"The document you signed, that homebrew XRO solution they call a 499? Well, it didn't take."

"What do you mean it didn't take?"

"The DOJ is going file a letter of intent."

"Intent to prosecute?"

"No, formally investigate, but that is serious enough."

Ken checked his inbox. There was to be a meeting in Jerome's office at 4. No messages from Margo. Oddly, while he had accumulated plenty of emails from XRO offices around the world, there was very little traffic from others at headquarters, even from Scooter.

Ken told Karin he had an offsite meeting and left at 11. He drove to the pink hotel and took a room. He shut the curtains and turned up the air. Ken undressed, slipped into bed under heavy covers, and day-dreamed about Caribbean beaches and brightly colored fish snapping one way, then the other. He fell into a deep, dreamless sleep. Awakened by his phone at 3 p.m., Ken showered—he wanted to be fresh—redressed and returned to headquarters at 3:45 p.m.

Jerome could have had a corner office on the third or fourth floors with the other executives, but he had chosen instead a small and unpleasant rectangle upstairs. What it lacked in size the little office made up for in location, prime real estate just outside the large, fortified glass doors that sealed off the occupants of the God Pod from the rest of the company. Of course, Jerome had the passcode and could enter the Pod at will. Ken like almost everyone else, had to be buzzed in to see the Chairman and his fellow deities.

Ken was not surprised to see the head of HR and someone from Legal. They had already taken their chairs. Ken sat in the little semi-circle in a chair that looked plush but was actually quite hard on the back.

"Ken, have a seat with us," Jerome said in an excessively polite tone. Ken felt relaxed, almost giddy. He would never again have to endure Jerome's faux empathy. He would never again have to steel himself to drive into this soul-crushing complex. Dubai was now somebody else's headache. Ken could say goodbye to the candy-stuffed, alcohol-free holiday parties and other corporate ticks shaped by the mores of the company's two dominant religions, Southern Baptism and Islam.

"I believe you know why you're here."

Ken said nothing, poker-faced.

"In regards to the possible sanctions violations, we've worked out a deal with the U.S. Justice Department we believe will benefit all parties," Jerome said. "They will suspend their promised investigation."

Jerome turned to Legal, the assistant general-counsel.

"We will require you, with your lawyer's permission of course, to sign some statements affirming that you've told us every detail about the incident," Legal said. "If Justice ratifies, then we're done with that."

"What does Margo say about this?"

There was an uncomfortable silence. Legal and HR exchanged glances.

"Ken," Jerome said, looking as if had just been gut shot and was heroically speaking through his pain, "Margo has left the company. She resigned while you were on vacation to take a position as an adjunct professor at the law school at San Francisco University, where her late husband was once the dean."

"Late husband? Current or late?"

"Margo had only one husband, Ken. Mike died, oh, five or six years ago," Jerome said. "I thought you would have known that."

Margo had worn a wedding ring. A widow's ring?

Jerome leaned forward and placed a smartphone in Ken's hand.

"I assume you also know about this."

Ken looked into the screen … two naked bodies, entwined, white shoulders and middle-age paunches contrasting with lean, tanned faces and shapely arms. There was a bit of color, the wide circles of Margo's pink-brown areolae and the gleam of Ken's gold wedding ring in the flash. A drop of fluid glinted in the bulb of Ken's slack penis. In the context of the picture, Margo's smile came across as a leer. Ken's face was blank, his eyes soulless red dots.

It was obscene.

"Before this, we were on the verge of firing her, discreetly of course," Jerome said. "Margo had long lost the confidence of the

Chairman and wouldn't take a hint."

"Now, of course, she has the basis to threaten us with a lawsuit," Legal said. "Title Seven, nonsense about quid pro quo, coerced sex. All manner of outlandish things about you implied. She threw in lurid hints about Iran and illegal deals just to rattle us. We're not buying any of it, of course. Justice will know all about this, for the sake of due diligence. But our, uh, inquiries have set to rest any thought that you had anything more than a garden variety affair. Our investigators revealed that Margo has a long history of sabotaging herself with men. She manages to squelch enough of it to keep moving upward ..."

"Just because we're not buying into what she's saying doesn't mean we're not paying her off," Jerome said. "The Chairman doesn't want to read any of this in the paper. Which he will if she files."

At her level, Ken calculated, Margo had to be looking at seven figures, plus all of her vested pension. With a sweet post in San Francisco and some work on the side, she would be doing quite well. The settlement would be secret, so she'd look like legal rock star on the West Coast, free to victimize someone new.

"Of course, we would like you to leave the premises today," Jerome said.

There was a polite discussion of distributing Ken's responsibilities among his several deputies until a replacement could be named. Any talk of payouts or severance would have to wait until the deal with Justice was done. Handshakes all around.

Ken returned to his office, packed up his pictures and a few knickknacks, all of which fit neatly into a company satchel. He called in Karin and told her he was leaving the company, effective immediately. She looked stricken.

"It's not a death sentence," Ken said. "Not in the least."

He gave Karin a moment to regain her composure, then he told her which deputy should handle which issue. She gave him a hug on his way out.

"At first, I thought I was fine," Ken said, a light breeze stirring the ragged palm frond behind him. "Of course, my marriage was over. Jane had the picture, don't know who emailed it to her.

Maybe Margo? In any event, when I got home, there was not much of a fight, just a cold and dispiriting settling of accounts. Jane was the one who moved out. She went to her sister's place in Highland Park.

"I sold the house, liquidated the vested portion of my pension they could not take away from me," Ken said. "With my firing, the Aztec priests on the high altar of the U.S. Department of Justice decided that one living, beating heart was enough. After I settled with Jane, and paid taxes, I had only about a million dollars left. Not a fortune, but enough for me.

"Like Caine in *Kung Fu*, I wandered the Earth. Or like Cain in the Bible, because everywhere I went I bore the mark. The mark of the Internet. Someone had found it necessary to post the cute little image of Margo and me, along with some choice details about my firing and dark inferences about 'dealings with Iran,' and tie it all to my search results. Maybe Jerome had it done? I still don't know why he hated me so much … maybe it was all just sport to him.

"Anyway, I am sure that everyone I know has by now seen it.

"I had thought about showing up at Margo's doorstep in San Francisco. What would be the point? At some level, she was crazy. At some level, so was I. So after the funds from the house cleared, I took a cheap sleeper bus deep into the Mexican interior.

"I could have stayed in Houston and found work. Not at another oil industry supermajor. Word gets around. But I could have found work in some weak, half-life of a consulting gig at the perimeters of the industry. I didn't want that. Partly, out of fear, I'll admit, of being seen by my peers in such a lowly station. Mostly because I had come to realize that the work I had done for the last twenty-seven years was a fucking bore I could no longer endure.

"So I wandered from expat community to expat community, the art studios and bistros of San Miguel Allende, Lake Chapala, Todos Santos. There were some dalliances, some with divorced women about my own age, some with younger women who mistook my rootlessness for something exotic. I ventured deep down into South America, fearlessly traveling into barrios I never would have seen, much less visited, when I was an executive.

"Then, while gazing at the last of the Andes tapering off at the very bottom of Patagonia, I had an inspired thought. I decided to go to Southeast Asia, where the living's easy and cheap. Once on the beach there, I fell in with a lady from Australia. She succeeded in doing something Jane never could, getting me into yoga, on the beach no less. Then her old flame, an Australian marine, got back from Afghanistan ready to marry. She left me. After that, I fell into every bad habit you can imagine and worse. I migrated from a few ryes at dinner to a fifth of rum a day. I trolled around the red light district from midnight to dawn, not really participating, just pointlessly milling around with all the drug vampires, sex ghouls, chunky German tourists, whores and lady boys. I got deep into hashish and smoked opium more than a few times. One night, a guy from Holland convinced me to drop acid. I can't recommend walking down the main thoroughfare of Patong, with its blinking lights and screaming whores, on acid. But when I got to the beach, I did feel a deep connection to … something … to everything and everyone. I stayed at the beach throughout the night, experiencing the sounds of the surf coming in and out as if I had my ear to the chest of the universe.

"Sounds stupid, I know, when I say it out loud like that.

"I remembered praying that night, to what and to whom I did not specify. I just prayed for clarity. I prayed for purpose. Above all, I prayed for a destination.

"Two nights later, my miracle came. I had a chance conversation with a couple, hipsters from Oakland, who turned me on to Freyja. The next day, I went to an Internet café and initiated contact, just like that. Soon, Freyja and I were texting back and forth. We eventually talked face to face, too, for endless hours. She convinced me to take the course. Which I did, adjusting the frequencies as she directed, taking the treatments she sent me, pouring over her blogs and taking in all her personal advice, therapy and counseling …

"Now don't think me stupid. I don't believe in Norse gods. There is a woman behind all of this. I can sense her, someone subtle, clever, wise. Someone who gets me. I do believe in symbols, in signs that lead to realities that can be perceived but to which access is quickly denied to those lacking in finesse. All along the way, I can't shake the notion that in Freyja, I am speaking not just with her, but with an aggregate wisdom, as if the Internet has some way of distilling the most sacred, the most revealing insights of man and woman and enriching it with the wisdom of all ages. Our relationship deepened, and I began to see her as a person, as someone who loves me and cares about me, who wants nothing but the very best for me, who understood what I wanted when I say I needed not just a destiny, but a destination, someone who invited me to a deeper level, a discussion not for everyone, but for—"

———————

Her smartphone buzzed. Elizabeth looked down. A text message with a phone number, a 732 area code.

>Urgent message: To the parents and/or guardian of Max Browne. Please contact the dean of students immediately. <

FIFTEEN

The Hudson River sweated upward into the air, a minor portion of which condensed into fat drops of humidity that rolled down the window of the ride-share limo. Elizabeth pulled her jacket tight. It was ice-cold inside with the air on high, but she knew that if she asked the driver to turn it down, they would soon be sweltering. At least he knew the best back route from Newark International. Within thirty minutes, the red brick walls and white steeple of Old Queens, Rutger's main administration building, rolled into view.

Elizabeth rolled her bag on sidewalks that rippled over ancient roots from the tall elms on the main quad. The trees looked weathered and the campus lawn washed out in summer sunlight filtered through city haze. There were few students. She dragged her bag over concrete steps to the building and found her way to the Dean of Students.

Max sat in a chair in the waiting room, madly clicking and flipping through something that commanded his absolute attention. Elizabeth studied her son for a moment. A nice-looking boy, anyone would say that. Black spikey hair, jaw blued by a missed shave, and Elizabeth's green eyes and white complexion—legacy of the Braunsteins, German and Russian Jews who had found a safe harbor in Brooklyn from the varied insanities of the previous century.

Max glanced up and had a little start at the sight of his mother silently standing before him.

"How are you?"

"Hungry."

"What do we need to do?"

"I'm all signed out. The dean wants you to call her later. I signed a waiver, so it's okay if you talk to her."

"I'll do that," Elizabeth said. "Let's go."

Max knew a nice little pizza place down on Easton Avenue, a family-owned joint with creaky wooden booths. They ordered a pepperoni pizza.

After the waitress left with their order, Elizabeth slowly reached out and placed her hand over her son's.

"Tell me, okay?"

Max had always had trouble looking people in the eye, but not with his mother. But this time he couldn't look at her.

"I took something I shouldn't have."

"What was it?"

"Some stuff. A drug."

"If you don't tell me, the dean will," she said. "It will be better if you tell me."

Their drinks came, a soda for Max, a light beer for his mother.

Max looked left and right, as if to escape and then spat it out: "DMT, okay, I took some DMT."

Elizabeth felt a rush of cold fear. She focused on her breathing, knowing from years of practice that calm and even was the tone for eliciting.

"That's unusual," she said. "I know from my practice that LSD is making a comeback at school, but DMT? Where did you get it?"

"Does it matter?"

"Yeah, humor me."

"It's kind of weird."

"That's okay, you can tell your mother the shrink."

"I got it in the mail."

"You ordered it?"

"Somebody sent it," he said. "I started getting these weird emails from a dot-tor address. At first I deleted them as spam. But there were really personal messages in the subject lines, stuff I did, stuff I was just thinking about, I mean from somebody who knew a lot about me. All about me."

"What was this person's name?"

"Freyja, you know, like the Norse goddess that became Friday," he chuckled. "The freaking Internet, okay? It's all weird all the time."

"And?"

"So we traded emails," he said. "Eventually, Freyja told me that I would benefit from taking something she recommends for people with social anxiety, you know, like I got. A week later, it came in a plain envelope, no note, no instructions, just a pill in a plastic bag."

"And so you just took it?"

"No," Max said. "I let it sit around. Finally, my roommate, Stuart, couldn't stand it, so he took it. He went into his room and tripped out. A day later, he told me it had to be DMT."

"What did it do for him?"

"He said he saw what users call machine elves. He said it was really cool."

"I know about the machine elves. And so …"

"Here is where it gets even weirder. Somehow Freyja knew I hadn't taken it. She knew it was my roommate who had taken it."

"How could she know that?"

"She'd hacked the peepholes in our laptops, obviously," he said. "She was not happy. She said I really messed up. But I could make it right my taking my treatment, she called it, which she'd send again. I didn't buy any of her shit, of course, but I was intrigued. Who was this person who knew and cared so much about me? And I have to admit, what Stuart described sounded pretty cool. I wanted to see for myself. A few days later, I had another envelope in the mail. So I took it."

"Do you still have the envelope?" Elizabeth asked.

"No, why?"

"Did it have foreign postage on it?"

"I didn't notice."

"So what happened?"

"Nothing, for about twenty minutes," Max said. "Then I started getting all paranoid, like Stuart and his girlfriend wouldn't stop looking at me. Like their eyes were boring into me. My body started feeling weird. I believed my heart had stopped and I was no longer breathing. Then I felt like I didn't have a body at all."

"Did Stuart help you?"

"Fuck no," Max said. "He was a real dick. So was his girlfriend. I think they were messing with me so I left."

"Left for where?"

"I went out into the quad and that's when things got too weird to handle," Max said. "There were things lurking behind the trees, dark things, bad things. They were all over and they were all cooperating to surround me. I didn't feel as if I still had a body, but as if I were just a floating mind that could see. And all I could see was evil stuff. I was afraid they'd take my spirit someplace bad."

"And then?"

"I don't remember much more," he said. "The campus police found me. Apparently, they're pretty used to this kind of thing. I remember being tied down, ceiling lights passing by as they rolled me down a hallway. I slowly came back and when I did, I felt pretty stupid."

"That's because you were stupid."

"You don't have to worry about me doing that or anything like that ever again," Max said. "I hated every second of it."

"Max, listen to me," she said. "The biggest danger isn't DMT, even though that's really dangerous. It is Freyja."

Elizabeth proceeded to tell her son everything that had happened in the last month, up to finding a colleague dead on a hill in Tromso.

Max listened to her, wide-eyed and anxious, but also clearly fascinated. He asked a few questions and Elizabeth held back very little.

"This person loves to trick people into committing suicide," she said. "This Freyja pretends to help when all she really wants to do is mess you up and get you to kill yourself. She knows about our investigation and is trying to get to me through you."

"The next time she contacts me, I'll tell her to kill herself for a change," Max said.

"No," Elizabeth said. "The next she contacts you tell her that you've got a message to pass along from your mother."

"What's the message?"

"Tell her this—'Elizabeth is ready.'"

"Welcome Elizabeth," Lars said. "How is New Jersey?"

Any number of responses came to mind, but Elizabeth knew he was really asking about her son. She had told him her son had an emergency to deal with, but nothing more.

"Everything is fine here," she said. "I am sorry to have missed Thor's funeral."

Lars rotated the laptop, letting Elizabeth greet every member of what had come to be known as the Preikestolen Investigative

Group, christened by Bowie as PIG. Nasrin looked striking, her black hair shining under the fluorescent ceiling lights, a bemused expression. Standing at the far end of the room was Thor's intern, Ingrid, looking small and undernourished at the end of the room. With her rings, runes and roostertails, Ingrid could have been a medieval waif orphaned by the Black Plague.

Someone else, a new member of the team, was seated along the table, too close to the lens for Elizabeth to see anything but two burly hands, lightly fidgeting.

"First order of business," Lars said, unseen behind the laptop. "While it is not yet official, I can tell you confidentially that the coroner believes that Thor died from a heart attack, likely the result of too much stress from running uphill, perhaps from fear as well."

"Whomever was chasing him was in shape," Nasrin said. "And physically formidable enough to scare Thor into running."

"Not necessarily," Agent Norris said. "Just in better shape than Thor."

"The coroner says, 'fear'— does that seem psychologically likely?" Lars asked.

Elizabeth quietly cleared her throat to speak, but was interrupted by a deep and familiar voice.

"If Thor knew that the chaser had a weapon, he'd have every incentive to flee," the newcomer said. "That would be a rational reaction any one of us would undertake."

The fingers of the two hands fidgeted a bit more.

It took a moment to register with Elizabeth. The voice of the unseen man came from George Adler Ableman.

"Ingrid, brief us," Lars said.

"It is like this," Ingrid's flat, heavily accented voice crackled with vocal fry. "Without access to Thor's stolen laptop, we cannot know for certain all that was on it. The items taken from his apartment and his mother's home in Tromso, his other computers, backup hard drives and memory sticks are yielding some data, but we believe there was more."

Elizabeth looked out the window of her hotel room at a gray desert of concrete and cars next to Newark International. She had spent two days with Max and was fully satisfied that he was stable. It was time to get back to the investigation.

"Everything we found related to the case," Ingrid said. "Thor had already reported to us—the dot-onion and tor domains, the testimonials of the victims and the like."

"What about the cloud?" Nasrin asked.

"We do not have Thor's password," Ingrid said. "We are contacting the companies to open his account for us."

"Thank you Ingrid. Anything else?"

"There is one other thing I should mention," Ingrid said. "There was a piece of paper on his desk, with hand-copied leads and web addresses, the same ones the criminal Karl Pedersen had provided."

"What about it?" Agent Norris asked.

"There was one new word written on it in different ink," Ingrid said. "Thor had written it."

"What was the word?"

"Halo," she said.

They met a day later in a Scottish restaurant along Karl Johans gate. George looked sporty in an open-collar shirt and khakis, shafts of chest hair poking over his top button like white wires.

They both ordered steaks, medium well, with Hasselback potatoes. They split a bottle of a lesser Bordeaux and a salad to start.

"So when were you going to tell me about this?" Elizabeth asked.

"Well, I knew you were away, with your son," George said. "I didn't want to inject myself into your personal crisis, at least not until asked."

"How did you become a formal part of the working group?"

"You mean PIG?" he smiled.

Elizabeth chuckled despite herself.

"As you know, Lars and I are acquainted," he said. "I was his therapist during my first Norwegian stay when he was divorcing. He arranged for me to join the team under his budget."

"But two shrinks?"

"On this case, Elizabeth, I think you need help from me, as I would from you," he said, leaning over, that charming half-smile.

"This one is a big stumper."

"It also has the makings of one big paper."

"You were right, there are no ethical conflicts here. Which is why I think you and I should collaborate in writing it."

"Really?" Elizabeth asked. "And who's name goes first?"

"Does it matter?"

Elizabeth took a bite of salad and a sip of wine.

"Tell me," George leaned forward, conspiratorially, "if it is not too intrusive, about your son. How is he doing?"

"It turned out to be just a bump in the road," Elizabeth said. "I will give you some news that reflects on the case, but you have to promise not to mention it until I've had a chance to present it to Lars and the group."

"I promise."

Elizabeth told George all about what had happened, the emails, the package, the pill, convincing Max not to interact with Freyja again … all except for the instructions she had left her son to tell Freyja that she was ready for contact.

"Are you sure it was a pill?"

Elizabeth nodded.

"Very unusual," he said. "DMT is almost always smoked, snorted or injected. To make it effective in pill form would require mixing it with a monoamine oxidase inhibitor. Someone went to a lot of trouble to make it easy and palatable."

"Which is what you'd need if you wanted to convince seven professional people to take it," Elizabeth said. "I can't imagine any of them shooting up, or even snorting or smoking anything."

"Freyja, whomever he or she is, has the shamanistic touch," George said. "It's all about pineal gland, you know."

Elizabeth remembered as a medical student pinching the tiny, red-brown endocrine gland between thumb and index fingers— a tough, fibrous pinecone-shaped organ not much larger than a grain of rice. She also remembered her professor having her trace the pathways of the optic nerves all the way from the back of a cadaver's eyes through the cortex to the gland, the pathway by which the gland helped regulate human sleep with melatonin.

"I remember Descartes had a lot of silly theories about the pineal gland," Elizabeth said. "Seat of the soul, as I recall."

"That's because it's the seat of all light," George said. "In evolutionary terms, the pineal gland is a vestigial photoreceptor, close enough to the skin in amphibians and reptiles to actually respond to light directly. Mystics and other pseudoscientists hold that in humans it evolved into our third eye, situated as it is in the midbrain behind the sixth chakra just above and between our eyes. Properly stimulated, it supposedly pulls back the curtain on hidden realities."

"What does this have to do with DMT?"

"DMT, ayahuasca and other harmala alkaloids hyper-stimulate the pineal gland," he said. "So users see strange beings in strange lands. The pineal itself also makes trace amounts of DMT, so it might be responsible for people who believe they've been abducted by demons or aliens and related hallucinations."

"Sounds like you know a lot about it," Elizabeth said.

"I tried it."

"George!"

"DMT, LSD and ketamine," he said. "Peyote as well. All part of my lifelong research into the human psyche."

"What about sound?" Elizabeth asked. "Can you stimulate the pineal gland with certain frequencies?"

George looked at her in silence for a moment.

"Interesting question."

"So?"

"Well, certain aural frequencies can stimulate various parts of the brain," he said. "I don't see why the pineal gland would be different."

"How?"

"Ever been to a tent revival?" George asked. "Ever wonder how a slick man in a suit who couldn't sell a used car manages to convince people to fork over their hard-won money by the fistful?"

"Have you?"

"I went to several tent revivals in the Central Valley when I was doing research at Stanford," he said, "just to study the technique. The preacher was a ghastly fellow, pasty, dough face, dripping sweat all over his black suit. Looked like an undertaker in a sauna. But in the end, he picked all their pockets."

Elizabeth had to laugh at the idea of George Adler Abelman in a tent revival.

"So what did you learn?"

"There's a lot of technique involved, but it's the music that sets up the pigeons," he said. "These preachers have an organist playing melodic hymns just as everyone is filing in, always at about 75 beats a minute, roughly the same frequency as the human heart. Even going in as an impartial observer, I couldn't help but feel the pull of the music. And when I looked around at my fellow congregants, everywhere I saw the glass-eye stare of people slipping into an alpha state. A waking dream state, almost hypnosis or a fugue state. Very suggestible."

"And if you paired the right frequency with, say, DMT?" Elizabeth asked.

"Effective," George said.

"Effective for what?"

"For control."

SIXTEEN

Ingrid did not look happy to see her, although Elizabeth doubted if Ingrid looked happy to see anyone in the morning.

The young woman led Elizabeth past Thor's office. It was already a bare cube with an empty desk and faded patches on the walls left by old concert posters. Elizabeth had a sad image of Thor's mother in Tromso opening the box of her late son's things. She wondered what Thor's mother would make of his nerdy knickknacks and toys.

She would dote over them, of course.

Ingrid showed Elizabeth to the same office and computer where she had earlier watched Ken Woods' testimonial. The young woman was wearing a sleeveless blouse and when she reached forward to plug in the computer, Elizabeth gasped. Ingrid's forearm sported a full-color tattoo with a realistic depiction of the underlying musculature of her arm. It was as if someone had peeled her skin off.

For all her understanding of people, Elizabeth could not grasp why so many young people were intent on disfiguring themselves like this for life.

Ingrid left. Now it was time to watch another victim explain why, despite good health and affluence, he or she felt the need to join with some new friends and leap off the edge of Preikestolen. Elizabeth started the computer. Before he had left for Tromso, Thor had created an interactive screensaver, one with images of the seven … fallen.

Elizabeth studied their faces.

Sophia Goddard? A mousey woman with a thin smile that failed to mask her lack of confidence.

Sandra Armstrong's face projected intelligence and confidence. That would be a very interesting one, a Fortune 500 CEO. But the playbar on her tile showed it was very long. PIG had a meeting in the late afternoon, so Elizabeth decided it was better to watch a shorter one. Elizabeth zeroed in on Daryl Parnell, the Atlanta restauranteur, a man with a square face and outthrust jaw. He stared straight into the computer lens, a stark, confused expression that was often the signature of deep depression.

Her eyes wandered down to Anne Shrewsbury. She would likely remain a mystery. Shrewsbury had left no recorded statement, just a cryptic note on her website that all she had to say to the world was in her books. The author had a smug, self-satisfied half-smile not in view when Elizabeth had last seen her laid out flat and naked on a steel autopsy table.

Elizabeth's eyes moved to Lionel Jacobson, the roundness of his head accentuated by salt-and-pepper hair shorn so close that it gave him the appearance of a tonsured monk. Jacobson's stare was intense, as if he had just discovered you doing something incriminating and he wanted you to know he was going to memorialize all your failings.

Elizabeth clicked the tile image of Jacobson and waited for it to load.

While the computer clicked and gurgled, Elizabeth's felt a flash of anger from the day before, when at the end of dinner George had pressed her to co-author his paper. She had demurred and now she was proud of herself for standing firm. It wasn't right for him to horn in on her like that, was it?

Of course, it was not clear that Elizabeth ultimately had any choice about accepting George as a co-signer. Given George's connections in Norway, and now his official involvement, what would happen if Elizabeth didn't write the paper with him? George had the bigger name. Unless she flatly refuted him on some point or another, it was likely his paper would bury hers.

But at least she could make George wait. It would feel good to make him wait, if for no other reason than to let George know how betrayed she felt.

"Sod off," Jacobson said. "Sod off you wanking tosser if the only reason you're watching this is to gain some masturbatory pleasure from my pain, you barking cunt … Sod off especially if you're grasping for a fat contract to be my biographer with some second-rate house with piles of cash and a readership of morons, you talentless pillock, how dare you try to use *words* to define my life … But if you're watching this for the right reason, to understand where I am at, where I am going, then settle in, pour yourself something tasty, for I have quite a tale to tell."

Lionel looked up from his beach lounge and scanned the waters of Cala Mastella Bay for any sign of Robert. He could, of course, go down to the water to check on the lad, but in this isolated—and quiet—corner of Ibiza (no English pubs here to turn out singing, puking, fighting drunks at 3 a.m.), the beaches were littered with white pebbles that required one to slip on rubber beach shoes.

Lionel had a pair of such shoes by his lounger … but drained of all energy by the sun and iced sherry, he could not summon the initiative required to slip into his beach shoes and stride into the placid bay. He scanned the waters, a riot of every slice of the blue end of the spectrum, from pale turquoise to violet. Lionel shrugged and took another sip of his ice-cold sherry-tini. The little orange umbrella in the drink bothered his nose, so he tossed it to the side, adding to the pile of them beside his lounge for the beach server to pick up.

If Robert had drowned, well, he had likely already drowned.

Robert's head and shoulders finally broke the water. He spat his snorkel out of his mouth and raised a pale, spiny lobster in the air, its antennae whirling madly. Robert smiled and expected Lionel to be pleased.

Lionel smiled back and nodded, any flatness of expression hidden by his sunglasses.

Robert walked out of the surf, his sandy hair plastered on his head, his lean hips well defined by his black bikini bottom, waving his prey in the air with the triumphant gestures of a child. He took a towel from his lounger with one hand, the other grasping the sea creature, its eyestalk rotating wildly out of sync with its antennae.

"I should put this in a tub of water, catch a few more, and throw them on the grill tonight," Robert said.

"You'll do nothing of the sort."

"Da fuck?"

Robert's command of the Queen's English had all the grace and originality one would expect of a former high school star quarterback from Torrance, California. He was a car dealer's son who had earned a degree at Cal State Long Beach in sports management, although he occasionally made earnest attempts to appreciate Lionel's plays and poems.

"I thought you might have drowned," Lionel said.

"Yeah?" Robert said. "And you just sat there sipping sherry? If I thought you had drowned, Lye, I'd be all over this bay. Do you realize how fuckin' tragic that shit would be?"

"If I were to drown swimming in the Mediterranean, Robert, it would not quite meet the definition of tragic, but some might consider it plagiarism."

Robert squinted at him, knowing that Lionel was once again speaking above him.

"Throw that thing back in the water. We've got dates tonight. With the girls."

One could say that the Peacock sisters were in rare form, but that would be inaccurate. They were always attired flamboyantly and spouting "I hear" rumors with the abandon of teens tossing empty bottles out of a speeding car.

"He really said that?" Robert asked.

"Does that surprise you?" Pam said.

"He's always popping off like that," Penny added.

Lionel did not bother to catch the identity of the victim of this latest bit of chinwag. He ignored them and just enjoyed the scene. The restaurant was well selected, a series of interconnected, high stone grottos that opened to a vista of blue sea. A mistral swept across that sea from Africa, bringing a delicious coolness to the room, though it also bore a film of microscopic grit from the Sahara that crunched between one's teeth.

Tired of hearing what passed for conversation between Robert and the Peacocks, Lionel finally had to say something.

"I see two more settings," Lionel said. "Who is joining us tonight?"

"You will be delighted, so let it be a surprise," Penny said. "Lionel, you're the dog's dinner this evening. What is that?"

"It's my old rowing blazer," Lionel said. His Cambridge crew blazer still fit him well, all dark red and blue stripes, with the heraldic shield of Gonville and Caius College sewed on the breast. Underneath, he wore a thin, light blue T-shirt matched by a snug pair of white shorts and leather sandals.

"What about me?" Robert asked.

Penny reached out and lightly caressed Robert's well sculpted cheekbones.

"You are always something else," Penny said softly. "My dear Robert."

Robert blushed and smiled. The truth was he liked women as much as men, perhaps even more.

"Yes, something else," Pam said tartly.

Penny withdrew her hand and giggled at Robert's canine satisfaction at being caressed. Lionel realized he'd better keep an eye on them tonight. Robert could slip away all too easily.

A bottle of Taittinger arrived, iced up in a silver bucket.

While Robert poured around the table, Lionel reclined in his chair of woven seagrass and regarded their dates for this evening. Pamela and Penelope Peacock were the daughters of a Texas computer magnate and a London socialite, a couple that was once society page fodder on several continents. Now the father was long dead and the mother was strumming her breastbone with *aums* in an Indonesian ashram, leaving her daughters to tend to the family fortune by making shrewd investments in clothes, travel and Mayfair flats.

"So when do our guests arrive?" Lionel asked. "I am hungry."

"You should be, with a frame like yours," Pam said.

"Quite a witticism, Pam," Lionel said. "I should write that down for my next play."

Pam and Penny looked up at someone behind him. The restaurant was sparse this early in the day, but there were enough patrons for Lionel to notice several heads turning around the room to stare at the new party entering the dining room.

"Oh good, they're here," Pam said.

Never one to relinquish his dignity over a scene, Lionel rose from his chair and slowly turned to greet whomever it was who was joining them for dinner.

Edward Lear, in the flesh, along with his wife, Judith Roberts.

Well practiced in stifling any sign of being impressed by celebrity, Lionel calmly welcomed them to dinner as if he had been expecting them all along, introduced them to Robert, who was almost choking with disbelief, and bid the pair to join them at the table.

Lionel had met them both before, of course, in the madness of some charity function at an ornate room rented out from the Royal Society of Medicine. Something about scoliosis, with several inebriated, inbred royals to boot. But this would be different, a chance for conversation, perhaps something more.

Edward buffed the cheeks of both Peacocks while Judith slipped around him and took a chair. A patron walked forward with phone in hand, seeking a selfie with one or both of them, but Judith gave the man a hard stare and shook her head. He returned to his table.

"Well, this is a rare privilege," Edward Lear said. "To have dinner with the Peacocks and with England's greatest living playwright … I'm referring to you, of course, Robert."

Giggles all round.

Over drinks, a polite discussion ensued about the best places to get away from the crowds on the island, favorite tapas and cities in Spain.

"So Edward, are you just off a job?" Lionel asked.

Edward turned to look at his wife, smiled at her over some private joke, and cast his green eyes straight back at Lionel.

"We both are just out of Pinewood, wrapping the last retakes of the latest comic book monstrosity."

Edward had one of those winsome mid-American accents reminiscent of the old stars.

"Exhausting, four-thirty in the morning to a martini take around nine. Some horrible misalignment with the green screen didn't show up in the dailies, so we had to completely redo some of the most intricate scenes. It felt like we were shooting pure shit, but I'm always amazed at what they can do when the computer animation gets plugged in."

"God, the fight scenes were such a slog," Judith shook her head and took a sip. "Try doing leg swings for six hours straight. I don't think I have it in me to do another one of those."

"So you won't do a leg swing for us now?" Lionel asked playfully.

Judith laughed. "More than that—I mean another superhero movie."

Edward looked at his wife with undisguised affection and raised a glass of champagne.

"Honey, with the stash we're getting from this one, you can do indies for the next decade."

She clinked his glass.

"Fine by me. And you can do multiplex blockbusters to your heart's content, Eddie. But they'll look like shit in a hundred years, and people will still be watching me in the indies."

"Yes," Edward said, "they'll be watching you in small, almost empty cubicles in the NYU Cinema Studies Department in the year 2121."

She gave her husband a superficial smile and the finger. He smiled back. They had only been married a year, just before they signed up for the blockbuster, and were still obviously in the teasing mood of newlyweds.

Ed turned to Lionel.

"What about you, Lionel, what are you up to?"

"We'll, I've just put the finishing touches on my latest play, *Holland Park*, the money says yes, and it looks like the Old Vic will give us six weeks in the fall season."

"Wow," Robert said. "You never said that."

Lionel shot him an irritated look.

"Of course, if the reviews are good and the crowds are thick, we can renew at the Vic for the spring or take it on the road."

"Did I ever tell you that the first contemporary play I ever did on a proper stage was *Canary Wharf*?" Edward said.

Lionel shook his head and smiled in response, overcome by a warm rush of satisfaction. *Canary Wharf* was his first, the one that had won him the Bruntwood and put him in profile pieces in every Sunday supplement. "If Shakespeare were alive today to write a play about sex, intrigue and high finance, he would have to change his name to Lionel Jacobson," *The Times* drama critic had gushed. A bit over the top, but one could never have enough of that.

In the train of that one play, and the millions in royalties that rolled in from its production throughout the English-speaking world, Lionel had gained entrée to a world he had long imagined. Then came further commercial success with *Marble Arch* and several other plays with London place names, though the reviews were not nearly as good. Not bad for the son of a Jewish mailman from York and a pint-pressing Scottish mother from the council houses of Glasgow.

"In that event, if you have got your fill dodging ray guns and killing robots, perhaps you ought to consider the lead," Lionel said to Edward. "The role of Stewart."

The actor turned to his wife, giving her a 'what-do-ya-think' look.

"We'd need to sound it out with Ira, but it sounds like it could be a good career move," Judith said. "Something to balance out the popcorn. Something I'd certainly be interested in— what's the female lead?"

"Charlotte," Lionel said.

"Yes, Charlotte," Judith said.

"Two for the price of one," Edward smiled. "Well, two for the price of two. It'd be a thrill to be back on stage with you, hon."

Lionel smiled and said something appropriate, masking his displeasure. Had he asked Judith to consider *that* role, in *his* play? The daughter of a press lord, Judith Roberts had clearly grown up taking what she wanted from the world as if it were her personal treasure chest. Did she think she could just barge in on whatever she wanted in one of his plays?

"Let me talk to the producers and I will have them get in touch with your Ira," Lionel said.

After dinner, the Peacocks begged Lionel to let them take Robert to a disco on the wild end of the island. Robert did not come home until five in the morning, stumbling about the villa, falling into Lionel's bed stinking of sweat, ouzo and Peacocks.

Lionel sent the boy back to California that very afternoon.

Elizabeth sighed, paused Jacobson's narrative and stretched out in her chair.

Over the years she had treated a number of such patients … intelligent, combative, always gnawing at some unseen bone … ravenous compulsions born of an inferiority complex that usually started in early childhood.

She took a bathroom break and to the office kitchenette. She wanted tea and while the kettle began to heat up, Elizabeth checked her email on her smartphone.

There were emails from Max—nothing urgent—Lars and Nasrin about PIG business, as well as a stream of emails from her dean at Georgetown, a water bill that was overdue, bank notifications and a lot of spam.

Elizabeth's thumb poised over one email for deletion when she froze.

The only word in the subject was "introduction." It was from freyjavanirlistens@onion.

The kettle screamed.

Elizabeth looked closer at the web address … Freyja Vanir, from the original tribe of Norse gods, of which Freyja was a survivor among the AEsir, the more celebrated tribe that includes Odin, Thor, Loki and the like.

Elizabeth rushed back to her office, opened her laptop and responded to the email with a simple, "got your message." The reply was near instant.

>I am glad, Elizabeth. I hope we can start a dialogue. <

Elizabeth coiled over her laptop as if she were preparing to leap off a high dive. She wanted to scream in capital letters to stay the hell away from her son, but instead she responded.

>I am glad, too. Freyja. What shall we talk about?<

**>I find email too impersonal, don't you? Why don't
we talk face-to-face?<**

Freyja wanted to meet? Didn't she know that anywhere she chose, a host of undercover police would be waiting as well?

>Where would you like to meet?<
>Right here. Let me send you some code to download onto your computer that will facilitate our talks.<

>I don't feel comfortable with that.<
>Elizabeth, dear, you're already an open book to me. So are Nasrin, Lars and all the others. I follow your

talks with PIG as if I were in the room. Believe me, you have got this all wrong. I want to help! If we can see each other, if we can make eye contact, that will make all the difference in the world.<

Eye contact?

>Very well, send it. <
>Thank you, Elizabeth. I shall not betray your trust. <

A moment later, a new email pinged in her inbox. Elizabeth opened it and stared at the long line of code.

Freyja, whomever or whatever it was, already had access to her computer and likely everyone else's. That much was clear.

Elizabeth clicked and the link activated, taking her to a site on the dark web with a simple rectangle with a green "go" sign in the middle. She clicked that as well. A bar told it would take thirty minutes to download the new software, so she put her laptop behind her, and returned to the office desktop and the life and death of Lionel Jacobson. She needed something to do to shunt aside the whirl of emotions that came with Freyja … anticipation at seeing her face-to-face, white-hot anger at Freyja's attack on her son, and … not quite fear, but dread … fear's awful herald, for the dread of something always felt worse to Elizabeth than the thing itself.

SEVENTEEN

They sat in the middle front. With the stage lights up, the ornate cavern of the Old Vic around them was invisible. Lionel sat between Charlie, the producer, Sheila, the ever-present face of the money, and Teddy, the director, who worked his jaw like a cow's cud. Teddy was always chewing on something, either a wad of gum or an actor. In front of them, Edward Lear deftly wended his way through a rehearsal scene in which he was the straight man to a Russian billionaire character, played for comic relief by one of London's most durable character actors.

Teddy's head rolled around and his jaw worked vigorously as he listened to Eddie read. The director, with a thick nimbus of rewoven hair dyed an improbable copper color, slowly revolved his head as he chewed and listened, reminding Lionel of a cleaning pad being stirred in a pot.

"So is this your club?" Eddie asked.

"*Myshka*, on this street they are all my clubs," the character actor replied in a thick accent and an expansive gesture, which would signal the audience to chuckle.

"There have to be a thousand people crammed inside. Aren't you afraid the fire inspector will shut you down?"

"*Myshka*, they are all my fire inspectors, too!"

That would get a roar.

They continued with another scene with a young woman just down from Stratford in the role of Charlotte. Eddie read with her. It sounded fine to both Lionel and Teddy, but Eddie felt it wasn't right and asked her to run through it with him again.

Teddy usually wouldn't allow an actor to take the lead that way. This time all he did was nod and continued chewing.

The Charlotte role, of course, had been promised to Judith Roberts. But Lionel didn't want her. He resented the insolence with which she claimed the part without even asking. Besides, she was not quite right for Charlotte, though he couldn't tell her that. A-list movie stars believed that they were right for anything. That went double for the daughters of press lords.

So Lionel bought her off.

It took some doing, but working through his network of directors, producers and fellow playwrights, Lionel had arranged for an offer to come to Judith without his fingerprints, a lead in one of the big rollouts on The Strand. He remembered with relish how she had come to him, wearing an anguished look on her pretty face to ask—she would understand if he said no—if she could beg off the role of Charlotte.

Lionel took his time, made a little speech about professionalism and why she was so perfect for the part, but finally … finally … he grudgingly relented and for his generosity, a grateful Judith had given him a hug.

"Can we get a little help here?" Eddie said.

The change in tone and diction snapped Lionel out of his reverie.

Eddie was out of character, hands on hip. The property master stood to the side of the actors, shame faced. He had been milling to around to check on the lights and had interrupted the flow of the rehearsal. The property master offered a wave of apology and left.

The actors resumed their readings.

Teddy was being unusually quiet, impressed by Edward Lear's performance on just a second read-through.

Lionel had lived among actors since he had begun to write skits for Footlights as a second-year at Cambridge. He had never known anyone like Eddie Lear. When they hear the name, most people naturally think Shakespeare. Edward Lear had in fact been named by his professor parents after a Victorian illustrator and nonsense poet of the same name, he of "they dined on mince and slices of quince" fame.

That distinctive name was the only thing about the man that stood out. In his resting state, Edward was remarkably unremarkable, a perfectly ordinary looking chap, with a slightly recessive chin, a gash of a mouth, expressive green eyes and a lop of dark hair. You would barely notice him on the street. But Edward's talent—his insane, over-the-top, once-in-a-generation talent—regularly transformed his slender, Midwestern towel boy self into a Richard III who throbbed with power and menace, into a movie superhero who could coolly put away a monster with athletic panache, into a lover whose aching need made you want to love him back.

There was magic to what he did, as if Eddie was an ordinary boy able to channel passionate and dangerous spirits. This vibrant, possessing talent, more than anything physical, made Eddie Lear far more attractive than a Robert could ever be.

Lionel's flat was near Covent Garden, with high bay windows that afforded a view of the city's more recent monstrosities—the Gherkin, which reminded so many of a pickle or a dildo but looked to Lionel like a giant upright bomb left over from the Blitz … the skyscraper with the ragged top everyone called the Shard, bringing to mind a bottle broken for a fight … the skyline still anchored, thankfully, by the graceful dome of Wren's masterpiece, the Baroque lines of St. Paul's.

There was still enough of the old London left, here and there amid the tech monstrosities of a global fintech sector gone mad. In twilight, the city cast a silver radiance on the low ceiling. The news said it might snow.

Lionel had spent a good half an hour tidying up, putting dirty glasses and dishes in the washer, frumping pillows and straightening up the papers in his office so his writing desk would make a serviceable showpiece.

For mood, Lionel turned off the lights in his office but kept the desk lamp on so it would cast a pool of light on a draft of his next play and the thick blue lines of a new poem composed with a fountain pen across Savoy stationery.

He stepped back to admire the effect—where the great man works his magic.

Lionel straightened an old framed photo in the office and stood back. He stared at his younger self, a student standing next to Seth Darby, a Cambridge don and a playwright himself, the two of them smiling contentedly next to the Porters' Lodge of their old school. They had had their time together, a time when it seemed as if Lionel would forever be Seth's student.

Lionel looked at their smiles, their contentment, no way for them to know how short that time would be. Within a year, Seth would be diagnosed with a particularly virulent strain of HIV that, thank God, had passed over Lionel but would rob Seth of his beauty, his intellect and eventually his will to live.

So many good days, back then Seth, we had no idea how good.

Lionel had an absurd wish, that somehow Eddie might allow him to take him under his wing as Seth had done for him. That Eddie could become someone to share an appreciation of the finest things that so few cared to understand these days. Someone who could be a friend. Not quite like Seth, of course. But Lionel had had precious few friends in his life. Whether such a friendship, such a love, ever became fully acknowledged was not important. The fact that they might share something would be enough.

The buzzer rang.

The fisheye camera of the intercom system sharpened Eddie's nose into a beak. He looked small, boyish and forlorn, with a scarf that could have been wrapped around his neck by his mother.

Lionel buzzed him in.

A minute later Eddie walked into the grand living room with its high ceilings and majestic panorama of London and whistled with delight, as if he were still just fresh from the outskirts of St. Louis.

"Lye, I had no idea that playwriting paid like this," he said.

"The difference between us is that a successful playwright can afford only one of these," Lionel said. "Drink?"

"What are you havin'?"

"Gin Rickey, soda, a dash of simple sugar and lime."

"Sure," Eddie said. "Sounds very … uh, limey."

Lionel chucked and made two drinks with a few brisk movements. They clinked glasses with a "cheers."

"I want to thank you for the part," Eddie said. "It is working out quite well, doncha think?"

The opening reviews had been good, though better for Eddie than for the play's author. That was a bother. Nothing Lionel had done had come close to the wild praise he had received for *Canary Wharf*.

Eddie turned to the bay window again, taking in the cityscape.

"I do love this town," he said.

"When you're tired of London …"

"I'll never be tired of life," Eddie said.

"Me neither," Lionel said, wondering if it were true.

"I've got something to ask of you," Eddie said.

"Ask."

That single word had come out of Lionel's mouth as overly tender, but Eddie had not seemed to notice, or bothered by it if he did.

"It looks like a second run is a sure thing," Eddie said.

It did indeed. Though the theater's calendar had a hold for the revival of an American rap musical about a colonial traitor, it looked like *Canary Wharf* would return in the heel season between spring and summer. But Eddie had yet to sign up for the second run.

"I certainly hope you will be with us when we do," Lionel said.

"About that," Eddie said. "How do you think our current Charlotte is doing?"

Quite well, Lionel wanted to say, if you go by what the critics and Teddy says. But the actress who played Charlotte was nothing compared to the clout of a movie star. Lionel stared at Eddie, knowing he could script the very words about to come out of his pretty face.

"Actually, I think it would be a hoot if Judith played Charlotte for the second run," Eddie said. "She'll be done with her current commitment, and is so looking forward to playing opposite me for the first time on stage."

Hoot. Well, at least there was one word in those two sentences that Lionel would not have imagined.

"Yes, a hoot … But of course, it's all up to Charlie."

"And you think the money will say 'no' to having two A-listers from Hollywood?" Eddie asked.

"No," Lionel said. "Sheila won't."

"Then it's a deal?"

"It's a deal that I will take it up with Charlie, Sheila and Teddy first thing in the morning," Lionel said.

Eddie pretend spat in his hand and Lionel shook it. Eddie's hand remained in Lionel's a beat longer than necessary. Eddie's smile was mild and comfortable as his touch lingered.

"Show me around this place," Eddie said. "Where do you put quill to parchment?"

Lionel smiled but couldn't speak. Eddie's touch had done something to him. His heart was hammering and his breathing was off. He was sick with desire.

"Come," was all he could muster with a weak smile. Lionel led Eddie upstairs and to the study.

"So this is where it all happens," Eddie said.

The desk lamp shone on Lionel's works in progress like a spotlight. His laptop, of course, was put away. Lionel felt embarrassed, suddenly worried that the room was too staged, the lighting too obvious and pretentious. He didn't want Eddie to think that he was preening for him.

Eddie craned his head around the room, his eyes squinting in the dim light, taking in photos of Lionel with world leaders and celebrity actors, framed letters from princes and potentates, and the burnished metal cone of the Bruntwood Prize on a shelf.

"Who is this?" Eddie asked.

"Seth," Lionel said. "My don at Gonville and Caius, the man who made me who I am. The man … who …"

To his embarrassment, Lionel's voice rose several octaves and trailed off. He felt an involuntary shudder pass through his body like an electric current and he began to sob a little.

"I don't know why … after all these years … in front of you of all people … dear God, what a silly sot I am."

Lionel wiped the corners of his eyes against his shirt sleeve and straightened himself up.

"I guess you didn't see that coming," Lionel said and coughed, padding his shirt sleeve against his cheek. "Neither did I."

"Tell me about Seth," Eddie said taking a seat on a small couch in the study. He patted a space next to himself, and Lionel sat close to Eddie while the whole story poured out him, one of the oldest and corniest stories of all, the one about the bright, young prodigy and his world-weary master unexpectedly finding devotion to each other and to their art. Then, cliché upon cliché, came tragedy, disease, death … The arc of a thousand bad plays lived out in Lionel's life.

They spoke for almost an hour about things Seth had taught Lionel about the stage, about writing, about life.

Eddie rested a hand on Lionel's shoulders and patted him.

"Thanks for telling me, Lye. Now I feel like I really know you."

Lionel's eyes had adjusted to the dim light. The desk lamp reflected a shimmer in Eddie's eyes. The boy understood. He cared.

"Let's go down and freshen those drinks," Lionel said.

As a light snow began to fall outside, the two sat side by side downstairs and talked for several hours more … old war stories, gossip about the industry, funny stories from Eddie's early life. Lionel shared some of his pet theories about the dramatic arts, some of which Eddie vehemently agreed with, and some that he vehemently argued against. They talked late into the night and when Eddie left, he pulled Lionel in with his strong arms and gave him a long and heartfelt hug.

———————

Lionel was beginning to take on the sound of a character delivering a soliloquy that had become overlong and tedious. He rhapsodized about Eddie's intelligent eyes, Eddie's humor, Eddie's way around a good story. Elizabeth noticed in the corner of her eye something bright and moving on her laptop screen. On the screen in front of her, Lionel was coming to the climax of his narrative, only a few minutes left. Elizabeth resolved to hear out rest of Lionel's story. It wouldn't hurt to make Freyja wait on her a few minutes.

What came next was no surprise. As soon as Judith had wormed her way back into the play, Eddie dropped Lionel like an infected needle.

After months of curt responses and minimal contact, Lionel tracked Eddie down on free night from the play. He had heard from a stage hand that Eddie had mentioned something about The Punchbowl, a fine old Georgian pub in Mayfair. Lionel walked through the crowded bar to the secluded restaurant booths in the back. His spirits sank when he saw Judith with Eddie, a hand wrapped tightly around Eddie's arm, a supercilious smile on her face and two half-empty beer steins in front of them.

Eddie had what the Yanks called a shit-eating grin.

"Fancy meeting you, Lye," Eddie said. "We'd ask you to join us for a beer, but the missus and I have some personal things to talk over."

"Don't mean to be a bother to the two of you, Eddie."

The pair of them broke out laughing.

"Oh Lionel, you are such a puppy dog," Judith said. "You can have a sit with us if you like."

"I'd rather stand."

"So what brings you out on such a cold night?" Judith asked.

"I was looking for Eddie."

"He's right here, what do you want to ask him?"

For once, Lionel could think of nothing to say.

"Something about the third act?" Judith said. "If that's it then I agree, there is something a bit patchy in the final exchange with Charlotte."

"No," Lionel finally replied. "I want to ask Eddie why is he suddenly being such a prick."

"You know Eddie is a such a talent …"

"I know."

"He can play anything."

"I know."

"Even a goddamn queer."

They sat smiling at him, holding Lionel's stare.

Eddie cleared his throat.

"With queer theory all the rage on the stage, Lye, I may have by now kissed more men than you have," Eddie said. "It's not easy for me. That's why I have to wash my mouth out with beer every time."

"It's all in a day's work," Judith said.

"Hardly a busman's holiday, right dear?" Eddie replied.

They clinked glasses and each took a swig.

"Well, Eddie, at least you didn't have to kiss me," Lionel said, trying to hold a confident smile.

"No, it was enough of an ordeal just wandering down memory lane with you," Eddie said. "It won't be long before you'll have to pay people to listen to your stories about dear, queer old Jeff."

"Seth, Eddie, Seth," Lionel said. "Shame on you Eddie. No need to be cruel."

Lionel turned and walked away with as much dignity as he could muster. He went outside, strolled down Farm Street and leaned against the cold stone walls of an old mews and wept a bitter cry that did not leave him feeling any better afterwards.

Lionel resolved to keep away from the Old Vic for the duration of the run.

A few days later, he let slip a catty remark in front of a gossip columnist about Judith being a temperamental bitch of an actor to work with. Almost downright unprofessional. A week after that, Lionel planted a story about Eddie being a terror with the stage hands, though it was far from the truth—he was notably well liked. The truth was never a deterrent to gossip columnists and bloggers. Before long, Lye had inspired a popular social media meme about the "Terror Two," with images of Judith and Eddie wielding bloody axes.

The bad blood between the playwright and the actors had become a commonplace of theater gossip, though the community split into two camps over who was responsible. After a successful run, a major studio came calling, interested in turning *Holland Park* into a movie. There would have to be changes, of course. Dialogue in a play wasn't a movie script, after all. Lionel would also have to agree to some other alterations, one of which was to change the name of the story from *Holland Park* to *Griffith Park* and set the whole thing in Los Angeles. With Judith Roberts and Eddie Lear, there was little doubt that they had a sure thing at the box office.

As the holder of the copyright, Lionel had the final say. All he had to do was sign a contract and cash a check for one million pounds.

Lionel said no.

"He goes on a bit more about lost love and spoiled opportunities for happiness, about not being appreciated."

The voice was feminine but strong, with the slight lilt of a Norwegian accent, and elongated "oo" sounds like those in 'lost' and 'love.'

The voice came from Elizabeth's laptop.

Elizabeth turned to her screen to behold Freyja. Behind the goddess was the same light, misty forest in gray-green silhouettes that Elizabeth had seen on the landing page. Freyja's blue eyes registered slight ticks, just like those of a real person, as if she were intently studying Elizabeth's face in return. Wind lifted and played with strands of her golden hair. The bejeweled torc of gold had depth and shadow against Freyja's neck.

The red light on Elizabeth's laptop was illuminated.

"You turned on my camera," Elizabeth.

"No, dear, I merely turned the light on your camera as a courtesy. I shall do this in the future, every time, just to let you know when I am watching you."

Freyja moved slightly with each breath and heartbeat. This was CGI, no doubt about that. The voice seemed only a little artificial. The realism of the simulation was near perfect.

"So that's it?" Elizabeth said. "Lionel leapt to his death because of heartbreak over a married man who was never going to go gay?"

Freyja stared at Elizabeth and smiled ever so slightly.

"He couldn't receive the love from the one person he desperately wanted love from," Freyja said.

"Eddie?"

"Himself," Freyja said. "Poor Lionel, I could not lead him to understand that his deep romantic feelings were actually reflections of his obsessive self-love, or the lack of it. I wanted to save him. Believe me, I tried so hard."

"What doesn't he say?"

"He attacked Judith and Eddie with several frivolous lawsuits about breach of contract and the like. He continued to drive attacks on them in social media and gossip pages."

"Who are you? Really?"

"I am a helpful spirit," Freyja said. "And I am so glad to finally be in dialogue with you. To converse with someone with your degree of learning and intellect is a delight for me. But to have an effective conversation with a goddess—" Freyja's smile was impish— "it is necessary to set a *mood*. The evenings are the best time for such talks. Will you engage with me, Elizabeth? Will you have some sessions with me?"

"I thought I was the one who held sessions."

Freyja's laugh sounded genuine.

"Perhaps we can help each other, *mein guter Doktor Braunstein.* I know you are busy today. Is there a good relaxed hour for you to speak with me, Elizabeth?"

"If I am going to speak with you, you must agree right now to never bother Max again," Elizabeth said.

"I got your message the first time," Freyja said. "The boy is fragile, I can see that now."

"I don't give a living fuck what you see. You are to leave him alone."

"I shall."

"Eight," Elizabeth said. "Tonight."

"Very well, Elizabeth, very well. Let us get to know one another tonight."

EIGHTEEN

They met again in the Directorate of the Environment in the conference room surrounded by blonde wood and clear glass. The day outside was bright and beautiful and Elizabeth felt an overwhelming desire to stand up and walk away from all of this.

"Good morning Elizabeth," George said, smiling with a cup of coffee in his hand. He took a seat next to her. Nasrin took a seat directly opposite.

Soon they were all there, Charlie Bowie, Agent Norris, Harold Kober of the PST, Lieutenant Dahl, Ingrid standing in front of a screen with a remote in her hand and, of course, Lars Stenstrom at the head of the table.

Nasrin made eye contact with Elizabeth and held it a beat longer than necessary. She wanted to talk to her about something.

Elizabeth pondered for a moment whether to tell everyone about Freyja, just as she had withheld exactly what had happened to Max from everyone except George. That first decision she could defend as a matter of privacy. She only told them she had a family emergency to attend to. But contact with the mastermind herself? It was possible that with the help of GCHQ that they would be able to track Freyja's ever-shifting array of mirror sites and zombie computers back to the original IP. Then again, why expect they could do so now after so many failures?

No, if Elizabeth told everyone, they would want to be in the room with her as she made contact, standing off to the side while she spoke with Freyja. They'd unleash digital hounds to try to track down Freyja's location that would spook her. Even in the unlikely event Freyja failed to detect that she was being watched, Elizabeth worried she would catch the deception in her voice.

Or would she? Was Elizabeth already buying into Freyja's pretensions of omniscience?

"The coroner's report has cardiac arrest as the cause of Thor's death," Lars said. "I need not say how badly Thor will be missed."

He let the words sink in and then had something else to say.

"Karl Pedersen pled guilty to three counts of reckless endangerment and possession of illegal firearms. He will serve no more than three years in prison."

"*Dritt!*" It was Inspector Dahl who had blurted out the word, no translation needed.

"Well, I hope they grant him full Internet access," Charlie Bowie said. "Otherwise we could have a human rights violation on our hands."

That remark only made Dahl look even more apoplectic.

"And I also expect he'll do well in photography class," Bowie added.

"Let us run through the cases," Lars said. "Kenneth Woods …"

He looked to Elizabeth to give a briefing.

"Ken Woods is an open book," Elizabeth said. "Classic breakdown. Loss of status, loss of career, financial hit, divorce … He got into recreational drugs. Living in a neon tourist center on the beach, mostly awake all night. He was susceptible."

"Lionel Jacobson?"

"We're far from a full picture," Elizabeth said. "The man was a narcissist. I'm not buying that he would leap off a cliff because he was heartbroken. Jacobson was the kind of man who would like to live to 120 just to see all his enemies suffer and die."

"But we think he jumped nevertheless," Nasrin said.

"Perhaps," Agent Norris said. "We've yet to find that body floating in the channel. Same with Woods."

"All I am saying is that there is more to Lionel Jacobson than he was willing to divulge," Elizabeth said.

"Have you done Sandra Armstrong yet?" Bowie said. "The whole Therapso saga?"

"No, I haven't *done* her yet," Elizabeth said.

"It's a doozey."

George spoke up.

"What I think we should be discussing is the role of DMT in the cultic initiation—"

"You mean brainwashing," Nasrin said.

"If you wish," George said. "We should look at how DMT rendered these people so pliable. We should also investigate the role of sound, perhaps even something subtle in the electromagnetic spectrum that might have allowed for some degree of remote control of their brains."

Lars and several others flashed embarrassed smiles, but Bowie stiffened in his chair. Elizabeth guessed he didn't like it that the conversation was turning so close to the CIA's MKULTRA experiments and his pet theories about RF.

"What about the note Thor had left behind?" Elizabeth asked.

"You mean 'halo'?" Lars replied.

"It's a common term used for atmospheric optics," Kober said. "Above the Arctic Circle, you see a bright circle in the clouds, especially in late summer."

"Could it be something else, perhaps taken from Norwegian mythology or archetypes?" George said. "I've seen images of Freyja where she appears to be wearing a halo."

"Loki, too," Ingrid said. "Beware the trickster."

The meeting went on for another hour as Lars spelled out in minute detail the open questions of the case and Ingrid gave a multimedia show about GCHQ's data and the email address from Pedersen—a lot of talk about mirror sites and packet switching—which presented many leads, but nothing definitive, at least so far. At the end of the meeting, Lars issued an invitation.

"We are all in shock over Thor's death. I thought perhaps we might need a welcome break. Tomorrow is Saturday and it is August in Norway. You have not been to Norway in the summer until you have swum in our fjords. My family has long had a cottage in Fredrikstad, just an hour west of here. I would like to invite you all out for a swim and enjoy some hot dogs and some beer."

"Sounds like a good bonding exercise," Bowie said. "Especially the part about the hot dogs and the beer."

Liberated from the meeting, Elizabeth walked out into the sunshine, only to find Nasrin scurrying to catch up.

"May I?"

"Okay."

Nasrin fell into step with her.

"Ever been to Frogner Park?"

"No."

"It's a total must-see and only a ten minute walk from here. Good place to stretch one's legs on a beautiful day like this."

They walked in silence down a broad street lined with shops that opened to an immense park of manicured lawns, stone bridges, and a French formal garden with low shrubs and a large stone fountain in its center.

Stone sculptures of nude bodies lined the walkways of the park, from toddlers to crones, but mostly Nordic men and women with heroic builds engaged in strenuous acts of labor, athletics and copulation. The walkways converged on stone steps that led to a circle with a stone obelisk made of writhing human forms.

These were all the handiworks of Gustav Vigeland, a world of the stout, the strong and the assertive.

"You know some people think his art is fascistic and he was kind of a Nazi."

"Vigeland?" Elizabeth said. "Or Karl Pedersen? They're still around you know, made all the bolder by social media. Do you have something in particular to talk about?"

"Your friend, George," Nasrin said. "He's become assertive, asking a lot of questions outside of the meetings with the other PIGers. He's obviously doing research."

"True enough, but so am I."

"There's more. In private, George is subtly dismissive of your contributions. He always finds ways to take something you've asserted and then layer a corrective opinion on top of it."

"That's George."

"I just thought you'd like to hear it."

"I do, Nasrin. I suspected as much, but it is good to know. Is that all?"

They walked over a curved footbridge. A few feet away was a stone toddler, with a pouting, angry scowl and his hands balled up into small fists.

"It's just … that I hope I haven't alienated you for good, Elizabeth, that's all. As I said before, I hope we can move on and work together and be good friends."

Elizabeth stopped and Nasrin turned to her, looking expectantly.

"We can work together Nasrin," Elizabeth said. "And with a little time, we will again be friends."

Charlie Bowie picked her up in a small, fire-engine red Ford. He was wearing blue jeans, a Hawaiian shirt, his broad face glistening with sunscreen.

"Did you remember to bring a bathing suit?"

Elizabeth nodded and threw her bag into the back and got in. Charlie was an aggressive driver, weaving in and out of traffic on the highway to Fredrikstad.

"So how's your friend?" he asked.

"George?"

"No," Bowie said.

"Is Lars really paying for George, or is it you?"

Bowie cast her a sideways glance.

"George was interested and so I asked Lars to get him on board and I'd pay for it. At least George reports to the people who pay him. If it was up to me, we'd let you go. But Lars insists that you are key to the investigation and I am not ready to rock that particular boat."

"So which friend are you asking about?"

"I meant Nasrin, Elizabeth. I saw the two of you walking away hand in hand yesterday."

"Fuck you."

"Later."

Elizabeth regretted accepting Bowie's offer of a ride. She wanted to get out of the car, but it was too late now. At least she could ride home with someone else, maybe Inspector Dahl.

"Seriously, tell me anything new that you have learned."

"I told you everything yesterday, in the meeting."

"What about the attempt on your son, Maxwell? When were you going to tell me about that?"

Elizabeth stared ahead at the ribbon of highway that cut through the coastal forest.

"I consulted George about it," she finally said. "I didn't tell PIG out of respect for Max's privacy."

"But there could be valuable evidence," Bowie said.

"There was nothing by the time I got there," Elizabeth said. "Max told me everything, and there were no forensic details worth relating."

"How do you know? You're a shrink, not a trained investigator. And besides, don't you owe it to everyone to tell them that their families might be targeted?"

"I'll tell Lars," she said.

"You should have told me. The Norwegian government is not paying you, we are. Remember, the good ole US of A, the country that you owe your allegiance to?"

"How did you know about Max?"

"We're Universal Exports, remember? We know everything."

Of course he had NSA pick up her international calls. It was perfectly legal for a case abroad.

Elizabeth chuckled inwardly over Charlie's belief that he can know everything.

Who did he think he was, Freyja?

———————

They circled Fredrikstad and headed west on a one-lane road to a place where the land sloped downward and splayed into jagged fingers of rock. Bowie followed a sandy path down one such peninsula until Lars' cottage emerged, a wooden clapboard house painted bright red with high sloping roof of dark ceramic tile. It sat on a small rise that overlooked a cove filled with gray-green water that opened to the Oslofjord and the North Sea. A wooden stairway ran down a rocky cliff from the cabin to a boathouse with a flat deck on its roof.

An elderly woman greeted them at the door. She wore her peasant braid like a crown, a few blond strands intermingling with the gray. Her blue eyes were bright and observant.

"You must be Elizabeth," the woman said. "I am Ingunn and you are most welcome. Lars has told me a lot about you."

Ingunn gave Bowie a perfunctory smile and invited them into the main room of the cabin. Perhaps twenty people of all ages stood around a long wooden table stacked with cold dishes of sliced salmon and canapes with cubes of white fish, a pot of meatballs and blocks of white and brown cheese ready to be plucked with toothpicks. A large ceramic bowl of berries sat next to jugs of ale and bottles of chilled white wine.

Mingled among the neighbors, relatives and children were most of the members of the Preikestolen Investigative Group, socializing with the family and friends of Lars and his mother.

George was engaged in an animated conversation about the existence or non-existence of free will with an elderly man who turned out to be a retired professor of philosophy. Inspector Dahl chatted with some local women, a glass of white wine in hand, looking more relaxed than Elizabeth had ever seen her. Agent Norris nibbled at some cheese in a corner of the room. Nasrin engaged one of Lars' neighbors in polite conversation, noting Elizabeth's arrival with a side glance. Ingrid, her eyes narrowed by pot and irony, stood aloof with a young man who sported a Hitler Youth haircut and a robust beard.

"Elizabeth, welcome," Lars said, beaming, his two children in tow, as blonde and beautiful in life as they were in the framed photo in his office.

Lars introduced his children, an eleven-year-old boy named Sven and an eight-year-old girl named Emilie. As Elizabeth made small talk with the children, she noticed a woman watching her closely from across the room. Blonde and pretty, with a pinched nose, the woman was catalog-hip, sporting a leather vest and an ornate silver necklace that looked like an Indian dream catcher. Lars called the woman over and introduced her to Elizabeth. She was his ex-wife, Anita, who introduced her husband, a reedy man who had immigrated from Greece.

"I am always pleased to meet any new friend of Lars," Anita said with what seemed a genuine smile. While she talked, Ingunn walked over and put an arm around Anita's waist as if the woman were still her daughter-in-law, even her child. There was a communal sharing of parentage and bonds in Norway. Divorced or not, Anita was still a member of the family tribe.

From the way they looked at them, Ingunn and Anita clearly thought Elizabeth and Lars were an item. Their attention began to make her uncomfortable. After a while, Elizabeth feigned interest in the buffet, begged off and circulated around the table.

"Elizabeth, good to see you off duty," George said as she speared a meatball. "I hope you relax today, you deserve it."

"Good to know that you have off duty moments of your own, George," Elizabeth said. "You've been so busy."

If George noticed any dig in that comment, he chose to ignore it.

"Are you coming for a swim?" he asked.

A few people were already beginning to depart for the water. Lars had changed into a bathing suit, a towel draped around his shoulders. He waved to her as he led his children outside. Elizabeth popped another meatball in her mouth, ate a square of cheese, then followed George and Lars and his children outside and down the wooden steps to the boathouse.

"You forgot something," Bowie said, pulling up next to her on the stairs. He had Elizabeth's bag with her bathing suit in it. Lobster red patches from the sun were already beginning to show on his white chest.

Lars and the children led them into the boathouse to an open dock with a small outboard on a lift.

"I guess I need to change," Elizabeth said.

While she spoke, she couldn't help but marvel at the whorls of blonde hair on Lars' perfectly formed chest. Lars smiled back and pointed to the structure's one interior room, a small office with sea charts, framed photos of Lars and his late father, sailing manuals, depth charts and books in Norwegian.

"I will guard the door," he said.

While she changed, Elizabeth noticed many classic books in English—not a mail-order library, but musty old covers, split and decaying, along with a whole shelf on Norse mythology. She pulled some down and found a few first editions. Odd, she hadn't figured on Lars being a reader of classics or a collector of books. There were hidden depths to this man.

When she emerged, Lars took a moment to admire her without his customary reserve.

"You do wonders for a bikini," Lars said, smiling in a way that had no hint of a leer.

"Show me the way."

He led her to wooden steps that led up to the deck, which the children and Charles Bowie were already using as a diving platform. Bowie cannonballed with a huge splash.

"There is really only one way to go in," Lars said with a smile.

He pivoted, ran across the deck and with a murderous yell leapt into the air and disappeared under blue-gray water.

Elizabeth looked down. She never cared for heights, not even a mere ten feet above the water. While she was looking down, Dahl brushed by her and dove straight in.

Ten feet down. A mere split second of falling.

"What the hell," she said to herself, walked to the back of the deck and made a running leap.

The North Sea water, warmed by the hot summer sun in the shallow cove, was cool but not the shocking cold she had expected. Bowie paddled around her and pulled himself out puffing and panting.

"Come on out," Lars shouted to her.

Lars had to be a good hundred feet away, dead in the middle of the cove. The water was feeling warmer, comfortable even, so Elizabeth swam out to him in clean breast strokes.

She turned back to see Ingrid sitting with her boyfriend on an outcropping to the side of the boathouse, passing a joint back and forth. George surveyed the scene from the top of the deck. His appearance was surprising. He was leaner than she imagined and far more muscular. He went to the back of the deck, bounded forward and made a clean headfirst dive.

"So why are you marginalizing me?" Elizabeth asked.

Lars paddled in the water, his blonde hair pasted on his head, his eyes almost squinted shut from the trickling water. Elizabeth couldn't shake the impression that he looked a bit like a Labrador retriever fetching something in the water.

"What do you mean?"

"I mean George," she said. "Why did you bring him in while I was away?"

"I didn't," Lars said. "Charles Bowie insisted. George is a consultant on his payroll. I think Bowie's unhappy with you and wants a second opinion. But I saw no problem signing off since George is a friend of yours."

"He is," Elizabeth said. "But he seems to be horning in on everything I do of late."

"I had no idea there was friction between you two," he said. "When Charlie asked my permission to bring him on board, George himself told me you were fine with it."

"He never asked me."

Lars took in that news with silence.

"I want to tell you some things," she said, "things you should know about."

She proceeded to tell Lars about Freyja's attempt to undermine

Max. He asked a few questions. Then she told him about the contact with Freyja the day before. Lars listened to her while he lightly paddled around her. As she spoke, Elizabeth noticed George climbing out of the water and back into the boathouse.

"And you don't want the others to know about Max and his private issues," Lars said. "I understand your thinking. At the very least, I have an obligation to warn the members of the group that their family members could be at risk."

"Fair enough."

"And I would like to ask Ingrid to look at your laptop," he said. "But I agree. This is a delicate thing. We should be very discreet for now. We need you to keep talking to Freyja. Just use your smartphone to record the conversations."

A sail rose over the water and sliced across the cove. George was standing on the board of a windsurfer, his back arched, his strong arms straining against the boom.

"I had forgotten about that," Lars said. "I am glad to see someone is shaking the dust off of that old thing."

George cut across to the bottom of the cove, made an awkward turn with trembling sails that almost deflated, caught a fresh wind and expertly shot across again. After several zigs and zags, he sailed to the center where Lars and Elizabeth were paddling. He released the boom and sail and slid gracefully into the water next to them.

"I saw this in the boathouse crying out to be used," George said. "I hope you don't mind."

"Not at all," Lars said. "I'm just surprised it still works. I think I tried it only a couple of times before giving up."

"I'm impressed, George," Elizabeth said.

"I had plenty of practice in the Long Island Sound," George said. "Elizabeth, you should try it."

Such a silly idea. She shook her head.

"Seriously, I will show you how."

"I couldn't."

"This is a slalom board, built for speed, which actually makes it more maneuverable and easy to use."

"I'd have to take a lesson first."

"This is your lesson. You just climb up on to the board, slide your feet into the straps while I stay in the water with Lars here, the two of us steadying the board. Then as you find your balance, pull the boom until the sail is perpendicular to the wind and take off."

"It's really that simple?"

"No, you will fall many times before your muscles learn the correct balance. But once you do …"

Elizabeth slid onto the board in one long, awkward motion. She pulled herself to her knees. There was a bit of wind, made more noticeable by its cooling contact with her wet bikini. With the strong grip of the two men holding the board level, she rose unsteadily to her feet, knees bobbing, and slid her feet into the straps, took hold of the boom and fell backwards into the water with a whoop. She came up spitting water and angry, as if the board had deliberately given her the slip. She tried it again. And again. On her fourth try, the wind caught the sail and Elizabeth shot forward, unsteady on the board but skittering over small waves before losing power and sinking back into the water.

On the next try, Elizabeth was able to get on the board without anyone's help. She wobbled and wavered into a turn, then caught a powerful burst of wind that shot her across the cove, skipping over small waves that slapped against the underside of the board.

It felt magnificent, like flying.

With time and practice she could master this sport. When George had first invited her, she had been afraid to try, but now she was glad. Mastery was the opposite of fear, a source of inner illumination that disinfected the dark corners of her mind. She kept at it for a good hour, long after George and Lars had paddled back, though she noted that the two men kept a watchful eye on her as they sipped beers at the dock while dangling their legs in the water.

Elizabeth fell many times, but sliding back on the board had become second nature. A good, brisk wind kept coming from the sea, while the geometry of the cove necessarily kept her runs short. As she got better at turning, Elizabeth learned how to zig and zag from the narrow end of the cove to the opening to the sound and back again.

While cutting inland, Elizabeth noticed some guests milling around the cabin above, plastic plates and cups in hand. She could go on for hours, but Elizabeth realized that her display was bordering on rudeness. She caught a strong wind that brought her to the boathouse. Bowie had now joined Lars and George, admiring her skill in cutting close to the dock and sliding off the board.

"You had to have done this before," Lars said.

"I've always had a knack for such things," she said. And it was true. Not long after the death of their parents, an aunt had begun taking Elizabeth and Mike snow skiing in Colorado every winter, then water skiing on big lakes in Vermont. Elizabeth had always been a quick study in any sport that involved balancing against wind, water and gravity.

George Abelman and Charlie Bowie started up the steps in their bathing suits to change into dry clothes in the cabin's bathroom. Elizabeth started to follow when she realized that her clothes were in the boathouse. She went into the small office and heard Lars outside folding and storing the windsurfer.

"Do you have a towel around here?" She almost shouted the words, thinking she needed to be loud to be heard through the door.

"Here," Lars spoke to her in a soft voice that easily penetrated the wood, sounding as if he were already in the room.

"Thank you," she said.

He cracked the door open, reaching one hand in with a beach towel. The door opened a little more. He stared into Elizabeth's eyes, reading her expression.

Lars came into the room and softly shut the door while Elizabeth peeled out of her cold bikini and left it in a wet pile on the wooden floor. Lars handed her the towel and Elizabeth dried herself. He shut the blinds, walked over to her and softly ran the towel down her back, over her buttocks, the backs of her legs. He placed his big hands on her bare shoulder.

Lars slowly turned Elizabeth and kissed her lightly. As they kissed more deeply, he traced his fingers down her side, stroking her ribs with her fingertips, then along her thighs.

He cupped her breasts, admired them, slipped out of his bathing suit and pulled her to him. Elizabeth felt her soft breasts pressed to his firm chest, felt those whorls of blonde hair brushing her nipples, just like she had imagined, felt his strong grip on her back. She wrapped her legs around his powerful thighs and curled her feet above his ankles. He entered her. She began to move up and down, slowly at first, leaning back at an angle while he held her in a firm grip by the small of her back.

They didn't last three minutes. They came together, making more noise than was prudent, hoping no one could hear but unable to stop themselves.

Elizabeth slid off him, struggled to catch her breath. She found a tissue, then slipped into her clothes.

"Well, that was not something I had envisioned as part of your morale-building lake outing," she said.

Lars laughed as he finished buttoning his short-sleeved shirt.

"I must have a fetish for windsurfers."

"That and a twitter account could get you a following."

He came close and gave Elizabeth a kiss.

"Thank you," he said.

"Thank you," she said.

"We should try this again sometime," Lars said.

Walking up the stairs, Elizabeth worried that the people standing around the outside of the house with their drinks and plates full of food would know what had just happened. But they were all deep in conversation, oblivious that Lars and Elizabeth had been alone in the boathouse for a few minutes.

Only Bowie had noticed something was amiss. He watched them as they came to the last steps, looking right into Elizabeth's eyes. Leave it to Bowie to have such a canine ability to sniff out her secrets.

"Everything all squared away in the old boathouse?" he asked.

Lars ignored him and went inside to get some food.

"Nothing that will ever concern you," Elizabeth said.

NINETEEN

Elizabeth poured herself a cold Ringnes from the mini-fridge, closed the curtains against the afternoon light of an Oslo summer evening and waited for her laptop to boot-up.

It was 7:47 pm.

She had showered, dressed and put on makeup, the irony not lost on her that she had spent the day au naturel among colleagues and a new lover, only to make herself presentable for a conversation with a monster. She inserted the thumb drive Ingrid had delivered. As promised, the tracking program took only a minute to load. Elizabeth had to reboot the computer.

It was 7:52 pm.

She felt her pulse quicken at the thought of speaking with Freyja, but without a return of the dreads. The day spent in sunshine, Elizabeth's mastery of the new sport, the sexual release with Lars, all that had unlocked months of tension and somehow banished the possibility that tonight would be lost to the bad feelings. Elizabeth was looking forward to this conversation, to pulling the smug mask from the monster's face, to make her pay for daring to lure Max into her orbit.

Elizabeth felt pumped, the hunter's élan.

The laptop was back up, fully loaded.

It was 7:55 pm.

She took a sip of beer and clicked the Freyja program. Her screen filled with the image of the misty forest, but dully illuminated, not yet active. Elizabeth hit the red 'record' button on a smartphone Ingrid had also left, a burner phone with no links to Elizabeth or her various social media addresses. It would give Lars a quick playback. The video and audio would automatically download to Ingrid's stick for a full record.

It was 7:58 p.m.

Who was this freak? Someone with deep technical skills. A psychopath with an appetite for manipulation, who enjoyed passive-aggressive murder, but capable of killing Walleen with a shotgun and Thor with terror.

Was Freyja a man hiding behind a woman's face and voice? Passive-aggressive violence argued for a feminine mentality, but not necessarily.

One thing was certain. Freyja had been deeply wounded. She wanted recompense for some ancient injury or personal injustice. What wound had Freyja suffered that had distorted her to such a degree?

"Good evening, Elizabeth, you look lovely this evening. And thank you for being on time."

"I wouldn't want to keep a goddess waiting."

"And the windsurfing! Elizabeth, I am impressed. You took to it so readily. This is a new side of you."

"Were you actually there?"

"I have more eyes than a spider."

It was probably true. Freyja could see through every camera of every smartphone carried by every person Elizabeth knew.

"So what's our agenda? How does this work?"

"I thought perhaps we might get to know one another, become friends first, and take it from there."

"But you already know all about me. I know next to nothing about you. So if we are to be friends, then tell me who you are."

Freyja titled her head in momentary contemplation.

"You must accept that I am many things. That I channel a collective wisdom born of the experience of many minds and the suffering of many hearts. I don't have an agenda, Elizabeth, but I do have a mission."

"Which is?"

"To help people, to enable them to discover who they truly are and what they are meant to become, and then guide them to become it."

"I saw some graduates of your program. All laid out on metal autopsy tables with Y-incisions on their chests."

"I don't control people, I just offer them guidance. Yes, I've suffered some failures. So have you, Elizabeth. Remember Jeremy?"

It was like a slap in the face.

"I didn't encourage him to jump, you silly bitch."

"At last, perfect candor from you. We're never going to get anywhere unless we are truly open with one another."

"And you are a bitch, even if you're really a fat slob wearing pajamas with one hand on your dick."

Freyja laughed.

"I like this side of you, Elizabeth. You are becoming more confident, more assertive. Tell me, how long has it been since your last episode?"

"What?"

"You know what I mean. By my count, your most recent episode was in that awful airport hotel in Newark. Was that the last time you had to self-medicate?"

Elizabeth wanted to slam the lid of her laptop shut and bolt out of the room.

Freyja continued.

"I mean, I do understand that you were afraid, and not for yourself. Max is a sweet boy. Smart, like you. Caring. Although I do think he does suffer from the family affliction."

"Stay the hell away from my son."

"Someone should monitor his progress."

"Like you? What about your promise? Get near him and I'll …"

"Kill me? Let it out Elizabeth, please. Cry havoc and let slip the dogs of war. Punch a fist through the screen and then have a good cry. But don't keep these feelings bottled up."

She wanted to say there was nothing working on her except for a psychopathic interloper.

"If you come near my son again, I swear to Almighty God that I actually will kill you … you fucking, fucking bitch."

"I see Lionel has rubbed off on you. And how would you kill me, Doctor Browne?"

Elizabeth came back to herself, suddenly aware she was grasping the edges of the desk, her fingers pressed bloodless white. She had been imagining wrapping her fingers around Freyja's slender throat. Elizabeth puffed out her breaths, almost hyperventilating.

This had gone very wrong. Never let them get inside your head. Never … Elizabeth had years of training to keep patients from doing that to her. And yet it had only taken Freyja a minute to get her raving. Of course, this was the first encounter she had ever had in which the other party knew her family history and had also threatened her son. That was still no excuse.

Elizabeth had to get control of her breathing and calm down.

She inhaled for four seconds, held her breath for seven, exhaled for eight. She did it again. Freyja stared at Elizabeth in beneficent silence while she did this several more times, calming down until she was ready to speak again.

"With my hands, Freyja, with my own hands. For what you did to those people, for what you tried to do to my Max."

"I understand, Elizabeth. And I accept your anger because I see how it all looks from your perspective. Truly, I do. And I can only admire you for it."

"Who gave you the right to manipulate people?"

"Elizabeth, you must understand, I am in a unique position. I have access to your inner life, to the unfolding story of you and Lars, to the unfolding story of you and Nasrin, the antics of Charles Bowie, from all angles, just as I can see and hear and know the trials and heartaches and secret desires of anyone I choose to know. And because I have this knowledge, this awful power, I feel responsible. That is why I feel driven to provide guidance to all who seek it."

Elizabeth had any number of responses to that sentiment, but she let them pass. It was time to start setting the agenda, to tease out clues that could accumulate like the dots in a pointillist portrait of Freyja's real identity. Elizabeth still felt like a mouse trying to turn the tables on an alley cat, but she had to try.

"Let's get back to Lionel Jacobson's last statement. I'm still not clear why he jumped."

"Oh poor dear Lionel. So much anger. Always trying to get back at the world."

"He did jump, didn't he?"

"Yes."

"And he didn't jump because of a broken heart."

"No, he didn't."

"Then why? There had to be a good reason for such a thorough narcissist to do something like that to himself."

"There was, but I cannot reveal it, not even to you. It was Lionel's secret to keep. Let's let him keep it."

"And Ken Woods?"

Freyja's laugh sounded pleasant.

"I truly loved Ken. Such an amiable sort. A genuine seeker."

"Of what?"

"Something more, something deeper, a newer and better world."

"And that's what you offered him? A ride on your comet?"

"I offered him a path to a finer level of insight, Elizabeth, just that. A methodology to the truth rooted in the hard-won, collective wisdom-algorithm born of a hurting world crying out online. Many of my graduates, as you put it, are doing better than ever."

"And I'm to be one of them?"

"That is up to you. This has been an honest introduction. I appreciate that. I do. We've managed to clear some rubbish between us. I think we shall be prepared to talk in earnest in our next session."

"That's it?"

"We'll talk again several days from now. In the meantime, I will soon be giving you a little homework assignment, something to make our next conversation more fruitful than this one has been."

Freyja faded away and the Norwegian forest behind her went from vivid to dull.

Elizabeth finished her beer.

Shit.

Freyja had expertly played every exposed key in her life. Elizabeth went into the bathroom and knocked back a benzo with a sip of water. She bowed her head over the sink and had a short cry.

Elizabeth blew her nose and washed her face.

She returned to the burner phone and emailed the conversation to the burner phones of Lars and Ingrid. No sooner did the file upload with a swoosh than the burner rang.

"Tell me about it." Lars asked.

"Freyja is a textbook psychopath with pretentions of omniscience. She expresses what I believe is a genuinely held delusion that she is the keeper of some gnostic wisdom created by the Internet. But those pretensions are backed by an ability to pull in so much data that she truly is close to all knowing, feeding her delusion and her power. There's so much about us online, in our emails, our texts, our calls, that it's practically mind-reading for her."

"How did it go?"

"Badly. Very badly."

"Tell me."

"She knew a lot about my past, even a traumatic case that ended in the patient killing himself right in front of me. She made me lose my temper by taunting me about my son. She got inside my head, an occupational hazard every shrink faces when confronted with a high-IQ psychopath. Lars, there's a lot of private stuff here. Please tell me you and Ingrid will keep it close-hold, that you won't share this recording with PIG."

"It is safe for now, but it may become public evidence in a trial, I must warn you of that. I am sure that even when you were on the defensive, you managed to extract some useful information."

"A few dots added to the portrait, I hope."

"So tell me, how are you, Elizabeth? Would you like me to come over?"

"I would love for you to come over, but not tonight Lars."

"Elizabeth, I …"

"I know. That's sweet of you. I will see you soon."

She felt the drug folding around her like a blanket, calming her restless heart, numbing her anguish. She would be all right for tonight. There was no sign of the Edge creeping up from the dark corners of the room. But she left the bathroom light on just to be on the safe side.

———————

The campus of Oslo University was an architectural mélange of severe Prussian classical architecture surrounded by upended glass rectangles. George had taken Elizabeth to the faculty lounge, plush and clubby, for lunch. Afterwards, they went to a small office the school had lent him as a courtesy.

It would do.

George hand-pressed dark roast coffee and handed a cup to Elizabeth. It was flavorful, much better than anything she had tasted in the States. Tall bookcases surrounded them, leaving just enough space for two comfortable chairs and a desk. The window was almost floor-to-ceiling, admitting dim light filtered through a thick layer of gray clouds, harbingers of a summer storm blowing in off the North Sea.

"So tell me about it."

Elizabeth recounted the conversation with Freyja, and reiterated the agreement with Lars not share it with the larger group.

"So why are you telling me?"

"Because I am getting in so deep, George. I have a rope around my waist as I descend into a very dark cave and you are the only person capable of holding the other end of the rope."

"You humble me, Elizabeth."

"You should be, humbled, George. You betrayed me."

George stiffened a bit in his chair.

"That's strong language."

"You've been crowding me on my research from day one."

"I only want to collaborate with you Elizabeth."

"And you do this by undercutting me around the investigative group?"

He cocked a white eyebrow.

"Nasrin? Is she the one who got you all wound up?"

"No one got me wound up. But if you're looking for a problem person, Bowie doesn't like me very much."

"Why?"

"Why do you think? I won't sleep with him. And now you're making it easy for him to get rid of me. Thanks to you, I am now connected to the group by a thread."

"I can make my continuation conditional upon yours," George said. "I've always felt that way, I just didn't feel the need to fully spell it out."

"What did you think, George, that I'm still your graduate assistant who'll write papers for you and let you take all the credit?"

George stiffened again. The presumption that she had anything to do with his success clearly threatened him.

"I treated you like all profs treat their TAs."

"Exactly."

"Very well, Elizabeth, if we write a paper together, and I hope that we do, your name can go above mine."

"That's not nearly enough. I know that you didn't get where you are today in the academy without some skill at intrigue. But I thought we were friends."

"We are," he said softly.

"Your role in my life has meant too much to me to lose it over a feud about turf."

"After a lifetime in faculty politics, perhaps my elbows have grown a little sharper than I realized."

"Your approach to this has really hurt me. I mean it, George, to the quick."

They sat in a silence for a moment.

George let out a sigh, mumbled something, then raked the corner of one eye with a knuckle.

"I am sorry," he said, his voice suddenly phlegmy. "I truly am. I cannot begin to tell you, Elizabeth, how much you mean to me. Yes, first as a mentee. But over the years, as my only true friend in this whole profession."

"You should be sorry. George, we are *friends*. More than that. Something deeper, special. You saved my life, remember? Then you gave me a career."

"And your research won me tenure, Elizabeth. I guess I can finally be man enough to admit that."

It was true. George had been going through a divorce with nasty accusations from his wife meant to keep him from their two daughters. Elizabeth had stepped in as a teaching assistant and kept George's classes running, compiled his research and helped in writing the published papers that eased George's way to tenure.

Grateful, George had pulled every string he had to help her get a place at Georgetown. They jointly published more papers and a book. Their stars had risen together, brighter—not diminished—by the other.

"I will go back to the States," George said.

"You don't need to do that."

"Then what?"

His face was blank, eyes a little watery.

"Cooperate with me, George. Be my ally. For real."

"If you will recall, that was my offer to you from the very first moment I arrived in Oslo."

"Yes, but you sprung it on me, made me feel cornered. I am doing research into the kind of rare case that you only encounter once in your career. I thought it was all mine."

"I can see that. I will turn my notes over to you and let you write the paper."

Outside, the wind was picking up, sending empty plastic bottles skittering down the alley.

"No, I will co-author the paper with you, George."

He brightened a bit, smiling.

"But this time, my name really will go above yours."

The room grew as gray and colorless as the darkening sky outside, rain beginning to pat against the windowpane. On a summer afternoon, the Department of Psychology building was near-empty. Few sounds echoed through the open transom window, just the occasional slamming door or pair of shoes clopping down the hall.

After their difficult conversation, this was not an ideal time for therapy. But Elizabeth needed it to fortify herself against Freyja.

George took her through the familiar routine … heaviness overtaking her eyelids, drawing them down … a wave of relaxation from the crown of her head, down her spine, the muscles of her back, her stomach, her thighs, her calves, her feet …

Elizabeth found herself standing on a tropical beach with yellow-white sand, azure sea and curving palms. Memory of a crescent beach in the Bahamas. It was her safe place, a world of flawless security and comfort. On the beach before her, as George explained, were five circles drawn in the sand. As she stepped into each circle, one by one, Elizabeth relaxed even more, until she stepped into the fifth circle and fell through the circle into the darkest recesses of inner earth, the deepest level of relaxation.

George had first used hypnosis on Elizabeth when she was an undergraduate traumatized by the suicide of her brother, the last surviving member of her family. She was used to the routine and had a suggestible nature perfect for being led through the process. She trusted George to protect her, to guide her through anything …

"Elizabeth, we are in a place where we can see everything and discuss it with no danger and no need for anxiety. Do you know this?"

"I know."

"Stand back from yourself, Elizabeth. See yourself as you talk with Freyja. Look at Elizabeth Browne. Tell me what she feels?"

"She is angry … almost a murderous rage … a desire to unmask her, to put Freyja down …"

"Put her down?"

"On the ground in handcuffs … dragged before a press conference in a police station."

"Why?"

"I want to humiliate her."

"Why?"

"Because she is arrogant. Because she plays with the very people I try so hard to save. Because she tried to get to my son."

"Elizabeth, I want you to look below that anger, lift that emotion like a lid and tell me what you see inside."

Her body clenched and she drew her knees to her chest. Elizabeth became smaller and her voice became a whine.

"I'm afraid."

"Why are you afraid?"

"I'm afraid."

"Why?"

"She knows everything."

"Why does that scare you."

"Because she might trick me."

"What would happen to you if she tricked you."

"She might bring back the bad feelings."

"You think she can do this?"

"She did do this. Last night, when I thought she couldn't."

He guided Elizabeth in her breathing, gave her imagery and suggestions that made her relax, causing her breathing to subside and feet return to the floor.

"Elizabeth, I am going to ask you a tough question. But it is only a question. It cannot hurt you."

"Okay."

"Are you afraid that Freyja might somehow get to you and make you commit suicide like the others?"

Elizabeth shook her head, but it was more in rejection of the question than an answer. She pushed her hands against the arm rest of her chair, body straining against the chairback.

"No."

"Why not."

"Because I won't let her win."

"You are safe here, Elizabeth, nothing will happen to you. Let us pull that mask from Freyja. What does your instinct tell you? Is Freyja a man or a woman?"

"A man, I think. A very clever man."

"Is he young or old?"

"He is experienced … highly intelligent and manipulative … both intuitive and technically able. Perhaps a scientist or technician of some sort. Middle-aged, at least … I think."

"Are you sure?"

"Yes, about the age, not about the gender. Freyja could be a woman. Men who like to kill do so outright. She toys with people like a cat torturing a mouse."

"Anything more?"

"A very dark heart … such anger … such malice … to manipulate people so … to make them parade for her, to fall and die in her circus … to take so much delight from tricking people."

"Elizabeth, I want you to listen to me and let what I say sink into your very bones. You are stronger than Freyja. You are smarter than Freyja. She may think she is hunting you, but you are smarter than she is. She is not hunting you. You are hunting her."

He let Elizabeth rest a moment and commanded her to relax, to release any anxiety or fear. George led her upward through ascending levels of consciousness. She followed him like a diver rising from the darkness into the lighter, shallower waters, until she opened her eyes, drew a deep breath and found herself once again in the little office.

"How do you feel?"

"Like catching this bitch and putting her away."

"Excellent."

George poured her some more coffee.

"She made me completely lose my shit you know," Elizabeth said.

"It can happen," George said. "It happened to me once. The divorce wasn't the only thing that was distracting me when you helped me get my tenure."

He handed her the cup.

"I never told you about this, but I had to take a brief medical leave."

"I had no idea."

"I was analyzing a psychopath sentenced to life in Atascadero who liked to do terrible things to little girls. He somehow intuited, from cold reading I suppose, that I had daughters. He kept needling me with questions, talking about outside friends who were … like him … about how he could escape Atascadero and join with them at any time. With every question I put to him, he came back with an insinuation about all the fun he and his friends were going to have with my daughters. I lost it. The guards had to pull me off him. In a panic, I sent my ex-wife tickets to take the girls to Europe and then I had a breakdown. Not for long, but seriously enough that I had to be medicated."

George losing control of himself, it was hard for Elizabeth to imagine. Strange, too, that even after all these years, and after sharing so much of her own life with George, Elizabeth had never met his daughters or knew much about them. She made a mental note to ask more about them at an appropriate time.

"Freyja said she would give me some kind of homework assignment," Elizabeth said.

"That is troubling. You cannot allow yourself to serve her. You must reverse the relationship and promote your dominance. Will you carry out her 'assignment'?"

"If it brings me closer."

TWENTY

Ingrid's eyes were gummy, red-rimmed, her greasy roostertail higher than usual. Elizabeth shook the rain off her umbrella and leaned it against a window in the stone entryway.

"So how does she know so much?" Elizabeth asked.

A second day of rain, coming down in heavy sheets.

"Freyja is just a very talented hacker, that is all," Ingrid said. "Anyone with the right skills could know what she knows. Imagine what I can learn about you from examining your searches … about your health, from your queries for remedies and medical questions … about your sexuality, from what you look at and who you flirt with … about your finances, your transactions."

"But Freyja knows more than that."

"She also sees," Ingrid said.

"She said she had more eyes than a spider."

"She reverses our smartphones, the fisheye lens in our laptops, and records all that," Ingrid said.

"Why do you think she records?"

"Most of life is boring. No one would have the time to watch it all. She's reviewing all her material from PIGers on fast-forward for anything that looks interesting."

"Which is why you gave us the burners. But is there more?"

Ingrid sunk teeth into her lower lip, causing her rings to protrude.

"Yes, I believe so. It is my guess she is hacking into CCTV systems in hotels, on streets, everywhere we go. She is probably in the police system, though we are always looking for that."

"So we're open secrets to her?"

Ingrid's smile was cocked and wicked.

"I do not mind being an open secret. If she wants to watch, let her get her rocks off on me. I only do what I want and I don't care who watches and how they judge. That is the only way to live."

Elizabeth smiled at the young woman's brio, then wondered if there had been a smartphone or laptop in Lars' boathouse. If so, there was a recording of her and Lars as well.

The little tile with Daryl Parnell's face came to life. He smiled shyly, rubbed his lantern jaw. He had a good head of hair, not much gray, and a friendly face with deep laugh lines around the eyes.

"Welcome to my story, if you can dignify it as a story."

His voice was masculine, deep, a cultured Southern accent.

"I grew up in these parts, went to the Virginia Military Institute, quarterbacked for two seasons, BA in English literature, Phi Beta Kappa, then served for twenty-seven years in the U.S. Army, stint in Special, before retiring as a colonel in Signals with service in Bosnia, Iraq, Afghanistan, all the cluster fucks of our young century, forgive my language if you're a lady.

"Married a great gal, Emily, three wonderful children, two boys, Sam and Richard, and our precious girl, Stacie. We had kids late. I guess I had half-expected to get killed overseas and by the time they assigned me to a cushy desk job in Fort Benning, we were finally a family. A very happy family.

"My father died on the day I retired from the service. So I sold his farm, spoke to a lot of smart money people about a good cash business I could get into, and after months of study decided to buy a restaurant from an old couple ready to take it easy.

"The Cloverdale, they call it. A fixture in the Glenwood Park neighborhood of Atlanta, an old neon sign out front that is a registered historic item, twelve feet long with distinctive lettering in six colors and chrome accents. Twelve booths inside, a giant S-shaped counter with more chrome and twenty-four swivel chairs. Twelve tables in the back. What's so special about all that? A lot. The Cloverdale is known for gourmet versions of diner fare, hanger steaks with flash-fried potatoes, blackened redfish with soy ginger and a side of risotto, fried chicken with collard greens covered in Mornay sauce.

"Best of all, when we bought the Cloverdale, we inherited all the cooks, the head cooks being three African-American brothers from the Old Fourth Ward who really ran the place. I learned to stay out of their hair and let them hire and fire and run the rest of the help ragged.

"It was a good business, the cash business I had hoped to acquire. I didn't have to worry if Emmie and I had picked the wrong location, or the wrong cooks, or the wrong menu. By buying into a long-standing enterprise, we had a loyal clientele of blue-collars, hipsters and techies. The Cloverdale kept the family busy. Kept us together."

———

"You gonna serve that plate or slobber over it?"

Darius Scott hung his face over the counter, his hair net almost touching the warming lamps. He gazed at Daryl with his customary scowl, as if the owner of the restaurant were a busboy in need of firing. But Daryl didn't mind. He appreciated that Darius wanted everything done right. And he didn't mind playing the subservient role. Restaurant help was notoriously unreliable. On this day, one of the waitresses had called in sick. Tomorrow, it could be anybody. An owner had to be ready at a moment's notice to be a cook, a waiter, a busboy or a cashier.

He was grateful for Darius and his two brothers.

"Twenty-three, right?" Daryl said.

"That's what it says." Darius turned back to a large griddle on which a dozen slices of bacon popped and trembled on the hot surface. Darius cracked another egg.

"Darius riding you, hon," Emmie said under her breath, turning from the counter where she had just poured coffee for a line of customers.

Daryl shook his head and smiled. At 49, Emmie had become a little matronly, but she was still quick on her feet and had that sarcastic, sideways look he loved. Daryl could still see the Auburn cheerleader Emmie had once been and would always be to him.

He delivered the plates to 23, a typical young Atlanta couple. The man had a long, pointed beard, hair shaved to white scalp on the sides and a mop of pomaded hair. Tats in colored ink ran up and down the length of one arm. His girlfriend was also well tattooed and sported a nose ring.

Daryl looked around at the clientele and saw young men who could have been Civil War generals, if generals had ever worn shorts with T-shirts. This one could be Jubal Early. That one,

Stonewall Jackson. And look, here comes old Nathan Bedford Forrest through the door with an ear gauge.

Not a good look, at least not in his book. But Daryl didn't care. He was grateful to have a steady clientele, hipsters who flocked to the Cloverdale because it was both retro and chic, old-style but with gourmet coffee and asiago instead of cheddar.

Daryl topped off their coffee and caught a glimpse of activity across the street. Four men huddled around the unfurled scroll of a blueprint. Behind them was the Atlanta Bankhead, a decaying office building that had once been the most glamourous building in Atlanta in the Twenties.

"Suzie, any idea what they're up to over there?"

The cashier was another relic of the Cloverdale, long past her prime, but she made up for it in what she knew about the business and the neighborhood.

"I don't know, Mister Parnell. Maybe they finally sold it?"

"Could be. Whatever comes next over there, it should be good for business."

"Should be."

"Hi Dad." It was Sam, at 14 his youngest son, homework done and ready to put in a few hours as a dishwasher.

"Richard has got a head start on you," Daryl said. "By a good half-hour."

Richard had come into work without so much as a glance at his father or mother. He had been a freshman at the University of Delaware while Daryl was finishing up his last tour with a career-capping ticket punch at Benning. With the family in Atlanta now, Daryl and Emmie insisted Richard transfer to be closer to them and to take advantage of in-state tuition at the University of Georgia.

It was a great school, they told him. All Richard had to do was leave his friends, his fraternity and a girl named Bernadette. For weeks now, all his son talked about was Burnie-this and Burnie-that. They were texting like crazy throughout the day, their conversation saddened by the fatal knowledge that their interest in each other was doomed to wane and die. Now Richard was in the back, letting the dishes clatter and the steel cutlery clang.

Sam was his own piece of work. He had his heart set on making the high school basketball team as a forward, only to be the last one cut from the try-outs. He was sullen, too, but in a different way, grieving over the death of a dream.

Stacie, their 13-year-old, kept in touch with Mom with the occasional text. She was excused from work, too immature to be of much use. Her time was better spent on Skype with her math tutor.

———————

Sunday was the family day for rest and worship because the Scott brothers managed the day in exchange for a management fee. All the orders for the next week were made on Thursdays and deliveries wouldn't come until Monday. The books were updated every Friday.

But Sunday was a day to sleep in, go to the 11 o'clock service, then … whatever. Go to the shooting range, see a movie, just sit at home and read in the sun room. But only after church.

Daryl was raised a Presbyterian. He preferred the old hymns, a dry exegesis from the pastor on the meaning of a given passage and the deep reverberance of the organ that a worshipper felt in one's chest as if God were humming. But Emmie and the kids favored the neighboring mega-church, an aircraft carrier with its own coffee bar, a basketball court, several dozen meeting rooms and a large amphitheater with multimedia displays and contemporary music.

A millennial pastor with Ambrose Burnside mutton chops was usually present on Sunday mornings to give an impassioned and intelligent talk on the need for faith in a culture distracted by vices and too many entertainments. During the sermon, Stacie kept sneaking a peek at her phone. Richard stared ahead glumly. Sam fidgeted, doodled on the church program, and seemed to intermittently pay attention to what was being said.

Afterwards, they would stop at the church coffee bar, a small counter selling beverages from the world's most popular coffee chain, and ordered coffees all around. Emmie let Stacie have a latte.

"I wonder …" Daryl said.

"Wonder what?" Emmie asked.

"Wonder what they're doing with the Bankhead?"

"You know what they're doing," she said. "Some hedge fund is gonna gut it, make it modern and rent it out for $200 a square foot."

"More bidness for the Cloverdale," Daryl said. He did that from time to time, slip into his grandpappy's backwoods accent to amuse her.

"More bidness, *sir*, and we might have to raise the prices on our menus."

"More bidness, *ma'am*, and the landlord will raise our rent."

"Kill joy," Emma said. "Party pooper."

Stacie sipped her latte, Sam played with his phone, Richard stared down the hallway at the ghost of Bernadette. And Daryl Parnell kissed his wife in the middle of church, smack on the lips.

Somebody must have pulled the food alarm on Tuesday afternoon. The front door was clotted with patrons. A line formed. Suzie got that thin-smiled, worried look when seating got sparse and customers became tense about waiting times.

"Did you remember to get the waters for nineteen?" Daryl asked Sam. His son froze, look stricken, and quick-walked to the counter to pour some ice waters.

One of the Cloverdale's best waiters, an older Hispanic man who went by Gus, had called in sick that morning. Gus was never sick, so you knew it was real. Daryl had no choice but to press both of his sons into service, Sam as a busboy, Richard as a waiter taking the place of Gus.

"How's your section?" he asked Richard.

"Behind but catching up."

Richard looked like he could use some help, but it was all Daryl could do to keep the counter running.

"Please do that son."

Across the street a knot of construction foremen and architects were using a can to spray-paint X-marks on the sidewalk in front of the Bankhead. This should be good news, but Daryl's gut told him otherwise. And he trusted his gut. It had kept him alive in wadis, forests and alleys around the world.

An elderly man at the counter wanted more ketchup and jam

for his biscuits. His wife nibbled at her omelet while hoping that no one noticed the tiny Yorkie in her purse that snapped when she offered it bits of sausage. Daryl didn't usually tolerate health code violations, but things were too busy today to make a scene.

He turned to see Cyrus, one of the Scott brothers, staring at him sullenly over the kitchen line, a rack of new meals under the heat lamps. Daryl bolted to the station, pulled the tickets and delivered the food. He came back and filled some more orders for Richard's station, told Sam where to refill coffees and sodas, and topped off everyone's drinks at the counter.

Daryl checked the coffee machine, pleased to find a fresh-brewed pot. He looked his station up and down, scanned the whole restaurant, and decided that this was a good window for a bathroom break. As he was coming out of the employees' bathroom in the back, still rubbing moisture off his hands, Emma waved him down.

"I can't reach the olives."

"Use the stool."

Emma licked her lips.

"I'm feelin' a little unsteady, hon."

"You okay?"

"Yeah. Just got dizzy, is all."

He followed his wife around the hallway behind the kitchen and the dishwasher, past the mandatory OSHA and state labor postings, the time clock, and their tiny office. Down one end of the hall was the cold storage room. Down the other end were two small rooms, little more than closets, where every square inch had been thought-through and maximized to the fullest. In the dry goods room were neat stacks of paper bags and plastic bowls, receipt paper and 25 percent cotton, glossy laser-print paper for the menus. In the storage room were the cans, ordered and stacked by food groups, vegetables, condiments, meats, garnishes.

The stepstool was already in place.

"Right there," Emma pointed to a spot on the top shelf.

"Okay," Daryl said, straining, trying to be quick. No matter how fast you were on a bathroom break, patrons quickly became impatient whenever their waiter disappeared from sight. There would already be new drink orders and at least one impatient patron waiting to pay a bill.

"Got it," he said.

Daryl heard the sound of a soft collapse, as if a sack of Idaho russets had tipped over. He looked down.

Emma was on the floor, sprawled out on her side, arms and legs moving in jigs and jerks, head lolling, eyes rolled up white, a rim of foam on her lips.

"I think you had best come forward," Ingrid said on the phone.

Elizabeth clicked Daryl Parnell to a stop in mid-sentence and went to the office's reception area. A young woman in a bike helmet and elastic bike-wear stood in the middle of the room, thin and still as a crane. Ingrid stood off to the side, hands on her hips, eyes locked on an envelope in the messenger's hands.

The young woman said something in Norwegian. Elizabeth caught only names—her name and "Freyja."

"I am Elizabeth."

The bike messenger handed over the envelope.

Ingrid signed and the messenger left.

"We should do this by the book, let forensics dust for fingerprints first …"

But Elizabeth was already tearing underneath the top flap with a fingernail. She shook it and a ticket slid into her palm. It had a long Norwegian word along the top and something underneath. A blue tornado was printed on the side.

"What does this say?" Elizabeth asked.

"It says, 'MegaJump.'"

"What does that mean?"

"Oslo Indoor Skydiving, good for one."

"Should I go?"

"If it helps catch the horse-dick who killed Thor."

TWENTY-ONE

The Uber Black driver was a polite young man with a red Porsche. Elizabeth settled into black leather and watched Oslo go by, the pier, City Hall, the angled steel and glass Oslo Opera House, until they entered a freeway that took them through that long tunnel that bore through a hillside. On the other side of the tunnel they slipped through suburbs with stucco houses and brightly colored flowers. It could have been Connecticut.

Almost.

The driver pulled into a strip mall with an appliance store that announced a sale in large neon colors. Next to it was the sign with the bright blue tornado.

The night before, Elizabeth had perused YouTube videos on indoor skydiving that included some discussion of techniques. She dreamed about real skydiving, twirling and twisting in the air over farmland. The thought that she'd be doing it now made her mouth go dry and her stomach twist a little, even if this wasn't quite the real thing.

Elizabeth felt as if she could never make herself jump from a great height, even with a parachute, unless perhaps she was in a burning airplane. Maybe not even then.

She thought of Jeremy and shuddered.

MegaJump was a tall cavern of concrete. Parents and kids, suspended by ropes and belays, skittered like spiders along an indoor cliff with plastic holds in bright colors. Deeper into the store was a tall cylinder of glass with two floating figures inside.

A store attendant, a young blonde, somehow sized up Elizabeth as an American before she said a word.

"Welcome to MegaJump," the girl said.

Elizabeth presented her ticket.

"Your friend is already in the chamber," she said.

"My friend?"

"Yes, he is right there," she pointed to the large glass rectangle. Elizabeth squinted, trying to identify the two men in red jumpsuits and black helmets as they bobbed up and down in a torrent of upward moving air.

Is Freyja here?

Elizabeth looked around, at the crowd of onlookers, mostly teens and their parents. She studied the climbers, other store attendants, and people coming in and out of the bathroom.

Elizabeth wanted to be sure this place was safe, that if Freyja was skydiving in front of her that she would not be harmed or kidnapped by some confederate. As she got closer to the glass wall, Elizabeth slid her hand into her purse and slowly retracted her smartphone.

Japanese electric dance music beat from speakers, providing a theme to the movements of the sky divers. It was loud but failed to mask the jet engine sound of air as it rushed upward through a trampoline-like floor.

Elizabeth glanced down at her phone and pushed a button that would call Lars.

She edged up to the glass. The two men rose and fell, gaining and losing height and gaining it again as they extended their arms and legs and molded the angles of their bodies to the air stream. One man was obviously an instructor, making hand signals and reaching out to adjust the other man's positioning of his arms and legs.

The customer was a well-built man, the muscles of his arms and legs apparent through the suit. Strings of blond hair poked out the sides and back of his helmet. All she saw of his face was the oval of his mouth as his lips flapped in the air, baring bright, white teeth.

Elizabeth listened to her phone, waiting for Lars to answer.

She heard the "vzzzzt" sound of a phone close by on vibrate. It came from a black, Swiss Army backpack set along the outside of the glass tunnel.

Elizabeth looked around to make sure no one was watching her, crouched down and lifted the phone from the backpack.

The man in the tunnel noticed her, pivoted her way and smiled. Lars.

He made eye contact then lost his balance and tumbled over, righting himself by extending his arms and legs in a perfect 'X.' The attendant gave him two thumbs up.

After a few minutes, the wind tunnel powered down and Lars

and his instructor gently descended to the floor.

Lars looked pleased with himself, his helmet in the crook of his arm, his blonde hair a swirling mess. He took her off to the side, away from the crowd.

"Lars, you bastard. The attendant told me someone I knew was here. You can imagine—"

"That should make you all even gladder to see me."

"How did you know? Ingrid? Of course."

"And I am not the only one."

Elizabeth looked around and realized that Inspector Dahl was behind her in jeans and a sweater, gazing at her smartphone as if she were checking on email. In actuality, the detective was regularly sweeping the room, capturing the faces of everyone there.

"And you think Freyja won't see through your subterfuge?" Elizabeth asked.

"Worth a shot. We tried to track back through the delivery girl and the purchase of the ticket, but Freyja always covers her tracks."

"It must be a drag following so many dead ends."

"She will make a mistake eventually. In the meantime, I have plenty of PST detectives assigned to this case to do the donkey work. Time to suit up, girl."

Elizabeth went to an attendant, who spied her tall and athletic figure and sized her up as a ladies' medium. Elizabeth folded her clothes in a locker. The red jumpsuit was clean and snug. She was given a pair of ear plugs in a plastic bag. She inserted them in her ears and slipped a black helmet over her head. It was tightfitting, like a motorcycle helmet, with clear plastic goggles.

The instructor was a muscular young man with a swarthy complexion and caramel hair that some Norwegians had. He had a big smile and waved.

"Have you done this before?" he asked.

"Only on YouTube," she said.

The enormous fans above them roared, propelling the column of air upward from the trampoline floor. Elizabeth pulled down her plastic visor from her helmet.

"First, I want you to take my hand, get down on one knee and slowly extend into the chamber," he said, shouting to be heard. "Then we will gently step forward and let the air lift us up."

Elizabeth was aware of a crowd around them. She was grateful now that Dahl was about, although it was far more likely that Freyja was present only as a disembodied watcher through the closed-circuit cameras inside the chamber.

Even through the heavy helmet pads and ear plugs, Elizabeth's ears rang from the thunderous roar. She took the instructor's hand, leaned forward and felt her whole body lighten as her uniform billowed and she lifted into the air.

Elizabeth shrieked with surprise and delight.

The instructor tugged at her arm and showed her how to make an X out of her body and scissor her way into the middle of the air column. She followed him to the center and took his hand, floating a good yard above the floor.

She moved her right hand inward, just a few inches, a perfectly spontaneous movement. In an instant, the airflow around her body changed and her left hand snapped away from the instructor. Elizabeth zoomed upward, a surprise that made her heart hammer. Elizabeth had the presence of mind to spread herself out and stabilize, and came to float almost ten feet above the floor.

The instructor grinned at her, pleased that she hadn't panicked and overcorrected.

He retracted his arms slightly and came parallel to her.

The instructor floated away from her, lowered his left elbow while raising the right. He began to gently spin to the left.

Elizabeth tried it, but began to spin out of control. She stretched out her limbs again and stabilized.

The instructor smiled and gave her a thumbs-up.

She did a slow spin to the left and stopped. Then she made a spin to the right.

The instructor winked at her and she watched him extend his legs and pull his arms to his chest and begin to move forward.

Elizabeth tried it and in an instant almost kissed the glass in front of her.

The instructor extended his arms and pulled his legs in, immediately retracting toward the back wall.

Elizabeth tried it.

The instructor extended his arms and legs, cupped his chest outward and rose to the very top of the chamber.

Elizabeth followed his example and soon found herself fifteen feet above the floor, the harsh lights of phones from onlookers capturing her performance.

The instructor reduced his body surface by pulling his chest in and bringing his arms closer to his torso. Elizabeth followed his example, and came down in a gentle decline to three feet above the floor.

She cupped her chest and extended her arms and flew up to the ceiling in a violent rush.

The instructor whipped his head up to see her from the floor, not at all pleased.

Elizabeth smiled at him in apology, pulled her arms inward and gently descended.

For the next fifteen minutes, she practiced all these moves. At the end of her session, she hovered at about eight feet above the floor, experimenting with tiny movements, slight deflections of her shoulder muscles, her arms, her outstretched hands, to get a feel for how they sculpted the air and altered her movements.

When it was over, she looked at up at the camera at the top of the cylinder.

Did you see all that Freyja, you fucking bitch?

After she finished changing back into her clothes, Lars was waiting for her.

"Would you like to get some lunch with me?" he said.

"Only if it's room service," Elizabeth replied.

———————

Elizabeth rested her head on his chest, content to be quiet. Lars finally broke the silence.

"We never did order anything."

"Room service is too expensive," she replied.

"So this was all just a ruse just to get me into bed?"

Elizabeth lifted her head just enough look him in the eye.

"No, you showing up at the MegaJump was a ruse to get me into bed."

She put her head back down and felt Lars laugh as much as she heard it, a deep rumble in his chest.

"I could say it was police business, but in truth you have me there. You do seem susceptible to seduction after athletic events."

"Why do you suppose that is?"

"Something about confidence, I would guess," he said, a smile in his voice.

"If athleticism makes me confident, then based on what just happened, I should now be very confident indeed. You never lack for confidence, do you?"

"No, I guess I never do."

Elizabeth turned her head to face him again, her chin digging into his ribs.

"Same with Nasrin. She is the most confident person I think I've ever met."

Elizabeth noticed an ever-so slight tremor in the corner of Lars' right eye when she voiced that name.

"Yes, I suppose she is."

"You really don't like her."

"And you really do?"

"No … yes … but not like that."

"Like what?"

"Like this."

"I am glad to hear it, Elizabeth."

"But let's be clear about us," she said. "These are early days for you and me. We should not get too far ahead of ourselves, okay?"

"Okay."

"Let us just take this gently and see where it takes us. Does that work for you?"

"Yes, early days," Lars said. "And besides, we may discover that we are both divorced and single for a reason."

Daryl Parnell scooped ice chips with a plastic spoon from the cup a nurse had brought him and gently fed them to his wife.

"There, honey."

The chips would rest on her sealed lips for a moment, saturate into deep crevices in her parched skin. When the ice had melted into a pool, she would open her mouth and take a painful swallow.

Her eyes were half-moons trying to peek from behind a black

cloud. From what he could see, Emma seemed to regard her husband with a kind of languid adoration, a look that reminded Daryl—he didn't like the comparison, but it came to mind anyway—of the eyes of their dog, Lucy, when the vet had started to put her down.

Emma was in a twilight state, the doctors called it. Daryl reckoned it a simple world without pain or fear, without past or future, just an appreciation of each passing moment, as if his wife—the most unlikely Buddhist he had ever known—had suddenly become a Zen master. Her life had now become one eternal now, a shadow play she followed from moment through moment through a morphine haze.

Of course, it had not always been like that. From the diagnosis—GBM, as the doctors called glioblastoma—through the chemo and until recently, Emma was alert and hyperactive, trying to cram years' worth of work, love and life into her final months.

The busyness helped, but tension and fear had pinched the corners of her mouth and kept her shoulders high. She radiated anxiety even when she tried to reassure the children. Many nights Emma curled up and gave into violent crying, giving into grief for the years she would miss with her husband and children.

He had tried to comfort her, but every word sounded false and patronizing. So Daryl gave up talking to his wife and just held her, stroked her hair, spooning his body around hers like they did when they were newlyweds.

There were visits to the church, spiritual counseling, healing hands ministries and prayer groups. Emma needed it, advocated for it, booked these activities on their shared calendar. But she never seemed to approach any of it with anything close to a spirit of hopefulness.

"This is it, hon," she had said to him more than once, "and there's no dancin' around it."

Just before admittance to the hospice, Emma had chosen plots for the two of them and planned her funeral right down to what she would wear and the hymns to be sung.

Daryl fed his wife more ice chips. Emma watched him dreamily, closed her eyes and turned away from him to sleep.

He felt tired, propped a pillow on the armrest of his chair and rested his head.

This was by far the worst thing that had ever happened to Daryl—it seemed the worst thing that could happen. But he had known times of sorrow and anxiety before … When his father had been drinking. Basic had been tough, but it had been summer camp compared to Ranger Training. Later, covert operations in damp, chilled forests in Kosovo. Clearing house-to-house in the mud-daubed labyrinths of Ramadi. Fighting in the high country in northeastern Afghanistan on one frigid spring morning, a battle in which he had lost two beloved comrades.

In each of these periods of his life, Daryl had observed something: You knew life was going badly when the highpoint of your day, the thing you most looked forward to, was sleep. And you were reminded of just how bad things were when you regretted waking up.

He set his head in the wing of the hospital chair and fell asleep. The near oblivion of a deep sleep felt like a warm blanket.

Daryl stirred and pulled himself up in his chair and cleared his throat.

How long had he been out?

He looked down at his phone. Twenty minutes. A bunch of new messages from the restaurant.

Emma was motionless, asleep now. He studied the profile of her hips under the covers. Her hips had been padded by middle age spread. They were now sharp and angular. Her arms were thinner. A few months ago, weight loss had made Emma's face leaner, accentuating her cheekbones. She had briefly looked younger, more like the Auburn cheerleader he had known.

But the process had continued and her face was now drawn, gaunt, aging her appearance by decades.

Daryl looked down at his phone to see the messages rolling in. He read the last one from Darius Scott titled "Decision needed." He typed:

> Okay, do it. Give her a month's pay <

The answer came back fast.

>A whole month's pay?<

>21 years<

Suzie was the most expendable of the ones who were left. They had reduced the cooks from seven to four, and the wait staff from eight to five. People could seat themselves, all that was needed was a sign giving them permission to do so. But Suzie would be missed. She had been, as they say, a fixture of the neighborhood, a familiar and pleasant face, a greeter who knew the regulars by name but on the second reference called them all "hon."

The cashier work could be done by Darius now that he had stepped in as manager. To make the arrangement work, however, Daryl had to sign over one-half of the ownership of the restaurant to the Scott brothers.

It was painful but necessary. As it turned out, the buyer of the Bankhead Building had not been a hedge fund, but rather an upstart technology company with a blockchain platform that had become the New Big Thing. And such a company, deep in the hippest part of Atlanta, had to be thoroughly wired … which meant the street had to be torn up, the asphalt lifted, the ancient plumbing and old cables replaced.

Then there would construction to completely gut the interior of the Bankhead, retaining only its brick façade, a mask of nostalgia while behind it a famous architect would oversee the construction of a courtyard and terraces sun-drenched by an array of solar mirrors.

The whole process would take six months.

And as construction started, business had dwindled to a trickle. Things would be fine once construction was done, but in the meantime, Daryl had to make his nut … mortgage, insurance, property taxes, water bills, electric bills, garbage collection, payroll and FICA, not to mention supplies of food, beverages and dry goods.

While she was still able, Emma went over the numbers. The only way to maintain even 50 percent ownership of the Cloverdale, she told her husband, was to flush out the college funds for the kids. They would also need to raid her 401(k), borrow against Daryl's Army pension … and with all of that, it still might not be enough.

Daryl stood up from Emma's bed, feeling nauseous.

He'd have to call Suzie before the day was over. There had to be something he could figure out for her. Someplace he could send her.

He walked out of the room and down the hallway, with its old green tile from the 1950's and busy nurses wearing starched, white uniforms with the green logo of this hospital named for an obscure saint few Catholics could identify. He went to the restroom and washed the sleep from his eyes. Stepping back into the hallway, Daryl realized he couldn't bring himself at that moment to go back to Emma.

It didn't matter. She was still probably asleep. Or if not, she'd barely know him.

So Daryl went for a walk, past the waiting room filled with nervous families, past the bank of vending machines stuffed with levels of sugar that put many people in the hospital in the first place, past some administrative offices. He turned a corner and noticed a small room with a plaque that read, Chapel.

He went inside.

It was hardly a chapel. It was barely a room. More like a large closet with a few chairs arranged in front of a non-denominational altar with a stick-on stained glass window.

Wearily, he fell into a chair and rested his forehead on the metal rim of the chair in front of him.

Daryl started to weep and then willed himself to stop.

He prayed as he had never prayed before, begging God to save his Emma … or, if it was His will, to take her mercifully. He begged the Lord to let him keep the restaurant because Daryl knew that with Emma gone, work would be the anchor needed to keep his family intact, his children busy and stable in the disorientation of grief.

He prayed more intently than he had ever prayed before an aerial drop or in a combat zone during the quiet moments just before first call.

He prayed and begged and beseeched. He bargained and promised.

Daryl Parnell had done his part. Now it was up to God to do His.

———

"We buried her three weeks later," he said. "She didn't suffer any more. Just went into a coma and faded away."

The flesh around Daryl's eyes looked bruised from rubbing and dabbing. His lower lip quivered like a hummingbird's wings.

"I tried to live up to the example of Job," he said. "Never once did I curse God. But I am not like Job. There is no reward God could give me now. Job got a new family, new wealth. I don't want a new family. I want the one I had …

"Had … you see, six weeks later, after the Scotts closed on all of the Cloverdale and I got out with just my shirt, my sons … my sons … Richard and Sam …"

Daryl looked down at the floor, snorted, raked tears from the corners of his eyes with knuckles and looked back up, starring right into the camera, voice strangled.

"They went … on a weekend trip to the University of Georgia to check it out, just a trip for two brothers. I thought it was a good idea. They needed to get away from me and the grief, two brothers having fun."

Involuntary twitches played across his face, at the corners of his lips and eyes, jerks of the flesh in his cheeks. His brown eyes were lustrous with pent-up tears. When he spoke again, Daryl's voice had become a croak.

"They didn't do anything wrong … no drinking or anything like that … It was a truck … at an intersection at the turnoff from eight-five to one twenty-nine … an eighteen-wheeler that plowed into them from the side … Oh God, oh Christ have mercy …"

He looked down and his head jerked as he stifled a cry. When Daryl looked up again, his eyes and cheeks glistened with tears and his voice was phlegmy.

"All I had left was Stacie … I tried with her … but everything that had happened had made it hard for us to talk to each other. She got into marijuana. She disappeared on me just after her sixteenth birthday. I finally tracked her down a year later … our little girl, working in a restaurant in Silver Lake, California, living with a drummer boyfriend, both of them covered in tattoos.

"I could have forced her to come home. But she was not glad to see me, as if I were somehow responsible for all that had happened to us. She was not going to come around. And I don't think she will ever want to see me again."

Daryl pulled a handkerchief and wiped his face. He blew his nose with a loud honk.

"Around that time, an old Army buddy turned me on to Freyja. Now, don't get me wrong. I am not naïve or stupid. I was once the darling of the VMI English department. I was a finalist for the Rhodes scholarship. I planned combat operations and led men into battle. So I'm no dummy. I do not believe in forest gods or ghosts on the Internet. But I do know literature well enough to appreciate Freyja's sly metaphors. And Freyja gives me something precious … in her methods, in her treatments, I am able to unravel my pain just enough to clear my vision and let me see where I need to go and what I need to do next."

Daryl cleared his throat.

"I need to move on, for I am done here. And I am done with the God of my fathers. But I am not done with all hope. If there is some sort of afterlife, or home that awaits us, I am ready to go there to be with Emma, to be with Richard and Sam. And if there isn't? If there is just nothing? Well, I'm ready to go there, too."

Elizabeth left the office at 6 p.m., though the summer sun declared it to be three hours earlier.

She could have worked longer, but Ingrid's shift was ending and the young woman needed to lock up the department's computer center. As Elizabeth watched Ingrid turn the two locks and key the alarm, it occurred to her how futile all these locks and alarms would be in stopping Freyja, who could pass through any doors or systems like a mist.

"Daryl Parnell struck me as the saddest of the lot," Ingrid said. "His testimony made me cry a bit."

"Yes, of them all, he had a good reason for suicide."

Ingrid's right eyebrow went up, and with it, a thin, tiny ring of gold.

"There are good reasons for suicide, doctor?"

Elizabeth felt a blush, surprised at the words that had come out of her mouth.

"What I meant was, he was the only one of them who had suffered genuine loss and grief. Most of the others had suffered blows to their self-esteem. They were selfish."

"I have never understood that," Ingrid said. "How can suicide be selfish? I am perhaps selfish. I am certainly always in pursuit of selfish pleasures. But flinging myself off a high cliff has never struck me as particularly pleasurable."

"That is because you are a very well-adjusted hedonist."

Ingrid smiled, taking Elizabeth's judgment of her as a compliment. The young woman's smile was a bit crooked, even lewd.

"You should come with me tonight to some clubs I know," Ingrid said.

"I'm too old for that."

"You're not that old," Ingrid said, looking her up and down. "We could have fun, you and I."

"Raincheck?"

———

Walking back to the hotel, Elizabeth received a text.

>Lizzie, wuz up in the Big O?<

Elizabeth briefly considered a like response, then decided to elevate the conversation.

>Still helping with police work<
>Gonna catch F?<
>Will put that bitch in prison<

She instantly regretted the text, realizing that Freyja would see it. She decided to change the topic.

>How's math going?<
>Got an 88 in final. Gonna pass it. Dang!<
>I'll take that as a win<
> now in grave danger of grad on time. I want to stay in school forever!!!<

Elizabeth laughed.

>No, you really don't<
>LOL, gotta go<

Elizabeth walked down Cort Adeler's gate to make a right on

Henrik Ibsens gate toward her hotel. She had been here long enough that Oslo was not only starting to become familiar, it was beginning to feel a bit like home.

A ringtone from Elizabeth's phone announced a call from someone not on her call list. The phone display read "No Caller ID." Elizabeth stopped, took a breath, answered and heard the womanly voice of Freyja, always composed, modulated and calm.

"Hello, Elizabeth, have I caught you at a good time?"

There was no telling if a Freyja call this close to her texting session was a coincidence. Elizabeth decided not to mention it to at least try to keep Max out of this mess.

"I always have time for you, dear goddess," she said.

Freyja laughed.

"I am truly glad to hear it. I am calling to tell you how impressed I was by your easy mastery of indoor skydiving. As with the windsurfing, you seem to have a talent for maneuver. Perhaps you have the makings of quite a goddess yourself?"

"I am flattered."

"I will send you more tickets, for morning runs before work."

"Why?"

"It is a pleasure to watch you in motion."

"Anything else you want to tell me?"

"Since you've come to Norway, you have done so much outside of your comfort zone. The parasail, the aeronautics at MegaJump, some interesting dalliances. You are learning to put aside your fear … the fear that has governed your life for too long. This progress is a powerful indicator of your far greater abilities. Are you ready to try something that can take you to the next level?"

"Depends on what it is. Does it involve flying in the air?"

"In a sense."

"What is it then?"

"Elizabeth, the next step you need to take is the inward journey, a deepening of your understanding, a quickening of your courage. We are on for tomorrow night, 8:30 in the evening, correct?"

Elizabeth started to answer, but realized the call had ended.

When she arrived at her hotel, there was a plain manila envelope waiting for her at the front desk. She opened it in her room. Inside was a plastic bag containing a tiny white pill.

TWENTY-TWO

Lars called another PIG meeting, once again in the conference room of the Directorate of the Environment HQ. Elizabeth took a chair at one end of the long table, directly facing Lars who sat at the other end, framed by the room's window overlooking Oslo in its late summer glory. One by one, the others arrived.

Lars looked around the conference table with a cheerful morning smile and called the meeting to order. The participants were by now familiar with each other and their joint routine. They gave reports from around the table as if they were in a board meeting, while Lieutenant Dahl took notes.

Harold Kober reported on recent developments on what remained of the Hommelvik Hammers. The war with the Night Wolves in Oslo had the predictable result of raining down law enforcement on both gangs. The Hammers and the Wolves had called a truce and both had gone deep underground. They were so dark, Ingrid failed to sniff a trace of the remnant Hammers and Freyja, not even on the dark web.

Charlie Bowie followed up by reading counselor notes on the release of the bodies of the American victims and their return to the United States for burial. He read his notes perfunctorily. For once, he made no wisecracks.

As they spoke, Elizabeth wondered how angry they would all be—Nasrin, Charlie and the rest—if they knew what was known only to herself, Lars, George and Ingrid, that Elizabeth had begun a regular conversation with Freyja.

It was now George's turn to speak. He smiled and deferred to Elizabeth, who had been more involved in the case analyses. Surprised and a little flustered by George's unexpectedly gentlemanly behavior, Elizabeth cleared her throat and offered her assessment of Daryl Parnell.

"Parnell is—was—a deeply religious man, a committed Christian," Elizabeth said. "He was well educated and highly intelligent. The loss of his business, then of his family, destroyed his happiness and shattered his belief system. I believe it was this challenge to his beliefs more than the tragedy itself that left him so vulnerable to Freyja."

"And Sandra Armstrong?" Lars asked.

"Sorry, I will finish that one today and all the rest this weekend," Elizabeth said.

"Please get all the case studies done," Lars said. "It is why you are here."

"Will do," she replied.

In meetings before the others, Lars was all business, with no hint of intimacy.

"About Sandra Armstrong," Agent Norris said, "you should know that our Delaware field office is investigating Therapso and Armstrong's activities, in conjunction with the FDA. Come by the embassy and I will let you read the case synopsis. If she weren't dead, Armstrong would likely be facing a grand jury by now."

Elizabeth turned to Nasrin. "Anything like that turn up on the background of Lionel Jacobson?"

Nasrin frowned, perplexed.

"No, should there be?"

"I continue to believe there's something off about his testimonial. Jacobson's account and personality do not add up to suicide."

"There is one thing," Nasrin said. "The Scotland Yard report on Lionel Jacobson mentioned something odd about the counter lawsuit for contract violations against him by Edward Lear and Judith Roberts. Their filing had snarky references and innuendo about Jacobson's mentor, a deceased don at Cambridge, Seth something. When the Yard asked, their barristers said their clients directed them to add that in. Lear and Roberts on are on location in Australia, and we haven't been able to catch up with them to ask what that's about."

"Jacobson's the weirdest of the lot," Bowie said. "We still don't have a body on that one."

"All we can say for sure is that one of his shoes was there," Agent Norris said.

Lars closed the meeting by noting that Agent Norris and Detective Inspector Jones would soon be needing to get back to their duties in their home countries.

"We need a suspect, at least enough evidence to get this person offline," Lars said. "I don't like the idea of Freyja potentially staying open for business. Is that possible, Ingrid, that she could still be trolling for victims in ways we don't know about?"

"It is very possible," Ingrid said. "Her versatile use of mirror sites and word-of-mouth networks to recruit fresh victims could certainly mean that she is still active on sites we have yet to detect."

As the meeting ended and they all stood, Bowie turned to Nasrin.

"How much longer will you grace us with your presence?" Bowie asked.

Nasrin's smile was a bearing of teeth.

"Ten days, Charlie, tops … although I will miss your endearing half-witticisms."

Bowie smiled back at her.

"And I will miss your wiles and charms."

Elizabeth ignored them. She was surprised to feel a mild sting from Lars' curt tone, even if it was wholly appropriate.

As they left the room, Lars stayed behind to talk with Lieutenant Dahl. Elizabeth left the room while Lars continued to play it cool, ignoring her. But then he would do that just to avoid gossip. As far as Elizabeth could tell, none of them suspected she and Lars were an item except, of course, for Bowie and his houndlike ability to sniff out personal secrets. As soon as Elizabeth got to the elevator with the others, her phone pinged with a text. She turned to the side to discreetly read it. It was from Lars.

> dinner tonight? <

For a moment, she thought about making a catty reply about having to do her case studies, but didn't. Lars was right. She was behind. The bigger problem was that Elizabeth had other plans. Should she tell Lars about the pill?

> Gotta spend some quality time with Max tonight on Skype.
tomorrow night? <

Lars sent her a smiley face reply.

She still felt a little irritated for his reprimand in front of the others.

The elevator slid to a stop, a mere two stories down to the ground floor. When the doors opened, Elizabeth lingered behind to grab George by the arm.

Nasrin walked away briskly with the others.

George stayed behind with Elizabeth in the lobby. After a minute's wait, they left the lobby and fell into lockstep on the sidewalk. As they walked, Elizabeth told George about the cellphone call and the pill.

"I do not approve of this, Elizabeth. It is dangerous."

"You know I too have some experience here."

It was true. As a grad student, Elizabeth had participated in an LSD study, a clinical experiment approved by the university and the DEA. Elizabeth had been given a mild dose and experienced her trip sitting on a comfortable couch in a safe room with a nurse ready to attend to her if the trip had turned unpleasant.

It hadn't been at all unpleasant. To Elizabeth's disappointment, it also hadn't been powerful or profound. She had experienced some visual disturbances, saw random letters of the alphabet and words floating by in rainbow colors, felt slightly euphoric. That was it. But the point of the experiment was, after all, to study the effects of a mild dose.

Elizabeth remembered George's paper: "Effects of Mild Treatments of Lysergic Acid Diethylamide on Ideation Among Survivors of Family Suicide."

The paper had been an important milestone in George's career, establishing some therapeutic value to psychedelics. Now it was Elizabeth's turn to be both guinea pig and primary author of a new paper that would startle the community, though it could go in many different directions … Religious Ideation and Group Suicide? … The Role of DMT and Sound Wave Indoctrination?

"I am going to do this, George," she said. "And I want you there, to talk me down or hospitalize me if it should turn bad."

"And you are not going to even tell Lars?"

"Possession of DMT is a criminal act in Norway and Lars is a policeman. I need to protect him from this."

"Are we even sure what's in this pill?"

"As you said, Freyja had to have concocted it herself to put DMT in pill form. She gave the same-looking pill to Max and to his roommate, and they both had classic DMT experiences. And besides, tripping people out with DMT is her MO."

"It could be poison for all you know."

"All the better reason to have a clinician like you at hand."

———————

Sandra Armstrong wore a bespoke business suit from a venerable tailor on Nathan Road in Hong Kong, the same family-owned shop that had crafted suits for her male predecessor, a habit she was more than glad to expropriate from someone she had helped stampede into early retirement to clear the way for herself.

Sandra had her suit of merino wool tailored for a snug fit, accentuating her tennis-trained body. She had chosen the fabric for this very meeting, so much like the dark-blue, lapis lazuli *rurikon*, with accents of white-silk brocade. She hoped it would trigger an association in the mind of her host of a *yukata* kimono, either subliminally, or as an overt metaphor for cooperation, with just a hint of submissiveness.

The driver of her limo turned a corner and came to a smooth stop in front of a large, modern office building.

"*Kōro-shō*," he said. The Ministry of Health, Labor and Welfare in Chiyoda City, the political heart of Tokyo near the Imperial Palace.

"*Arigatou gozaimashita*," she said with a slight nod.

A polite young woman was waiting for Sandra at curbside, ready to take her past security and up the express elevator to the office of the Director General of the Health Policy Bureau, Takahito Watabe.

Sandra stepped into the elevator and felt pythons coil in her stomach. Out of a dozen years of research fueled by $2 billion of investment, Therapso's lab in Switzerland had discovered a magic balance of platinum-based, antineoplastic molecules that had become the basis of the company signature pharmaceutical, a new pediatric that resulted in a 23-percent remission rate in children with certain common types of leukemia, while having the unexpected side effect of reducing the nausea brought on by chemotherapy.

Armed with a blockbuster drug, the Board had sent its best salesperson on the road, Therapso's own CEO. With a little support from the two Delaware senators, Sandra Armstrong had won FDA approval in half the usual time and got the drug on the schedule in the U.S. The precedent allowed her to clean up in India, roll over the EU, and win over Brazil.

She had saved Japan for the last. Japan was always the toughest negotiator. Sandra hoped that by knocking down all the other bowling pins, Japan would go down easy.

Takahito's office was as she remembered, with carpet the hue of dried seaweed and light, wood paneled walls. Only Takahito's large, antique desk of teakwood stained to a blue-black, a mounted samurai sword and several gorgeous Ukiyo-e prints spoke of his taste and cultivation. Everything else in the room, the plaques, awards and honorifics, right down to a photo of Takahito receiving his commission from the prime minister, announced him to be a servant of the people.

As she entered, Takahito smiled warmly, rose from his desk and walked around to face her, his spine aligned exactly with the center of his desk behind him. Sandra bowed and he returned the bow. Takahito offered his hand to shake.

"Watashi o goran itadki arigatogozaimasu," she said, and shook his hand.

"It is no trouble at all, Sandra," Takahito said. "I am always delighted to see you."

They were cordial friends, meeting often at health science conferences around the world. Takahito and his wife had once entertained Sandra with an elaborate dinner at his home.

"How are your children, Watabe-san?"

"They are doing well. My son is thriving in New York and my daughter is engaged to be married. And please, let us not be too Japanese. I am always Taki to you."

"Thank you, Taki, it is a pleasure to be back."

There was a moment of awkward silence. Takahito was trying to think of a reciprocal question to ask, but Sandra had no children.

"I hope your many travels have been pleasurable," he finally said.

"They have, but none so interesting as Japan," she said. "In fact, after our meeting, I intend to take a ten-day vacation and see the archipelago from stem to stern, so to speak."

Takahito's face softened for a moment. He was flattered and a little touched that Sandra's interest in his country was more than business. He motioned for her to sit in one of the two chairs before his immense desk. An American would have taken the seat next to her. Takahito walked around to sit behind his desk, yanking down on the bottom seam of his jacket to prevent it from bunching.

"So, let us get down to brass attacks," he said.

Sandra stifled a giggle and replied with a soft smile, "let's."

"Our evaluation team has had several months to review the raw data you have provided," he said. "The randomized tests from FDA conform to the independent findings of the PFSB."

That was expected, but it was a relief to hear that Japan's Pharmaceutical and Food Safety Bureau agreed with FDA. A hitch here and negotiations would be near impossible.

Takahito smiled.

"And it further pleases me to say that the process of registration is all but complete. There is no reason why the Health Policy Bureau cannot include your new drug when we announce our new schedule in two weeks … of course, this after we come to terms on the listed price."

The price list was everything. Every one-percentile deviation from the world price would deny Therapso roughly $30 million in revenue, pure gravy on top of all the other sign-ups.

He named his price and the pythons in Sandra's gut twisted in agony.

"Takahito … well, that's … that's 20 percent off the world price."

"The Ministry will pay that full amount," he said, smiling again, as if he were doing her a favor. "And we do not mind paying up front."

Sandra drew in a breath and steeled herself for combat.

"First, Watabe-san, I am honored that the Ministry has taken our offer so seriously as to conduct your own tests. I was unaware of this and when I inform the Board, they will be immensely pleased."

Takahito's formal smile broadened. This gaijin had modulated her tone perfectly.

"They will also be disappointed," Sandra said.

Takahito nodded thoughtfully. Of course, she had to express this thought.

"In order for us to continue to pursue innovations, we must have a robust return on investment," Sandra added. "Therefore, as a representative of the Board, I must tell you Watabe-san … with great respect for you and reverence for the Ministry … that Therapso declines this gracious offer and requests that you withdraw our drug from consideration on your schedule."

A blush rose in Takahito's cheeks. A corner of his mouth trembled. He brought a fist down on his desk with a bang that resonated off the wood panels around the room. Sandra was prepared for this. She did not flinch.

"Goddammit, Sandra," he yelled, spittle flying over the middle of his desk, "children will die." Over the corner of his shoulder, the gleam on his mounted sword seemed to brighten. Sandra guessed that many a bureaucrat had quailed in the face of Takahito Watabe's strategic outbursts.

"With great respect, Taki, if we degrade the innovation cycle, more children in the future will ultimately die."

Takahito leaned back in his executive chair, eyelids narrowing.

"This is a big market in a rich country," he said. "Our price, even at a discount, is worth several Brazils."

"We appreciate the importance of Nippon to our market. We respect your role as the guardian of the nation's patrimony. But I am afraid that my response is final."

"Very well, then," he said. "You are excused, Armstrong-san."

Sandra stood up, bowed, and set a newly printed business card down on the broad expanse of Takahito's magnificent desk.

"What is this?"

Their mutual exchange of cards had taken place years ago. This seemed inappropriate.

"As I mentioned, I will be enjoying your lovely country as a tourist," Sandra said. "My local cellphone number is on this card. If you have a desire to discuss this further, please do not hesitate to call me, Watabe-san."

She bowed again and walked out.

———————

"I wanted," Sandra said, eyes locked onto the computer's camera, "to make my mark on the world … My own unique success.

I achieved it. And the gods made me pay for it."

Elizabeth froze Sandra Armstrong and regarded her for a moment. The CEO was sitting at a desk, dressed casually, probably in her home study.

As Elizabeth had remembered her from that years-ago conference, she was an impressive-looking woman with a firm jaw line, dark-blonde hair done in a casual style, and large blue eyes that projected intelligence. Sandra had a calm expression, but when her file had been playing, Elizabeth had seen micro-tics around the eyes and slight downturn twists at the corners of her mouth, signatures of disappointment, perhaps self-loathing.

Elizabeth shuddered to imagine what could do such a thing to this utterly self-possessed executive. And to think that this magnificent woman had spent her last night on earth in the hotel bed in Stavanger that Elizabeth had slept in.

Elizabeth put the computer in sleep mode.

Earlier in the day, Elizabeth had reviewed the last statement of Sophia Goddard, the 24-year-old executive assistant. Her message had been brief, something about a search for something greater than this life had to offer. What came through Sophia's testimony, despite the young woman's nose rings and colored streaks in her hair and somewhat pretentious manner, was a perfectly ordinary girl who had been crushed by a breakup and humiliated by being pigeon-holed as a mediocrity in school and at work.

Elizabeth had also watched the statement of Mike Drummond, the former PR executive turned outdoor enthusiast. Drummond gave a short, agitated speech about finding God in rocks, water and all living things. The burn in his eyes and pace of his speech were the signatures of someone in desperate need of admittance to care and medication. Elizabeth would tell PIG that of all the victims, Drummond was the only one who displayed signs of chronic mental illness.

The others were reacting to events, not disease. Each had a unique trauma that had made them existentially disappointed with life and with themselves. Ken Woods had been fatally disappointed over how his marriage and career had turned out. For Daryl Parnell, it was the worst of all traumas, the loss of his wife and two sons, and then the alienation from his daughter, Stacie.

Freyja cultivated people of stature who had been brought low. She had a talent for finding and exploiting them.

So far, only Lionel Jacobson stood out as a case that didn't add up. At least, not yet. Maybe Sandra Armstrong would remain a mystery as well. Elizabeth decided to complete the Armstrong testimony in the morning. She had something else to do tonight.

Before leaving for the day, Elizabeth performed one last analytical task. She scanned Sandra Armstrong's FBI file on her desk, a copy that Agent Norris had allowed Elizabeth to take with her on the promise that she would shred it.

Sandra had been raised on a farm in Nebraska, accustomed to discipline and chores from an early age, rising to sanitize the milk system, milk the cows and clean the milk parlor hours before dawn. Sandra had disdained the local beauty pageant for 4-H. At age 16, she had won a ribbon for her raising of a prize cow, then another for developing a program that involved residents of a senior citizen home to teach elementary school children how to care for animals in the local petting zoo. The local paper was wowed by her high school valedictory speech.

Sandra went on to earn undergraduate and Master's degrees in biochemistry at Stanford, then an MBA at Harvard Business School, marketing track. There had been a brief marriage to a British investment banker while working in Hong Kong. The divorce records were spare, no mention of adulteries or abuses, just an apparent lack of passion. Perhaps her husband had realized that Sandra Armstrong was already married to her career.

Elizabeth put the file to the side; there was more to read about legal action against Therapso. She looked at the envelope on her desk, the one that contained the pill.

It was almost time.

She folded the envelope into her pocket, bid Ingrid goodnight—moving fast to avoid an unwanted invitation—and went to a pub for a hamburger. Elizabeth ordered a diet soda instead of a beer. It wouldn't do to have any alcohol in her bloodstream tonight. But having protein in her stomach was necessary.

It was seven in the evening by the time she finished dinner and walked outside. The sun was still high, but noticeably lower at seven than it been when Elizabeth had arrived in Norway—had it been a month already? She walked for twenty minutes past shops and bars until she came to the entrance of Frogner Park, that vast expanse of green lawns and straight avenues lined with maple trees.

The declining sun inflamed the maple leaves and cast buttery light on the gravel walkways. Elizabeth walked to the Vigeland installation centered around a large rectangle of grass and stone walkways edged by granite walls topped with the artist's bronze and granite nudes … that truculent toddler, children running, playing, teasing bears and wolves … one man chasing another, beating him on the back of the head … elderly men with hollow chests, sunken cheeks, toothless mouths … elderly women with thin arms and breasts like spent balloons … muscular mothers and fathers rolling babies around their arms and swinging them in the air … a young woman running and playfully pulling her braids in opposite directions …

Ahead was the monumental fountain surrounded by twenty statue-trees of bronze, their narrow, almost tentacle-like trunks capped by bushy leaves with green streaks of verdigris. Human infants grew inside the cavity of dying trees, a woman dove downward from a growing tree, lovers intertwined with determination in mature trees. The larger trees contained more of the elderly and infirm, with the fullest tree of all holding a skeleton.

Elizabeth took a seat on a stone bench.

Her phone vibrated. A message from Freyja.

>I am so glad you are ready to take the next step on your journey<

Elizabeth responded.

>What next?<

>Please download the app I made just for you and play it while you are on your dream journey<

A moment later, George appeared out of the low light, loping between the trees. He sat next to her.

"Circle of life," he said, "the oldest and most persistent theme. And then there's that."

Elizabeth turned to the direction George was looking. Stone steps beyond the fountain rose to a platform that supported the monolith that she had walked around before with Nasrin, a granite totem pole. She took a harder look at it. It was, she had read somewhere, composed of 121 human figures of both genders and every age from infants to withered elderly. Their limbs and torsos writhed and intertwined around the cylinder.

"I've been thinking this through. I can't let you do this."

"You can't stop me," Elizabeth said.

"Why here of all places? Some of these images are disturbing. And if you act out, people will see you."

"I might feel claustrophobic in my room. I think I will need the air. Besides, I like being outdoors for something like this. I want it to feel expansive."

"What do you hope to achieve, Miss Expansive?"

"To understand Freyja's brain hacking, for one."

"So you're going to risk your life for a paper?"

"I am going to risk my life to prevent her from killing future victims. I will learn something that will help us catch her. I know it."

"Maybe she will catch you."

Elizabeth went to the attachment Freyja had sent her, an app represented by the image of a human head with a third eye, large and blue. She downloaded it. A minute later, she played the app for George with the speakers on.

Her phone emitted oscillating electronic beats at a very high pitch.

George listened closely with interest and then asked her to stop.

"That's a binaural beat," George said. "Two sine waves, pure tones oscillating regularly. I bet when you put on your earphones, you will hear a third beat. That's pure illusion the brain fills in when the two beats are almost in sync, one beat just a few hertz lower than the other."

"So tell me again, how does this work?" Elizabeth asked.

"It stimulates the pituitary gland. Shamans the world over use metal tambourines, throat singing choruses, chanting and the like to create such a binaural rhythm. The sound produces alpha and theta waves in the brain that can sometimes induce a non-ordinary state of consciousness, one in which experiencers believe they have conversed with various spiritual and demonic entities."

"What is the result?"

"Sometimes insight. Sometimes terror. Usually just a headache."

"I'm banking on insight. Into Freyja."

"What about the Edge?"

"What about it?"

"Aren't you afraid this experience will trigger it?"

Elizabeth looked away from him and nodded gently.

She reached into her purse and pulled out a short bottle of water and the envelope. She removed the pill and held it up against the twilight sky.

"Doesn't look like much."

For a moment she contemplated biting it in half.

"Elizabeth, you don't have to do this."

She put the whole pill on her tongue and swallowed it with a gulp of water.

George fished a flask out of his back pants pocket and took a pull.

"Scotch?" she asked.

"If I am going to have to be in this park for a few hours to watch you rave and talk to goddesses, I will need a little toddy to keep me comfortable on this park bench. Give me your room key."

Elizabeth handed George her key card. He pocketed it and patted her on the arm.

"I'll be here with you at every moment," he said, voice lower, more intimate, fatherly. "Just relax and go gently with this ride."

Elizabeth declined George's flask and took another swig of water. It was closer to night than dusk now, the shadows between the trees joining into gloom.

"Tell me about Lars," she asked.

"You know I cannot do that. Especially if you two might get involved."

"No secrets … just tell me about him."

"I will tell you what anyone who knows him well would say," George said, taking another swig. "Lars is very stern on himself. His father was stern on him … very stern … and he internalized that. He has a deep-seated need for control. Of himself. Of other people."

"And he came to you?"

"He came to me after the disintegration of his marriage. His wife left because of that controlling nature. And he was disappointed that he had been passed over for a promotion from the Department of the Environment to the Justice Ministry or the PST."

"I guess that all fits."

"Now tell me about Nasrin," he said.

"She has a crush on me."

"Is that all?"

"No."

Elizabeth told George about what had happened on the plane. She recalled the incident slowly, trying not to let emotion get into her voice.

"And you were asleep?"

Even in the twilight, she could see that George's face had colored with anger.

"Goddamn her, I'll report her, that's—"

"If anybody does any reporting, it will be me," Elizabeth said. "Besides, I was in a very light sleep, dreaming … so I think I was, well, you know … responsive."

"With your eyes closed?"

"Yes, in a very light sleep."

George took a brisk pull on his flask.

"Still, I don't think I will ever look at Nasrin the same way."

"Neither will I." Elizabeth realized how silly that sounded. They both laughed.

The sun was just above the low buildings now, shafts of gold penetrating the trees and casting a supernatural light on the immense mountain face of a thunderhead over the city. Once again, Elizabeth could see why ancient peoples were certain gods lived in the sky. The clouds, carved in golden light and purpled shadows, were vessels ferrying the gods as they chased the sinking sun.

Chariots in the sky.

The sun winked out, falling beneath the distant profile of the Royal Palace adjacent to the park. Darkness spread between the trees. It was like a rain, a curtain of wetness that blackened the grass and moved toward her as fast as a car. Elizabeth jumped up onto the bench to keep her feet from getting wet.

"Get up George!"

"Elizabeth … Elizabeth … look at me dear."

She looked at George, at his sweet walrus face.

"Elizabeth, you are starting to hallucinate. Please understand that. Give in and don't fight it. But always understand that you are simply watching your own mind at work, just like in hypnosis."

Elizabeth nodded and put her feet back on the sidewalk. It was dry.

She connected her earphones and put them in her ears.

The piercing binaural beats permeated her mind and body, shearing and reshaping her thoughts. She watched a screen of abstract patterns merge and divide, paramecium shapes with fractal fringes that throbbed and pulsed with the obscenity of flesh.

The sound was too much. Elizabeth took out her earphones and opened her eyes. The quiet was better. There was enough going on with what she could see.

The darkness was now made flesh. It pulsed and rippled between the trees. Elizabeth did not want to think about that so she got up from the park bench and walked over to the statues where the lamp light was strongest.

The statues were moving, of course. Elizabeth knew that they would be, and this did not surprise or alarm her. The babies rolled around the muscular arms of their parents. The wasted-thin elderly reclined while letting out deep sighs of resignation. The girl with the braids chittered nonsense. Elizabeth looked closely at her and saw that she was Sophia Goddard.

She looked away.

The bronze trees swayed over their granite trunks while the statues writhed beneath them. The diving woman dove and met an updraft, an air column on which she floated and manipulated the currents with subtle movements of her hands, with twists of her hips and arches of her back.

The diving woman had been afraid. Now she swam through the air with the confidence and poise of a dolphin.

The dying man was Daryl Parnell, moaning, bereft and abandoned by the God he had tried to please. Now he wanted nothing more than annihilation. He begged for it.

George's face emerged out of the gloom, his eyes bright and concerned.

"George, why are you here?"

"I will not leave you, my dear."

"Oh George, I see them."

"Who are they?"

"The victims."

She turned from him and he stayed behind her as she toured the statuary, made more dramatic in the chiaroscuro of bright lamp light in the night.

Elizabeth came to a new section of the park she had never visited before. Human forms struggled with lizards the size of wolves. Some held them off, prying open their jaws like Hercules. Some curled and meekly submitted to their fate, while others screamed as fangs were sunk into their necks.

"George … is this … am I?"

George wrapped his strong arms around her and placed his chin on the top of her head.

"You are not making this up. These grotesques were left here by Vigeland."

"Why did he do it?"

"It is only an expression of the human unconscious. His monsters are not real."

But Vigeland's monsters had been real. They had been as real as these creatures the artist had liberated from the stone with a chisel, as real as the metal he had molded in his studio. In the afternoon, Vigeland's monsters would take hostages—men, women and children pulled from the routines of their days—and line them up in back alleys and mow them down with Mausers. In the early evening, these very same monsters came calling on the great artist, ingratiating and polite, happy to sip aquavit and talk of the Aryan aesthetic.

"Monsters," Elizabeth said.

"Are not real."

"Are."

George released her and she walked in the lamplight around a corner to come face to face with the truculent toddler.

Sinnataggen, she had learned the name, Angry Boy, his fists curled, feet stamping and mouth an ugly downward curl.

This was one of the smaller and more modest of Vigeland's creations. And yet it was by far the most famous one of all, the statute every visitor had to see and touch. Out of a small block of granite, the artist had somehow crafted the purest expression of the most primal of emotions.

Elizabeth lingered. The boy's foot was raised for a stomp, shoulders pinched, fists turned into small hammers, mouth a downward gash, eyes narrow slits.

Anger radiated from the boy, waves of wrath that washed over her.

"I see her."

"See who?"

"Freyja. This is her heart."

TWENTY-THREE

Sandra Armstrong stood before the dozen men and women who made up Therapso's board of directors. The directors looked up to her, literally, from their seats, at their tall and commanding CEO in her dark-blue business suit.

It was all a bit of virtual reality magic. Sandra was still in Japan in a crummy little office in downtown Tokyo while the board met at its annual offsite in Scottsdale. She had gone to considerable trouble to make sure her projection would be slightly elevated above them.

Sandra was officially on her Japanese vacation. She had met with some old friends from Nebraska and Stanford to hike Mount Fuji, tour the castles of Kyoto and take pictures of the snow monkeys of Jigokudani. It had been a swell time, the first real vacation she had taken in years. And it was all theater, ostentatiously enjoying Watabe-san's country while the old bureaucrat sat in his hard-back executive chair in Tokyo and squirmed.

Sandra had even emailed Takahito a few selfies of herself on top of Fuji and in front of a country ryokan. Each email came with a jocular note about how much fun she was having, just to rub it in.

Now Sandra stood in that small, cramped company office in downtown Tokyo in late afternoon. She stared into a screen the size and shape of a full-length mirror ringed by tiny cameras that streamed her HD, 3-D image to the other side of the world, where the board was taking up the first issue on its morning agenda.

"Sandra, why aren't you here?"

The question came from the non-voting executive chairman of the board, an eminent attorney and former secretary of state.

It did not sound like a friendly question, but it was.

Sandra explained her strategy. If you net out Japan, she said, it is still a smaller loss than having to renegotiate all the other contracts around the world downward. Worse, capitulating to Watabe's demands would inflict reputational damage on Therapso, a tacit agreement with their worst critics that the company does, in fact, hold countries hostage and extract exorbitant payouts.

You had to keep politicians and regulators in their place, or they would own you for good.

Sandra stopped speaking and stood in silence. There was a slight delay for her words to resonate around the world.

"It still makes no sense," said another board member, a man in his late thirties who was never expected to wear a tie because he was the founder of a tech company. "By value, Japan is the largest market outside of the U.S. and EU. Are we supposed to wave goodbye as this huge chunk of our future calves away?"

"Instead of waving, you should expect handshakes and signing ceremonies," Sandra said. "There has been a lot of press of late about the impact the Ministry's decision will have on Japan."

She did not have to explain how that press had come about. A premier Japanese public relations firm had spread some cash, called in some chits and placed human interest stories throughout key social media sites, TV news and newspapers. Millions of impressions had been made about anxious families praying that the cruel Ministry would decide to spare their beloved little Harotu or Yui. Bee hives of bloggers had been unleashed on Watabe, resulting in letters of protest from opposition politicians and an official query from the Prime Minister's office.

There was even a rumor afoot that the Empress herself was concerned. It was not true, of course. But it was a useful rumor.

"Within one more day, two tops, my phone will ring and I will be asked to make another visit to see Watabe-san," Sandra said. "After the usual nested courtesies, the distinguished minister will pound his table and demand that Therapso supply training for his physicians and fresh IV equipment at cost. This demand, of course, will be a face-saving capitulation to our price."

The following day, Sandra's phone did ring. Watabe went further, demanding that Therapso provide the training and equipment for free. Two days later, the two of them held a press conference and shook hands after making their announcement before the Foreign Correspondence Club of Japan in the Ginza.

That evening, Sandra Armstrong relaxed into her seat and glanced out the window as her chartered Bombardier Global jet rumbled east. Beads of light festooned the Sea of Japan, night-fishing boats lined up in phosphorescent strings as elaborate as lace.

Japan had been interesting, she had decided. But overall, it was nothing special.

Alonso Fernández de Avellaneda was a handsome man, lithe and fit at 60, with olive skin, swept back white hair and a white nib of goatee. A biochemist who also held a degree in computer engineering from Cal-Tech, Alonso had been Therapso's Chief Science Officer for eight years. He sported casual dress—dark jeans and a thin sweater worn like a shirt—but he stood before Sandra's desk with the posture of a military officer reporting to his commander, waiting for his CEO to speak first.

Sandra bade him to speak with a wave of her hand.

"We have completed all the round one assay comparisons against all the best machines and clinical laboratory professionals," Alonso said.

"Standard deviation?"

"Z-score of zero," Alonso broke out into a smile. "Sandra, we have built a near-perfect machine."

Sandra rose from her desk, too agitated to sit. Out her third-floor windows one could admire the sweep of Brandywine forest beyond the company parking lot. The leaves were already beginning to turn. Soon the C-Suite's view of the Delaware countryside would be a pointillistic masterpiece of red and orange dots.

"Show me."

The work was being done two floors down, away from the main bio labs where there would be too many curious eyes. It was kept in a simple rectangle of an office with no windows and a guard posted in front of the door.

Despite the human guard, Alonso's handprint and retinal scan were still required to gain entry.

The machine was not impressive to look at, just a black box resting on a metal desk. It had the size and heft of a heavy-duty office laser printer, an oblong piece of molded plastic whose black surface glistened under the lights. It had a touchscreen that for now said only "Therapso," but with just one minute of analysis would spit out readings: liver function, A1C blood sugar, complete blood count, blood protein tests, tumor markers, the usual markers for anemia and infection ranging from bacterial STDs to the viral, including HIV. It would also produce more detailed results for the presence of tumor cells and signs of cancer, as well as forms of inflammation and genetic markers for Alzheimer's and other degenerative diseases.

It was two hundred laboratories in one machine, the universal assay test, the Golden Fleece of high-tech medicine.

"Have you come up with a name yet?" Alonso asked. He knew his boss would want the naming rights.

Sandra ran her hands along the smooth sides of the machine and pressed the button that opened the tray that would hold the samples under lasers, glucometers and tiny test strips.

"It needs something warm, catchy. I've got just the name."

"Before we get started, I thought you would like to see how it works."

Sandra had not worn her customary business jacket, just a shirt of white cotton and a pair of brand new, nicely pressed blue jeans. Her communications director thought the casual look would make for a better photo op.

A good twenty of the nation's top health and business reporters filled the room before her, with the blinding lights stabbing at Sandra's eyes. There were cameras from major-market East Coast television at the back of the room.

Sandra rolled up one sleeve while Alonso stood to her left and the company nurse stood to her right. In front of them was a standing phlebotomy chair so Sandra could remain on her feet throughout the procedure.

The nurse slipped on sterile gloves, applied a rubber tube tourniquet, swabbed her boss's inner arm with alcohol and inserted a needle.

Sandra watched with calm fascination as dark fluid spurt out and filled one specimen tube. It looked like a tiny sea, a turbulence of waves and eddies while the tube filled. As the nurse filled two more tubes of her boss's blood, Sandra smiled at a memory from the last office blood draw. There were men who worked for her, senior executives who bedeviled the office with their endless macho jokes about the office basketball pool, who could not bear to watch blood coming out of their arms.

The news people watched Sandra's blood drawing procedure in reverent silence, as if they were witnesses to open heart surgery. Sandra looked around the room to make eye contact with beat reporters she knew. The digital cameras flashed and emitted programmed whirling sounds as if they had film inside them.

After the third collection, the nurse stamped a round bandage over the puncture wound in Sandra's inner arm and taped a cotton pad over it. She removed the tourniquet tubing. Sandra flexed her arm while the nurse handed a small tray with the samples to Alonso. Of course, Sandra Armstrong had taken the test before, just to make sure she would not be hit with a surprise diagnosis before the eyes and ears of the world. She also had to sign a number of HIPPA and other releases regarding her medical privacy.

Alonso pressed a tab on the machine and the room filled with a whirring sound as the machine's built-in centrifuges spun and separated plasma, red blood cells, white blood cells and platelets. The sound ebbed and the machine emitted clicks and guttural glunks as it began to analyze Sandra's blood.

The panel illuminated.

"What do you see Alonso?"

"Sandra, I can see many things about you. You are O-negative, so you would make a good universal red cell donor. Your white blood cell count is in the average zone, so you have no worries about anemia or infection. The markers for inflammation are low, non-existent for cancer. Your risk for Alzheimer's disease would be graded downward based on this test."

Sandra had breathed a sigh of relief the first time she had taken the test. Her father was living—if it could be called that—in a "memory care facility" in Nebraska. She knew that the blood test was not final, and that she would live with genetic Russian roulette throughout her life.

"But Sandra ..." Alonso shook his head and tut-tutted in the way he had done several times before in the practice session ...

"Your A1C is slightly elevated."

Sandra scanned the expectant faces in the room.

"From now on," Sandra said, "I am declaring it will be corporate policy to forbid doughnuts in the conference rooms."

The line was rehearsed, but it won her the expected chuckles.

It was now time to present. Sandra stepped forward.

"Ladies and gentlemen of the press, it is my honor and distinct pleasure to introduce to you—Betsy—the world's first comprehensive, universal blood assay machine," Sandra said. "For the cost of a movie and a tub of popcorn, Betsy can bring immediate and highly accurate diagnoses for a range of the common disorders to any human being on earth."

Questions erupted around the room.

The health-care beat reporters wanted to know about independent verification.

"We have tested each function ourselves against every major machine and human lab," Sandra said. "And then we beta-tested our results against the same comparisons made by Empirca Labs in Mountain View. In each instance, Betsy scored as good or better as each comparison form of assay."

"Why don't you say the tests are perfect?" a young woman from *The Huffington Post* asked.

"No instrument or test can be 100 percent perfect," Sandra said. "Ours is 99.99966 percent accurate, a six sigma level of performance that exceeds any other assay by orders of magnitude."

The remaining questions came from business-beat reporters who wanted to know about ROI, expansion plans, franchising and interaction with the new health care system and if Medicare would pay for it.

The last question came from a Delaware health care blogger, a chunky woman with a purple strand in her blonde hair. Her name was Gillian, Sandra remembered, whose blog tended to attract a lot of Therapso ads, and whose editorial policy in return reliably sold Therapso messages. Sandra was ready for Gillian's question because she had made sure that her communications office had planted it.

"Who is the inventor of this remarkable device?" Gillian asked.

Sandra cocked her head and smiled, as if surprised at such a perfect question.

"Well, Gillian, I am deeply honored to be considered the co-inventor of the Betsy universal blood assay machine … a set of discoveries and solutions that would not have been possible without the drive and vision of my co-inventor, our Chief Science Officer, Alonso Fernández.

She turned to Alonso appreciatively and nodded.

On that note, the press conference was over. While heading back to the third floor, Sandra imagined an evening three to five years into the future when she would be standing shoulder-to-shoulder with Alonso in Stockholm to accept the Nobel Prize in Medicine.

Should she let him speak first?

Elizabeth had slept in late, a hangover from the DMT. The evening before, George had brought her back to her room and waited with her until he was sure she was ready to sleep. George was concerned. On the walk back from the park, Elizabeth had seen suggestions of things creeping in the shadows of the alleys, between the trees of parks, nimbly following them down the street.

When Elizabeth awakened at 11, she felt as if the frontal portion of her brain had been removed and the space stuffed with cotton. Her visual perception was still off. The shower stall was out of plumb, the contours rubbery and undependable. After the shower, Elizabeth caught a glimpse in the steamed mirror of a feral version of herself, wolf's fur running along the side of her neck and her eyes nothing but dark iris.

After coffee and eggs downstairs, Elizabeth felt clear enough to go to Thor's old office and return to Sandra Armstrong's long testimony. It was not a pleasant experience. As the executive told the story of her life—really, the story of her death—she spoke with clinical detachment, as if the crash of her spectacular career were a business school case study of a storied corporation that lost its share value to a strategic error, or an analysis of a touted pharmaceutical that tested well but had bad side effects. There was much Sandra Armstrong had left out, of course, but Elizabeth was good at reading between the lines.

In the afternoon, Elizabeth had had enough of the CEO. She

placed her head on Thor's old desk to take a nap. A few minutes later, her phone rang. She raised her head lazily. It was Lars calling to ask her to dinner. Elizabeth went back to her hotel. She took a real nap this time. She lingered in a warm shower and took extra care in applying her makeup. Elizabeth slipped into the one evening dress she had brought across the Atlantic, a suitable black dress she had worn the night she had sat next to the ambassador and given her speech in London.

Elizabeth met Lars at a white table cloth restaurant on the harbor. Lars looked comfortable in civilian clothing, a black woolen jacket and dress shirt. Something about civilian attire made his blond hair look longer, a little shaggier.

They lingered over dinner, sipping wine, talking of family.

Lars gave a brief account of his ten years of marriage to Anita, who worked at an NGO dedicated to helping immigrants. He voiced his suspicions that his wife had had an affair with a coworker, while she had accused him of having a controlling nature.

"And do you?"

Lars' smile was winning.

"She is not the only one to make that observation," he said. "I just like to see things done properly, promptly and in a way that tidies up."

Elizabeth laughed.

"You're textbook, Lars."

"So I guess that was a confession," Lars said, laughing, then turning serious. "I have struggled with depression over that and some other career issues. You might be surprised to know that I once saw George—"

He paused to scan Elizabeth's face for any sign of surprise.

"But it was really time—time and hard work—that pulled me out of it."

Elizabeth took his hand in hers.

"I know that you saw George. Of course, he's a professional …"

"So the two of you don't tell tales when you're in your cups?"

"Never. I have placed the same confidence in him, as I think you know."

"I do," Lars said. "Tell me more about yourself. How did you come to be the great doctor Browne?"

And so Elizabeth did.

She spoke of how her mother's death had thrown father for a loop, how he had eased back from work and started to live on savings, how he spent hours on end putting on those large earphones and listening to music, letting his hair and beard go wild and his hygiene lapse. His obvious disinterest in their homework and school activities only made Elizabeth and Michael want to excel in school, if only to separate themselves from him.

Elizabeth and her brother Michael thought that their father had gone to seed without the guidance and structure mother brought to the household. Now, of course, she can see that her father was profoundly depressed.

Father's suicide affected Mike more than his sister. Mike got into drugs, and that did no good for his mental stability. In his freshman year at the University of Michigan, Mike grew depressed. Elizabeth would later learn that he had gone three weeks without showing up in class. How can that happen and the university not check in with someone?

She had graduated from Smith in three years and was already into her medical studies at Harvard when Mike had cut his wrists. Michael's suicide devastated her. It kept her out of school for half a year. It could have taken everything from her. It was only due to the friendship and strenuous efforts of her academic mentor, George Abelman, that kept her from completing the family tableaux and ending the last of the Brownes.

Telling Lars all this did not feel like one of her speech confessionals. The stories welled up inside her, telling themselves. She had to excuse herself and go to the restroom.

When she came back to the table, Lars looked shamefaced.

"I am sorry I put you through that," he said.

"You didn't," Elizabeth said. "I did. No bother. You deserve to know who I am."

"Two broken people," Lars said.

Elizabeth smiled and finished the last of the wine.

"You are not broken Lars. Just a little scarred, like most people."

The bill was 3,500 kroner, almost $400, for two branzino filets and the wine. Restaurants were ridiculously expensive in Oslo. Elizabeth offered to split the bill—Lars, after all, lived on a public official's salary—but he shook his head.

"Everything has a 25 percent VAT tax here, the prices are astronomical, how do people live here?" Elizabeth asked.

"I pay nothing for health care," Lars said with obvious pride. "I need not put away a penny for retirement, and the state will take care of my children's college tuition. In Norway, money is made to be spent."

After dinner, they had walked in the cool of the evening around the glowing lights of the courtyard fountain of the Oslo City Hall. They waded through a crowd to find a chorus of African children dressed in school uniforms singing melodic songs accompanied with hand instruments. One child tapped out a strong and infectious beat on a goblet drum.

They held hands and Elizabeth rested her head on Lars' shoulder.

After walking her back to the hotel, it seemed only reasonable that he see her up to her room, and even more reasonable that she let him in. Lars kissed her as soon as they entered the room, spun her around and unzipped her dress, snapped off her bra, yanked her panties down and rushed into her. No man had ever quite taken command of her like that, with such assuredness and ferocity. When they were done, and resting in bed, Elizabeth nestled her head on his chest.

"What are your thoughts on the case now?" he asked.

"Wondering if Freyja is someone we know."

"Could it be Karl Pedersen?"

"You mean Freyja? How?"

"He has access to computers in prison."

"Doesn't fit his MO," she said.

Lars frowned.

"What about Charles Bowie?"

"He's weird enough," Elizabeth said. "But no. Charlie is, at root, quite simple. Even his deviousness is straightforward."

"What about Nasrin?"

Elizabeth laughed.

"Well, Freyja is the right gender for a goddess," she said. "She certainly has the attitude."

"But is Nasrin feminine enough to be a goddess?"

After a pause, Elizabeth replied, "Essentially."

"What about our good and mutual therapist, George?"

"George Abelman? Don't be silly."

She looked up at Lars.

"What about you?" she asked.

"Me?"

"Yes, you, mister policeman. It makes dramatic sense, after all, the macho detective who turns out to be a secret digital cross-dresser."

Lars laughed, making his ribs vibrate. He quit laughing and took on a mock-fierce look.

"Now I know who it is. It is you after all, Elizabeth-Freyja."

"You've got me."

Lars kept eye contact.

"Yes, indeed, I've got you."

He molded her face and neck with his fingers. His hands drifted down, a light touch, and they made love a second time, gentler this time, more considerate. They came to a soft climax together and were soon asleep in each other's arms.

In the morning, Elizabeth fumbled around the bed with one hand, searching for Lars. All she found was a warm spot. She sat up. A bright day outside, typical Oslo. It was 7 a.m.

Lars had left a note on the bedside table.

"Didn't want to wake you," Lars had written. "Got to go home to get fresh clothes— wouldn't want to set off gossip among the PIGers."

Elizabeth smiled at his thoughtfulness.

There was another line under Lars' signature.

"You really do need to finish the Sandra Armstrong testimony today."

TWENTY-FOUR

Sandra loved Palo Alto— who didn't? The spreading sycamores and broad aspens, the town's once-ordinary main street enchanted by wealth, the eternal spring weather great for a morning's run. Sandra had bounded out of her corporate condo early Saturday to jog across El Camino Real, winding through Stanford's exotic sandstone courtyards and Moorish archways, around the History Corner, past the business school for nostalgia's sake, down the sprawling green to cross El Camino Real to finally rest her aching body in a coffee shop.

She checked her phone.

Therapso's stock had ended on a high Friday afternoon, the latest in a steady seven-week upward march. The company had now doubled its value since the day the board had tapped Sandra to become CEO.

A long queue of emails popped up—a request to give a TED Talk on Betsy, an invitation to join the Council on Foreign Relations, knotty issues from the CFO and HR, some notes from the Armstrong family office. Sandra sent the invitations to her chief of staff with instructions to reply in the affirmative, and attached the TED Talk request to her speechwriter, a gnomish sixty-something former White House speechwriter who lived in Austin.

> I want something bold, futurey, optimistic <

The evening before, Sandra had dined with two household-name tech billionaires and a hedge fund manager who had initiated her into the select group of Extropians—tech titans feverishly funding research into ways to slow cell death, rewind telomeres, print organs and find other ways to slow aging and extend human life. Their goal was not just to live long, but to live forever, or at least as long as they wished. With any luck, they could all be practically in their infancy, with centuries of life ahead.

Sandra was flattered, and more than a little astonished, that the

Extropians had reached out to her.

The Extropians were a handful of men—and all of them were men—who had pioneered new technologies with disruptive business models that upended whole sectors. They were all billionaires many times over. Sandra had not founded her company. She was an *employee* who could actually be fired by her board, as unlikely as that was. When Sandra eventually retired, even with stock options at greatly increased value, she could not expect to be worth anything more than two-tenths of a billion dollars. And yet they had taken her in, inviting Sandra to contribute some of her expertise to their quest for immortality.

And it had all happened because of Betsy.

Keep up the momentum, she told herself, while saving her emails. Everything depended upon it. After dinner with the Extropians, maybe more than she had imagined.

It was imperative that the Betsy launch go well.

She cleaned up, put on pair of new jeans and a casual blouse and ordered a car to take her to Alonso's new home on Sand Hill Road. Sandra brought with her a wrapped gift box containing high-end cosmetics that she had picked out the evening before.

Within minutes, the driver was following Sand Hill Road west, winding through forest and pasture land along the coastal range. Sandra opened the window to savor the cool, misty sea air filtered through evergreen trees. She congratulated herself for a wise move, shifting Betsy operations to this place where the greatest concentration of scientific and computer talent resided. Alonso did not complain about the move and seemed ensconced comfortably in his two-story Spanish-style adobe house deep in the woods.

Balloons tied to a mailbox signaled a party.

Alonso answered the door, looking handsome and fit in jeans and a light sweater. Sandra couldn't help but find him attractive. But she didn't have time for such thoughts and never, of course, would consider even flirtation with a subordinate or colleague. But she couldn't help but wonder if Alonso found her attractive as well. And if so, did that generate a little cognitive dissonance with a superior who at times rode him hard?

Who knows, she thought. Maybe someday, on holiday in Spain perhaps, after we've both won the Nobel Prize.

"Where's the birthday girl?" Sandra asked.

"Out back, surrounded by friends."

The interior of the home was classic California faux-Spanish, with dark, ornate tiles, wooden bookcases stained black, white-washed walls and dark beams crossing the ceiling. Loud music reverberated off the windows. The back lawn was lush and green, the area around the pool a riot of teenagers running around under the watchful eye of a lifeguard hired for the day.

"There she is," Sandra said.

Carmen turned around, a slight girl with straight black hair, olive skin and dark and pretty eyes that missed nothing.

"Hello, Ms. Armstrong," she said. "I am honored to have you here."

"Here's a little something I think you might appreciate," Sandra said. "Happy birthday."

Carmen thanked her. Alonso took the package to set it with the pile of others on a table at the end of the pool by a large chocolate cake under a plastic cover.

"This could be your *quinceañera*," Sandra said.

Carmen smiled but shook her head.

"I'm sixteen today, not fifteen, and we really don't do that where we come from in Spain," she replied. "But it sure feels like a *quinceañera*."

A girl ran screaming past them, chased by a boy with a squirt gun the size of a machine gun.

"How's chemistry going?"

"I've just started advanced placement," she said. "If I can manage an 'A' in those, they'll let me start at Stanford a year early."

"Do you think you will be ready for college?"

"I've felt ready for college since I was eleven," Carmen said.

After more small talk, Carmen rounded the pool, spoke with her friends, and came to the table just in time for Alonso to light the candles on the cake and prompt everyone to sing "Happy Birthday."

Sandra studied her. The young woman was thin, too thin, and moved with more deliberation than you'd expect for a person her age. But her face was radiant. It was hard to believe that Carmen had recently been so close to death.

Alonso was divorced, but childless. Carmen was his niece, whom he took into his house to care for after her mother—his sister—had died of cancer. Carmen's father, wherever he was, remained out of the picture. So Alonso took charge of raising Carmen, helping with homework, preparing her for college and managing her wellbeing.

A year ago, Carmen had begun losing weight and suffering night sweats. She had been diagnosed at Stanford Hospital as having large granular lymphocytic leukemia, very rare for someone as young as she. With conventional treatment, Carmen could expect to live as many years as she had behind her. And along the way, the disease promised debilitation and pain.

There were, thankfully, new treatments coming into the labs that were anything but conventional. One of them involved a new Therapso experiment in CRISPR gene-editing that transformed ordinary white blood cells into microscopic superheroes. There were only so many slots at the experiment at the Stanford Medical School for test subjects. Sandra had made sure that Carmen was one of them and that she would not be in the control group. It was a violation of policy, perhaps even California and federal law, but Sandra had moved subtly, leaving no tracks. She had been careful not to order anyone to do anything. She had simply apprised them of the facts and left them to intuit the right course of action.

After the cake was passed around and her friends left, Carmen would need to rest for the remainder of the day. Sandra took a couple of bites of cake, sipped from a cold bottle of beer and talked with the other adults. She stayed just long enough to be polite.

When she was ready to leave, Alonso ushered her to the door.

"Thank you so much for coming, you have no idea how much Carmen looks up to you," he said.

"Thank you Alonso." She leaned in and whispered. "And how is she doing?"

Alonso looked around to make sure they were out of earshot.

"The T-cells are still aggressive, but the therapy has already saved her spleen. And she seems to have more energy."

"We're going to beat that bastard of a disease and that girl is going on to do great things," Sandra said. "And when that particular therapy is validated, we're going to give it away to the world."

"Give it away, Sandra?"

"Why not? The PR value will be greater than the revenue on a therapy for such a rare disease. And besides, it's not all about money, you know."

"No, it isn't," Alonso said. "Sandra, thank you."

TWENTY-FIVE

Sandra labored over her TED Talk. The speechwriter in Austin had done a serviceable job of capturing the conversational style of the format. He had expertly retold Sandra's farm stories and memories of Nebraska, but he was off on a lot of the details and operational doctrines about Betsy. Sandra crossed out a line that seemed too crassly commercial in its meaning, scribbling "don't go there." She added in a few more lines at the end about the future of health and humanity.

Sandra had just set down her pen when Alonso entered her office. She remembered he had called the day before and asked to use the corporate jet to see her.

"You must have come straight from the airport," Sandra said, smiling, not rising from behind her desk. Alonso stood almost perfectly still before her, gathering courage.

"I have some news and it isn't good," he said, his voice softer than usual.

Sandra steeled herself. She had heard that statement many times before in her career and she had always persevered. She nodded for him to continue.

"It's not official, not yet, but our lobbyists caught word that the FDA will reject this round of testing," he said. "They believe Empirca Labs cut some corners."

The Food and Drug Administration requires any new test to be analyzed by the same exact methods and procedures as the regular testing for patient sampling. Empirca had to make some adjustments, but it was believed that the FDA would go along. They had said as much in back channel conversations.

"You know Empirca," she said. "Is this just a minor compliance issue? Or is it something more serious? Do they see Betsy and the test labs as apples and oranges?"

"More like apples and baseballs," Alonso replied.

"But how could it be otherwise?" Sandra asked, walking out from behind her desk. "This is a machine that prods atoms with a laser and sniffs molecules. It is not conventional laboratory bloodwork. What else could we compare ourselves to? Are they crazy?"

"They're the government."

"What about the other labs we used?"

"Same problem."

"Is there any way to comply?"

"Yes, there is one way," he said. "Siemens has sniffers that test for most of the same panels as Betsy, about a dozen machines in all. They're not as good. But to keep the schedule from slipping any more than it has, we need to immediately task Empirca to purchase their sniffers and verify Betsy against Siemens, every one of their machines, line by line—"

"How much time will that take?"

"If we go all out, two more months."

"And the cost?"

"Two million, maybe three."

"Do it."

Alonso nodded. They spoke some more of budget and personnel issues and then he was gone, racing back to the airport to begin the laborious process of designing a test that had never been attempted before.

Sandra paced on heavy carpet. The only sound in the room was the distant thrum of heavy engines starting. A credit card company had purchased her view—the Delaware forest she had looked out over for years—stripping it out for its new headquarters.

———

Sandra entered Carmen's hospital room slowly, an outward show of respect that was really the result of her natural trepidation around the ill. Alonso was standing over his niece, speaking softly to her with a smile that seemed to Sandra to be false.

The girl's room in the Stanford Children's Health Center looked more like a suite in a high-end hotel than a hospital room. The furniture was plush and comfortable. A flat wall screen flashed video images, but with the sound on mute.

Carmen noticed Sandra and smiled.

"Hello Carmen," Sandra said.

"Hello." The skin on her face was waxen, but her eyes were bright and her smile genuine.

"I heard about Stanford."

"I start in September," the girl said. "Can't wait."

"I'm sure you can't."

Carmen suddenly looked serious.

"I've been meaning to ask you, do you think I should take organic chemistry in my first year? I'd like to get it out of the way early and, you know, actually enjoy my college experience, but I'd be lying if I told you I wasn't a little intimidated."

"You'd be a fool not to be," Sandra said. "I got an 'A' in organic chemistry, but I had to cut sleep and skate by in my other classes. Needless to say, weekends were for catching up. So I waited until I was a sophomore and took the second class as a junior."

"Thanks," Carmen said. "So will I."

After a long silence, Sandra said, "This is a nice room." It was all she could think to say.

"Even a nice hospital stay is still a hospital stay," Carmen said. "I get out tomorrow. Uncle Al is taking the weekend off and we're driving up to Tahoe."

"That should do you wonders."

They talked for a good half hour about school, biomedicine, Carmen's possible future as a biomedical scientist, maybe an entrepreneur. When it was time to leave, Alonso excused himself from Carmen and walked Sandra toward the elevator.

When they were out of earshot of Carmen's room, Sandra asked about the girl's prognosis.

"Small cell tests came back not so good," Alonso said. "But we start the second round next week. We're really hopeful about that. All the prelims show that you usually need to get to the second round to start seeing results, so we've got that in our corner."

"Yes," Sandra said.

"Along the way, we need to make sure that there will be no obstacles or questions about our participation for a second round."

"There will not be, I will see to that personally," Sandra said. "A few years from now, you and I will be attending Carmen's graduation party."

Alonso stared at her.

"Thank you Sandra."

"Now, if we can talk a moment about Betsy."

He swallowed hard and struggled to compose his features.

"Of course. Yes. The news is still not good. Empirca is having trouble getting the Siemens machines to reproduce our results."

"That simply means they are not as good."

"Even so, we still have a compliance issue with the testing."

They had come to the elevator.

"Alonso, can you get inside Empirca?"

"What do you mean?"

She asked Alonso how well he knew the head of the team dedicated to Therapso and Betsy. She already knew the answer. Alonso had a long-time friend, Jim Achenbach, at Empirca who had worked on several start-ups with him.

"I've been over to Jim's house a few times for dinner in the last year," he said.

"I know him only by reputation," Sandra says. "He sounds like he would be quite a catch for Therapso. Let him know that in two years' time our head of research will be retiring. Salary alone is two mil, with annual stock options that are multiples of that. We could add a signing bonus as well."

Alonso stared at her, at first not sure what she was saying.

"I just want you to talk with your friend. And then the two of you could do a code by code comparison, perform some reverse engineering and make sure that the comparison tests reflect all the real-world attributes of Betsy."

Alonso looked down at his shoes.

"Can you do that for me?"

Alonso answered her with a shrug.

"In the meanwhile, I will be moving heaven and earth to secure that second round for Carmen."

Alonso finally looked up at her.

The elevator chimed and the door opened.

"To rig the test," he whispered.

"To make sure that this great technology ticks all the bureaucratic boxes of the FDA so it can save lives."

Alonso said nothing in response. He searched Sandra's eyes, looking for validation that he had heard her correctly.

"If you do that, I will do my part, and we shall all come through this passage better than ever—you, me, Carmen, Betsy. Do we understand each other?"

Alonso nodded.

The door closed.

Sandra waved away an assistant bringing her another short glass of warm water. She took a few deep breaths and thought of a beloved family cow, a gentle Brown Swiss named Betsy, the one that had helped win her first 4-H ribbon.

This was just another test, no different than the first, just another milestone in her rise. There would be other milestones at Davos, at the New York Economic Club, and eventually Stockholm. Then she could cash out her stock, retire and maybe run for the Senate in Delaware or take a Cabinet post. How far could Sandra Armstrong go with a Nobel Prize behind her?

The assistant checked the lavalier mike clipped to Sandra's shirt. Sandra cleared her throat while the music swelled. She stepped out on to the stage to sharp applause that made her feel as if she were about to address a stadium.

The venue was in fact an old theater near Carnegie-Mellon in Pittsburgh with only about 150 people. But they were all seated close for the cameras, making it look like a vast attendance. The lights were too bright to see anything more than just the suggestion of an audience, which was just fine by Sandra. Behind her was an enormous video screen with a depiction of a massive cell against a background of fluid pulses of dark and light red.

"Blood," she said.

Sandra walked toward the audience at a slow, thoughtful pace, hands interlaced in front of her chest, two fingers pointing toward the ceiling.

"The ocean of life within us."

She continued to pace forward until she hit her mark. She spoke her lines conversationally, addressing the silhouettes before her. Many in the audience were, she knew, Therapso investors and Wall Streeters looking for the Next Big Thing. So this was a twofer—selling Sandra as a public intellectual while boosting Betsy and the share price.

"Blood bathes the cells of our bodies in nutrients. It carries oxygen to our brains and delivers carbon dioxide to our lungs for us to exhale. And it contains within it multitudes of organisms … parts of ourselves we barely know exist … armies of white blood cells with specialized spotters ready to detect an alien bacteria or rogue cell turning cancerous … suicide soldiers ready to dig into these errant cells and explode them … and platelets ready to come to the scene of any injury, our first-responders who seal our wounds with coagulants."

Sandra was on a semi-circular stage set just high enough so she could glance down at the words of her speech scrolling on screens inset in the floor, while appearing to be merely looking straight down to make eye contact with her audience. But Sandra did not need to read her lines. She had rehearsed them so well the words poured out of her.

Her Austin speechwriter had told her that when a speaker focuses on merely getting the words out, the result seems predictably forced. But when a speaker dwells on the rich meaning of her words, she invites her listeners to dwell on those meanings with her.

Sandra was good at this, so good that the format's chin-stroking asides and flashes of revelatory insights seemed to flow naturally from her.

"The handiwork of billions of years of evolution in our blood is majestic, a thing of wonder," she said. "But it isn't perfect. We are not perfect. We are vulnerable to diabetes. Cancers. Immune disorders. Anemia. Alzheimer's."

Sandra repeated statistics about early death from these scourges of mankind.

There are tests and markers, she said, for each of these scourges. But not one practical, affordable universal assay for all diseases detectable in the human blood … until now.

Sandra spoke of how one day she was sitting at her desk, pouring over statistics about how many people died for lack of early detection, when she looked beyond the numbers to think with fondness and sadness of a young woman she had known for years … the niece of a friend … a bright and clever young lady Sandra had mentored … who had been accepted to Stanford and started working on a degree in biochemistry … only to be forced to withdraw from school just a month in her first quarter … This young lady, her name was Carmen, soon lost her life to one of the very diseases she had hoped to one day cure.

A commotion in the audience. Someone speaking loudly. Sandra ignored it, like a good actress should and continued.

"That was when I determined that I would dedicate whatever number of years I have left on this earth to saving the Carmens of the future."

"Cunt."

Sandra paused. Whatever it was, security would take care of it. With a flurry of fright, she realized she had lost her place, but remembered the screens. She glanced down and found her place. They could edit out the interruption.

"The tragedy is that most diseases are easily cured with early detection. But we can't go to the clinic every week to have every little imperfection checked and double-checked. What was needed was a way to read a record of the body in one glance … in one drop of blood. What was needed was … Betsy."

"Liar."

The silhouettes were moving. There was a scuffle, someone being grabbed by the arm and pulled back.

"Tell them Sandra, tell them about our little deal."

Sandra put it out of her mind. He was being taken care of … being ushered out. She had to get on with it. She had to tell the story of how she had devised this new technology and then close strong.

"It was Alonso, of course. I had not been able to keep up my part of the bargain. Believe me, I tried. We had Jim at Empirca Labs on board. But a stubborn faculty physician blocked Carmen at the last minute, indignant about compromising the purity of the leukemia test. He was right, of course. But what would it have hurt to have at least added Carmen to the test and scrubbed out of her data later? After all I've given to that school …"

The skin around her eyes looked bruised. Sandra looked older, her eyelids pinched.

"They escorted Alonso out of the auditorium without arresting him. If they had, the story would have spilled out right then and there. TED told me that my presentation was spoiled by the interruption. I asked them if they could edit it out, but they said that was against the rules.

"Several days later, the FBI paid me a little visit. The FDA suspended Betsy. The board fired me but made it look like a retirement. So I sat at home, talking with lawyers, preparing myself for the story to break and the subpoenas to arrive. After that would come trial and retrial, testimony, getting yelled at by congressmen, scandal. Then this …"

Sandra picked up the report from her desk.

"While I was steeling myself to weather this storm, I found that I was having trouble concentrating, thinking clearly. Not surprising, given all I was going through. But I took a vacation to Italy and realized it was not just stress. It was something else, something that felt different inside me. So I went in for testing and was diagnosed with early onset Alzheimer's."

Sandra set down the report. She took a sip from a cocktail glass, for a long time the only sound the tinkling of ice.

She put the drink down.

"So Betsy couldn't even get that right."

Her lips fluttered and eyes welled over with tears. Sandra composed herself and looked straight into the computer camera.

"So that's it. That's the end of me. This is where I wind up. As I traveled around the world striking items off my bucket list—there weren't many left—I heard about Freyja. I got in touch. Freyja and I had some useful conversations, though I don't buy her bullshit for one minute. I do detect someone very clever and intuitive. A week ago, when I received her invitation, I instantly accepted. So I am going to go to Norway. I will probably not do it with the others, at least not that way. If I don't put an end to myself then, no one will see this little confessional of mine.

"But I might. I am not so much looking forward to following Freyja as I am to meeting her other disciples. To break bread with those fellows of mine who have been to the top and are now on their way down."

She chuckled, realizing the aptness of her metaphor.

"I don't want to be sentenced to prison, even if my condition prevents them from actually sending me there. I'll have to do *something*, while I still can. I don't want to end up like my father. That's another kind of prison."

She took another drink and set it down with a slam.

"All my life I wanted to be remembered for something … Now I don't. I don't want to be remembered. I don't want to exist anymore. I don't even want to have existed."

TWENTY-SIX

Elizabeth slipped into the box man, the neutral position of freefall, with her back in a relaxed arch, legs wide apart and up-lifted behind her, head up, arms straight out from her shoulders.

It was a position of power from which she could initiate radical changes in direction with the slight bend of an arm or leg, making her limbs the ailerons and flaps of an airplane. Left arm tilted down with a pull of her right arm up, she found herself banking at an angle like a pivoting aircraft.

She tilted her arm even more and executed a complete turn. She halted and executed a turn in the other direction.

To move forward, all Elizabeth had to do was to pull her arms in, straighten her legs and dip her head down, and she was descending as gracefully as a jet toward landing.

Bored with technique, she curled into a ball and shot up twenty feet to just beneath the padded ceiling. Elizabeth straightened and descended to the middle of the chamber and pivoted to hang upside down. She righted herself and stood straight again.

Elizabeth folded her arms and settled her hands over one another and let the wind circulate her around until she spun around the chamber like a centrifuge. With quick extension of her hands, she came to a gentle stop and hovered like an angel.

The instructor tapped on the glass. Her half-hour was up. The wind lessened and she came to a light landing on her feet.

"You are a natural at this," the instructor said.

"Nothing like it," she replied.

Elizabeth went to the changing room, helmet tucked under one arm. This was her sixth session. Freyja kept sending tickets and Elizabeth kept working in sessions in the mornings.

After each indoor skydive, Elizabeth felt better. It felt good to have such complete mastery of one's body in a world with such strange physics, the next best thing to space tourism. She was beginning to look forward to the arrival of a new ticket—and it was good therapy for anxiety, as the oceanic sensation of the drug had been—good therapy, even if the prescribing physician in this instance was a psychopath.

And what, precisely, was the agenda in sending Elizabeth to this chamber, again and again?

But Lars did not object. In fact, he wanted Elizabeth to use each ticket, and go alone, in case Freyja might be lured in to showing her face. Ingrid had a live tap into the many cameras set up within MegaJump, running the feed through facial recognition software against known cyber criminals. Elizabeth knew, of course, that Freyja would never risk herself that way. She, too, would be tapping into that feed, watching Elizabeth's progress so the goddess could occasionally send text messages of congratulations when her student did particularly well.

Elizabeth waited outside for her ride to come. The morning was brilliant, but the sun was rising into an arc that was noticeably flatter than it had been when Elizabeth had first arrived in Norway. She would soon need to get back home for fall classes. And there was Max as well. They had a text storm the evening before. Max had nothing important to text about, but she could read the need behind his words. Max was fragile. He needed his mother a short train ride away.

The thought of leaving Norway without reaching Freyja bothered her. But there was no reason why she should could not continue the digital contact from America. She might still be helpful to the investigation and her fellow PIGers. And Max ... and Max.

Another sunny Oslo day, taunting all who work indoors.

Lars took a seat at the end of the table, framed by the large window that looked out over the city and harbor. One by one, the PIGers took their seats, most bearing big mugs of coffee. Nasrin was composed and pretty, in an elegant black business suit. George looked his age, perhaps he had had a sleepless night. His bow tie and suspenders did not make him look any younger. Ingrid had pressed her hair down, looking more presentable and not at all hungover or sleep deprived.

Bowie was his usual smirking self.

"Elizabeth, what is your evaluation of Sandra Armstrong?"

Lars asked.

All eyes were on her.

"Well, when I started on Sandra, I couldn't believe she was one of the suicides," she said. "Someone of that caliber getting into such an unlikely cult. But beneath all that polished steel was a brittle and surprisingly defenseless ego. The prospect of disgrace was too much for Sandra to bear and the likelihood of a prison sentence came as an additional, unacceptable horror. Her diagnosis clinched it. Sandra was going to commit suicide one way or another. Freyja just happened to get inside her decision cycle."

"And the others?"

"Sophia Goddard was a narcissistic young woman who could not live up to the impossible expectations she had of herself. You might call her callow. If she had been a few years older, I don't believe Sophia would have signed up. Mike Drummond, well, he's the only one in this whole group who showed positive signs of mental illness. He was clearly borderline psychotic. All remain explained except for Jacobson."

"Remind us."

"Because he was too self-absorbed to kill himself over a mere crush gone bad."

"What about the indoor skydiving?" Norris asked.

All heads turned to the FBI agent, the group surprised that he had spoken up. This much, she had divulged to the whole group.

"What's that about?"

"It may be metaphorically connected in Freyja's mind with the suicides from such a high place," Elizabeth replied. "Or it may be another way of her trying to jack into my head."

She instantly regretted her words.

Lars stiffened in his seat. Bowie raised an eyebrow. Only Lars, George, Ingrid and Nasrin knew about her nocturnal conversations with Freyja. Elizabeth followed up quickly, hoping to cover her tracks.

"I mean, since she's observing us all, it may be that Freyja believes that getting me to undertake some kind of vigorous activity might bring me into her orbit."

"As an informant?" Bowie asked.

"No, I think as one of her victims," Elizabeth said. "She believes I'm susceptible."

Agent Norris leaned forward, sniffing a nuance like a truffle pig.

"Miss Browne, you used the words 'another way' to get inside your head," Norris said. "Are you in some kind of communication with Freyja that you have not told us about?"

In the bright light of the office, Elizabeth was sure everyone could see the strawberries blooming on her cheeks.

"She is," Lars finally answered.

"Care to tell us about it?" Bowie asked.

For the next five minutes Lars gave a concise and accurate description of Freyja's online avatar and its conversation with Elizabeth. As she listened, Elizabeth was grateful that he omitted personal details about Max and her anxiety attacks.

"Why didn't you tell us?" Norris asked.

"We kept this close-hold because we wanted to create as little feedback as possible," Lars replied.

"What does that mean?" Norris asked.

"If there is one thing we can be confident of, Freyja is always listening to us, always watching us," Lars said. "I didn't want the larger group adding comment and complexity to this early stage of dialogue with Freyja."

"When were you going to tell us?" Bowie asked.

"Soon, but now it doesn't matter."

"Matters a fuckload to me," Bowie said.

"It doesn't matter because now I know who Freyja is. She has revealed herself."

All eyes locked on Lars.

"She is Karl Pedersen."

"And you know this how?" Nasrin asked.

"Because Pedersen has escaped."

Nasrin laughed. "How does one escape from that prison we toured— call an Uber, or just ask the warden for a lift?"

"Karl got over a wall. That's an automatic three years to his sentence, and not concurrent either."

"And?"

"He left behind all his devices, each one with digital traces of the site used to converse with Elizabeth as Freyja."

"They have all since gone dark," Ingrid said. "But I documented the TOR addresses and took screenshots. Here is Freyja."

Ingrid swiveled her laptop to show them Freyja, every freckle on her pale skin, wisps of blonde hair roiled by a light wind. Freyja had a subtle smile that matched the good humor of her blue eyes.

"So that's her," Bowie said. "I must say, Karl the Killer must have quite a woman inside him trying to get out."

"What do you think Elizabeth?" Nasrin asked.

"I have my doubts about Karl Pedersen," Elizabeth said. "He's a psychopath, to be sure, but he prefers to kill people face to face. Using dialogue to lure people to their deaths would be a strange hobby for such an accomplished criminal."

"It would not be all that unusual," George said, one hand raised by his chin, a habitual gesture from the days when he would be sucking a pipe. "Sometimes even criminal masterminds have their secrets. And the digital evidence is compelling."

Harold Kober, the PST agent, briefed them on the details of the comprehensive manhunt for Karl Pedersen. It was assumed that Pedersen had a network of helpers and probably had already exited the country. There was a little more talk of Pedersen, then Lars closed the meeting. He thanked everyone for their assistance and observed that the working group was almost done.

"Anything else?" Lars asked.

"I am almost done," Elizabeth said. "I have to return stateside in a week, tops, to prepare for my fall classes."

As she spoke, she caught a micro-expression on Lars' face, a drawing of the eyebrows and narrowing of the mouth. Was Lars angry? He had to have known this was coming. They had talked about it.

"Well." Lars cleared his throat. "We will miss you and your good work."

"Yes, indeed," Nasrin said, leaning sideways to get a good look at Elizabeth.

"I thought you might want to stay for the interrogation?" George asked.

"I might be able to come back for that," Elizabeth said. "If not, George, we shall have to share notes."

"Walk back with you to the hotel?"

"Sure."

Nasrin fell into stride with Elizabeth.

"Are you going to miss Norway?" she asked.

"Yes," Elizabeth said. "No. I have a lot of memories to take back, some of them wonderful. Some not."

Elizabeth realized that it sounded as if she were speaking of the unpleasantness that had transpired between her and Nasrin on the plane and afterwards. But she didn't mean that and didn't want to dredge all that up again.

"Until I met you Nasrin, I had never actually been in the middle of a gun battle," Elizabeth explained. "Nor almost raped and murdered by a master criminal in my hotel room."

"Stick with me and you will see the world."

"At the moment, I feel that I have seen quite enough of it to last a while."

"And will you miss Lars?"

Nasrin was studying Elizabeth intently, gauging her every reaction.

"Same answer. Yes. No."

"Well, it's a Friday and all the efforts of Lars and PIG will be focused on Karl."

They came to the entrance of their hotel.

"If you find yourself at loose ends this weekend," Nasrin said, "I could sure use a friend to go shopping with, maybe a glass of wine or spot of dinner?"

"Let's play it by ear and see where we are tomorrow."

Nasrin went straight to her room. Another envelope was waiting for Elizabeth at the front desk. Yet another MegaJump ticket?

Elizabeth took the envelope and walked from the lobby toward the hallway that led to the elevator. A strong hand grabbed her by the inside of her elbow, tight enough to pinch a nerve.

Lars spun her around.

"Elizabeth, what the hell are you doing?"

"Excuse me?"

"What are you doing?"

"I'm going up to my room. What are you doing?"

Lars stepped back, confused, embarrassed, as if he were surprised by himself.

"You were so abrupt this morning, like you wanted to slam a door in my face."

"You just hurt me," she said, rubbing the inside of her arm.

His face reddened.

"I'm sorry."

"I mean it, Lars, it really hurts."

"I am sorry. That is not who I am."

Elizabeth let him hang for a few beats.

"Okay," she said. "I will let you off. This one time. Got it?"

"Yes, I have got it."

"Lars, I told you not to take me for granted," she said. "You always knew I had to go back for my classes, my research office, my son."

"In theory, yes. But the way you said it this morning, announcing it so publicly. It felt like a rejection, almost a slap in the face."

"I'm sorry for that," she said. "I did not mean it that way."

Another micro-expression, an ever-so brief flutter.

"Elizabeth."

He put his strong hands on her shoulders, drew her close and rested his forehead on hers. She let him hold her like that for a good half a minute, then she withdrew and his hands dropped to his side.

"You know it would never work, not long term," she said. "Not as rooted as we are in our respective worlds."

"I could retire," he said.

"It's not just being in different places," she said. "You know that we're both way too intense, in very different ways. And what would you be without your position? You are still young enough to be promoted, to rise in the government. Are you willing to throw all that away?"

Lars shook his head. He recognized that she was right, even if he didn't like it.

"Okay," he said. "I shall be on my way."

He turned, shoulders slumped, looking forlorn.

"Lars?"

He turned slowly.

"Call me tomorrow morning. We could have dinner tomorrow night if you like. Talk all this out like the adults we are."

"That would be good," he said without enthusiasm. "One more

thing. We are going to post plainclothes in the lobby tonight and have the staff keep a watchful eye on the employee's entrances. Just to stop Karl in case he decides to pay you another visit."

"Thank you."

The elevator dinged and Elizabeth went up to her room.

Elizabeth went for an early evening run around the park, returning to her room aching and sweaty but feeling all the better for it. She showered, slipped into a comfortable pair of jeans and a Georgetown Bulldogs T-shirt and resolved to order in. She had enough of her colleagues, even George, who had asked her to dinner and was a little perturbed when she politely declined.

There was text message on her phone. It was Freyja, confirming their "session" at eight tonight. Elizabeth thought about it for a moment. She'd be on her own, no Lars or George watching out for her. But she was leaving soon. She might learn something. And if it was Karl, maybe he would give up his location.

But Freyja wasn't Karl, of that she was sure. Elizabeth had no idea who was behind this digital simulacrum of a goddess, but it wasn't him.

Elizabeth ordered in and within half an hour a young man arrived with a tray bearing a cheeseburger with a Ringnes that came with a tall, icy glass. For dessert, there were berries floating in crème fraiche.

"Good thing I ran today," she said to the young man, placing forty kroner in his hand.

Elizabeth ate quickly, greedily, downing the thick cheeseburger with beer, before devouring all the berries with a spoon. Done, Elizabeth went to the wash basin to rub the grease off her face and hands. She belched.

No, this is not a night to be with company.

As Elizabeth put her tray in the hallway, she was grateful that Lars had posted plainclothes watchers down below. Would that stop someone as clever and determined as Karl? The thought of Karl in her room again prompted Elizabeth to turn the deadbolt on her door. She wedged a chair against the handle of the door, just for good measure.

It was almost time.

As before, she went through the ritual of powdering her face, applying a little blush, a light coat of lipstick and a slight tinge of color above her eyes. She put on a shirt and her nice jeans. She did not feel at all silly for doing this. It felt like putting on armor before battle.

Elizabeth hit "record" on her burner phone. Her laptop pinged precisely at eight.

"Hello, Elizabeth, you are looking lovely tonight."

"You too," she said. "As always."

"I was as surprised as Lars that you announced that you are leaving us so soon. Did you catch the look on his face? He had left his smartphone on and set it up at a nice angle for me on the conference table. I had to replay it several times to fully gauge the depth of his emotion. I am afraid you and he are parting. But I hope that just because you are on the other side of the sea, dear, that we will not fall out of touch. It may surprise you to hear this, but I truly look forward to our little sessions. They mean a lot to me, as I hope they mean to you."

"Are you Karl Pedersen?"

Freya laughed.

"I am exactly who you see. I am always who you need me to be."

The image of the goddess pulsed with electric vitality. Her head turned and she cast a soft and gentle smile.

"But enough about me, dear, let's get down to brass tacks. I want to talk to you about taking the next step on our journey. Please open your envelope."

"Before I do, why the indoor skydiving?"

"We discussed this before. To help you conquer your biggest foe, the fear that holds you back. By floating, we disconnect ourselves from the fatal pull of gravity, the ground truths that have been gripping us, holding us fast to the earth."

"And you think I am afraid?"

"I have been with you my dear Elizabeth when you were overcome like a little girl. I so wanted to hold your hand and stroke your hair. I just want to help."

"And what do you think I am afraid of?"

The smile dropped. The goddess receded slightly. The corners of her eyes and mouth drooped.

"Oh darling, why do you make me state the obvious? You are afraid of the Edge itself … that you will follow the others, just as your father and your brother did."

"I want no such thing."

"Of course not. I don't believe that you would want that, not for a minute. But it is all the worse for the fact that you might do something you do not want to do."

Elizabeth wanted to scream at her. Instead, she turned away and focused on her breathing.

"And so what is this?" she said, holding up the envelope.

"Please see for yourself."

Elizabeth ripped the envelope's seal, held it upside down and tapped it. A pill in a plastic bag fell into her lap.

"Another trip?"

"Another journey."

"Why? What are you trying to show me?"

Freyja paused, strands of hair roiling in the light wind of her digital paradise.

"I am trying to show you, Elizabeth, that what you take for reality is but a screen, that there are deeper realities not in some other mystical or supernatural realm, but right here, just underneath what we usually touch and perceive. It is all around you, now, and you can choose many paths to open it up and use it to go wherever you want to go."

"By leaping to my death?"

"Only if you believe in death. If you do, then you will die. If you don't you can find the truth of your existence in that. But there are other ways. Through meditation. Or prayer. Or by taking this pill and letting your inner eye open to the truth that is all around you throughout the day as you work, eat, drink, make love and sleep."

Elizabeth again wanted to tell her that she believed in the reality of death. She had seen it many times on metal tables with runnels. It stank.

"You want me to kill myself for you, just like the others. That would be your ultimate sick joke, wouldn't it?"

"Is what I am talking about really so outlandish? Science today talks about quantum consciousness, multiverses, near death experiences. No, Elizabeth, you don't have to take extreme measures to see what I am talking about. But if you take this pill, I promise that you will finally see where I live … and if you still believe I should be brought to justice, well, then I shall turn myself in."

Elizabeth took the pill out of the bag and held it up in a vise between her thumb and index finger.

"Is this the same pill as before?"

"The very same chemical."

"And you will turn yourself in if I come across the rainbow bridge and still cry 'bullshit?'"

A long pause.

"Elizabeth, I am confident you will come to see the value of what I am doing. But if not, I will end all my contacts now."

"So you are still doing this, with others?"

"Many. All around the world."

"And you promise to stop?"

"Yes."

"And you promise to turn yourself in?"

"Yes."

Elizabeth put the pill on her tongue.

It was a small pill, after all. She swallowed it without water.

––––––––––

Elizabeth closed the shell of her computer and turned off the power. She turned off her smartphone as well. She did not want Freyja messing with her head while she tripped. She read for a good twenty minutes and then set her book down.

Nothing yet.

She thought about calling George, but couldn't bring herself to do it. He would be upset that she had taken the pill and she didn't want to have to endure his disapproval. Besides, she could handle this. And if taking the pill succeeded in unmasking Freyja, or at least getting her to lay off a fresh round of victims, it would be well worth it.

Elizabeth poured herself a water and used the bathroom. She looked up from the washbasin to regard herself in the bathroom mirror.

The surface of the bathroom mirror shimmered, as if she were looking down at it through an inch of water. She poked an index finger in the water and made quicksilver ripples. She turned off the bathroom light and looked around her hotel room.

Everything was in place, the bed, the furniture, the lamps, her computer. But something was different, a flattening of reality, as if she had just realized that all the dimensions between these objects was an illusion, a whole world projected on a screen. She was living in a hologram that was really a flat world, one that hid a greater, more numinous world underneath the surface of things, just like Freyja had said.

Elizabeth went to the window to look down at the street. More flat world illusion. People and cars and street lights and stores. All projected on a screen, a movie she had mistaken for reality.

The pedestrians and the traffic sped up and slowed down, sped up and slowed down. She could will them to do that. She willed them to stop. And they did.

Amid the stopped cars and frozen people, a blue SUV tore up the middle of the road and came to a screeching halt. A naked man stepped out from the driver's seat onto the pavement. Jeremy looked up at her, the top of his head flattened and his face crushed by the fall.

"Oh dear Jesus."

Elizabeth turned from the window and fell into a crouch.

That was too much. She had not expected anything like that.

She should call George. He would be angry, but she needed him. Where was her phone? She heard someone in the bathroom, calling out to her.

"George?"

She could hear someone, a man.

"George?"

She turned on the bathroom light.

It wasn't George. It was Mike, her brother. He rested on the lip of the large bathtub of the shower stall with a small razor in his lap. Mike's cheeks glistened with tears as bright red blood spurt from his wrists, pumping into to a large, black clot coagulating in the basin.

Elizabeth's scream welled up in her gut and rushed out of her like a gale. She fell to her knees and drew in a breath as if someone had punched her in the stomach. Mike couldn't speak either.

All he could do is look at her and sob, eyes brimming with tears and regret and shame and horror.

She wanted to hold him, grasp him and pull him back.

But there was no approaching Mike, no saving him from the invisible boundary that separates the damned in hell from their loved ones.

So Elizabeth squatted in front of Mike on her knees, keeping faith, brother and sister sobbing together.

The bedside phone rang.

Elizabeth went down on all fours, still sobbing, and looked up.

Mike was gone.

She pulled herself up, went to the table and lifted the receiver. The voice on the phone sounded tinny, a man in a bathysphere who said he was the assistant manager and that there had been reports of noise from her room.

"I'll turn down the television," Elizabeth said and hung up.

The room was too small. It brought things too close to her. The phone rang again and Elizabeth ran out of the room, down the stairwell and through the lobby.

It was dark and cool outside. It felt better. It had to be better to be outside.

She passed a curio shop, the front window with a shelf full of cute plastic trolls for tourists. The plastic trolls watched her, their blue heads turning as she passed them by, keeping track of her so she could be followed by their kin.

Elizabeth stepped up her gait.

The people on the street seemed bothered by her. Sometimes they stared, sometimes they looked away. An attendant at a petrol station glared at Elizabeth as she walked by, his head also turning with her as she passed.

She looked away from him.

Mustn't look into people's eyes.

The colors of fabrics, sweaters and scarfs, snow equipment and candy in the shop windows were vivid, as if she realized that apparently solid objects were no more than the solid manifestations of colors. It was color that was real, not the world. The edges of the stone buildings seemed sharper, almost like gray razors. The bright lights of the store fronts guttered like candle flames, announcing the transience of material existence, a vibratory reality behind this one, a juddering skull beneath the placid face of the apparent world.

Then there were the things, the *nisse*, little people in the shadows. They tracked her in perfect silence, always staying on the periphery of her vision, darting behind trash cans and cars whenever she dared to look directly at them.

"My lover is the sun, golden and warm," she said to a passerby, an older man who started walking faster to get away. "But get too close to the sun and he will burn you."

Elizabeth was unable to feel her legs moving and feet connecting with the sidewalk. She was floating smoothly above the concrete, riding on a current that flowed along the street to lead her into the park.

"My lover is the moon, cool and beautiful," she said to an elderly woman who looked startled. "But get too close to the moon and she will freeze you."

She came to the park entrance and went inside, following the well-lit walkway to the place where the statues writhed, while the little people slithered and bunched like weasels in the dark recesses of the park. The talk between the statues was almost overwhelming, a din of cackles, laughter, moans, cries and whispers coming from all directions.

Elizabeth walked up to her father hanging from a bronze tree.

"Are you happy now? Is this what you wanted?"

Asshole. Selfish fucker. Look at what you did to Michael you fucking fuck with the earphones and the silly haircut for a dad you asshole, look at what you've done to us … all because mom died …

Look at what you did to us.

"Look."

Someone was screaming. Maybe it was her.

TWENTY-SEVEN

The holes in the ceiling tiles were tiny pores in the epidermis of a giant that dripped a mist of humid sweat throughout the night. The pores themselves were nothing. And nothing has a way of expanding and meeting until it transcends and engulfs all dimensions.

If she could float upward, Elizabeth could enter through one of those holes to coast in cool, liberated space. But she couldn't float. The restraints on her wrists kept her firmly anchored to the metal bars of a hospital bed.

This left her at the mercy of the nurses. She watched them, the way they looked at her, the knowing looks they exchanged when they passed by her room. The nurses were telepaths who shared thoughts about her, to trick Elizabeth, to keep her here and contained, to keep her from discovering the truth about Freyja.

Elizabeth read the little tag on the plastic bag of her IV.

Thorazine.

That explained the dryness in the back of her mouth, the slight pounding headache. Of course they would give her that, the prescribed anti-psychotic administered around the world. Another one of their clichés.

What they didn't realize is that sanity is relative. The DMT pill she had taken had accelerated Elizabeth closer to the speed of light, making all her motions and words appear bizarre and distorted only to those left behind in the slow world. The nurses could not understand that in Elizabeth's frame of reference, everything was proportional, everything made sense.

And so the nurses conspired, sending each other telepathic messages to keep the charade going, moving up and down the hall outside her room with tennis shoes that squeaked on the tile floor.

Nice touch, that, the tennis shoes. Keeping it real.

The Thorazine made her sleepy. Elizabeth patted down pine needles and leaves around her nest, scrunched her arms as close to her body as her restraints would allow, and curled up and went to sleep like a momma bear.

Hibernation.

———————

George was walrus faced again, his large blue eyes intent with walrus concerns, his grey mustache drooping with walrus worries.

"Elizabeth, how are you doing now?"

"The Thorazine is drying me out. A nap did me good. Still a bit trippy."

"You seem to be better than you were even just an hour ago."

"You were here an hour ago?"

"Elizabeth, I have been with you practically all night."

She had no idea.

"I guess you want to know why."

George said nothing, his body stiff and erect, expression stern, eyes bloodshot from lack of sleep.

"Freyja promised me that if I took her pill, she would terminate her communication with any other potential victim."

"You cannot know what promises Freyja will or will not honor," George said. "She is the soul of deceit."

"I guess in the back of my mind I am still worried about Max, and that if I took the pill it would encourage Freyja to keep her word to stay away from my son."

George's posture and expression softened.

"I suppose I can understand that."

Powerful emotions welled up in her chest. Elizabeth gave into a brief cry. She knew her face and voice were distorted, making her ugly, but she was not embarrassed to cry in front of George. As she moved in her bed, her hands pulled against the restraints, which did embarrass her.

"I'm sorry … I'm so sorry, George, I should have trusted you."

"You sure should have, Elizabeth."

George leaned over the rail and dabbed her eyes with a tissue.

"I'll get them to take these damned things off you," he said gently.

The cry had passed through her like a sudden squall that left a clear sky. Elizabeth felt all business now.

"George, she had to have upped the dose," she said.

"Based on what I saw, I'd say by three times."

"So let's get back to work. It's not Karl, you know that. We're close, I know it, let's catch this bitch once and for all."

George leaned back and stiffened again.

"Elizabeth, once you are released, I am to settle you in for the night in your hotel. Tomorrow morning, Charlie Bowie will escort you to the airport for your return home."

It should not have come as a surprise, but it did.

"And Lars?"

"He is beside himself with anger at you. He refuses to come see you. Possession of DMT is a Schedule I drug violation in Norway, a major felony. His superiors are all over him. He had to disclose your relationship. He told me he feels that you made him out to be a fool."

"Is it really that bad?"

"Elizabeth, by the time they came for you, you were in the park shaking your fist in rage at statues and screaming at them."

Elizabeth felt empty and groggy, the DMT burned out of her system, dopamine wrung out from her traumatized brain. A good night's sleep would do her wonders. Then she could sleep some more on the plane.

George checked her out of the hospital. She had to endure a lecture about the dangers of psychedelics from a young physician who could have been one of her graduate students. George promised to watch over her.

They took a cab to her hotel. As the driver maneuvered through late afternoon traffic, Elizabeth leaned over and rested her head on George's shoulder.

"Screaming in the park where the bronze trees are?" she said.

"Yes."

"I was berating my father," she said.

"I would suppose so."

"Vigeland's bronze trees?"

"Yes."

"I think I remember. I was reasoning with my father. Trying to make him understand."

"I know that, Elizabeth."

"So you will carry on here, with PIG?"

"Until we catch Freyja. In the meantime, I will Skype with you and keep you apprised of developments."

"Is that wise?"

Any digital communications could be picked up by Freyja.

"No," he said, shaking his head, "I suppose not, now that you mention it. But at the correct time, at least we can begin to share notes on the case. For our paper."

Elizabeth watched the storefronts slide by. She no longer cared about the paper.

"You do it, George. It's yours."

"Don't make any hasty decisions. Think it over."

"I've got a lot to think over."

———————

George helped Elizabeth pack most of her things. He offered to sleep on the couch and keep an eye on her, but Elizabeth declined. Satisfied that she was in for the night, he gave her a hug, kissed her on the forehead, made her promise to call as soon as she was stateside and left.

Elizabeth appreciated all that George had done, but she didn't need him hovering. She was fine. And besides, he had suffered a mostly sleepless night. He deserved better than to sleep on a couch.

An hour later, there was a soft knock on the door. Elizabeth looked out the peephole and saw Nasrin standing in the hallway.

"Come in," she said.

Nasrin entered. She looked crisp and prepared for anything in one of her dark business suits.

"I am so sorry, Elizabeth, about what has happened," she said. "Lars is truly stupid to boot you out of the country like this. I guess I'm lucky he's not booting me along with you."

"Why would he expel you now?" Elizabeth asked.

"Because he's jealous, dear. Always has been. And I bet if you went back to him now, and batted those pretty eyes of yours, he'd take you back."

"That's not going to happen. Besides, Lars has come to appreciate how much he depends on you, Nasrin."

"Drink?"

Elizabeth nodded. Nasrin smiled, took off her jacket and arranged it neatly on the back of one of the two chairs by the writing desk. She took a seat. Elizabeth fixed two scotches, one with ice, one neat.

They clinked glasses.

"I must say, Elizabeth, I am impressed that you and George had this little side operation going on with the drugs. A real corker, that was."

"It turned out to be one of the stupidest things I've ever done."

"I suppose it was, with you yelling at those brass trees in the park. Sorry I introduced you to Gustav Vigeland. Any new insights from your experience?"

"Just what we already had guessed— Freyja uses DMT to break down her victim's sense of reality and personal boundaries. Enough 'treatments' and anyone would begin to lose their sense of self."

"She penetrated some tough personalities." Nasrin took a sip of scotch. "Freyja knows psychology. Maybe she's a shrink like you?"

"She knows a lot about the mind. The binaural beats that go with the drug resonate with the pituitary gland, making the DMT even more effective. No telling where I'd be now if I had let her use the sound on me as well."

"Want some dinner?"

"Thanks, but I am still a bit woozy," Elizabeth said. "I am going to order in tonight."

Elizabeth took a sip.

"And besides, I have to be at my best tomorrow morning for my little date at the airport with Charlie Bowie."

Nasrin's laugh was splendidly derisive.

"Could you use some company on your last night in Norway?" Nasrin asked.

Elizabeth opened the drawer of the writing table and pulled out a menu.

"Okay, here are our options."

———

After steaks, fries and a few Ringnes beers, they talked a good hour about Lars, about PIG, about their respective futures. They each had another beer. Nasrin divulged a little more about her life, about how it was with her English father, now deceased, who was convinced to the end of his days that she was simply working too hard to find the right man. Elizabeth opened up about her family, the edge of sadness that rings even the happiest moments of her life.

If it wasn't for Max …

A long silence. This was the time for Nasrin to leave, but she showed no sign of stirring.

"Penny for your thoughts."

"Just hate leaving Norway like this …"

"You haven't left yet."

Nasrin rose, hooked a bang of Elizabeth's hair behind one ear and softly stroked her cheek with the edge of one finger.

"You are anything but stupid. I think you are brave."

Nasrin pulled her in close for a kiss. Elizabeth did not resist. They kissed for a good long while, lips parted, hands roaming. Nasrin's lips explored Elizabeth's face, the hollow of her throat, the tender point of her neck just under her jaw.

Nasrin pulled back, a little breathless.

"Tell me you don't feel something for me."

"I do," Elizabeth said softly.

"But not enough?"

"Not enough for what you want."

"I am fine with that, just to be your friend … and to have truly known what it was like to have kissed you like that. That's all I need, dear. But don't think for one minute that I am leaving you alone tonight."

Nasrin took off her boots, unbuckled her belt and loosened her pants. She made a stack of pillows and leaned back on them, beckoning Elizabeth to join her. Elizabeth removed her shoes and her blouse, leaving on a T-shirt and old jeans. She nestled.

"You're quite a good snogger, you know."

"Snogger?"

"Kisser, love. Kisser."

"Thanks."

She felt Nasrin's heart beating, heard her blood coursing, felt her own head rise and fall on the woman's chest just as it had done with Lars. The softness of Nasrin's breast, the gentle stroking of her hair, made Elizabeth think of her mother, long lost, long ago …

Elizabeth snapped awake an hour later. The lights were out and Nasrin had rolled over, asleep in her clothes.

Elizabeth had been dreaming of something, a dream centered around an image …

"Brass trees," Elizabeth said aloud.

Nasrin pulled up, startled, as if Karl Pedersen might again be in the room.

"Yes?"

"They're really bronze trees. But you said brass trees."

"So?"

"Brass trees … bronze trees and brass *what*?"

Nasrin was fully awake now, quiet, waiting for Elizabeth to make a point. Perhaps she wondered if the drugs were still working on her.

Bronze trees and brass *what*?

A gossamer thought fluttered around Elizabeth's brain, gently evading her grasp. The DMT had kicked something lose in Elizabeth's memory, a random connection. She could sense the outline of what her unconscious mind knew, but just that. Words swirling, the agony of them almost connecting.

Bronze trees and brass what?

Brass what?

The connection closer than ever, Elizabeth quit trying and let it settle in her grasp. She closed her eyes and focused on her breathing. She let her mind go still, watching ideas float by like leaves on the surface of a gentle stream.

Brass tacks.

It had to do with something Sandra had related in one of her stories. The Japanese ministry official, who otherwise had spoken perfect English, had said, "brass attacks" instead of "brass tacks." It was funny the way Sandra had told it.

"Nasrin, what would you say if I told you we need to get down to brass tacks?"

"I would say it sounds painful."

"People in the UK don't say that, do they?"

"No. But now that I think about it, I am familiar with the term from watching so many American movies. It means getting down to business or some such, doesn't it?"

"Right. And a Norwegian wouldn't use that phrase, either."

"I don't suppose so. Their accent is more American when they speak English, but their vocabulary is standard UK."

Elizabeth rose, found her smartphone and searched for the etymology of the phrase. The earliest documented use of "brass tacks" was in a newspaper in Texas in 1863.

"Freyja used that very phrase."

"So?"

"Freyja is an American."

"Unless Freyja is Lionel Jacobson, who is a skillful writer of dialogue. It would be just like the playwright to throw something like that in, just to confuse you."

"Why do you think of Jacobson now?" Elizabeth asked.

"No body found. And as you said, his motive for suicide was far weaker than the others, for someone so self-absorbed."

"No. Freyja made a mistake. She let the mask slip and accidentally let me see that she is an American. What do you think, Inspector?"

"Possibly," Nasrin said. "Can we go back to sleep now?"

Elizabeth felt calm, satisfied that she had located her revelation, hoping that it meant something. In the light of early morning, Elizabeth was awakened by someone trying to close the door to her room as softly as possible.

A sheet with hotel letterhead rested on the bedside table. It had a large heart drawn in red lipstick. Nasrin's jasmine scent permeated her side of the bed.

Elizabeth rose, performed her yoga stretches and short meditation, bathed and dressed, and finished packing. She felt clear and happy and ready to start the next chapter in her life, whatever it was going to be. She put on a pair of blue jeans, a comfortable shirt and shoes, and took her bags downstairs. She went to the hotel café for a hearty breakfast of sausages, eggs and coffee while waiting for her date to pick her up.

Only one more ordeal to endure and then home.

Charlie Bowie came threading through the restaurant, thick red hair pointing in every direction, his tie too short and swung to the side, his navel peeking out through the space left by an open button on the bottom of his shirt.

Was it sadism on the part of Lars to assign Bowie to escort her to the airport? No, Elizabeth decided, it was protocol. The embassy would have insisted on it. They had, after all, been paying her way.

Bowie motioned for her. Elizabeth rose and followed him outside to a black Ford SUV with a driver. They slid into the back and the driver took off.

"Did you and Nasrin have a nice rubdown last night?"

"Charlie is that the kind of image you need to get off? If so, knock yourself out."

"What I will be getting off on is seeing your backside receding away from my proximity at just under the speed of sound. You have no idea the kind of shit storm you have unleashed. No one had you pegged as a drug abuser, although your freak out in the park did not come completely unexpected, given your history. The ambassador in London is particularly embarrassed for having vouched for you."

"Charlie, I have cared about only one thing, and that is stopping Freyja from doing more harm."

"Your extracurricular activities may have only encouraged her."

"Most of those activities were approved by Lars."

"I know that, now. But not the drugs, Lizzy, not the drugs. That little mess you managed to do all on your own."

"So what do you want from me? Want to banish me? Done. Want to humiliate me? Done. What else do you want Charlie?"

"All my life I've worked alongside people like you, the best schools, the smart set. Always cleaning up after you. Never an apology. Never any accountability. No. Accountability applies only to people like me."

Elizabeth could have said that he had just given her his entire psychological case history in twenty seconds but thought better of it.

"So what, Charlie?"

"I want to hear you say that you're sorry."

"I am sorry, Charlie, for any trouble I've caused you."

Bowie started to say something, then realized there was nothing more to say. They rode in silence.

A good twenty minutes later, they arrived at the airport, but the driver skirted past the Oslo main terminal. He came to a stop in front of a small terminal for private planes.

"What's this?"

"Here's the deal," Charlie said. "We're sending you back on a charter plane from Bergen. The big oil companies run flights to the East Coast for their engineers and executives. We kick in a little cash and seed the flight with our people. So I am to fly you to Bergen, make sure you get on that second plane, and wave bye-bye, forever."

"Why not just send me commercial?"

"Because we have extra seats and the jets are paid for. You wouldn't believe how hard the bean counters ride us. And it lets us move our people without putting their names on airline manifests, which are confidential but hackable."

Elizabeth rolled her bag behind Charlie, who had a briefcase. He led her through the terminal to a waiting plane, a Bombardier Learjet 70. The sounds of the airport were muffled, almost extinguished, by the plush interior. There were seven seats in all, three of them occupied—two men and a woman who sat near the back. The men had beards several days old. They looked exhausted from a rough tour in—Syria? Iraq? Ukraine? The men watched Elizabeth through narrow eyes. The woman, lean, athletic and hard-looking, in a turtle neck and jeans, simply glared at her.

"Sit here." Bowie pointed to a seat near the front, well away from the agents in the back.

Elizabeth sat and Bowie took a seat across from her.

The co-pilot pulled a lever and the ramp folded into the plane. He closed and locked the door and went to the cockpit. There were no announcements. A moment later, they were taxiing toward the runway.

Elizabeth checked her smartphone for messages. The night before, she had sent an email to Max informing him that her work was done and that she would be home in a day. He should expect her to visit him at Rutgers in two days.

There was a text. From Max.

"Turn off your phone," Bowie said.

The plane was taxing at speed, preparing to roll around a corner to line up at the end of a runway and take-off.

"What are you, the FAA?"

"No, I just don't want you taking pictures of our people on this plane, or the next one. Got it?"

"Got it. Just need to check my messages."

There was a message.

>No way, Lizzie! I have come all the way to Norway. Was going to surprise u and now u coming back?<

Elizabeth felt her heart flutter. What the hell was this? She sent him a text.

>Please don't joke. Where are you?<
>Here, amazing views<

>Alone? <
>With Freyja. She's cool, not what you think.<
Elizabeth set her phone in her lap. The plane lifted off the tarmac and shot like a needle through low clouds.

She looked down again.

>She says not to tell anyone. That would be bad.<
Elizabeth exhaled loudly and tried to focus on her breathing. Panic does no good, no good, no good.

>Tell me exactly where you are<

>Near a place called Tyssedal. U won't believe how it looks here<
She called Max's number but only got his voicemail. She left a message, struggling to control her breathing, trying not to sound desperate or pleading, turning her head toward the window so Bowie wouldn't overhear.

"Max, honey, please extricate yourself safely from that situation and call me. Please. Just listen to me this time as an expert."

A few seconds later, her smartphone tingled. There was another text. This time from Freyja.

>Max is resting now. I shall send you directions where you can meet us. Please follow them and tell no one.<

>Please have mercy on us<
>No worries, if you tell no one<

Elizabeth typed, "I promise," but the text went nowhere. The bars on her phone had disappeared. They were above the service ceiling.

"I'm telling you, if you take a picture with that thing, or even point it at the back of the plane, I swear I will smash it into tiny pieces," Bowie said.

"I understand."

Elizabeth turned off her phone to save power and pocketed it.

Everything that had happened recently—the fright of her hallucinations, her humiliation, being sent home early—all of it now seemed so petty compared to the enormity of what was happening now. Elizabeth looked down at nibs of white ice on sharp mountains separated by wide rivers coursing through green valleys. It was all sliding under her, away from her, life itself, out to sea.

Elizabeth never prayed. She prayed now, silently, in a way that Charlie might think was her taking a nap or meditating. It was a propitiatory prayer of the most childish sort—*please, please, please God.*

She kept her eyes closed, focusing again on her breath-calming exercise.

What could she do?

She couldn't tell anyone. Freyja had thoroughly infiltrated her phone. Freyja would know. Elizabeth could slip a note to Bowie or police at the airport, explaining her situation. But once someone called Lars, or Nasrin, or maybe even Ingrid, Freyja would know. Or would she? She again wondered if they were all too willing to grant Freyja omniscience?

Perhaps, but Elizabeth wasn't going to gamble Max's life on it.

No, she was going to follow Freyja's rules, for now. When they met, if they met, Elizabeth would have to find some way to get into her head before she could … what?

Had it been truly Freyja who killed Walleen with a shotgun? Maybe that gruesome murder was the handiwork of the Night Wolves.

The flight was only an hour but it seemed longer. The jet finally descended toward the Bergen airport, a wide, flat space between two mountains next to a fjord. In the distance, she could see the grey mass of the city. It was still early, only 10 a.m.

Once they had taxied to a stop, Elizabeth saw the plane that would take them home, a Boeing 757 with the unfamiliar brand of a charter company on its tail. A cluster of people waited on the tarmac to board on a metal stair ramp.

It was a private airport, so there was no security to go through.

"Give me your passport," Bowie said.

Elizabeth handed it over while the pilot and copilot left the Learjet to watch the bags being moved from its hold to the 757. Bowie reached into his briefcase, pulled out a kit and embossed Elizabeth's passport with an exit stamp.

"You can do that?"

"I can do that. Now I need to see you get into your plane and watch you leave."

"I never asked where I am going?"

"Dulles, then you're on your own. Wouldn't recommend coming back here. You're PNG in this little kingdom."

Elizabeth moved to join the waiting passengers. The wind blew cold spittle from low, gray clouds.

She thumbed the "on" button of her smartphone.

Elizabeth took her place in line behind the other twenty or so waiting passengers. Most of them were men in casual shirts and jeans, most likely oil industry engineers. None were obvious CIA operatives like those on the Learjet. The agents from the back of the Learjet stood behind her in line, Charlie to her left side.

Elizabeth's smartphone rang with an illuminated tile image that identified the caller.

"I've got to take this."

"Elizabeth, how are you doing?" Freyja's voice was as soft and friendly as ever.

Bowie studied her, curious about the call, his canine instincts as active as ever. Elizabeth turned away from him and focused on her response to Freyja. She resolved to take a minute to think. Don't try to reason with Freyja, just talk to her psyche.

The line was not moving yet, so it was natural for Elizabeth to move a few yards to the side for privacy.

"I must admit, I have gone up against you only to learn how second rate I really am compared to a player like you," Elizabeth said. "You really took me down. I am being sent home, disgraced, kicked off the investigation for good as you must surely know by now."

"Yes, I am sorry the way things have turned out."

"Remember what I said about taking pictures," Bowie said loudly. Elizabeth hunched over, hoping that his voice didn't carry.

"I think along the way I've acquired quite a lot of respect for you. For your intellect, your perceptiveness. I know now that you really care about people, that you've only been trying to help me."

"Why thank you, Elizabeth. That means a lot coming from you."

"It would be a gesture of supreme magnanimity for you to send Max to the nearest train station … so he can …" she felt her breath slip out of sync, inhalations somehow failing to fill her lungs. It was as if Freyja was there, watching with her pitiless, unearthly eyes as her victim started to beg. Elizabeth's legs felt weak and she went down to the tarmac on her knees.

"… so he can join his mother and we can go home together."

The pitch of her voice had risen almost to a squeak. She hated herself for losing control.

Elizabeth looked up. Bowie was standing over her now. She nodded at him, smiled weakly, as if to say *situation normal*, which must have looked ridiculous.

"Oh Elizabeth, that is a lovely vision. Max insists that you come to us first."

"Please do this one thing for me."

"Relax, dear, we can finally meet in the flesh and talk everything out, just us two girls. Here's what Max and I want you to do. Rent a car and we shall send you directions. Do not alert Lars, or Nasrin, or may the gods forbid, Charlie Bowie, or any other stupid policeman. Just come alone. If you do, I promise—I swear on all that is sacred—Max will be joining you on a flight home tomorrow."

Elizabeth was almost on all fours now, one hand on the rough, black surface, the other clutching the phone to her face.

"Please be truthful with me, just this once."

Bowie looked away, embarrassed by the scene she was making.

"Once you have our directions, input them into the GPS of your rental and pull the battery out of your phone. This will ensure a discreet meeting. Don't you want to see me in the flesh, as Max is doing now?"

"Yes."

"You are stronger than you think, Elizabeth. See you soon."

The face of the smartphone went dark.

Elizabeth took Charlie Bowie's outstretched hand to pull herself up.

"What is going on? Do you need a doctor?"

"No. Devastating medical news, for a friend. I guess I am still weak from the … you know."

Elizabeth slipped her phone into her pocket and took her place back in line. Bowie studied her intently. The three CIA agents were locked on to her like retrievers following a falling duck.

"Really, just bad news from home and some wobbliness from the hospital. Once I get settled into a seat on that jet, well, I will have a good nap all the way home. You can rest easy, now, Charlie."

Bowie nodded slowly, not believing anything she said. The three CIA agents behind him scanned her face intently, wondering who this problem child could be.

The line began to move, people climbing the stair ramp to the open door at the front of the plane.

"Is there anything you need to tell me?"

"No, just a family matter."

"Goodbye," Bowie said.

When it was Elizabeth's turn to put a foot on the steel staircase, she turned, attempted a natural smile and said goodbye. She tried to say it as firmly, as definitively as possible. Maybe it would make Charlie Bowie leave.

She willed herself up the metal stairs, reluctance weighing down her feet with every step. There was no one to welcome her. The charter plane showed its age, cracks in the plastic interior, the hiss of air nozzles and whine of electrical systems louder than in the smaller jet. There was open seating, with most seats empty, so Elizabeth took an aisle seat near the open door. The CIA woman gave her a sharp glance and took a seat directly behind her.

The door remained opened. Within a minute or two, a flight attendant would close it.

Elizabeth lifted the window shade. Charlie Bowie stood on the tarmac, briefcase on the ground, staring at the 757. He was not going to leave until he saw a steward lock and arm the door and the plane begin to roll.

Her racing mind slowed. An idea.

Elizabeth opened her purse, fished out her wallet and removed her driver's license, credit cards and insurance cards, and slipped them into her jeans pocket. She retrieved her passport and put it into her other pocket, under her smartphone. Elizabeth rose, turned and smiled at the CIA agent behind her. The woman looked at Elizabeth as if she might be a jihadist ready to explode.

"I forgot to tell Charlie something important. Would you mind holding on to my purse for a moment? I'll meet him on the stairs and be back in a jiff."

The CIA agent nodded. Elizabeth handed the woman her empty purse and went to the airplane door. She glanced to her side on the way out and saw that the woman had put her head down, texting something.

As Elizabeth descended, Charlie Bowie looked down at his phone, studying the rippling ellipses that announced that a message was coming through from his fellow agent in the plane. While he waited and read, Elizabeth quickly bounded down the stairs. She always wore flexible walking shoes whenever she traveled and was now supremely grateful for that fact.

As she hit the bottom step, Bowie's head snapped up, his eyes contracted, mouth drawn in fury.

Elizabeth doubled back under the ramp and the belly of the plane. A baggage handler shouted a protest in Norwegian. She ran past the nose of the craft and along the side of a fuel truck. Out the corner of one eye, she caught a glimpse of Bowie chugging around the ramp. Behind him a figure bolted forward, a woman in a turtleneck sweater and blue jeans.

It was the CIA agent who had been sitting behind her, ready for just such a surprise. The woman was all angles, sharp elbows and pumping knees.

Elizabeth sprinted toward the small lounge of the private airport, pushed through the doors and continued at speed past the counter, weaving to avoid passengers milling about.

She did not have to look back. She could see from the startled looks of the desk agents that someone was on her heels.

Elizabeth raced to the entrance doors.

There was a single taxi, just emptied of passengers. Elizabeth opened the door of the cab, slid inside, shut the door and depressed the lock.

"Main terminal," she shouted.

A second later, the agent was on the taxi door, rattling it, banging her palms on the roof.

"What is this?" The driver was a portly man of sixty with droopy mustache and bulging eyes. "Do I need to call the police?"

"No, she just doesn't want me to leave her. Lover's quarrel."

The driver smiled at the thought and gently eased forward. Elizabeth looked back. The agent planted her hands on her hips, a gesture that gave Elizabeth a tickle of satisfaction. A second later, Charlie Bowie came bounding behind her, his tie flapping and shirttail twisting as he ran.

"Actually, take me to the rental cars."

Elizabeth realized that she was drawing satisfaction from getting away from two people who could help her so she could deliver herself into the hands of a psychopathic murderer.

She could think of nothing else to do.

Elizabeth picked one of the premium American car rental companies, showed her passport and a credit card, and ordered a Jeep Cherokee with GPS.

While the rental agent scanned her computer, Elizabeth checked her phone. Nothing new.

Then a ping.

>Nice escape<

Then,

**>Odda to Tyssedal, 4834 Skjeggedal,
up Hardangerfjord Trail,**

1.8 k to Old Cabin Trail <

The Jeep Cherokee was dark blue with khaki-colored leather interior. Elizabeth settled into the driver's seat and took a few minutes to get the feel of the car. The impulse to quickly text Lars or Nasrin was almost overwhelming, but she forced herself to stay with the fact that Freyja would instantly know if she did. And then what would the crazy bitch do to Max?

Besides, she still didn't know if the directions told her exactly where Freyja was holding Max.

Elizabeth turned the ignition, waited for the GPS to illuminate, selected English and pecked in directions with an index finger. She clicked her seatbelt and slid the SUV out of its stall.

It was 10:30 a.m.

The GPS told her it was a three-hour drive to her destination. She resolved to make better time than that but was grateful for a few quiet hours to think.

Elizabeth had a lifetime of experience working with troubled people. How to get to Freyja before she could harm her son? Assuming she hadn't done something to Max already.

Approach her with a calm mind. Talk to her psyche but don't patronize or beg like you did on the tarmac.

A winning approach would depend on guessing the identity of the psychopath hiding behind the Freyja mask before they met, so Elizabeth would have time to exploit her weaknesses. But who?

Lionel Jacobson? That's what Nasrin thought.

But Elizabeth knew that Freyja was an American.

Sandra Armstrong?

Maybe brain disease had already begun to make her insane. Or Ken Woods? Hard to picture, but not out of the question.

She had forgotten something. Elizabeth pulled over, pulled her smartphone from her pocket and removed the batteries. She put both together in her right front pocket and began to drive again. She was going to do this by the book, Freyja's book, so the goddess would have nothing to hold against her.

The road cut through the outskirts of Bergen. Elizabeth had two lanes to herself, the opposing traffic divided by a greenway. The road moved inland, taking her into highlands and giving her a glimpse of mountains and bright glaciers. It was some of the most scenic land on earth, but it might as well have been a featureless desert.

"Okay," she said out loud, "so I don't know who she is yet, but what do I know?"

Freyja gets her reward from manipulating strong people and breaking them. What's the motivation for doing that? Anger at elites? A desire to humble people who are more successful than she is?

No, this feels like something beyond class envy, though there seems to be an element of that. This is a rage emanating out of a deep wound. Why a goddess? The underlying grievance is spiritual, a metaphysical protest of the ways things are. Deep hurt mixed with disappointment.

Disappointment with what?

Her mind played the angles. Elizabeth debated the points aloud, working through those whose bodies had not been recovered. More likely than not, however, Freyja was someone else, someone she didn't know, a squalid Internet troll who had been at this game for a long time. Elizabeth's eyes and hands controlled the car, freeing her mind to chew on the problem. She was lost in thought while making the prescribed turns around Odda when the GPS told her to do so, gliding up sharp hills and pumping the brakes on the downhills, so that when she finally arrived at Tyssedal in just under 2 hours and 45 minutes, it came as a surprise.

A tourist would be awed by Tyssedal set deep in a fjord, facing a giant plug of a mountain reflected in a serpentine lake of deep blue. On the undulating highlands above were glimpses of alpine forest. There was a concrete arch dam where a helicopter with the royal seal had landed on its roadway. The city had a large smelter of some sort and a hydroelectric plant, but the industrial side of town was offset by plank board homes and churches, all painted bright red.

She had no time for any of it. The GPS led her on the road above town, then down a side road between Tyssedal and an incline that led into Hordaland, a national forest. The GPS told her to make a right onto a gravel road where several other cars were parked at the beginning of a hiking trail.

A sign, "Gamle Hytte Stien."

Elizabeth reinserted her batteries back into her phone and translated it. "Old Cabin Trail."

Elizabeth locked her car and started up the trail, using the phone to track her movements so she would know when she had reached 1.8 kilometers. She periodically checked to see if Freyja or Max had sent her a new message, but there were none.

The trail led through humid lowland forest. As Elizabeth's shoes crackled on the gravel trail she glanced through breaks in the trees at fields of heather and tall hyacinth, purple against the bright green forest floor. She moved in and out of the shade of tall elms and aspens.

The grass glistened with dew. Sunlight transformed spider webs into brilliant filigrees of glow diamonds. On the trail, the sun was harsh in the gaps between the trees. Deep in the forest, Elizabeth could see dark, cooler places, perfect dwellings for trolls and *nisse*.

The incline rose and Elizabeth began to feel winded from the climb. As always, she knew, that if she pressed on her breathing would regularize and she would be in a strong rhythm to move upward with efficiency.

She checked her phone.

She had come 1.2 kilometers in twenty minutes. Almost there.

Her heart began to hammer, not from the climb but from anticipation. Elizabeth would soon come face to face with Freyja and engage in contest of wills to free her son.

Up ahead, she saw movement, a figure passing behind the trees, coming around the bend above her. Another figure. Two millennial hikers emerged on the road above her, a young man with a wispy beard and red bandanna, a young blond woman. Both wore hiking shorts, swinging walking sticks.

They smiled as they approached her. Elizabeth smiled back.

She checked her phone, but it had quit working. She guessed she had come more than 1.5 kilometers.

Elizabeth took to the left side of the trail and walked cautiously toward the bend, which cut to her left. She looked up the trail and around the trees, seeing nothing ... not that she necessarily would. She continued, this time taking the right side of the trail as it wove inward more steeply toward the higher land. She looked up to her right and saw a cabin.

It was back on the left side of the road, where the land rose steadily but not treacherously. She doubled back far enough to where she was sure she would not be seen and crossed the trail into the forest.

Elizabeth again removed the battery from her smartphone and stowed it in her jeans pocket. Moving upward through the forest was not easy. She stepped over mossy rocks that one could slip on, rotting limbs one could trip over. Despite her best efforts, she occasionally stumbled into a bramble and was rewarded with a slap on the face with a sweaty frond and a scratch on a cheek.

The forest was wet and buzzing with fat horseflies that nipped at the corners of her eyes.

Elizabeth walked slowly, stepping carefully to avoid making a sound.

Her plan was simple. She would observe the cabin. Find out who Freyja was and see if she was armed. Locate Max and confirm he was okay. And then she would decide whether to confront Freyja or snap her battery back into her smartphone and call for help.

She would turn the tables.

The old cabin came into view between the trees. Elizabeth crept to the backside of it. The cabin had a small backyard patio with deck chairs that overlooked a clearing with a magnificent view.

Elizabeth moved further around toward the back of the cabin.

She waited and watched, no hurry, concern for her son feeding her patience.

As her eyes adjusted to the harsh sun reflecting off glass windows, she noticed shadows moving inside the cabin. How many people were inside she could not tell.

She heard a screen door yawn open and snap closed.

An older man came bounding around the side of the cabin with an axe slung over one shoulder. He took off his shirt to reveal big shoulders and powerful arm muscles. He had a large, gray mustache. The man picked up a birch log, set it upright on a chopping block and split it neat.

He cast the two pieces to the side, picked up another log and split it. He split another. He bent over to roll the logs into his strong arms and against his chest and turned toward the entrance of the cabin.

The man stopped. He turned around. He looked out at the trees, observant, as if he had caught a glimpse of someone in the forest.

Elizabeth froze, hoping the shadows and greenery would mask her.

The man shrugged and turned and made a graceful dip to retrieve his shirt with a finger, while balancing the thinned logs. It wasn't until he was almost gone that Elizabeth realized that she had been watching George.

TWENTY-EIGHT

She retreated further into the forest and found a fallen tree to sit on.

It made sense, in a way. In their last therapy session, George had revealed darkness in his life, the end of his marriage and loss of custody of his two daughters … the breakdown he suffered under the threats of a sociopathic killer.

Still … George?

If George was Freyja that meant he had humored her the first time she had taken DMT, sitting with her in the park, pretending to be concerned about her taking a narcotic that he had sent her.

If George was Freyja, that meant that the second time he had given her a triple dose of DMT.

If George was Freyja his claim to authorship of the paper would have him writing about himself, an act of recursive insanity.

If George was Freyja, he had used all his skill and knowledge of the human psyche to lure seven people to their deaths.

If George was Freyja, he might have used a shotgun to blow the top off of Everett Walleen's head and chased Thor to his death.

If George was Freyja, he was holding her son hostage in a cabin in the middle of Norway.

Elizabeth could not believe any of that. But then she had not recognized the George she had just seen, shirtless, with a frenzied expression as he swung the axe. And why else would he be here?

There was an upside. She could not believe that George would hurt her. She could not imagine George harming Max. This was a cry for help. She would talk him down with gentleness. The mentor would become the patient.

Elizabeth walked out of the forest, along the side of the cabin. She wanted to learn as much as she could before George saw her. She glanced in a window and saw movement again, the forms of several people, and heard a murmur of conversation.

There was nothing to do now but go straight in. Elizabeth walked up the frail wooden steps, the sound of her feet on hollow wood now unmistakably heard by anyone inside. She gave the door three hard knocks, slowly turned the handle and swung the door open.

In front of her, Karl Pedersen leaned against a long wooden table, a toothpick twirling from one side of his mouth to the other.

"Good to see you again, *mia cara*," Karl said.

The black leather belt of a holster crossed his chest, clasping a small black pistol to his hip.

"You are looking truly magnificent today."

Elizabeth stepped backward, tripped on the front steps and fell flat on her backside. She pulled herself up on her elbows and looked for the best direction to run.

"Relax," Nasrin said, stepping outside. "All is well. Karl is not in a particularly rapey mood this afternoon."

Elizabeth rose, crouching, still ready to run.

Nasrin leaned over her smiling.

"Besides, I'd have the drop on him anyway," she said and pointed to the dainty side holster on her belt that held her 'Lady Glock.' "Come inside. George has started a fire to brew us all some tea."

———————————

"It makes my heart glad to see you again," George said to Elizabeth, buttoning the last button on his shirt. "I know you've been through quite an ordeal this morning."

A kettle popped and clanged and finally whistled. George lifted it from the top of the old wood-burning iron stove. Elizabeth looked around at the crude, wooden structure. She could make out enough cognates in a plaque to see that it had been built by park service volunteers for the Norwegian Guide and Scout Association. The wooden walls were gnarled and a weathered gray, as if the structure had been constructed from driftwood.

Elizabeth cast a wary glance at Karl, who sat on a wooden bench opposite her on a long bench against a well-worn pine table.

"Care to tell me what is going on?" Elizabeth asked.

Nasrin retrieved old cups in a cupboard. She washed them out with water from a canteen and set them out.

"The park service does a pretty good job stocking this place," Nasrin said as George poured tea in each cup. "But I'm afraid there is no sugar."

"Damn it," Karl said. "I like sugar."

"Mind telling me what the fuck is going on?"

"Very well," Nasrin said, sitting next to Karl, while George put the kettle on the cool side of the stove. "Let's step out back, why don't we?"

Three Adirondack-style wooden chairs sat on the rock and concrete patio. There was a grill and cooking pit to the side.

"Have a seat," Nasrin said. "You look thoroughly knackered."

Nasrin handed Elizabeth a cup of tea. They all took seats except for Karl, who paced behind them.

The view opened over Tyssedal and a lake, Ringedalsvatnet. Afternoon sun beat down on cliffs opposite them and made the navy-blue water sparkle. It had to be 2 p.m. already.

"I had secured us some of these," Nasrin said, waving a cellphone with an antenna as wide as Elizabeth's thumb.

She pushed a button and Elizabeth heard the tune of an auto dial.

A man's voice answered. Lars.

"She's here," Nasrin said, "only a little worse for the wear."

Nasrin listened, nodded at what sounded only like murmurings to Elizabeth.

"We shall, thank you." Nasrin pushed the off button.

"Sat phone, new Inmarsat model straight from GCHQ, encryption most nation-states couldn't beat," Nasrin said. "We shared these around PIG the day you left. We also kept your devices under surveillance, Elizabeth, so Ingrid picked up all your messages from Freyja soon as you did. Within half an hour, Lars had us all on a helicopter that shot us from Oslo to land on that hydroelectric dam in Tyssedal. We were on a Land Rover up here before you even left the Bergen Airport in your rental. Fancy moves, by the way. I bet Charlie will get reamed out by Langley for that."

"And Max?"

Nasrin chuckled and smiled.

"Elizabeth," George said. "Max is fine. He always has been. He has not left the United States."

"I don't understand."

"You never actually spoke with Max, did you?" Nasrin asked. "Freyja just took control of his devices to trick you into coming here. She knows his diction, his verbal ticks, even his nickname for you—Lizzie."

"Max is okay?"

"A pair of FBI agents checked in on him at Rutgers. They were amused at the clumsy way he tried to distract them from the bong in his living room."

"Oh God."

Elizabeth cradled her face in her hands, her cup fell and shattered on the stones. It all came out at once, racking sobs, all the day's terror and stress. Nasrin went inside and returned with picnic napkins.

"Oh that changes everything." Elizabeth wiped the corners of her eyes and blew her nose. "Oh thank God."

"And Karl?" Elizabeth asked, not looking at him, just at Nasrin, who had returned to her chair. She was leaning close, one hand on Elizabeth's shoulder.

"Karl is working for me now," Nasrin said.

"It is okay for him to have a gun?"

"I am glad he does," Nasrin said.

"Were there signs Freyja had been here?"

"Come inside," Karl said.

Elizabeth pulled herself up and reluctantly followed Karl Pedersen alone into the cabin. Karl pointed to a narrow strip of wall. "Just that."

A white sheet of paper hung from a nail next to the door. A laser-printed note in large, black font read, "Elizabeth: Take the Trolltunga trail up to the rock." The signature, "Freyja," was in the same black font.

On the floor below were a new pair of hiking boots with thick, waterproof socks. A canteen leaned against one of the boots. Elizabeth was certain the fit of the boots would be perfect.

Karl stared at her, saying nothing, as if he expected her to tell him something. He slowly pulled a flask from his back pocket and poured gin into his tea and then smiled at her. Elizabeth went back outside to sit by Nasrin again.

"Are you sure Freyja did not see you come up here?"

"Lars, Dahl and a gaggle of young rangers were first up with binoculars and rifles. They scouted the cabin and the area and determined that there was no one around except for a few legitimate hikers. They secured the cabin and found no devices left behind by Freyja."

"So this was another one of her ruses?"

"We don't think so," George said. "We're pretty confident she is up at Trolltunga."

"Troll what?"

"The Troll's tongue," Karl said. He had followed Elizabeth back outside. He slurped his teacup full of gin. "A high precipice much like Preikestolen. If you take a side road off this trail up from here, you hit the main trail up to Trolltunga, a good three-hour hike if we go all out."

"The rangers are cordoning off all the trails and scouting the forest," Nasrin said. "Rangers in plainclothes have already gone to the top to identify every hiker and tell them that a criminal is loose and to come down and call if they see anything or anyone unusual."

"So Lars and the rangers will tighten the noose?"

"No," Karl said. "They are leaving Freyja no avenue of escape. Nasrin and I, we're the noose."

Nasrin shook her head, irritated with Karl's lack of discretion. She turned to Elizabeth.

"George and I are delighted to see you so well and to give you the good news about Max," Nasrin said. "But you are a complication, a civilian complication. You will go back down and wait for the police in Tyssedal."

"George is also a civilian," she said. "Why is he with you?"

"He's still on PIG, you are not. Besides, he's here to assess anything we could have learned from the cabin, not go up with us to confront Freyja."

"You need me," Elizabeth said. "I am the only one here who has held conversations with Freyja. I know her like no one else."

"You can't come up with us."

"I could go up, help with negotiations if needed," George said.

"You're strong, George, but I think you'd find the climb too much for a man your age," Elizabeth said.

"I could outrun any of you," he said. "No, I think I see what's going on. The implications of your unfolding plan are becoming clear to me. If Freyja can be talked down, we have a legal and moral obligation to do that."

"Very well," Nasrin said. "So if we do need a negotiator shrink, which I hope we don't, then I choose Elizabeth."

"Choose me," George said.

"Elizabeth is right, she knows Freyja like no one else," Nasrin said. "And besides, you really would find the mountain to be too much."

George went to make himself another tea, sulking in the corner by the stove.

Elizabeth didn't wait. She laced up her shoes and poured water from a plastic jug into her canteen and stopped cold.

"What if Freyja laced my canteen with DMT or something?"

"Good point," Nasrin said. "Leave it and you can drink from mine."

She turned to George. "What will you do?"

"I suppose I shall have to trudge back to Tyssedal and use my analytical skills to locate the best place for lunch."

Nasrin nodded and stepped outside, joining Karl, who had already laced up and was scanning the scenery as if the enemy could be watching them.

"You thought I was Freyja, didn't you?" George asked.

"George ... when I saw you up here, such a shock ..."

"Well, I suppose you have every reason to feel disoriented by what has happened. It has been a hell of a day, and it's only two o'clock in the afternoon."

He walked across the cabin and wrapped strong arms around Elizabeth.

"Come back to me."

He kissed her forehead.

Elizabeth nodded and stepped outside. She followed Karl and Nasrin as they set off on the upward trail. After a ten minute climb they came to a spur that opened to a narrow trail cutting deep into the woods. Nasrin and Karl consulted a map on the digital display of the sat phone and decided it was the correct path.

The climb was steep. Elizabeth again felt her breathing slip out of control and regularize. After a good hour of climbing a steep trail through more dense, humid forest, Elizabeth reached out and touched Nasrin lightly on the wrist. They slowed a bit, letting Karl bound forward out of earshot.

"Explain Karl," Elizabeth asked.

"He escaped because the Russian Night Wolves had put a contract out on him," Nasrin said. "He is clearly not Freyja. He had simply been contacted by Freyja, who tried to play her games with him, which is why his devices were linked to hers. He contacted me and we made a deal."

"What kind of deal?"

The trail rose sharply. After ten minutes of silent effort, they came to a cliff, the trail now a thin ledge overlooking a forested valley a good five hundred feet below. The ledge was covered with slate, slippery from algae and runoff.

The three of them focused on their footfalls. The trail widened and they relaxed.

"It will be late in the day when we get up there," Elizabeth said. "How are we getting back down?"

"There is an old funicular," Nasrin said. "Lars' people think they can get it running again. If not, rangers will meet us and we'll be sleeping in tents tonight."

The ledge widened into a trail, and the trail came to a wide meadow. The forest was boreal, thinner, the grass high and tall with only a few flowers. Karl was still well ahead of them, walking fast to a beat only he could hear.

"So tell me, what kind of deal?"

Nasrin's cheek twitched.

"This whole episode is an embarrassment for both countries. And Lars' career is on the line. He doesn't want a trial. He doesn't want Freyja's methods sorted out there in the press for terrorists or other lunatics to pick up. This country has suffered quite a bit from such people."

"And so Karl shoots Freyja."

"Your words, not mine, Doctor Browne."

"But you couldn't condone ..."

"In my current line of work, I've learned to condone a lot of things I never would have before."

"Then what happens to Karl? Now he has an escape record and a murder rap. I know he hates Freyja, but why would he do that?"

"Did he escape, or was he released for cooperation?" Nasrin

asked.

"Even in Norway, some crimes are considered serious, like murder."

"For smoking a non-existent fairy goddess?"

"There will be a body, an identity."

"And an explanation."

"Then what will you do with Karl?"

"He'll have his uses."

"Uses?"

"In other, less refined parts of the world."

"And you think MI6 can control him?"

"We think he can be of use."

"Because you backed him down, right, in my room? Now you think you own him because you're his alpha."

"My knowledge of people doesn't come from a couch and a pad."

"It won't work Nasrin. He's a psychopath. He'll wind up owning you all."

Nasrin cracked a smile.

"Assuming we don't get up there and find that he's Freyja after all," Nasrin said. "And we've just given him a gun."

"You're pretty causal about all of this."

"You have to be a good sport, or it doesn't work."

The trail took a sharp descent by a small lake surrounded by mountains. In the distance were several small cabins, emergency shelters for winter hikers. Elizabeth's calves felt sore and hot. It was a relief to be walking downhill, but it didn't last. The trail rose again, promising a harder climb ahead.

"Let's stop a moment and replenish," Nasrin said.

Karl and Nasrin pulled out ham and cheese sandwiches in plastic wrap and chocolate bars. Nasrin tore her sandwich in half and threw the slices of ham in the tall grass. Something out here would have a feast. Elizabeth ate too quickly and had to swallow precious canteen water to wash it down.

"Here," Karl said, handing Elizabeth his chocolate bar, "you can have the rest of mine."

She took it and ate the whole thing without guilt. She would need the calories.

The trail led them through a wide, muddy pasture. The trail rose again, steep climbs followed by short dips, and steep climbs again. Through the trees, Elizabeth caught glimpses of mountains and a winding lake stretching to the horizon. She felt small against the inhuman, geologic scale of the summits and the sky.

Elizabeth had become so fixated on the scenery breaking through the trees that she was late to notice a man with a rifle stepping out on the trail.

He was a ranger, a blonde beast no older than 25.

"We have activity," he said.

"How close?" Nasrin asked.

"Just off the trail, several sightings of someone carrying a handgun."

"What's the plan?" she asked.

"The Chief Inspector believes this is our suspect. He has ordered us to sweep the area."

Karl banged his fist against a thigh. "So we are to go down, after all this!"

"No," the ranger said. "The Chief Inspector judges it too dangerous for you to stay here or go back. Trolltunga is just ahead. It is the most defensible area around here. You are to take a secure position and hold out there until it is safe."

"On a bloody rock jutting out into space?"

"It is a clear area. No one can approach you without being seen."

"Very well, then," Nasrin said. "We have our marching orders. Literally."

"I will secure your flank," the young ranger said as they began to move.

"Secure your own bloody flank."

They wove around boulders in the trail, some the size of medicine balls, some the size of small cars. The leaves of the thinning forest shivered in the wind. Elizabeth caught more flashes of blue sky and white glacier.

The trail cut back into the forest and split into two trails that cut around a wall of rock that rose a good twenty meters above them.

"We should separate," Nasrin said to Karl.

"Doesn't sound like a good idea," Elizabeth said.

"We're just behind the ledge," Nasrin said. "If Freyja's around here, we can clear both sides before joining on the other side at

Trolltunga."

Karl pulled his gun and thumbed the safety. Elizabeth had scant experience with guns, but by now she could recognize the kind of pistol Nasrin used.

"I thought that was a lady's gun?"

"Nasrin has convinced me of its virtues. It is light and easy to handle."

"I'll see you on the other side," Nasrin said.

Karl began to move away. His pace was slow, deliberate, gun out.

Nasrin took the same stance. Elizabeth crept behind her through the forest for ten minutes. There was a high rock wall to edge around. And then they were there.

A series of ledges rolled down to Trolltunga like a shattered staircase. The formation itself would be called a tongue in any language on earth, an elongated rock slab about 70 feet in length that curled slightly upward and narrowed to a rounded tip. Beyond it, an ice-blue lake cut through a canyon with high, gray cliffs. The tops of the mountains below them were flat, covered with black moraine streaked with ice.

"We're two thousand, three hundred feet above the lake," Nasrin said. "Ringesdalsvatnet, I think."

Elizabeth looked up at the dark blue sky and down at the fjordlands. It was a mistake. She wavered from vertigo and was forced to squat.

"But no Freyja," Nasrin said.

Nasrin sat on a ledge of rock at the last of the staircase, at the base of the tongue. She set her small backpack by her feet and rested her gun in her lap. The wind was uncomfortably strong, giving Elizabeth the same feeling she had felt at Preikestolen, that the wind might catch her and sweep her into space.

"Water?"

Nasrin handed her canteen to Elizabeth. It felt light.

"It's almost dry."

"I'm fine, take the last of it."

Elizabeth did.

"Where's Karl?"

"Good question," Nasrin said. She pulled her sat phone from her backpack and hit auto dial and held it up to her ear. No answer.

"I don't like this," she said.

"Maybe Karl's had second thoughts about being in your service," Elizabeth said. "Maybe he's halfway to the border."

"He wouldn't do that, we've offered him too much," Nasrin said. "And besides, if he were going to go solo, he wouldn't do it on a bloody mountain that takes hours to get off and is surrounded by police."

"Okay."

Elizabeth scooted closer to Nasrin. It was silly, but it made her feel anchored against the wind.

Ten minutes passed and Nasrin hit the autodial again. No answer.

She waited a few more minutes and tried again. No answer.

"I've got to go," Nasrin said, rising, her gun out now, safety off.

"Why don't you just wait here like we've been told?"

"Karl may be a nasty piece of work, but he's my Joe now," Nasrin said. "I have to see about him."

"Do you have an extra gun for me?"

"No."

"Then I am coming with you."

"You are safer here."

"Not without a gun."

Elizabeth was afraid of the forest, but she was even more afraid of being thrown off the Troll's Tongue.

"Stay behind me," Nasrin said. "And if you hear any shooting, I want you to fly away in a running crouch down the trail and not stop running until you see an armed ranger. Got it?"

"Got it."

They went around the wall of rock that separated the two trails, rounding the opposite side from where they had arrived. Soon they were again in the shade of the high forest.

Nasrin stepped lightly, gun outstretched, head turning rhythmically, eyes scanning for a flash of color or movement. Perhaps the greatest danger, Elizabeth realized, is that Nasrin and Karl would shoot each other. She hoped they were each alert to the danger of friendly fire.

Nasrin gingerly rolled around a large boulder and stepped over a deep puddle in the middle of the trail. Elizabeth followed.

"Karl?" Nasrin had not shouted, but her voice was loud and firm.

"Karl?"

They descended for another minute and Elizabeth saw Karl, leaning causally against a tree, looking as if he had just had a pleasant smoke.

It was a typically insolent Karl gesture. He was standing upright, arms relaxed at his side, looking straight ahead as if he had not a care in the world.

Nasrin went into a crouch, pacing around to scan the forest in all directions, arms extended, the Glock now clutched in both hands.

The realization did not come to Elizabeth all at once. It developed like a photo in a chemical tray as they closed in on him and Elizabeth saw that Karl's eyes were wide and unblinking. A silver thread cut into his throat, holding his body upright.

Karl's expression showed no remnant of the agony of strangulation, just an intense stare, as if he were looking in the distance for help. Midges danced inside his half-opened mouth. His Glock rested on an exposed root at his feet.

The silver thread ran around a small birch tree behind him, a bowstring of steel with a crossing knot and two rubber handles.

Nasrin kept her posture, gun sweeping the forest, as she methodically wound her way around Karl and tree. The need to stay within Nasrin's perimeter forced Elizabeth uncomfortably close to the body.

"Reach into my backpack and pull the sat phone."

The fat antenna made it easy to find.

"Call Lars."

Elizabeth went to "recent calls" and touched the number. Lars answered.

While Elizabeth held the phone on speaker, Nasrin explained what had happened in clear, unemotional terms.

"It will be a half an hour before we can be there," Lars said. "At least."

"We're going back to the ledge," Nasrin said. "You're right, it is the most defensible."

"The trail back will highlight you as a target," Lars said.

"I know," Nasrin replied. "We will shadow it in the forest."

"Is Elizabeth with you?"

"Yes."

"Please take care of her. And yourself."

"Deal." Nasrin ended the call and handed the phone back to Elizabeth. "Keep a finger on auto dial. Stay behind me. I will need to continue to circle around you to see."

"I know who it is."

Nasrin continued to scan the forest. It took her a moment to process what Elizabeth was saying.

"You mean Freyja?"

Elizabeth told her.

Nasrin bit her lip in concentration as she continued to look around.

"Shit, that is bad news. I have to admit, it makes sense. Whoever Freyja is, she or he had better keep some distance. I'm ready to send that tosser to Valhalla."

"Fólkvangr."

"Can we agree on hell?"

Elizabeth looked down at the sat phone.

"How do I get an open line?"

Nasrin told her.

Elizabeth punched in the country code for the United States and directory assistance.

"Keep looking out, I need a few minutes on the phone before we start back."

TWENTY-NINE

The return trip took twice as long. They followed the trail from a good twenty feet to the side, stepping over branches and rocks and fallen trees. Nasrin was not able to orbit Elizabeth as she had planned, so every minute or so she would stop to perform a slow pivot to scan the forest.

Elizabeth tripped over a root and landed on her side. Nasrin stood over her protectively, continuing to scan.

After a good twenty minutes of climbing they returned to the back wall. There was a short distance now to the top, the trail leading between the rock face and a large boulder. It would be easy for someone to hide on either side, waiting to ambush them.

They crept to the trail and moved upward as quietly as they could. Elizabeth clutched the sat phone in her left hand and Karl's Glock in her right.

She looked down at the gun and thumbed the safety. She had shot a pistol once before, at a shooting range with her father and brother.

Could that have been a quarter-century ago?

They were now close to the walkway between the rocks that opened to Trolltunga. Nasrin moved quickly now along the side of the trail, gun out, checking around the sides of the rock while Elizabeth swept the forest with her right hand, not confident at all in her ability to spot and shoot someone, feeling like an actor with a toy gun in a police drama.

"Clear," Nasrin said.

They crossed between the rocks and out into the late afternoon sunlight of Trolltunga.

Not a soul.

"We'll take a position at the base of the rock. Lars and company will be here soon. Everything is open, no one would dare to step out into our line of fire, not even a god."

They walked backwards carefully over the irregular face of the rock toward the stone ledge, guns still out. Elizabeth stepped over the last ledge and sat down, cross legged, at the base of Trolltunga. Nasrin joined her.

They relaxed and rested their guns on the edge of their laps, barrels pointing outward. There was nothing behind them but rock and infinite space. No one could come close to them now.

"Hand me that." Elizabeth passed the sat phone to Nasrin, who hit a button to make a report to Lars. His voice was strained from the exertion of quick movement uphill.

"It is taking us longer than expected," Lars said. "It will take us another twenty minutes."

"That is not a problem," Nasrin replied. "We are safe now."

Nasrin handed the phone back to Elizabeth, who held it in one hand. It was in truth the only weapon she knew how to use.

Elizabeth redialed the phone and connected again to the same number in the United States.

"Please stand by, we may need you soon."

She pushed the off button.

"Well, love, it's been quite a ride now, hasn't it?"

"Yes," Elizabeth said. "But frankly, from the moment I knew Max was okay, nothing has seemed quite as frightening."

"Of course. I want to meet this little man of yours. Would I like him?"

"Let's just say he's a unique individual."

"Are you looking forward to getting back home?"

"Yes. I've had quite enough of this, whatever this is. And you?"

"I live such a peripatetic life, I've forgotten what home feels like. London is more like a refueling station for me, though I do miss my mum."

The wind was strong, but Elizabeth felt safe sitting so low on the ground.

"Horrible thing done to Karl," Elizabeth said. "Although I can't feel sorry that he is gone."

"I will give you that, the world is safer place. What about Lars? You will be seeing him again, soon."

"Lars and I are done. He didn't even come by to see me in the hospital."

"He is part asshole," Nasrin said.

"You're part asshole."

Nasrin laughed.

"I guess it's an occupational hazard. When Lars gets up here, we'll reveal our theory about Freyja and they can put out an APW."

"A what?"

"An All Ports Warning. Before I got into this life, as a young policewoman in Manchester I went into service determined to—"

Nasrin puffed out as if someone had slapped her on the back and knocked all the air out of her lungs.

Her arms went wide, hands tremoring like felled doves. She looked down with astonishment at a silver cylinder that had appeared in the center of her chest. Elizabeth turned and saw the rest of the arrow sticking out of Nasrin's back, the steel of the shaft and fletching shining in the sunlight.

Elizabeth screamed.

Nasrin clasped Elizabeth's forearm and gripped tight, eyes wide with terror and pleading. She tried to speak but could only make a gurgling sound. A splash of blood, bright and red, gushed out her mouth and onto her shirt. Nasrin's whole body shuddered and her eyes rolled up. Her body dropped backwards on the arrow, which jammed straight up from the rock to hold her in a grotesque arch, head back, arms dangling like discarded puppet.

Elizabeth screamed again.

Gravity slowly forced the tip of the arrow to fully emerge as Nasrin slid down the shaft, until the fletching halted her movement. She made a final groaning noise as her lungs collapsed.

Elizabeth closed her eyes and spoke to herself … calm mind, be strong, speak to the psyche. She turned her head slowly and saw him with both feet confidently planted at the tip of the Troll's Tongue.

"How … how … how did you?"

"Easy peasy," Daryl Parnell said. "A little top roping around the edge, that's all. Learned it in a stint with the 10th Mountain Division. These rocks are nothing compared to some of the hairy inclines I encountered in Afghanistan. I'm going to miss Nasrin Jones. Quite an impressive gal, that one."

Daryl was dressed in a form-fitting, two-piece undersuit, half of it in camo colors and the rest in dark brown. He wore green gloves, one hand gripping a thin bow of black carbon, the other hand clasping another metal arrow glinting in the sunlight.

"I'd like to see your gun go over the side, if you please."

Elizabeth lifted the gun off her leg and knew that she could not possibly fully turn, aim and shoot Daryl Parnell before he put an arrow through her chest. But if she didn't shoot him he'd throw her off the side.

Nasrin had said it was 2,300 feet down, about half a mile.

Where Daryl stood, a good thirty feet from her, the rock was barely a yard wide and a slight incline up, as if the stone tongue were licking a giant ice cream cone. From where Elizabeth sat, she had a good ten feet of clearance on either side.

The urge to run toward the trail, to Lars and the others, to go home to Max, was an urgent, physical desire.

Elizabeth stood, faced Daryl and hurled the gun over the side, just as he had asked.

He was a little squatter and more compact than Elizabeth had pictured him, and a little grayer now. But he had the same strong, stubbled jaw, the same friendly looking cast about the eyes. He had the body of a man who spends several hours every day in the gym. He rested the arrow on the cable of his bow and motioned for Elizabeth to come forward.

She had no choice, so she did, taking the phone with her.

Everything now fit. Daryl Parnell had been a Rhodes Scholar finalist at VMI, an English major who would have acquired a love of Norse myth and literature. As colloquial and Southern as he was, he had the education to easily shift to the elevated, womanly diction of Freyja.

He had also been Special Forces with combat decorations from Kosovo, Iraq, Afghanistan, and likely other places not recorded in his bio. He had finished his career in SIGNIT, where he would have acquired a sophisticated understanding of cyberwar, which included Internet hacking and the darker uses of social media and psychological warfare.

"Why the binaural beat?"

"Something I was inspired to create by old CIA mind experiments. I had a high clearance level for classified material, back in the day."

"And the DMT?"

"It loosens the mind, makes even strong-willed people suggestible. I found a kid in Oslo who can make it into pill form."

Daryl threw the bow and arrow on the ground with the indifference of a god. He stepped forward to meet Elizabeth five feet from the tip of the tongue. He unclipped a backpack, pulled it around and let it fall to the ground between them.

The wind rustled her hair, making it wave and flutter in her eyes. The wind caught Daryl's odor. He stank of exertion and sweat.

"Are you going to kill me now?"

"You don't have to die today, Elizabeth, not if you are brave. Unzip the bag."

Elizabeth again wanted to turn and run but knew she couldn't outrun him. She bent down and unzipped the backpack. There was a canteen inside, crampons and two yellow suits.

"Pull them out."

She did. The suits were complicated, a stitch work of advanced synthetic material with many Velcro straps, metal rings and zippers.

"These are wing suits?"

"Elizabeth, my dear, would you care to join me for a little afternoon ride?"

"This is how you …?"

"Yes," he said. "Without a parachute, no less."

"How is that possible?"

"A wingsuit landing has only been done once before, and it wasn't into water. A brave—or foolhardy—man landed safely into 18,000 empty cardboard boxes set up to cushion his fall. I was the second to attempt it, and the world's first and only water lander. You see, Elizabeth, the hardest part for me was not maintaining control down to the ground. It was leveling off and hitting the water at a precise angle so that I would skip like a stone, losing energy without breaking a bone."

"Halo," Elizabeth said aloud, remembering the word Thor had jotted down on his note. She had guessed it was some ironic reference to saints or imagery from Norse gods.

"That's right," Daryl said. "High Altitude Low Opening, one of the more poetic acronyms of our military."

"And the others who jumped knew you were going to do this?" she asked.

"I told them the truth about my odds. I had extensive HALO training and had done a wingsuit a couple of times with a parachute. I told them my chance of survival was about one in a hundred. I plunged straight down the cliff as the others rolled and screamed. I pulled up over the rocks and shot straight out into the fjord. That was the moment, if I had packed a parachute, that I would have cobraed up and pulled the ripcord. I improvised. I did spiral turns, cresting and falling, losing altitude, getting a little burbled now and then, but keeping steady. As I came in just over a hundred feet, I felt calm, assured, gliding over the face of the waters."

Elizabeth noted the Biblical resonance in his choice of words.

"I squeezed my butt cheeks and stretched my elevators between my feet and leveled out just close enough to almost feel the wetness of the lake on my face. I trailed the toes of my booties in the water for just an instant, pulled up, leveled off, and did it again. And again, until I had bled enough speed to go into the drink bruised but not broken. I kicked off my heavy booties, swam to a trail head and that's that."

"And if you had died?"

"I am ready to die—will die—soon. So why not make it interesting? I was wrong about my odds, though. On that day, it was more like one in ten. I give myself one in five today. I give you about one in ten thousand."

Elizabeth took a step back.

"On the plus side, you do have some training. You know how to feather, how to pivot, how to make a graceful descent."

"In a small chamber, ten feet above soft material."

"Still, it's less certain than this Ruger." Daryl produced a small pistol out of his backpack.

Lars was coming. Elizabeth had to slow this down.

"That was a dirty trick you played on me with Max."

"I could continue to mess with Max, but I don't like shooting fish in a barrel. Now that would be really dirty."

"You went to dinner with them—Lionel, Sandra, Ken, the others. Did you ever tell them that you were Freyja?"

"No, they believed me to be a fellow seeker, that's all. Which I am, of sorts."

"Why did Lionel Jacobson kill himself?"

"I see what you're doing. But I'll give you the quick answer. Because Lionel was about to be revealed as a plagiarist in a countersuit by his Hollywood enemies. They discovered that the play that had made him famous was an unpublished work his professor lover had toyed with for years. That's why none of Lionel's subsequent plays quite measured up. He could bear almost anything except that particular form of disgrace. Time to suit up."

"You think you can get me to jump?"

Daryl's head cocked in a quizzical manner.

"I'm not sure. You see, that's the interesting part, the point of our little experiment, Elizabeth. Which will you choose, certain but painless death with a bullet to the head or a brave leap into the void with a microscopic chance that your amateur skills will put you in the record books for all time?"

"With you gloating over me all the way down."

"Take this suit." He handed her the smaller of the two suits. "Strip down to your undies."

Elizabeth slowly pulled off her shirt, yanked off her hiking boots and her socks.

"Pants."

She stepped out of her jeans. She was now standing on a platform in the sky wearing a T-shirt and panties rippling in the wind.

"I've already attached our suits to their main rigs, so we have very little to do. Lay out your suit and sit down at the top end."

Elizabeth wanted to let the wind catch the suit and take it away from her, but she knew that would mean a bullet to the brain. If she took her time, Lars might come.

She sat down and inserted her feet into the suit. The fabric was smooth, light, insubstantial. Her torso was to be her fuselage, with her head as nose, hands as ailerons, feet as rudders. The fabric between her arms would be her wings, and the fabric between her legs her elevators.

She felt as if she could repeat those terms, it might make all the pieces work together.

Daryl set out the other suit and sat down, gun next to him on the rock.

If Lars did not come soon, Elizabeth had only one move she could think of, one tiny chance to slow Daryl down, maybe stop him cold, if he didn't shoot her first.

"Pull all the way through, like this, until your feet stick out …

Good. Pull the suit up and now stand.”

He stood and she stood.

“Now thread your arms through the harness.”

She did as he did.

“Fasten your leg straps like this.”

She fastened the straps and squeezed the clamps hard.

“Fasten your chest straps, tight, hard on the buckle.”

Elizabeth watched him closely, intently, trying to get it right.

“Pull on the main zipper, all the way up.”

She did it.

“Slip on your booties and zip the ankle grips around them.”

She mimicked his actions.

Daryl tucked his pistol in the belt of his suit to check her suit. He zipped a zipper that went up her arms. He checked her up and down, pulling hard on all her straps, zips and handles, testing them.

“Slip on your gloves and we’re good to go.”

Daryl stretched his arms and spread his legs to show her his wings.

“See, there’s a carbon grip here by your hand. You’ll want to hold on to that for dear life.”

“All you want, Daryl, is to trick me into committing suicide in front of you.”

“The choice is yours. Quick, painless and certain, or terrifying and just barely possible, Elizabeth, but possible.”

“Why?”

“To challenge your fear. To see what you’re made of.”

“And you think you can get away?”

“If I heave everything over the side, you included and make it to the shore alive, yes, no one will be the wiser.”

The wind ruffled the rills of Elizabeth’s suit, pushing her toward the edge. As she righted herself, she knew this was the moment. She drew in a breath and bent over to press a button on the sat phone. She hit speaker and it began to ring.

“Turn that thing off,” he said, thrusting the gun toward her face.

“Daddy?”

Daryl stiffened, paralyzed by indecision.

It was a young woman’s voice. Elizabeth hit another button and Stacie Parnell appeared, barely visible in the late afternoon sunlight against the little screen. Elizabeth held her arm out straight so Daryl could see his daughter and she could see him. She knew from the last call what Daryl was seeing—a young woman, now, thin and pretty, hair shaved on one side of her head, a delicate nose ring and a small Chinese symbol tattooed on the side of her slender neck. Behind her would be a patio door that revealed an apartment complex and a swimming pool.

It was already morning in Silver Lake, California.

"Daddy?"

Daryl's eyes went wild. He looked from side to side, seeking escape.

"Oh my God, Elizabeth, what have you done to me?"

"Daddy, this lady, this doctor, tells me that you're in trouble."

"Stacie, no honey, no, there's nothing like that."

"Is that a gun?"

He tucked it back in his suit.

"Where are you? I see mountains. Is that a cliff? What are you wearing?"

"Stacie, love, I'm just doing some jumping, like I did in the Army."

"From what the doctor told me, I worry that you might kill yourself. Come home. We're still family. I miss you now."

"Stacie darling, I just … it's not, it's not …"

Daryl's eyes welled up.

"She says you're in Europe? Is that Switzerland?"

"I am traveling."

"Come home, Daddy."

His mouth curled down, his face reddened and he began to sob.

"I can't darling. Daddy can't."

"Come home."

"I'm sorry."

"Come home."

"So, so sorry, about all that's happened to us. I love you."

Daryl went silent. He had nothing else to say to his daughter. He reached out and swatted the phone from Elizabeth's hands. It rattled across the rocks and went over the edge. He pulled his gun again. His jaw clenched, face like a knotted fist.

"Now or die."

His tight expression squeezed tears into deep creases around his eyes.

"Listen to you daughter."

"Count of three."

"Okay, which edge is best?"

Daryl pointed to the left-hand side of the tip of the tongue.

"Some last advice." Daryl's voice was a croak. "You're going to want to spread out immediately. You will plunge at first, straight down, but try to keep your eyes on the horizon and bow your body, pulling hard up like a cobra to try to level off."

"And then what?"

"You know as much now as you'll ever know."

Elizabeth stepped back a good dozen feet from the edge and went into a crouch, preparing to sprint to the tip and dive head first.

"One," he said, aiming the pistol at her.

She calmed her mind, focused on her breathing. This was the end of her life, but she was doing something brave. She was doing it for Max. She would choose the fall because that would give her at least a tiny chance to see her son again. To accept the bullet would be to accept suicide. Somehow, she hoped Max would know that.

"Two."

Daryl fired into the sky. The report of the pistol made her whole body flinch.

"Three."

"I'm going. I'm doing it. Let them know I did it for Max."

"Go now or die now."

He stretched his arm and aimed the pistol at her, smiled through his tears and spoke.

"If you make me shoot you, I promise to do it in the side of your head. Small caliber. You will still be pretty."

Elizabeth puffed several short breaths and began to sprint toward the cliff.

A rifle shot, behind her. She fell flat, skittering and scraping hard across the rocks, a few feet from the edge. She looked up and saw Daryl running. He spread his arms and soared out over the fjord at the same instant as a second report boomed from the rifle.

Daryl plunged out of sight.

Lars, Lieutenant Dahl, Agent Norris and half-a-dozen rangers ran around Nasrin's body and out onto the rock.

Lars pulled Elizabeth up. Her suit was shredded in front, streaks of blood where the scrape had gone through to bare stomach.

"Are you wounded?"

"We've got to see," Elizabeth said, moving toward the tip in a crouch.

She crept toward the edge on all fours, then scooted up to it. Elizabeth looked out over the fjord and felt a flash of vertigo terror. Wearing this suit, the wind could truly take her over the edge. Lars laid down next to her. She grabbed Lars by the belt and held on tight.

Lieutenant Dahl scanned the rocks below but saw no one. Lars whipped out a small pair of binoculars.

"Five o'clock."

Elizabeth looked to where Lars was pointing.

A yellow mote shot out over the lake. It slowed, pivoted and made a downturn and plunged, righted, and plunged again. The mote was attempting a wide corkscrew spiral but kept losing control and cutting inward.

"He's in trouble," Elizabeth said.

"I think I blew a hole in his right wing," Lars said.

Lieutenant Dahl handed Elizabeth a pair of binoculars.

The mote leveled off and kept a straight line over the length of the lake. The mote's descent now seemed better controlled. It was hard to believe that this particle shooting through the air was a man. The particle gracefully descended, as Daryl had said he would, over the face of the waters.

He slowed, fell and wobbled upward, fell and wobbled upward. He moved upward and stalled, flapping his arms and pumping his legs as if he were on a bicycle.

"He could easily be going 200 kilometers per hour," Dahl said.

Daryl slammed into the lake, bounded into an arc heels over head, and hit the water again. He was not skipping over the water like a tossed stone. He was a human cannonball repeatedly slamming into the lake at the hardest angle, bouncing upwards, and hitting it again, for a quarter of a mile until he came to rest.

The mote became still as it floated, arms and legs spread-eagled, face down. It reminded Elizabeth of a tiny bug in a water glass.

THIRTY

Elizabeth paced when she lectured but kept herself to the side of the screen to give her students a clear view of the PET scans of two human brains. She always saved the most interesting part of her lectures for the last minutes before the bell. It kept students alert and off their phones.

One of the brains was lit up like a war zone, explosions of reds and yellows in the cerebral cortex that extended downward in a crescent of color.

"The orbitofrontal cortex, or OFC, is the lower portion of the cortex," Elizabeth said. "It is where we govern our emotions, impulses and moral choices."

The other brain was also bright in the high, frontal portions, but in the OFC region there was only an archipelago of tiny islands of color. The rest was dark and quiet.

"This is a PET scan of a serial killer," she said. "A psychopath lacks processing power in this part of the brain."

"So our moral choices are determined by our brains?" A young man asked.

The students were a mix of pre-med biology majors, a few Georgetown School of Medicine residents and some curious, undergraduate liberal arts majors. This question came from an earnest looking pre-med type.

"There is no doubt that people are born with genetic predispositions to these patterns," Elizabeth replied. "But could it also work the other way around? Could the way we live, the choices we make throughout our lives, affect our brain patterns, turn a dormant gene on or an active gene off, reinforcing a tendency through an act of will?"

"This leads us to an even deeper question."

The speaker, sitting high up in the small auditorium, had a deep, booming voice.

"Can someone be normal, happy, well-adjusted and socially moral, only to lapse to psychopathy late in life due to deep trauma?"

"Students, this is George Abelman, one of the most distinguished scholars in this field," Elizabeth said. "We're writing a paper together on this very subject, though we have yet to agree on a conclusion. Yes, George, as we have seen in our case study, that can happen."

The bell rang. Elizabeth remained behind to answer a few questions from students, most of them about the questionable morality of grading on a curve. She met George outside of White-Gravenor Hall. Students were walking fast to their next class. October had arrived in full, the air pleasantly crisp, the trees shimmering with their own explosions of red and orange against the blue-gray stones of the university.

"Take a walk?"

They fell into lockstep.

"The essential remaining issue in our paper is ideation," he said.

"I've got a theory," Elizabeth replied. "Daryl had been committed to his family and went to church, for years. I postulate that he never stopped believing in God. He was an angry Job who wanted to pile one stinking corpse on top of another under the very nostrils of the Lord. He was saying to God, 'See. See what you do to us.' The Norse imagery just a pagan wrapper for his calculated insult."

"As an insult to God?"

"Yes."

"And so he became a killer, just like that?"

"He had been a killer for years for Uncle Sam. It was his peaceful years in Atlanta that were the anomaly."

They passed through the iron gates of the university and took the sidewalk that led down to M Street in the direction of Martin's Tavern, their default bar whenever George came to Georgetown.

He shook his head.

"My, how much all this God nonsense has cost humanity over the centuries. Even intelligent people still fall for it."

"Yes they do," Elizabeth said. "You should know, George, I have my moments on that question as well."

George stopped walking for a moment.

"Really? And I thought I had educated you so well."

"Let's save that talk for another time. All I am prepared to say right now is that I don't believe in Daryl's God, a fundamentalist deity not that much different from Odin. He saw God as his father figure who had betrayed him, tortured him, and he wanted payback."

"And so Daryl Parnell's brain switched, at middle age, to that of a psychopath? Just like that?"

"Another way to put it is that he gave in to an evil impulse—to medicate his intense pain by enjoying the many clever ways he could mete out God's punishment to others. He allowed himself to become degraded by grief."

"We were talking brains earlier. Now you sound like you're defending the idea of a soul."

"If you take a computer apart and examine its circuits it will tell you nothing about the meanings of the movies, books and blogs that flicker across its screen. The device should not be mistaken for its content."

"I can see that our paper is going to take longer than we thought."

They walked on to Martin's. They had a lot to talk about. They always had.

Max waited for her in a chain coffee shop by their gate.

She hugged him. He let her do this, confident that none of his friends were around to witness the act.

"Are you excited about seeing California?"

"Yeah, but it's going to be kinda weird being alone for part of the time," he said.

"I just need a few hours on Saturday and Sunday mornings. We'll have the afternoons and all day Monday."

"I'm cool," he said. "I can sleep in, I guess."

"I bet you can."

They went to their gate, waiting for their flight to be called.

The last time Elizabeth had flown had been to attend a memorial service for Nasrin Jones on an appropriately dreary London day. The service had been held in one of the older and more established mosques in England, one that had the dark atmospherics of a Victorian church.

She met Nasrin's mother, beautiful in old age, who despite her grief displayed a similarly canny expression and offhand sense of humor.

All pretense that Nasrin had worked for Scotland Yard had been abandoned. The congregation was packed with men and women whose dark suits matched their glowering expressions. But MI6 had done a good job overall, delivering a train full of Nasrin's old Manchester police colleagues, complete with the customary bagpipers who played patriotic and mournful tunes.

Lars had met Elizabeth outside after the service. The conversation was awkward as they held their umbrellas upright and had to move now and then to let fellow mourners pass. On Trolltunga, Lars had been sweet, holding Elizabeth tight and not letting her look at Nasrin as he led her away. Lars stayed with Elizabeth for several days until it was time for her to fly home. Now, all he really seemed to want to talk about was being promoted and elevated into the PST. If he played his cards right, he might someday become the director. She could have said something cutting, but he had saved her life. They talked awhile, hugged and parted.

They had run out of things to say to each other.

Now Elizabeth was going to spend a long weekend in LA. She would do fun things with her son, make up for all the time she had been gone and for almost leaving him forever. They would go to the beach, do a studio tour and eat at fancy restaurants with outdoor seating.

But in the mornings Elizabeth had business to attend to in Silver Lake. She had someone to see, a young woman who had lost her entire family to tragedy and suicide and who needed to know that it is always possible to come back, even from something like that.

END

 **Mark Davis** is a former White House speechwriter and frequent lecturer, writer and blogger on politics, technology and the future. He divides his time between Austin, Texas, and Washington, D.C. Davis is the author of two science-fiction novels. *Seven Shoes* is his first crime novel.